T0285387

LANDSLIDE

ALSO BY ADAM SIKES

Open Skies:
My Life as Afghanistan's First Female Pilot
(coauthor)

LANDSLIDE

A NOVEL

ADAM SIKES

OCEANVIEW (C) PUBLISHING
SARASOTA, FLORIDA

ISBN 978-1-60809-504-9

Published in the United States of America by Oceanview Publishing

Sarasota, Florida

www.oceanviewpub.com

10 9 8 7 6 5 4 3 2

PRINTED IN THE UNITED STATES OF AMERICA

"An intelligence service is the ideal vehicle for a conspiracy."

—ALLEN DULLES,
Director of Central Intelligence 1953–1961

AUTHOR'S NOTE

Landslide is a work of fiction, and all the characters and events in this novel are products of my imagination. Additionally, as a former member of the intelligence community, this book was reviewed by a board to ensure the manuscript did not contain any classified or sensitive information. However, like most every author, I write about what I know. Thus, key elements of this story and the characters in it were inspired by true events and people I encountered during my time in the military and as an intelligence officer.

The realms of warfare, espionage, and the international criminal underworld can be cruel, twisted, and unforgiving. Those souls who live and work in these spaces—the *good guys*—must lie and manipulate and constantly look over their shoulder, while at the same time adhere to a complicated and at times conflicting sense of integrity, honor, and loyalty. It is not easy, nor is it clean, and often the lines between right and wrong are blurred, and sometimes there is no right answer or good option, only something less bad.

Having seen this world up close, my hope, then, was to tell an entertaining story with a taste of realism. Tragically, as this book was in the pre-production process in February 2022, Russia invaded Ukraine, launching an unprovoked war of aggression. As I write this, the war continues to rage with Russian forces inflicting immense suffering on the Ukrainian people. Fortunately, the international community has rallied against Vladimir Putin's ill-gotten war, but the future is unclear.

I pray hostilities end soon—no one wins in war, no one.

LANDSLIDE

PROLOGUE

A man calling himself Henry Delgado stared out the window of the two-room farmhouse that sat abandoned on the outskirts of Kumachove, Ukraine. He surveyed the Russian frontier a little over a mile away, where the biting wind had cracked the barren earth. Crops may have grown in the fields at one time, but now the grass and weeds had withered to walnut-colored razors and needles.

"Who does he think I am?" Henry asked the Ukrainian standing next to him.

"I tell you already—journalist. As you tell me, I tell him journalist," replied Fedir, a man with pale, Eastern European features and a scruffy, short beard with black whiskers that ran down his neck under his shirt, mixing with his chest hair. Although his skin was ashen white, the man seemed oily. Greasy was probably a better description, like his best suit would be a set of grime-smeared overalls.

"I know. You said that, but that's not my question. Who does he *think* I am?" Henry repeated, folding his arms across his chest. In contrast, his features were dark, akin to someone born on the Mediterranean or in South America. His black hair and brown eyes accented the natural olive tone of his skin. Built like a swimmer, with a trim yet sturdy frame, he stood a little over six foot two. He wore tan cargo pants and a navy sweater, and his boots had the grit of too many far-off places ground into the soles.

Fedir took a drag on his cigarette, breaking Henry's gaze. When he expelled the smoke it slammed into the window like a wave hitting a seawall. The man had been lighting butt after butt for the past hour, and a soft haze now hung inches from the ceiling.

"He think journalist," Fedir finally said, shrugging his shoulders. "From big New York newspaper. Just like you tell me, I tell him. Journalist from big newspaper."

Henry sensed too much assurance in the Ukrainian's voice, like he was trying to convince him everything was fine, as if he needed to keep smoking to calm his nerves because of the lies he told or the secrets he held back. And he did it again, lighting another damn smoke with the cherry from the last.

Henry touched the edge of the CZ-75 pistol under his oversized sweater, confirming it was still there and accessible. He always did that, consciously and unconsciously, a habit of his going back twenty years. Pistol or rifle, it didn't matter, he always checked to make sure his weapon was within reach even in his sleep. He mused that one day he'd shoot his balls off in the middle of the night. A simple roll to the left and a finger pull to the right and *pop*, there they go.

But he knew that would never happen—just as someone couldn't chew off his or her thumb while asleep—his weapon served as an extension of his limbs. It was a part of him.

"Right. Sure," Henry said. "He's late."

"He's coming. I promise."

Henry pursed his lips and checked his watch again. Nearly thirty minutes late. Had this been Africa or the Middle East, being late wouldn't be unusual. But here, in Ukraine, punctuality was the norm.

He trawled his eyes around the empty bedroom once more. He hadn't used this location before and he was still committing every corner to memory. Two windows facing east, no windows on the northern or southern walls, a pathetic heater making the space only slightly warmer than the outside, and a single door leading to the other half of the house.

The meeting would happen through there, the main room, once Boris arrived. If he arrived.

Boris, a Russian businessman, sold medical supplies to the hospitals and clinics peppered on both sides of the border in the disputed region. He ran a nice business, low-level, regional stuff. Very humanitarian, making sure the wounded, maimed, and crippled on both sides of the conflict got what they needed. The money was good but never flaunted. That would be ill-mannered.

Henry, however, didn't give a rat's ass for the man's business. Rather, it was to whom Boris could introduce him that prompted this meeting: Oleg Tolesky, an arms dealer who, like Boris, liked to play both sides of this conflict, and any other conflict where he could sell his wares. His business was more international in scope. The Congo, Syria, Colombia—Tolesky endeavored to be Amazon .com for the warlords and self-designated colonels and generals running insurgencies and civil wars.

The irony was not lost on Henry. The weapons dealers and medical providers were in cahoots, profiting handsomely from their complementary services. The more shooting, the more casualties, the greater the need for medical supplies, then back into the mix to shoot each other up again. A bit of yin and yang.

But Tolesky wasn't the main target either, just another stepping stone Henry had to navigate to reach the real issue, which was elusive. It was barely a hunch, but concerning enough to compel him to venture all this way. And if it were true, it meant the world had changed—out with the old and in with the new. The international corporations and the people who ran them were, in some ways, becoming just as influential as governments themselves. And for some that meant unregulated, destabilizing players deciding who went to war, who had food, who survived, who had freedom . . .

"There he is," Fedir announced louder than necessary.

Henry scanned the horizon and spotted a lone vehicle bouncing over the gravel road toward the house. He brought his mini-binoculars to his eyes and focused on the vehicle's cab: a blue Toyota with one occupant.

Henry returned the binos to his bag, which had PRESS stenciled on it in big letters. "Come on," he said, entering the front room and pulling out his notepad. He set three bottles of water on the table and checked the pot simmering on the propane stove—a goulash of sorts. If things started off well, they'd crack open the bottle of vodka, too, even if he hated the stuff.

The sound of a car's engine revving could be heard as the vehicle traversed Ukraine's rolling landscape. The engine had a low grind that kept getting louder and louder. It was the only sound coming from the outside, aside from the wind.

Henry stole another glance out the window and saw the Toyota pulling around to the front of the house, its tires crunching over the frozen dirt. He shifted the pistol from his right hip to the small of his back, fully concealing it from anyone in front of him, and cracked his knuckles.

How many times had he met people under similar conditions? After all these years it had to be in the hundreds. But this time it was different. It had never been like this.

A car door slammed and Henry wiped the perspiration from his upper lip. He thought about his escape plan in the event things went south. If that happened, he and Fedir would need to get out fast. Boris may have a free pass to stroll around the separatist region, but they didn't.

A knock came at the door. Fedir looked at Henry, who gave him the go-ahead.

Fedir called out, "One moment." He cracked the door to peer out, then opened it all the way, revealing a tall man with chalky skin and sharp eyes. He wore the typical uniform of a Russian business-man: black shoes, black pants, white shirt, black jacket. The man, presumably Boris, stepped inside and surveyed the small room's contents. His eyes settled on Henry, who stood beside the circular table with his hand resting on the back of a chair.

"Hello, I'm Henry Delgado with the Associated Press. Are you Boris Volkov?"

The Russian turned to Fedir. "You said he was a reporter with a New York paper."

Fedir started to respond, but Henry spoke up. "The AP is based in New York, and I contribute to the *New York Times* and others. I'm freelance, which is the only reason I can travel to a place like this to meet you. Too high-risk for a staff writer."

Boris grunted. "You look Spanish, or Greek. Not like from New York."

"It's an international city. I was born in Madrid," lied Henry.

"Ha. Yes. International. Spanish."

Henry wanted to search Boris, check for weapons or anything unusual—a unique phone, a recording device, some over-engineered piece of tech—but he couldn't. Only certain kinds of people demanded searches. As a journalist, he wasn't among them.

"Would you like to sit down?" Henry asked.

"Yes. What are you cooking?"

"Stew. Would you like some?"

"It smells like shit. Vodka."

"Right," Henry replied, already feeling his stomach turn.

Henry put the bottle and two glasses on the table and sat down. Boris reached for the vodka and poured. Not waiting for Henry, he raised his glass to his lips and said, "To our meeting." He downed the vodka in one swig. Henry let his glass linger by his lips for a second, then followed suit, the alcohol biting his throat as it went down.

Boris refilled their glasses and leaned back. "So, you're going to write a good story about me and I will get publicity, yes?"

"That's the idea, among other things."

"What other things?" Boris downed another glass and poured again. He then put his right hand in his jacket pocket, where he seemed to clutch hold of something small. His other hand rested on his thigh, his fingers struggling not to tap his pant leg.

He's anxious, thought Henry. But why shouldn't he be? He could freely cross the border and move throughout the Russian-controlled areas in Ukraine, but he was still meeting with a Western journalist. As a rule, the Russians weren't fond of the BBC, CNN, Reuters— biased anti-Russian propaganda filth, as put by one Muscovite.

"What things?" Boris repeated. "You will write a big story. It's good publicity for me. More contracts."

"Yes," Henry answered. "But for me to write the story, I need to understand what it is you do and how you do it. I'll need to ask a lot of questions. I'd like to know the other people you work with too. You okay with that?"

"I tell you whatever you want to know. Sure. But first," Boris said, raising a finger, "I need to ask *you* some questions."

"Of course," agreed Henry.

"Good. Then we will talk more."

The Russian shifted in his seat but didn't take his hand out of his pocket. He didn't have a pistol in there; Henry was sure of it. Too small. But he was definitely holding something.

"You say your name is Henry Delgado," Boris began, pronouncing the name slowly. "You say you work for Western press, but I checked. I have friends in Ukrainian government. You're not listed as an accredited journalist."

Henry frowned. He knew Boris would have questions. No one would open up without first getting a sense of whom they were sitting across from. But he'd hoped Fedir's brokering of the meeting would have been sufficient.

"Like I said, I'm freelance. Different status," Henry replied.

Boris scrunched his brow. "Okay. Sure. So you say. What kind of status?"

"Tourist. Removes the minders and the red tape."

Henry thought he heard something scrape outside, like footsteps. The hair on the back of his neck stood up.

"Tourist?" Boris balked. "You're a funny guy. Spaniard. Journalist from New York. Tourist."

Henry eyed the Russian, listening to his guttural tone, listening to the pot on the stove simmer, and listening to the wind howl. Something wasn't right. He looked at Fedir, who'd been standing by the opposite window. Fedir hadn't made eye contact with him since Boris arrived.

Then, without a word, Fedir went into the back room. Henry started to say something but refrained when he saw a bead of sweat drip down the side of Boris's cheek. The Russian sat motionless, stone-faced, like a statue, sweating in a room lacking heat.

Alarm exploded inside Henry. He stood, reaching for his pistol. But before he could get up, the front door burst open.

Men in masks and mismatched camouflage uniforms rushed inside. Some had weapons raised. Others had their gloved hands outstretched.

Henry barely cleared the chair when powerful arms grabbed him from behind. It wasn't Boris; it was someone else who'd gotten in the house another way . . .

That shit Fedir let someone in through the back window!

Rough hands yanked a hood over Henry's head. Everything went black. He struggled to take in air. He tried to break free from the arms locked around his chest, but he couldn't move.

Fists pummeled his head, face, and stomach. He lost his balance and slipped to the floor. Kicks replaced punches. He raised his hands to protect his face. He tried to pull the hood off but failed, the onslaught unrelenting.

One of the assailants rolled him over, wrenched his arms behind his back, and bound his wrists. They tied his feet next. Someone using what must have been a hammer whacked his outer thighs, giving him leg-numbing charley horses.

Henry couldn't move, he couldn't breathe, he couldn't cry out. The last thought that went through his mind before losing consciousness was he'd been betrayed.

CHAPTER ONE

MINISTRY OF ECONOMIC AFFAIRS AND ENERGY,
FRANKFURT, GERMANY

The man sitting across the table from me was a representative from the German Federal Ministry of Economic Affairs and Energy. He embodied the quintessential German bureaucrat: shiny bald head, wire-rimmed glasses, slender physique, and a crisp gray suit. He spoke methodically, laying out everything in an organized and unambiguous fashion, his pronunciation precise and curt. He was clear and direct—emotionless—getting right to the point.

I preferred working with people like him. I didn't have to sift through any convoluted nonsense obscuring the crux of a matter.

My boss, Alistair Ruttfield III, sent me to meet with this man. It wasn't my usual sort of trip—no conflict zones or crime bosses—but I didn't mind. I go where the firm tells me. Jack Thompson, the partner who typically handles government interactions, had a personal thing so he couldn't go. I think his wife is leaving him, or he's leaving her. I'm not sure and it's none of my business.

Nonetheless, this trip is a nice reprieve. I like Germany: the efficiency, the logical organization, the simplicity, not to mention the beer and the food. And unlike my usual trips, there aren't many triggers here to conjure up the demons. I can enjoy some blissful forgetfulness. Tonight I'll go to Apfelwein Solzer; they have an excellent roasted pork knuckle that's sure to give me heartburn, but it's worth it. There are worse things in life.

So, here I am in Frankfurt—one of Europe's great financial hubs—on behalf of Ruttfield & Leason (Ruttfield for short), a global financial firm based in the City of London. We occupy floors thirty-seven through forty of the Leadenhall Building and handle corporate accounts for international defense firms and energy multinationals. They may be the robber barons of the twenty-first century, but someone has to invest their money. We also manage a few state funds for a select number of small Middle Eastern and South American countries. We do a solid business, and there are certain inquiries we don't make.

But unlike the financial giants Goldman Sachs, Deutsche Bank, and Credit Suisse—massive firms in the bulge bracket offering a fifty-page menu of services—Ruttfield is a boutique. It's not everything for everybody and it doesn't need to be to do what it does well. Like I said before, it's good to keep things simple.

As for my position in the firm, I'm not a senior partner, nor a top analyst. I can crunch numbers and read the markets—one can't survive in this arena without knowing that stuff—but my expertise falls elsewhere.

I go to the places other bankers won't: the warlord-controlled rare earth mines in South Africa, the pirate-infested shipping lanes in the Gulf of Aden, the lawless border regions of the former Soviet satellite states, and most recently the war-ravaged Syrian Desert. In these garden spots I talk with the local businessmen and government officials, but I also seek out the paramilitary power brokers and mafia-types who wield as much leverage on international markets as the bureaucrats and corporations. It's this *ground truth* that gives Ruttfield a nice edge over its competitors, and they pay me handsomely for doing what I do, which I don't mind even if sometimes I wonder if I deserve it.

Not surprisingly, although most of the senior partners find value in the information I gather, they also whisper about me at the holiday parties and as I pass by their offices. I don't make a show of things, I keep to myself quite well, but they know the rumors. Whether there's any truth to this or that story—and allegedly there are some doozies—it doesn't matter; I'm not keen on setting the record straight. I don't see the point.

Consider me however you want. I'm an American, a rebel colonial from across the pond and a former US Marine. I fought in Bush's wars, and after twenty years of picking a fight with just about every country on the planet, the Brits view us Americans differently now. It might take a generation or two to get back to being the chummy cousins we once were, if ever. I hope we do.

My meeting commenced within an hour of my arrival in Frankfurt.

I took British Airways flight 902 out of Heathrow, which I've already taken twenty times this year alone, usually with a connection sending me elsewhere. I had a chance to chat with Trish for a spell while we were in the air. I've known her for quite a while—she's a flight attendant—and this is her route. She's a nice gal, a bit younger than my thirty-eight years, but she likes me for some reason. I suspect she found me amusing—or took pity on me—the second time we met when I fumbled through the Russian language with the passenger next to me and then skewered my French bantering with her fellow flight attendant.

The plane touched down in Frankfurt at 9:45 a.m., and an analyst from Ruttfield's satellite office, Klaus, picked me up from the airport and drove me straight here. The briefing by the ministry official had been droning on for the past thirty minutes, but I'd heard everything I needed in the first five.

Germany is actively pursuing deeper relationships with the Russian Federation's energy sector. The situation in the Middle East is too volatile, and like the rest of Europe, Germany needs stable energy supplies. Relations with the United States have become unpredictable in recent years, which doesn't help matters. It's our own fault and I can only shake my head, but thankfully the circus is ending.

Russia—despite its provocative foreign policy—is a much safer bet for oil and natural gas. International politics and trade are funny that way. *I may not like your record on human rights, but you have something I want that I can't get anywhere else, so I'm going to do business with you. We just won't talk about it.*

It was obvious to me that Germany's move would reshape Europe's energy market and upset the old order. Consequently, Ruttfield & Leason will need to restructure quite a few investments. It's for others to assess whether that's a good or a bad thing.

I don't particularly care for the Russian government—conveniently chopped down to *the Russians*. I was raised against them—a product of growing up in the final days of the Cold War and hearing the stories about how my uncle died in an air force training accident when his plane went down near the East German border. I've always viewed them warily, a brutal bunch of thugs. And in recent years I've seen the Russians return to their coveted status as adversary number one, sharing the spot with China and Iran. North Korea is the annoying child everyone wishes would go away; the enemy everyone loves to hate.

Germany's new direction, however, means investment opportunities. Only a fool would ignore them, and Alistair and the rest of the partners at Ruttfield are no fools.

While the German talked, I let my eyes wander to the flat-screen television mounted on the far wall. The day's financial stats were scrolling at the bottom.

The main newscast was about the conflict in eastern Ukraine, which was ironic given the substance of our meeting. As the ministry official explained Germany's intention to broaden economic ties with Moscow, BBC World News was reporting on Russian aggression in the region. The annexation of Crimea a few years back had only been the start. Incursions and support to separatists in Donetsk and Luhansk had been next. Off and on, off and on, cease-fire and then return fire, pull back and move up. It never ended. That shit never does.

Only now the Russian steamroller—formerly limited to soldiers and tanks—included businessmen and conglomerates with offshore bank accounts and commanding positions on the stock exchange. Once the Kremlin's security forces established control—if not outright occupation—the economic tentacles slithered in. It was all very imperial-like, maybe a little Hobbesian, if I were to dust off and consult the tomes from my graduate studies.

From the closed captions I could discern the talking heads were reporting on the detention of a Western journalist by pro-Russian militants. A freelancer had been near the border when he was kidnapped. Rumors gleaned from the locals indicated the militants suspected he was spying and not a legitimate journalist, but that was typical. Every foreigner is a spy in places like that.

When I visited Ukraine a while back, I'd been careful to register with the right offices, bribe the right officials, and make it abundantly clear I was with a financial investment firm, not any government. The last thing I ever wanted was to get tossed into a Ukrainian or Russian prison cell. After the perfunctory beating to get things going, they enjoy drilling holes in your teeth and hammering your knees to loosen the tongue. No thank you.

But when the BBC displayed a picture of the missing journalist on the screen, a vice clamped down on my chest and I stopped breathing. I stared, riveted, unable to tear my eyes from the screen.

I recognized the hair, those eyes, that jaw, and the bold-ass grin. It was *his* face: my best friend, my comrade in arms, the man I twice

went to war with, and the man I'd risked my life trying to save. I'd
know his face anywhere, but that guy is dead.

Kevin Gomez died over fifteen years ago on a blood-soaked gur-
ney in the heart of darkness. Yet his picture appeared on the television plain as day and, apparently, he was alive but with someone
else's name.

CHAPTER TWO

The meeting ended awkwardly, with the ministry official asking if I had any questions. I didn't, not about Germany's energy prospects or anything else that concerned him. I was trapped in near silence, uttering one-word responses. I either came across as rude or an idiot.

We left the ministry to go to Ruttfield's Frankfurt satellite office, and Klaus tried to review the substance of what we'd learned—he's a dutiful analyst and will probably go far—but I didn't engage him either. I couldn't shake what I'd seen on the television and I wasn't about to try and explain. Seeing what I thought was Gomez's picture had sent my mind into a frenzy with too many memories emerging from the dark holes I'd stashed them in: bombed-out buildings, machine-gun fire that was too close, IEDs going off and blowing my men to pieces, the blood on my hands.

Now in the back seat of the sedan and making the short drive through Frankfurt's downtown, I pulled out my tablet to see what I could glean from the news websites. But I soon slammed the cover shut, the connection excruciatingly slow and the screen locking up for eternity as the webpage loaded. I wanted to chuck the technical piece of garbage out the window but chose to stare at nothing instead.

Had it really been a picture of Gomez on the television? Kevin Gomez? A second-generation immigrant from Sinaloa, Mexico, who grew up in the barrios outside San Diego and whose mother feared he'd either join a gang or be murdered by one. A smart kid who chose a third option and attended the University of Southern California, then joined the Marine Corps. My bunkmate during officer training and fellow infantry platoon commander in Fifth Marines out of Camp Pendleton. My best friend . . . the man I saw die on a blood-soaked stretcher in Ramadi, Iraq, fifteen years ago. The man whose parents I sat beside during the funeral, whose father I saw weep while the mother numbly stroked a strand of gray hair.

It couldn't be him on the TV. That was impossible. Gomez was dead. He was killed in action on the second of September, 2004. The doc found so many holes in him he stopped counting. I watched him die. I saw the life fade from his eyes and drip out of his body onto a concrete slab floor. The man was dead.

There must be a mistake. The picture of the journalist on the TV had to be a doppelgänger or an unrelated twin. Perhaps a long-lost brother Gomez never spoke of. He'd said his family had been small, only three sisters. Maybe a cousin?

But the face—it looked exactly like him.

"How much further?" I asked, drumming my fingers on the armrest.

"Just another few minutes, Mr. Hackett," replied Klaus, still confused.

Silence filled the car once again.

Seven minutes later we stopped in front of the Main Tower building. I jumped out of the back seat and hastened toward the skyscraper's main entrance. The heels of my shoes cracked against the sidewalk, sounding like I was back on the parade deck at Quantico as I weaved in and around the citizenry out for lunch and midday errands. If someone had been unfortunate enough to get in my way, I probably would have plowed over him or her without as much as a stutter step.

"Mr. Hackett! Mr. Hackett!" called Klaus from somewhere behind me. I turned to see the analyst struggling to keep up. He looked like a child, shoulder bag and papers all catawampus, rushing to class before the teacher shut the door and called attendance.

"My apologies, Klaus, but I need to check something. Let's reconvene in an hour."

"Yes. But, Mr. Hackett, is everything all right?"

I responded with a halting wave of my hand. "It's nothing."

I lengthened my stride to pull away from Klaus. I entered the lobby, breezed through security, and slipped into an elevator as the doors closed. Fifty-three floors up and two halls later, I shut my office door and fired up my computer.

After forty-three seconds, the screen finally lit up and I opened a web browser. In the search bar I typed *Ukraine pro-Russian militants journalist detained* and stabbed the return key. A list of results appeared and I started scrolling through them.

Multiple news sites carried the story. *Pro-Russian separatists, pro-Russian militants, DPR paramilitaries* . . . The headlines varied but the theme was consistent.

An AP journalist had been detained in a village outside Mariupol', a city in southeastern Ukraine on the northern coast of the Sea of Azov, which is on the edge of the separatist Donetsk People's Republic and just a few miles from the Russian border. Some sites displayed a stock photo of the journalist, but others rotated numerous shots. Close-ups, formals, candids, shots from the side while interviewing someone.

I blinked, struggling to believe my eyes. The face, the smile, the intensity—the man looked identical to Gomez. I knew his face like my own; I'd awakened to see it first thing in the morning more often than I care to admit.

We'd practically been brothers. Best friends. Do anything for the other guy kind of friends. Drop everything and come to each other's aid kind of friends. Best man at a wedding and eulogy at a funeral kind of shit.

We'd joined the Corps for the same naïve, idealistic reasons too. Willing to fight when others can't. Prepared to protect the nation at all costs. Unit, Corps, God, country, and all that. Parades, medals, honors. Ready to die to preserve the American way of life.

The pictures were of Gomez. I was positive. I'd bet my life on it. But the name . . .

The news identified the detained journalist as *Henry Delgado*, a freelance journalist with the Associated Press out of New York. Who the hell was Henry Delgado?

Could it be something as crazy as a doppelgänger or a near-perfect look-alike? Celebrities and the rich and powerful employed them, using them for security and to throw off the paparazzi. This could be a simple coincidence, unnerving as it was.

But something about the face forced me to think otherwise. The same squint, the same curl of the mouth, the smile he flashed when earnestly shaking someone's hand. Those were Gomez's quirks, his and his alone, like a fingerprint.

I kept searching, reading and rereading every article I found.

This Henry Delgado had ostensibly been reporting on the conflict in Ukraine, and when I expanded my search, multiple articles attributed to Delgado popped up. I read each word, not interested in the news, but instead hunting for clues about the author.

Every writer has a style—even bad ones—and with every sentence and paragraph I analyzed, the heaviness in my chest grew worse. I found turns of phrase only someone with Gomez's background would use—*in order to*, *outstanding*, *orient*, and others. They were the subtle—and awkward—tells of a writer who had been corrupted by years of military writing and questionable grammar. I should know since I suffered from the same deficiency.

Continuing through the tangle of internet links, I found other articles by Delgado out of Somalia, Syria, and Libya. A profile in the *New Yorker* called him a seasoned war correspondent, often alone and unafraid, and undeterred even by the most dangerous of places. Delgado was about the same age as Gomez would have been, in his late thirties. Delgado was Spanish, but in the last few years he'd worked out of New York. No family to speak of.

This was crazy, I thought.

I stood up and paced around my office to settle down, telling myself Gomez was dead. He'd died on a stretcher in that damned army med unit. His team had been surrounded and cut off, and he'd called *Landslide*, the call for immediate help, because they were about to be overrun by the muj and needed everything the American military machine could throw into the fight.

But the man who was supposed to help him, the commander of the battalion's quick reaction force, me—First Lieutenant Mason Hackett—had been too slow. On the way to the fight, I'd lost Humvee after Humvee to IED blasts, my own marines getting wounded and killed on the way, men I'd been responsible for. I was supposed to keep them alive. But I kept going, balls to the wall into the fire, following orders, because that's what we do.

In the two-hour gunfight, Gomez was shot multiple times and perforated by chunks of hot shrapnel. When my platoon finally arrived, the building he was atop collapsed. I saw it happen, staring slack-jawed as two rocket-propelled grenades—RPGs—hurtled through the air and slammed into the last remains of the building's load-bearing walls.

An RPG came at me too, detonating on the other side of the wall I was hunkered behind, peppering me with shrapnel and killing my one rifleman still standing, PFC Villa. Villa was just nineteen, not even old enough to drink, a kid. He was inches from me. He died and I lived.

The reserve platoon eventually came and transported all the dead and wounded back to Camp Ramadi to the med unit. Barely conscious myself, I watched the broken bodies getting wheeled in. They were my marines, some incapacitated, some screaming, others in shock, some already dead and getting zipped up in body bags. And there were marines from the other companies, some missing limbs, some with bullet holes aerating their chests and bellies.

And Gomez's men. He'd been the commander of the battalion's scout sniper platoon. Most of his boys were dead, but they carried the proof of fighting to the last breath. The majority had been shot multiple times, slapping on tourniquets and pressure bandages so they could keep fighting. Gomez had done the same.

I spotted him across the med unit lying on a stretcher. Somebody gave him a shot of something, then moved on to the next casualty. It seemed to help. Gomez actually smiled, the crazy son of a bitch. But then his chest rose and fell like a deflated balloon, then nothing. Lifeless.

The army doc closed Gomez's eyes and pulled a sheet over him.

It was my fault Gomez died that day, and my fault eleven of the men from my platoon died trying to help him. Mine. Lieutenant Mason *goddamned* Hackett. My fault. I'd led my marines down those IED-filled streets and ultimately failed to reach the stranded platoon—Gomez's platoon—before it was too late. There were over thirty-five parents, spouses, children, brothers, and sisters who lost someone dear to them because of me. My fault.

I closed my eyes to halt the tears. I slowed my breathing, inhaling and exhaling, counting to three. I needed to push those memories away. I had to ignore them like I did every other day. I had to shove them back down like I did each morning when I woke up with my pulse hammering like a liquid piston. I'd get up to stare at myself in the mirror, eventually splashing water against my face, and begin shaving, trying not to nick the scars on my neck with my razor. The scars, my souvenirs, my visible reminders.

Reliving that day wouldn't help anything, I told myself. Force it back down for god's sake.

"A bit of standing yoga?"

The woman's voice startled me and my head snapped toward the door.

"What? Yeah. Just taking a moment," I replied, taking a deep breath.

"Sure," said the woman, giving me a curious smile before continuing, "Klaus gave me the highlights."

"Highlights? I'm sorry, what?"

"The highlights from your meeting with the ministry this morning."

"Oh, yes. Right," I said, dragging my hands down my cheeks and forcing myself to suppress everything I'd been thinking about.

The woman's name was Hannah, a senior account manager based in Frankfurt, whom I'd known since my first week at Ruttfield over ten years ago.

Caroline, my ex-girlfriend of two years in London whom I'd just broken up with last week and whom I'd never deserved, hadn't liked Hannah. She probably had good reason given how I was when it came to relationships, but that wasn't an issue anymore, was it. What's done is done.

"Not very surprising," I offered, "but the firm can act with more certainty, now."

"I agree," she replied, crossing her arms. "So, discuss over lunch?"

I hesitated, admiring Hannah's almost smile and intelligent eyes. She regularly invited me to lunch and on occasion to dinner. She had a decidedly attractive presence about her—shoulder-length auburn hair, blue eyes, medium lips, attractive body bordering on athletic, and a confidence in her about everything she said or did.

The offer for lunch was tempting; we knew each other well and it would be nice to chat now that Caroline and I were done. I almost said yes. I normally *would* have said yes.

"I wish I had time," I replied, "but I really must attend to something. Can we do a fast thirty-minute review later this afternoon?"

Hannah's face didn't reveal a thing; neither did her voice. Her Prussian heritage wouldn't allow it. She had no idea what was going on in my head, but she took my rejection in stride. She's measured like that. "Of course. Four thirty, my office," she said.

"I'll be there."

"Good."

She closed the door to leave me in silence, though the interruption had been good. I no longer felt myself dropping into the darkness.

Gomez was dead, I repeated to myself. I watched him die, saw the doc zip up the body bag, heard the teeth clip together with a tic-tic-tic-tic, and watched two corpsmen carry him away to the idling mortuary affairs truck. Days later I'd stood at attention during the battlefield funeral; I can still picture the empty boots, upside-down rifle, and helmet resting on the buttstock. And six months later I visited Gomez's grave at Arlington, the inscription on the headstone etched into my mind.

KEVIN J. GOMEZ

LT   US MARINE CORPS   IRAQ

JUL 17 1979   SEP 2 2004

Navy Cross   Bronze Star   Purple Heart

My friend is dead; it's a fact.

This individual named Henry Delgado was exactly that—someone else entirely. Nature's failure at variety. It was anyone but Gomez.

I shook my head once more and sat back down in the chair behind my desk. I had work to do, the German matter one thing among the fray. Opening up my email, I began triaging the urgent from the mundane, all thoughts of Gomez and Mr. Delgado receding.

I read a few messages from the team back in London, a couple from Ruttfield's regional office in Tokyo, my travel facilitator in Bucharest inquiring about any future trips, a ministry official from Istanbul fishing for a bribe.

Then I spotted a subject line that read *Past Debts 1 of 1*, which struck me as odd. I didn't recognize the sender's address and was about to hit delete assuming it was spam, but the preview pane stopped me.

The weight that had been lifted moments ago suddenly fell back on my shoulders and the air left my lungs, making me light-headed. I double-clicked on the message and the words jumped off the screen. I saw nothing else.

Brother Hackett,

It's been a long time, and no doubt you think I've crossed to the other side, but it's me. If you're getting this, it means something has gone wrong and I need your help. Remember that promise we made in the desert sitting on the berm? I'm calling it in— Landslide.

SF,
KG

P.S. Start with Doug.

CHAPTER THREE

For how long I remained transfixed by the computer screen, I don't know. Ten, fifteen minutes—time slipped away from me. I read the email over and over again, picking apart the words as if there should be a hidden meaning beyond their simplicity. It took the buzz of my desk intercom to snap me out of it, the office manager asking if I wanted lunch brought in.

"No, not right now," I muttered.

I looked at the time stamp on the email and saw it hit my inbox at 11:52 a.m. this morning, after my meeting with the ministry but before getting back to the office. The address had the mark of a random account generated by Google, but the content of the message was anything but.

Only Gomez—or someone with whom Gomez had shared intimate details—could have written the email. Gomez was the only person who'd ever called me *Brother Hackett*, and only Gomez and I had been on that berm in the Kuwaiti desert. No one else knew what we'd promised each other that morning as we watched the sun come up to roast the desert sands.

A red warning light started flashing in the back of my mind. A dead man was speaking from beyond the grave, and the correlation with Henry Delgado blared painfully right beside it.

But unlike before where I'd been grossly unsettled because of a damned picture on the television, I took a deep breath and exhaled slowly, focusing on a spot on the far wall, looking through it. Something real was happening, I thought, the coincidences too many.

I calmly reached into my briefcase and removed a narrow leather portfolio, placing it on the desk in front of me. It contained old-fashioned business cards, an antiquated thing, but suitable for those moments when people still shook hands and presented contact info with pretentious flare.

I flipped to the back of the portfolio where I stored the cards for those individuals I never intended to call but had known not to toss. I quickly found the one I was searching for with its white background, embossed black lettering, and gold seal in the upper left corner. I took out my mobile phone and dialed the number, bringing the handset to my ear.

After one ring the line came alive. "This is Doug."

The voice hit my ears with a despised familiarity. "Doug Mitchell?" I asked.

"Yes. Who's this?"

"Mason Hackett."

"Mason? Mason Hackett? How are you, man? What's it been, like two years?"

"Something like that. Barcelona," I said.

"That's right. You still in finance? What's the name of the firm? Muttfield and . . . ?"

"Ruttfield and Leason."

"Ah. That's right. Sorry. How's things? How's business? I'm still waiting for my stock tip."

The man's insincerity grated on me, just as it had in Iraq, just as it had that day in the Pentagon, and just as it had during a random encounter at a restaurant in Barcelona two years ago. Doug was one of the few people in this world who irritated me so deeply, I could feel my blood pressure rise like a thermometer over a blue flame.

"Don't hold your breath. I'm not calling to catch up. It's something else."

"Ha. Sounds ominous. What can I do for you?"

"You still telling folks you're a diplomat?"

"I *am* a diplomat, Mason."

"Yeah, sure. You back stateside or still in Paris?"

"Paris, obviously. This is my office line."

I knew it was but wanted him to say it. In the fifteen years I'd known Doug, trust never characterized our interaction. But it made our relationship straightforward, believe it or not. If you know you can't trust someone, you're never caught off guard.

"Why?" asked Doug. "You eager for some inside scoop on the next G8 or something?"

"No."

"Then what? I've got a meeting in ten and then I'm meeting my daughter for lunch, so either spit it out or call me back in a few hours. How'd you get this number, anyway?"

"You gave me your card, remember?"

"That's right. Figured you would have burned it. So, come on. What's up?"

"Have you seen the news today?"

"You'll need to be more specific. I watch a lot of news."

"Did you see the story about a journalist getting detained in Ukraine?"

"There's been a few. Which one are you talking about?"

"It just happened today. The news is saying it's a guy named Henry Delgado."

"Yeah, I think I saw it. So?"

"They showed his picture."

"Okay?"

"It looks exactly like Kevin Gomez," I said, pronouncing each syllable of his name so it was unmistakable.

Doug didn't respond, his pause breaking the back-and-forth of our conversation.

"Doug? You there?"

"Mason, Gomez died. Remember? You were there, so was I."

"I know where I was, and I know he died. But I'm telling you, this guy Delgado looks just like him. Spitting image."

"Okay, so what?"

"Why did you hesitate when I said the picture looked just like Gomez?" I asked.

"Because Gomez is dead and, to be frank, you sound off."

"I can assure you I'm not."

"Fine. What gives? You saw someone on TV who *looks* like Gomez," Doug said with a huff. "I got a meeting, so come on."

"Your meeting can wait. I'm not calling about what I saw on the TV."

"Then spit it out, man. Goddamn. I should be the last person you'd call about that guy."

"I got an email," I said flatly, once again staring at the cryptic words on the screen coming from beyond the grave.

"An email?"

"Yeah, and it said to call you."

"What? Why? What'd it say?"

"It said I should start with you."

"Start with me? You're sounding crazy, man. Who sent the email?"

I waited a second before responding, intentionally letting the air between us go dead so my response would hit Doug like a brick. "Gomez."

There was another pause before Doug uttered, "Mason, Gomez is dead and—"

"I know he's dead, but he wrote it. It landed in my inbox this morning, and he said start with *Doug*. You."

"Mason, I have no idea what you're talking about."

"Don't fuck with me," I said steadily. "You're a shitty liar, and don't think for one second I believe you're a trade rep or some other bullshit diplomat. I saw you in Iraq. Your crap didn't fly then, it didn't fly during that fucking inquisition after we got back, and it's not flying now. Why am I getting an email from a dead man, and why does he say I should start with you?"

"That's enough," Doug snapped. "Where are you?"

"Frankfurt."

"Frankfurt. Right. Then if you're not an idiot, you know not to talk about this shit over the phone and definitely not on my work line."

"I don't care," I replied. "You know something. I can hear it every time you stop to think about what to say next. Gomez? Delgado? What's going on?"

"We're done talking about this. As far as I know, Gomez is dead, and this email and this Delgado shit is nuts. You should see someone, Mason."

"Don't make any plans tonight. I'm getting on the next plane and will be in Paris in a few hours. Meet me at Le Bonaparte on Rue Guillaume Apollinaire. Six o'clock."

"What?"

"You heard me. You don't want to talk on the phone, fine. That's the beauty of Europe. You're never really that far away."

"Mason, wait—"

I hung up, setting my mobile phone down next to the keyboard. I then picked up my desk line. "Hi, Marta . . . Please get me on the next flight to Paris . . . I believe it departs in a few hours . . . Thanks."

I leaned back in my chair, lacing my fingers behind my head and stretching my neck and back. I felt a few pops, releasing the tension in my spine and shoulders. I then stood and looked out my window at the gray sky.

Doug knew something. I just needed to get it out of him.

CHAPTER FOUR

The flight from Frankfurt to Paris took one hour and fifteen minutes. Without luggage, I expedited myself through immigration and customs like an entitled ass and grabbed a taxi.

I arrived at restaurant Le Bonaparte on Rue Guillaume Apollinaire just after six to find Doug waiting for me, sitting outside in a row of twenty other tables and chairs filled by the evening crowd. It was open-air, agreeable, and public, across from a pedestrian square with the pointy tower of Église de Saint Germain de Prés staring down at everything.

I surveyed the street once more before sitting down beside Doug, wondering how many eyes, cameras, spotter scopes, and directional microphones were on me. They were the tools nosy, scrutinizing, and intrusive people used—intelligence officers and surveillants—tearing open people's lives like a can opener exposing the ragged edges. I hated being under a microscope. Hated it.

Doug had spy written all over him from the first moment I had the displeasure of meeting him fifteen years ago. CIA, DIA, NSA—it could have been any one of them. Given our exchange over the phone, the spooks were probably out in force right now, watching the crazy guy—me—who believes his friend has come back from the dead.

"How was the flight?" asked Doug, a pleasant smile on his face, as if martinis and oysters were coming right out. It'd been a few years, but he hadn't aged all that much. He was a well-built black man approaching fifty, but it was hard to tell he was over forty. Maybe a line or two around the eyes, a strand of gray struggling like a weed in his closely trimmed hair, and a gray suit that was almost too tight.

"Fine," I said, leaning back in my chair and assuming the necessary café pose, feeling the bamboo seatback cut into my shoulder blades.

"Glad to hear it. The afternoon Lufthansa flight?"

"Yes."

"I've never taken that one. Whenever I need to go to Germany, it's Berlin. But it's comparable, I'm sure." Doug slid a menu across the table. "You like wine? I recommend the Syrah, third one down on the right."

"Water's fine."

The phony smile remained etched on Doug's face. He signaled the waiter, ordered himself a scotch and soda and a Perrier for me.

"It's good to see you, Mason."

"Of course, and you," I replied disingenuously. "But let's skip the small talk."

"Sure. All business. Still," Doug went on, keeping his deportment pleasant, "always good to catch up. Especially with someone from the war."

The war? Is that how it's referred to now? The modern-day equivalent of saying, *Back in Nam?* Fuckin-A.

When our unit arrived in Ramadi, someone from on high assigned Doug to my platoon as an observer, whatever the hell that means. No one *observes* in war—you're either in it or you're not. Even if you're an aid worker with a bleeding heart rather than a soulless one, you can't simply observe. Bombs and bullets don't ask whether you're there to watch or participate—getting killed is equal opportunity for everyone.

With just three weeks on the ground, orders were issued from somewhere outside the battalion. My platoon went on an op that went sideways; lots of people died who shouldn't have. Similar missions happened six more times during that deployment to the sandbox.

Then, when I got back to the States, battered and scarred, three suits with no names grilled me in the basement of the Pentagon. Doug was connected to all of it, including the final ripping, the entire razing giving off a deceptive stink. Doug was present the day Gomez died too.

Now the email.

Too many coincidences.

"We just got off the phone a few hours ago," I said, meeting Doug's eyes. "What's going on?"

"With what?" he asked innocently.

"Quit the game. With Gomez. A dead man who apparently isn't."

Doug pressed his lips into a thin line, seeming to weigh how to respond. His eyes flitted about scrutinizing the surrounding company. Glasses of wine tipping back, small plates of cheese or sliced duck resting on tables, and charming laughter behind chic sunglasses. Paris in the fall.

"That's right," Doug remarked as if he suddenly remembered. "You think some reporter who got his ass detained in Ukraine looks like Gomez."

"Yes, Henry Delgado. A Spaniard."

"I don't know what to tell you, man. Weird. But Gomez is dead. You saw him die. So did I."

"Yeah, I know what I saw back then, and I know what I saw this morning."

"Then what? You saw it with your own eyes, in person, back in that hellhole. Fucking Ramadi. Yet here you are, convinced it's your buddy on TV, back from the grave. Never mind the name or nationality." Doug cocked his head. "The war finally catching up with you? Guilt, PTSD?"

The waiter arrived with the drinks, setting them down indifferently along with a small, black plastic tray holding the bill. Rather than firing back at Doug, I took advantage of the interruption and picked up my glass of Perrier to take a sip. I then set it back down but did not remove my fingers from around the glass. I rotated it on the table in short counterclockwise movements—twist, twist, twist—letting the perspiration form a wet ring on the tablecloth. "You're forgetting the email I received."

"Right. The email." Doug reached for his own drink and swirled it. "What'd it say, again?"

"It said to start with you."

Doug laughed awkwardly, like a teenager trying to appear more in control than youth would allow. "Mason, you sure someone isn't playing a joke on you, fucking with you? I mean, if it was Gomez but you think he's actually Delgado, or is it that Delgado is Gomez? I'm confused, but whatever." Doug shook his head to break free from his condescending logic. "The guy who's been detained, how did he send the email if he was captured?"

I rotated my glass again, not smiling or frowning. It was a good question, a nice counterpoint, and one I'd already contemplated but hadn't sussed out yet. But I would. Doug was acting too coy for there not to be an explanation.

"You're CIA, right?" I said, redirecting. "All that crap about government observer, now a trade rep. You gave it away when you sat on the board digging into why the ops went wrong. No diplomat acts that way. It's bullshit, right?"

Doug cringed at the mention of those three letters: C-I-A. His eyes once again bounced around the patrons sitting nearby—three young girls in jeans wearing floral and solid-color blouses, a young man in a navy suit with curly blond hair, two older gentlemen wearing jackets that were worn at the seams and elbows—looking for any sign they might have overheard those forbidden three letters.

"Don't worry, Doug. I'm not about to expose you to all these nice folks. But I am tired of the BS. I know enough to know you're lying and something isn't right."

I could see Doug contemplating the direction of the conversation and his role in it. I continued rotating my glass, slowly turning it once, twice, three times. Waiters weaved in and around tables, and conversations clucked with few discernible words. The occasional car horn echoed across the square, and the angels of God looked down from Église de Saint Germain de Prés, judging it all.

"Let's take a walk," Doug finally said.

* * *

Doug knocked back the remainder of his scotch and popped up from his chair before tossing a few euros on the table. The tenor of our meeting instantly changed.

I remained seated for an additional moment. I honestly hadn't known what to expect coming here to confront Doug. Perhaps denial, perhaps a refusal to talk at all. But this . . . I had a suspicion Doug felt compelled to reveal something to me but loathed to do so, like a professor having to give a student an "A" on a paper even though the haughty child, barely an adult, never bothered to attend class.

A sense of wariness—mixed with a strong notion of curiosity—crept inside me. I stood and took up a position abreast of Doug. We crossed the intersection and headed east along Rue de l'Abbaye.

"I need you to listen very carefully," Doug began, the afternoon shadows making it seem later than it actually was. "I'm about to break a whole host of rules by telling you this. But, ya know, fuck it. I'm tired of the charade myself."

I studied Doug and saw the tautness of his jawline, the movement of his eyes against corners, windows, and cars, and the speed of his walk, which was a hair faster than a relaxed stroll. His demeanor gave me a small sense of hope as well as apprehension, as if on the edge of a great precipice. A cliff, perhaps, which up until a few hours ago hadn't existed, but which now brought into question the events surrounding one of the most painful memories of my life.

"Yes, I'm CIA, have been since we first met. But you already knew that," Doug began. "What I'm about to tell you is highly classified. The majority of people who pass through CIA's halls know nothing of what I'll call *the Program*, and most presidents don't find out until their second year in office, after being vetted, so to speak. You following me?"

I nodded, keeping pace with Doug, with my gaze focused straight ahead at the avenue before us.

"All right. For the past twenty years I've been involved in the Program, which goes all the way back to the end of World War II. When our forefathers drafted the charter for CIA and enshrined into law the intel community's authorities, they were very precise about one authority in particular—covert action.

"Not that crap you see on TV—black masks and guns and rock-star spies—but real covert action. Knocking the crap out of the Reds, but with deniability. Hiding the hand of the US government. Shaping the world according to our wants and desires—all in the name of freedom and democracy, fucking city on a high hill—and making the masses and their leaders think someone else was behind it or that it just happened. Still with me?"

"I've read a bit of history."

"Right, sure you have. But what you haven't read about is the *real* covert action we do. The Bay of Pigs, the Phoenix Program—they were all big CIA covert ops, but the deniability was in statement only. Paper-thin. Perfectly transparent. Everyone knew it was us.

"No, what I'm talking about is the real deal. Complete, total, and utter deniability and nonattribution. So secret only a handful of people ever know the truth. Records so classified and vague no one will ever get at them or leak whatever they think they might find.

"You see, even back in the forties they knew we'd have to do some very sensitive stuff. Nasty stuff. Stuff maybe the American people couldn't stomach, going against everything we think we are—the righteous beacon of democracy—so we could defeat our enemies and protect our allies, and so the world would go the way we needed it to go. You understand?"

"Yes," I replied, a witness to America's virtuous influence long ago and still sickened by it.

"Good. So, this—"

"Are you in charge of it?" I interrupted.

"The Program? No. Let's say I'm involved."

"Right," I muttered, wondering if *involved* was the same as *observe*.

"So, the Program, it's a long-term type of operation, generational. We need people with unquestionable loyalty and dedication, with certain skills, but who have no ties to America, who can go forth and do God's work. But the typical idea of recruiting foreigners to do our bidding was found . . . problematic. We needed full control with no uncertainty. Beyond reproach. So how do we do this? Where do we find these people?" Doug asked rhetorically.

I didn't answer, and we rounded the corner onto Rue de Buci.

"We *make* them."

"You make them?"

"Yeah. These people with special skills, with loyalty, who are willing to give up everything—they have to die so they can live."

"What?"

"Since the 1950s we've been faking the deaths of special operatives so they could assume the identity of someone else entirely. But not merely a made-up name with a passport and pictures of kids on swing sets who don't exist. They needed to assume the life of someone *real*. Everything had to be real."

"I'm not following."

"Someone who'd been born, who had parents, a job, hobbies, a hairstyle, a background that if checked would turn up a bona fide history. But as you can imagine, only certain types of profiles are suitable. Candidates' lives had to be foreign, minimal social and familial ties, of similar ages and appearances to the American operative whom they were paired with. I won't go through it all, but you get the idea."

"Yeah, sure. I'm just, I guess, skeptical about you switching out lives like that. Wouldn't the candidate's friends and family know?"

"It takes the right kind of profile, where there isn't a risk."

"No ties, no family left?"

"In a sense, yeah."

"And what happens to these people—the candidates—whose lives you're taking over?"

"Good question. They have to disappear. Sometimes people are willing to give up their identity for a new one, then settle in the heart of America. Back in the day, Soviet defectors coming out from behind the Iron Curtain fit that bill nicely."

"And what if someone didn't want to give up their life?"

Doug shrugged. "We find a different candidate. We don't kill them if that's what you're inferring. A lot of preparation goes into this thing, and we know long before we approach someone whether they'll do it or not."

"So sure of yourselves."

"Yes," replied Doug firmly.

"I'm guessing Gomez is part of this?"

"Yes. Gomez, now Delgado, is what we call a *consultant*—all people like Delgado are—and his former life ended on that stretcher back in Ramadi. His heart really did stop—medically controlled, of course—and he was put in a body bag. There was a battlefield funeral and a burial at Arlington. And his next of kin—a father and mother, I think—were presented an American flag on behalf of a grateful nation. For all intents and purposes, he died and was reborn in the life of another—Henry Delgado—to continue serving his country."

"Wait. Gomez knew this was going to happen?"

"Of course he did. We'd been planning his disappearance for about a year. We recruited him, and he agreed to join the Program to become a consultant."

"What?" I tried to hide my astonishment, but my voice betrayed me.

"I know you two were close. He told us, and it's part of his file."

"File . . . wait. Back up." The fact that Doug knew Gomez and I had been tight meant nothing. It was the other thing he'd said. "It doesn't surprise me Gomez volunteered for this thing. I get it. He was that kind of guy. But are you telling me you orchestrated his fake death in Ramadi in the middle of a war?"

"No. We're good, but we're not that good."

"And the risk," I went on. "If the people you recruit for this Program are so special, top operatives—*consultants*—how could you risk him leading a scout sniper platoon in the heart of darkness? He could have been killed for real any day out there."

"Let me explain."

"Yes. Please do."

"Gomez insisted he deploy with you guys one last time. And he knew the risk, and so did we. He couldn't back out. Wouldn't be right. He owed it to you guys even though he knew eventually he'd have to disappear. And that's one of the reasons we wanted him for the Program: loyalty and dedication."

"But that battle . . . the day he died . . ."

"Don't think for a moment we staged a battle and got all those people killed only to fake a death. That day was real, every bit of it, including Gomez's injuries."

"And my injuries, and those of my men."

"Yeah. That was a real op, planned and executed by you and your battalion."

"And what about those ops the men in suits questioned me on? Are they connected to this?"

"No. Those were different. Unrelated to Gomez."

I exhaled, making my lungs go empty, refusing to allow my mind to fall into those dark memories but also trying to digest what I was hearing.

"Back to Gomez," continued Doug. "Once things turned out the way they did, we took advantage of the opportunity. We're agile in that regard. Our docs came in, regulated the appearance of his death with a shot in the arm, and Kevin Gomez disappeared forever, fated to live again as someone else."

"And Henry Delgado?"

"The real *Henrique* Delgado was a near-perfect twin of Gomez. All of us have them, people who look almost identical. Maybe someone who lives on the other side of the world, or someone who lived fifty years ago, but they exist. Just so happens Henrique Delgado fit all the other requirements too."

"And what happened to him?"

"He was from Spain, a loner with no family. We helped him disappear the same year. I hear he's living a quiet life in the Rockies in a nice cabin courtesy of US taxpayers."

I stayed silent for a time, walking, looking but not seeing anything, trying to make sense of what Doug had told me. But I couldn't, not yet. Hours from now, once everything had settled, I might make sense of it, but I'd have a million questions. At the moment what resonated with me was Gomez's involvement in covert operations so secret, he erased his entire past to do . . . what?

"Why was he in Ukraine?" I asked.

"He was on a mission. That's all I'll say."

"Really? That's all you'll say? A mission. *The big mish.*"

"He was looking into something. Something that threatens the balance of power between governments and international corporations. Don't ask any more questions."

I shot Doug a look, wondering what the hell he meant by *the balance of power between governments and corporations*, but chose not to press the matter. "Okay, fine. But why tell me the other stuff?"

"I have immense respect for Delgado—the man you knew as Gomez—and he obviously wanted you to know the truth, particularly if he thought he might never have an opportunity to tell you himself."

"What do you mean?"

"Just that. I suspect he wanted you to know the truth."

"But . . . my God." A realization hit me like a hammer. "You're not going to get him, are you?"

"No, we're not," Doug replied flatly.

"Why not? If everything you told me is true, that Gomez and the other *consultants* like him are sooo special, how can you abandon him?"

"Tough choices. It's the mission."

"It's disgraceful."

"Think what you want. Delgado knew the deal. We all do."

"Oh, don't give me that shit. You make it sound all selfless and pure. For the good of the country, you abandon your best people? You could get him out if you wanted to, couldn't you?" I said, levying the question more as a challenge.

Doug shrugged.

"Right. 'Course you won't, because it might compromise the Program."

"It's more than that."

"Is it?"

"Yes. What do you think he was doing over there?"

"I don't know. You won't tell me."

"He was going up against the fucking Russians and the bloody mercenaries and conglomerates of death undermining the world and threatening mom and apple pie. Serious business and I bet a hell of a lot worse than we think."

"Yeah, I've seen the news. Governments and international financiers aren't playing by the rules anymore either. Big surprise. Glad to hear you're on top of it."

"Fuck off. Let me put it this way for you. The Russians are invading their neighbors on an annual basis, knocking off their enemies with plutonium appetizers, using your traditional GRU and SVR types, but also employing the new-age mercenary companies to do the real dirty work that even Putin doesn't want to be associated with. He likes hobnobbing with the international business types—the oligarchs and international citizens who owe loyalty to no nation—and then covertly backing them for cutthroat shit that turns a profit.

"And when I say cutthroat, I mean it, literally and figuratively depending on who and where. And if you ask me, there's men and women out there—beyond the Kremlin's heavy hand—who may be worse because they are rewriting the playbook as we try to catch up. Where we see borders and talk about international relations and norms, they see none of it—borders and national loyalties are antiquated ways of thinking. Power is shifting elsewhere.

"So, if we got caught trying to rescue Delgado in the mix of something we don't fully understand, the blowback would be catastrophic. The enemy might not nuke Washington, but don't think for a second they won't launch a stray rocket in Syria or run a live-fire exercise in the North Sea too close to one of our ships. And targeting our own spies, officials, and economic interests would be a given. Show up on the doorstep of the family home in Arlington, Virginia, kill everyone inside with a spray of gunfire from a suppressed submachine gun, and then sabotage a natural gas pipeline so they can scoop up the market. Putin could back it, or someone else we don't know anything about could order it.

"We're not prepared to go down that road for one man. It'd compromise everything else we have going on."

"It's disgraceful, what you're doing. Or let me rephrase, what you're unwilling to do."

"You were a marine, so I'll cut you some slack. Things were black and white for you, *loyalty and honor, leave no man behind.* You can do that when the marines hit the beach because everyone knows you're there, nothing to hide. You plant fucking flags on mountains. But this is the world of espionage and covert action. Lies, double-crosses, admit nothing, deny everything—it's on the recruiting poster."

"Even against your own people," I said, my disgust catching in my throat.

"Like I said, Kevin knew the game. That's the reason he was out there on the edge. He was under no illusion what would happen if he got caught. Everyone in the Program knows."

"So that's it?"

"Think whatever you want. I've already told you more than I should have, but I did it because Delgado liked you and I know you from Iraq."

"You know they'll torture and kill him, right? You just said it—you think it's the fucking Russians or some merc outfit who have him. Torture, extracting information, a convenient bullet to the head—it's a national sport for them."

"Yeah. But let me ask this—why do you care? Your friend has been dead for over fifteen years and he chose this life, and he didn't tell you anything. He chose to keep you in the dark, until now. So why do you care about someone who did that?"

I paused, finding Doug's words sharp. I couldn't deny his point, but it wasn't that plain for me. I understood what Gomez did, choosing that life. He was a natural. Talented, with instincts that let him walk away from tight spots he shouldn't have. And he must have known severing his past life was how it had to be . . . but now things had changed. He'd reached out to a trusted friend—me.

"The email," I finally said.

"I wouldn't read too much into it. I think he wanted you to know the truth, but nothing more. He told me as much," Doug remarked with a shrug.

I noted a change in his tone like he was making an effort to sound indifferent. Moments ago he'd been wound tighter than my Catholic grandmother when she met Billy Graham. Doug's words and movements had been measured and rehearsed; but now, nonchalance had entered the mix.

"What happens if Gomez—ehh—Delgado talks?" I asked. "Won't that expose everything?"

"Delgado is tough, you know that, and his cover is one of the best. Plus, we won't acknowledge anything."

"Do you know if they caught him in the act, whatever he was doing?"

"Sources indicate he was caught under suspicious conditions."

"What the fuck does that mean?"

"Exactly what you think it means. Suspicious circumstances."

"Do you think they'll kill him?"

"I won't speculate."

"I'm asking what you think."

Doug hesitated another moment, then offered, "They will eventually."

"But not till they squeeze what they can out of him."

Doug nodded slowly.

I snorted, looking up at the street signs. We'd ended up at the intersection of Quai des Grands Augustins and the bridge of Pont Neuf. I shook my head and veered off, stopping by the wall overseeing the River Seine. I rested my palms on the cool stone and watched a riverboat pass underneath the bridge, hearing the ding of the captain's bell.

Doug came up beside me, his hands in his pockets, a small tear forming in his eye from the wind scraping his face. I was at a loss about what to say, so disgusted and confused by what he'd told me. Angry, too.

Truth is, I didn't know what to think. Part of me was hurt, maybe even mad. My best friend faked his death and I, consequently, had carried around a numbing guilt for over fifteen years. Since then, I'd woken up just about every morning with sweat-soaked sheets and my heart racing like I was hooked up to an electric chair.

I'd drunk myself into a stupor an embarrassing number of times. I'd punched walls, yelled, shaken my fists in such a rage I'd scared off more than one nice girl who didn't deserve to be burdened by anyone as broken as me, not to mention the friends I'd lost because of my shit.

Gomez, my men who died, and the horror before and after that day, it was all linked. I could see their faces, the dead and the living, and hear their voices. I'd held the hands of their next of kin as they wept. Mothers, daughters, brothers. I wept too. The guilt that haunts me, it eats away at my soul with a slow rot.

I don't know if *forgiving myself* or *getting past it* are even the right ways to think about these things. I don't know how to think about any of it, and talking about it sure as shit doesn't help. It makes it worse.

Forgive myself? Get past it? And now this? Goddammit, Gomez! Goddammit!

Yet the man reached out, I repeated to myself. *He* reached out to *me*. He sent me an email—a call for help. The bastard had called in a pact we'd both sworn to uphold, no matter the odds or what stood in the way. A battlefield debt drawn up on a berm in the middle of nowhere in the Kuwaiti desert with the rising sun as witness.

How the hell could I ignore it? How could I live with myself if I did?

"What's going through that mind of yours, Hackett?"

"Nothing," I said curtly.

"Don't bullshit me. You have the face of someone thinking about their next move."

"I don't have a next move."

"You better not."

I kept watching the river flow by.

"You hear me? You need to let this go. Just let it go."

Again I didn't respond.

"I need you to give me your word you'll let this go. Don't think about doing anything to find out more or to help Delgado. The issue is over. You hear me?"

I finally turned to face Doug. There was something genuine in the CIA man's face, like he was pleading. It made me want to punch him, drive my knuckles into the man's jaw. I wanted to explode, yet I held back, my mind elsewhere, on other things I hadn't fully thought through yet.

Maybe I never would think through them. It was just an idea.

"Do you hear me, Mason? Drop it."

"Fine," I replied, wanting the man to shut up.

CHAPTER FIVE

The guard smacked Delgado across the face. The impact drove his skin into an even deeper shade of red, and his brain rattled from the blow.

However, despite being severely dazed, he noticed the oaf had used an open palm this time rather than a closed fist.

Up to this point, it had only been closed, knuckled fists, along with booted kicks and some asshole with a baton. If he ever got the chance, he'd shove that baton so far up the man's ass it'd make the bastard's head pop up like a jack-in-the-box.

The guard smacked Delgado again before taking a step back, like a well-trained dog unable to think for himself, merely attack and heel. Delgado wanted to smirk. Perhaps his captors were getting tired, his bruised and broken body wearing them down. He would have laughed if he could, a stupid cocky laugh like an action hero in a B-grade movie.

With the momentary pause, he struggled to adjust his wrists, which were bound behind his back with oversized zip ties that sliced into his flesh. The restraints were the kind specially designed to bind human limbs, and he knew the type all too well. His captors had also bound his legs to the chair with rope and added a strap around his waist to secure him to the seat. They'd wrapped him so tight he doubted he could fart.

A gloved hand grabbed Delgado's hair and yanked his head back. Another guard dumped a bucket of icy water on his face and chest, the frigid cold jump-starting all his senses and bringing him back from his odyssey of pain.

He remembered when they unloaded him in this square room, he could feel a draft from somewhere, though he didn't see any windows. There was only a single metal hatch and a concrete floor with a drain surrounded by puddles of oily water. A bright fluorescent bulb hung from the ceiling with a headache-inducing hum, the light searing his eyes.

The pain he felt from the nearly continuous beatings was excruciating. Where in the beginning it had been broad soreness from the punches and kicks, it had started to localize in precise, pointed locations. Sharp, dull, burning, and throbbing pain invaded his arms, legs, ankles, stomach, ribs, face, and every joint in his body. He couldn't tell if anything had been fractured but he wouldn't doubt it.

"Wake up! Wake up!" yelled a deep voice with a thick Slavic accent. "You fucking man. Open your eyes."

Delgado managed to crack his lids, never realizing his eyelashes could hurt.

"Wake up!" The guard smacked him again. Two hands grabbed his face while coarse fingers pried open his eyes.

Delgado cried out, "I'm awake! I'm awake!"

Even to his own ears his voice sounded rough and labored. He struggled to focus and found the guard's face inches from his. The man looked wild with unkempt hair, black eyes, and an unshaven face.

The guard stepped back again, allowing Delgado to see at least three other men in the room. All of them wore mismatched camouflage clothing, but not from any specific military. Two held AK-74s; the other had a pistol on his hip.

Another bucket of water hit his face, causing him to shake his head and blink. When he opened his eyes, a different man stood before him. Less brutish, more intense, and with a suggestion of intelligence.

"Henry Delgado, journalist," said this new man in a more controlled voice. Delgado noticed his clothing was crisper than the others, and he seemed to wear a rank on his shoulder boards. Major, perhaps.

"Is that your name?" the major inquired. "Henry Delgado, journalist?"

"Where am I? What's going on?" asked Delgado.

"Mr. Delgado. I do not think that is your name. I do not think you are a journalist."

"Please, where am I? What's going on?" Delgado tried to make his voice sound weak and pleading. He couldn't appear strong, nor in any way that might imply he was anything other than *Henry Delgado*: a terrified reporter about to shit his pants.

"You've been taken into custody by the Patriotic Forces of Donbas, of the Donetsk People's Republic. This is for your safety. The area we rescue you from is a dangerous place, disputed territory, with many Ukrainian criminals and terrorists. You are safe now."

"Safe?" asked Delgado, the irony of the question hanging in the air. "Where am I?"

"The actual location does not matter. You're under the protection of PFD. You know PFD, yes?"

"Please, I'm a reporter with the Associated Press. Out of New York. My wallet has my credentials."

"Yes. It says Henry Delgado, journalist, Spaniard."

"That's right. I'm a reporter."

"Journalists carry pistols, yes?" The major held up the CZ-75, which Delgado recognized was the same one he'd had tucked in his pants when they took him. He'd known if caught with it, possession of the pistol would be incriminating. He'd thought through these things between the beatings, car ride, and being dragged into this room. The sight of his pistol in the major's hand, however, made his heart sink.

"I do not know much about Western journalism, but I do not think a pistol is normal."

Delgado stayed silent.

"I will be very easy with you and you will speak the truth to me, okay? I do not think your name is Henry Delgado, nor are you a journalist. We know about fake news, as your ex-president says," quipped the major with a small laugh.

"Please," Delgado pleaded again, "just call my office. They will ex—"

The major raised his hand to silence him. "I will not call any office. I don't have to. I already spoke with someone."

Delgado scrunched his beaten face, confused.

"Your friend Fedir told me many things. You remember Fedir? He knows lots of things, and he says you're not a journalist."

Delgado knew the accusation would come and he felt the virtual noose tightening around his neck. Fedir had sold him out—betrayed him. But how far? Had he simply revealed he wasn't a journalist? Or had he divulged everything: what they were doing, who they were meeting, and that he'd been . . .

"I know you are an American, and I know Delgado is not your real name. Therefore, we will talk until I am satisfied you are speaking the truth. Okay?"

Delgado took a deep breath and braced himself.

CHAPTER SIX

Mikhail Petrov wore a GRU colonel's uniform that still smelled of the previous owner and hung too loosely off his wiry frame. The rank fabric chafed his skin, while the damp air of the building's interior carried a cold odor of wet dust and rusty pipes that oppressed his lungs. The conditions reminded him of the farm he grew up on in the Volga, except back then the floors had been covered with animal blood and hacks of tissue from the slaughter.

It had been a wretched life on that farm—for him and his sisters— and he pitied his drunk of a father for having slogged through it until his unsurprising death at forty-six. After that meaningless event, Petrov had left them all, vowing never to go back to an existence ever resembling the toil demanded by unforgiving land, and he'd been deeply satisfied once he'd reached his calling in life—a vocation that he willingly let consume him.

That was a long time ago.

Here, he sat on a folding chair behind a bare metal desk with his boots placed squarely on the crumbling concrete floor. The only light in the hollow room came from the desk lamp, which cast a malignant glow on the paper file spread before him. Clipped to the top left corner of the folder was a small photo of a man in his late thirties with short brown hair, caramel skin, blue eyes, and the chiseled face of someone inclined to . . . how would the Americans say it . . . *extreme sports*. Or maybe the outdoors. Either way, it wasn't important. The papers underneath held the real value, and they numbered about fifty, detailing the particulars of this individual's life.

On the opposite side of the folder was another stack of papers, but instead of documenting personal data like place of birth, college transcripts, and narratives about the man's hedonistic retreats, these papers described a highly secretive operation run by American intelligence. There were more unknowns than confirmed facts about the operation, but there was enough information to illustrate the substantial scope of the program, the man's involvement with it, and the threat he in particular posed to Petrov's business.

Over the past year, Petrov had read this file at least thirty times, picking through each morsel of information over and over again, and comparing and contrasting this one to that. He'd also added a few pages of his own to the pile, which went beyond what the clumsy shits in Moscow had put together. His people were so much more skilled at this kind of thing. His people had a thoroughness that a bureaucrat—even a well-trained one—couldn't match. Money made many things possible when it came to selecting talent.

Yet despite everything his contacts in the Kremlin had provided and what he'd formulated on his own, he still found the man and the operation an enigma. And they would most likely remain so until Mr. Henry Delgado broke. And he *had* to break—it was the only way.

Petrov had only checked in on Mr. Delgado once to confirm it was him; he kept out of sight for the most part. The game he was constructing was delicate, and he needed to handle the situation like a director would a stage performance, with each actor playing his or her role at precisely the right time and place with the exact amount of emotion and vigor or lack thereof. If Mr. Delgado really was who he believed him to be, he couldn't permit any mistakes. Mistakes were unforgivable, even for him—Delgado's actions were a threat to the latest deal Petrov and his partners were building—one of many—and Petrov needed to know why he was here.

A knock came at the door much harder than necessary, disturbing his concentration.

Petrov knew who it was by the rhythm of the *bang, bang, bang* which, in his view, spoke volumes about the temperament of the offender. A person of unmerited arrogance. The man warranted a bullet to the knee.

"Enter," Petrov called.

The door swung open and in walked a man wearing a mismatched camouflage uniform and a major's rank on his shoulder boards. His name was Mykola Klymenko, but he expected—no, rather this shit of a man demanded—that others call him *Major*.

Accordingly, Petrov chose to call him by his given name.

"Shut the door, Mykola," Petrov said, returning his attention to the file.

Mykola gave Petrov a slow glare, then dutifully closed the door. He looked around the room, searching for a place to sit but was unaware Petrov had removed all the chairs except for his.

"What do you have?" asked Petrov.

Mykola frowned as he approached the desk, stopping a few feet away. He stood straight with his arms by his side as a well-disciplined soldier should, but Petrov detected a sea of defiance under the man's skin.

Major Mykola Klymenko wasn't a real soldier, not anymore, fifteen years having gone by since he wore a private's uniform in the Ukrainian Army. But the passage of time and low rank hadn't stopped Mykola from fashioning himself as a senior commander in the Donbas when the fighting broke out a few years ago, and he no doubt expected the customary respect of the rank he'd appropriated. His particular insecurities compelled him to exert power over others.

Petrov, however, would never accord him the basic military courtesies a real major would receive. In fact, Petrov was under no obligation to render anyone military courtesies. Even though he wore a GRU uniform, he'd hadn't officially been in the ranks for over a decade. He only wore this rag to keep Mykola and people like him in check. They'd never know the truth about who he was and who his real partners were—the minds of Mykola and his Ukrainian thugs too feeble to realize how the world had changed.

Petrov closed the file and met Mykola's deep-set eyes. "Well, what do you have?" he repeated.

"Nothing new, Colonel. The man will not break so easily."

"Did you expect him to?" asked Petrov, leaning back and crossing his arms. "It's only been a few hours."

Mykola cocked his head. "You know this man more than you have revealed, yes?"

"Your skills of deduction should be commended. Your men are lucky to have a commander such as you."

Mykola spat. "Who is this man, this Henry Delgado? We did this man's capture for you, and we did so with no information about who he is or why."

"Do you think you deserve to know? Such a small favor—detaining this man—yet we have given you so much. We stand with you when the rest of the world denies your claims. Is it really so much to ask for such a little thing?"

"But *is* it such a little thing? The man believed he was going to arrange a meeting with Oleg Tolesky, one of the largest arms suppliers in the Caucasus and the Middle East. The Americans have wanted him disposed of for decades, most recently because of his work in Syria. So we set up the operation for you with Boris and his medical business, and now I hear Oleg is under house arrest in Sochi."

Mykola waited for a moment, but Petrov didn't react.

"No response? Okay, I have many questions, you see. I don't expect you to answer all of them, but I do wonder why—if this Henry Delgado is important—why do you not bring him back to Moscow? Surely Lubyanka has better facilities than here." Mykola glanced around the dilapidated room.

"You make interesting connections, Mykola. But you are correct—you don't need to know many things. Except that, yes, Mr. Delgado must remain here for the time being. He *is* very important, and he knows things we must learn more about. Things very powerful men are worried about."

"What things?"

Petrov scrunched his lips as he contemplated what to say next. If he expected Mykola and his men to compel Delgado to talk—to break—they needed something to work with. But how much to reveal was the question. A little truth, a few lies, a little misguided confusion could be good. But too much and matters could get complicated.

"Henry Delgado is a very special operative for American intelligence," Petrov began. "We have monitored him for many years, and we know Henry Delgado is not his real name, nor his true identity. A few years ago we learned he is actually a man by the name of Kevin Gomez. It confirms what we suspected about him and the operation we believe he is a member of. We think he was here trying to meet with Tolesky because of concerns about something inside the American defense industry."

"What concerns?"

Petrov shrugged, comfortable with what he'd disclosed but unwilling to go any further.

"You tell me so little as if it is so much. Why tell me these things at all?"

"Because we must break Mr. Delgado, but it cannot be men like myself. He knows he is captured, but he doesn't know how interested the Kremlin is in him. It would make him behave differently, you know, if he knew it was not Ukrainian separatists holding him, yes?" And it would cause you to behave differently if you knew it was more than just the Kremlin who had interest in this man Delgado, thought Petrov.

Mykola nodded. "Yes, you are GRU, and it would not be good to present yourself."

"No, it wouldn't," Petrov replied both truthfully and falsely at the same time, always amused when such a dichotomy existed.

"Of course," Mykola said, though only partially satisfied. But there was nothing else he could do, and there never would be for a man like him.

"Good. Now, so there is no misunderstanding, you must break him. But physical torture will not be enough, and going too far would be counterproductive. I don't want him turned into ground meat missing too many fingers and toes, with ice picks through his shins. Besides, he has been trained to withstand such things. He is very special, like I said. You understand?"

"Yes."

"Good. I need you to grind him down psychologically so there is no resistance."

"My men are skilled at this. We learned well from our Russian mentors. I have ideas."

"We shall see."

CHAPTER SEVEN

I shot up in bed, my heart pounding, my skin clammy. Darkness surrounded me and I didn't know where I was. My fists scrunched the sheets as I steadied myself. I blinked, forcing my eyes to bring my surroundings into focus. The bed, the nightstand, the television on an unfamiliar dresser, a single window with drapery I didn't recognize.

Then I remembered. Last night I'd checked into Hotel du Chadran a few blocks from Champ de Mars. A simple place I'd stayed in once or twice while on business. I was in Europe—Paris—not in some backwater village or on the edge of a war zone. No one was about to burst through the door, and I wouldn't be picking up any body parts from the street after a mortar barrage. There would be none of that. I was someplace normal, the civilized world.

I managed to swing my feet off the bed, rubbing my eyes hard, grinding the sleep away. With my breathing almost back to a reasonable rhythm, I went into the bathroom to splash water on my face. I stared at my haunted image in the mirror, trying to recall what I'd been dreaming about and thinking I needed a shave, a shower, and a cup of coffee as black as midnight.

The dream had been vivid and real, more so than usual. I'd seen Villa, Nance, Blake, Rupp, Felsmann, Hubbeard, Brian, Lench . . .

and more. Their faces flashed before me like an old-fashioned 8mm home movie, mixed with bloody streets and smoked-out buildings. Dead kids. I could hear their screams, others groaning, and everything moving so quickly, as if God had hit fast forward. And then everything went white in a flash.

I splashed cold water on my face again before patting myself dry, taking another deep breath. I didn't always wake up this way, but it happened enough to make me undecided about sleep. It's like a hangover. Knocking a few back the night before feels great, then you wake up wondering why the hell you'd had that last drink. Then you do it all over again.

I emerged from the bathroom and used the phone by the bedside to call the front desk.

"Good morning, Monsieur Hackett," said the hotelier on the other end. "It's a pleasure to have you with us again. How may I be of assistance?"

"Bonjour," I said. "Can you please send up some breakfast and my dry cleaning? Housekeeping picked it up last night."

"Right away, monsieur. Is there anything else?"

"No, thank you."

I replaced the receiver and grabbed the TV remote. I tuned to France 24, where a broadcaster was discussing the previous day's sports highlights. Frowning, I flipped to Sky News, then CNN International, then the BBC, but none of them were covering the situation in Ukraine or the day's headlines.

Glancing at the clock, I saw it was between the hours.

I powered up my laptop and searched for any updates about Henry Delgado, aka Kevin Gomez, but I didn't find anything new. The same headlines, the same articles, the same damn photos.

My conversation with Doug filtered back into my thoughts. Whoever had detained Gomez had probably killed him by now . . .

right? Why not? A few too many bats to the head or a quick, clean bullet through the nose. Done. Easy. Over.

No doubt Gomez had stared defiantly down the barrel, his final words likely some crass riposte laced with bravado. It's how he would have wanted to go out, a proverbial finger in your face.

Then, *crack*! Gomez's brains splattered against the wall, drooping like a painting by Salvador Dalí. Ciao.

I slammed my laptop closed and got up to pace around the room. Even if Gomez were still alive, he'd be dead soon. The CIA—his own country—had abandoned him. Disavowed and left to die. An operation too secret to ever acknowledge. A medal presented to no one during a ceremony in the Agency awards suite, then locked away in a cabinet with an anonymous citation. A star on the wall without a name in the book, just a blank entry.

I wanted to vomit.

Yet, I knew it had to be this way.

If the US claimed Gomez, the fallout would be complicated. Like Doug said, the confrontation wouldn't be direct; too risky for everyone. An all-out shooting war between the US and Russia—or whoever the hell was involved—would wreck the world, and not even the crazies in the Kremlin or the profit-driven conglomerates wanted that. They're too greedy now that communism proved a disappointment and CEOs can send their operations across borders with the flick of a pen. Stand toe-to-toe on the street like a neighborhood bully, sure, Moscow enjoyed throwing some weight around and giving the US the finger, but the real brawls occurred on the sidelines and in the back alleys.

The flavors of the month were proxies who didn't play by the traditional rules. Surrogates, paramilitary groups, private security firms—operatives who could murder diplomats in hotels, poison the water in a family's house in Georgetown, and set off a bomb in a beer garden in Munich. Go after the easy targets that barely make the news, but which scare the crap out of the feds because there's no more professional courtesy. War as business didn't have ethics.

The same would be true for a rescue operation, which would incur similar responses. The US government wouldn't send in a special operations team to rescue someone who wasn't theirs. Who knew where the counterpunch would come from.

A knock at the door broke my ruminations. "Room service," came the voice in the hall.

I opened the door. An attendant said good morning and wheeled in a breakfast cart while another deposited my freshly cleaned and pressed clothes in the closet. I tipped and thanked them both, recognizing one of them from a previous stay when things weren't so complicated.

Removing the metal cover from one of the plates, I found a generous European-style breakfast of fresh cheeses, cured meats, smoked fish, pastries, rolls, and spreads, but I instantly regretted ordering it. I didn't have an appetite, feeling like I had a poisoned stomach.

I settled for a cup of coffee with milk, then returned to the bathroom to clean up and get dressed. My flight back to London departed in two hours.

*   *   *

Showered, dressed, and duly caffeinated, I dropped my key at the front desk and took a car to Charles de Gaulle Airport. Checked in and through security, I headed to the business-class lounge to await my flight home.

The absence of food finally set in, and from the well-stocked buffet, I selected a croissant with jam and grabbed another coffee. I took a seat with a view of the television and picked up a newspaper from the side table, flipping to the business section. But try as I might, I found it difficult to read articles about mergers and earnings reports. I couldn't give a damn, really. Thoughts about Gomez and my chat with Doug rumbled in the back of my mind, like the aftershocks of an earthquake continuing for days.

Then, as if on cue, the broadcaster on the TV started reviewing the hour's top stories, with a segment about the detention of freelance journalist Henry Delgado number three in the lineup. The report didn't have anything new, but hearing the familiar headline persuaded me to slide the plate with the croissant away.

"I don't blame you," said a man sitting down beside me. He had an American accent and wore a pair of khakis and a striped shirt that should never have been allowed out of the Midwest. "I've never been a fan of airport food, myself. Always afraid to know how long something's been sitting out."

I regarded the man, always finding it curious how Americans, which I count myself among, like to strike up conversations beyond a polite hello with random strangers in random places, simply due to proximity or a need to talk. It's an American quality, for sure, and I'd done it myself more than once. But not today.

"Yes," I replied, returning my attention to the newspaper.

"And given the news out of Ukraine," the man continued, making an apparent effort to let his gaze wander around the lounge, "I can understand your lack of appetite."

The man's words smacked against my ears and a familiar tightness formed in my chest. Pulling my attention from the paper, I studied the man: middle-aged, more than a little overweight, a trimmed goatee to hide his double chin, and beyond the khakis and shirt, a pair of cheap shoes he probably bought at a bankrupt department store during the year-end closeout. "Do I know you?"

"No. We've never met in person and I suspect this is the first time you've ever laid eyes on me."

"Come again?"

"Tragic stuff, if you ask me. That reporter the Ukrainian separatists got," remarked the stranger shaking his head from side to side. "Let's not kid ourselves—they're probably giving him a rough time."

My disposition hardened as I shifted in my seat to face the man. "Who are you?"

"Nobody you'll need to care about for too long. I'm Garrett," he replied dishonestly.

"What do you want?"

"Nothing. I'm simply here to remind you Mr. Delgado is not your concern."

"Not my concern? What the fuck are you talking about?"

The man calling himself Garrett cocked his head. "Last night you met with a colleague of mine and you mistakenly thought Delgado was a friend of yours. Let me assure you, Mr. Delgado isn't anyone you know, and it would be a very bad idea to try anything to assist him. It would only make the situation worse, for him and you."

I leaned forward, feeling my jaw clench. In seconds, this man had pushed all the right buttons to set me off. My blood began to boil and I fought the urge to stand up and jam my finger in the bastard's face. "Did that fuck Doug send you? Is this the Pentagon inquisition all over again?"

Garrett shrugged.

"Did he send you here to threaten me?" I asked.

I hated threats. My dad hated threats; my grandfather hated threats. It was in my DNA to hate threats. Bullies make threats, and I despise bullies with every essence of my being. That was one of the reasons I joined the marines, to fight the world's bullies. Ironically, I found the Corps full of bullies, but that's beside the point. Now this clown was sitting next to me *suggesting* it would be a bad idea for me to do anything about Delgado, aka Gomez. Well zip-a-dee-doo-dah.

Doug had pulled similar shenanigans when we got back from Ramadi. But I wasn't going to stand for it this time. They put me on the chopping block back then and I had to shut up and take it like a good little boy, but not this time. I no longer wore the uniform.

"Spit it out," I said. "Are you here to threaten me to keep my mouth shut?"

"No. We don't make threats. As I said, I'm a reminder," Garrett replied.

I gritted my teeth. "Get the hell away from me before I smash your face with that fucking glass."

"No reason to be rude," Garrett said, holding up his hands in mock protest. "I'm a friend."

I flexed my fingers then told myself to calm down. The man was intentionally provoking me, doing so quite easily, and I was letting him do it. I leaned back in my chair and in a measured tone said, "You, Doug, and the lot of your kind are spineless cowards. Tell me, are you trained to fuck your own, or is it part of the hiring criteria? *Must be willing to hang your coworkers out to dry.*"

Garrett didn't flinch, his eyes still wandering about the lounge.

A woman's voice announced over the intercom, "British Airways flight three-zero-seven to London Heathrow now boarding. All passengers please proceed to the courtesy jet bridge for expedited boarding."

"I believe that's your flight," Garrett said. "Don't want to miss it."

I raised myself out of the chair without a word but kept my glare fixed on Garrett.

"Glad we had this chat, Mr. Hackett. Please remember what Doug and I said."

I remained silent, knowing I was hovering at a near boil. After a moment's pause, I turned on my heels and headed toward the gate.

"Safe travels," Garrett called behind me.

As I walked away, it took all of my self-control not to turn around, grab Garrett by the shirt, and slam him against the wall. I would have enjoyed seeing him bounce off it.

CHAPTER EIGHT

When the Airbus A319 touched down at Heathrow Airport, I had four voicemails waiting for me. One was from the office in Frankfurt, asking if I wanted any more meetings before heading back to London. The second message was from Hannah, chafed by my no-show at our appointment but suggestive in her demand for dinner the next time I was in town as recompense. My boss, Alistair, left the third message inquiring about how things were going. And the final voicemail was Caroline's, asking when I planned to pick up the last of my crap from her flat. I needed to give her the key back too.

Wholly consumed by the events of the past twenty-four hours, it was apparent I'd stepped away from my life as I never had since moving to London twelve years ago. Part of me thought I should head to my office in the city and get back at it, doing as suggested—let the matter go. But thoughts of Gomez and my apparent impotence burned in my throat like a hot coal.

The rational side of me knew Doug and that clumsy ass Garrett were right. Gomez made a choice, leaving behind his old life to become someone else to run covert ops. He was running the most sensitive kind, according to Doug, a *consultant*. He'd made his choice and I wasn't going to judge him for it, not now anyway. We all have to make choices and we have to do what's right for ourselves.

He chose to roll deeper into the filth and I applaud him for it. I chose differently.

And Doug, even for being a pompous turd, I'd always had the impression he knew his job. I don't like him or his approach, but Doug possessed a manner indicating that, despite being a shifty prick, he was a competent prick.

But knowing Gomez had been abandoned—most likely left to die—I struggled to shake it.

I had to do something to snap myself out of this circular state. I needed to work. Work was the only way I'd get my mind right; that's how I'd walked away from the Corps fifteen years ago.

I'd resigned my commission, jumped on a plane to fly across the Atlantic, and landed in a graduate program at the London School of Economics. When Ruttfield picked me up, I'd dived in full throttle eager to start fresh and put anything complicated behind me. Ignore it, forget it, and never speak of it again. Move on like a wagon train heading west.

I'd learned these special traits from my father. He'd buried himself in work to hide from personal struggles too. In fact, he buried himself in work to hide from everything.

When I was a junior in high school, my dad showed up at football practice, something he'd never done before. Coming to watch his only son play sports wasn't his thing. Work took priority, *the cat's in the cradle and the silver spoon* humming in the background. Nevertheless, he stood there on the edge of the field in his suit, the sun going down, and his shadow extending across the field like something drawn from a comic strip. My coach already knew what happened, and he told me to hustle over and go talk to him.

When I got there, no hello, no nothing, my helmet dangling in my hand by my side and me trying to catch my breath from the last play. *Your mom's gone*, my father said. That's how it started. *She's dead. Her heart stopped a few hours ago. The housekeeper found her on the kitchen floor.*

The old man told me just like that, all matter-of-fact like. Then he pulled me in for a hug, one of the rare times he'd ever done so. I can count on one hand how many times that man hugged me and it never felt right, always stiff. I started to cry and ask more questions, but Pops wanted none of it. *Mom's dead. Heart attack. You know she had a weak heart,* he said.

Of course I did. I'd gone to the hospital every time we had scares, held her hand while she told me not to worry. But I was sixteen. What the fuck do you know about weak hearts and death when you're sixteen? Not a damn thing. But he gripped my arms and said now wasn't the time for tears. *Later. Man up.* He'd been a marine too, thus the compassion.

But later never came because Mr. Robert "Rob" Hackett was a strong man, self-reliant and stoic like true men are, and he needed to get back to work. *It's best just to accept the reality and move on. No sense dwelling on what can't be changed.* And down came the hand on my shoulder, smack! *Best get on with it, that's what she would have wanted.*

I used to wonder how the hell he knew what she wanted. He was always working, no time for her either. Conveniently absent like *true men* are. Asshole.

But I got on with it like he told me to do, a boy of sixteen—I got on with it as expected. Two days later, I was back at practice. A good friend of mine named Mike, our star fullback, asked how I was doing. I said fine, then proceeded to tackle and hit anyone who came near me on the field.

I bloodied Mike's chin during a blitz. Drove the top of my helmet up underneath his facemask, but he didn't mind. I didn't mean to hurt him and he knew it. Still, he told me it was a good hit and smacked my shoulder pad. I don't think he saw the tears in my eyes, but he knew because good friends can feel that shit.

And now, as horrible as it sounds, I can't do anything for Gomez and I have to accept the situation for what it is. The Gomez I knew died in Ramadi fifteen years ago. Doug was right; the email had simply been so I would know the truth. Anything else was crazy, and best to let the crazy fizzle out.

*   *   *

When I emerged from baggage claim, the midday sun shone high in the sky. I'd neglected to call Ike—a facilitator from the firm whom I was probably closer to than I should be—to arrange a pickup, so I hailed a cab and headed straight to the Leadenhall Building. With a swift ascent to the fortieth floor, I proceeded straight to Alistair's office to check in, my usual routine after traveling.

"My dear Mason, do come in." Alistair stood behind his massive mahogany desk, leaning forward with his arms behind his back reading a spread of papers arrayed neatly before him. With his pure white hair, slate gray suit, French cuffs, and sixty-plus years, he might as well have worked for the East India Company in the time of Kipling.

I entered his office, and as I always did, admired the deep maroon Persian rug, built-in bookcases, wingback and captain's chairs, and brass bar cart tucked against the wall adorned with bottles of gin and scotch I could never afford. The classic grandeur of the place made me immensely uncomfortable, but I couldn't help but marvel at it. Old school, like my grandpa had been.

"So, Mason. How'd it go? Are the Germans really jumping in the sack with the Russians?"

I nodded and proceeded to outline all the details the ministry official had shared with Klaus and me. It only took a few minutes, and Alistair must have noticed me eyeing his scotch because once I was finished delivering my report, he got up and fixed us both a few fingers.

"I'm not surprised," he said, handing me one of the tumblers. "Was bound to happen sooner or later given all the capital Putin's funneling into the energy sector."

"Yes," I replied, taking a sip and rolling it around in my mouth.

"And the trip itself, a nice change?"

"Nice enough. I like Germany," I replied, not daring to mention anything else. I doubt Alistair would have cared I stopped in Paris, but I wanted to save myself the embarrassment of explaining why. I didn't feel like reviving the matter either, given I'd started to put it behind me.

"Good," remarked Alistair. "I thought you could have used a little break after your last adventure."

I allowed a thin, knowing smile. "It's what you hired me for."

"Yes. Still, I don't care for Syrian radicals pointing guns at my employees."

An image of a short, scruffy-faced Syrian border guard pushing the barrel of his AK-47 against my sternum came to mind. The incident occurred during my last trip just before Frankfurt as I was trying to cross the Lebanese–Syrian border, and I probably could have been a little more compliant. But waiting three hours with all the right paperwork had made me irritable. Things may not have worked out so well if the guard's supervisor hadn't shown up, realizing the prospect of a fat bribe.

"It's fine, sir. I've seen worse."

Alistair nodded. "Yes, I know."

"Is that all, sir?"

"Not yet. This move by Germany got me thinking, and speaking of Syria, I forgot to ask, or maybe you put it in your trip report."

"What, sir?"

"Did you come across any Russian paramilitary types when you surveyed the Syrian oil fields? You know, my little hobby interest."

I cocked my head, recalling a conversation we had during a company retreat a few years back when he asked that I remain attuned to the presence of private military contractors during my travels. He assessed that they—private companies offering military-like services, guns for hire—were a new variable in international business and of particular interest to Ruttfield's clients in the defense and energy sectors. It made me think that if circumstances were different, I should arrange a lunch for Alistair and Doug so they could compare notes. It reiterated for me that government intelligence and industrial espionage are not that far apart.

"Yes," I replied, "but only at a distance. They appeared to be running some kind of mobile security."

"At a distance. Are you sure they were Russian?"

"Yes. I recognized their weapons and equipment—too high-speed for any regime nugs—and the markings on their trucks."

"Right. Very well."

"Is there something wrong?" I asked.

"No, no. Like I said, this latest move merely got me thinking. The world's changing."

"Right, sir," my own thoughts falling to Gomez again. "Is there anything else?"

"No," replied Alistair with a smile. "Thank you."

I nodded curtly and stood, feeling a need to get moving. "I'm going to finish out the day and take the weekend, sir."

"Very well. Heading up to Yorkshire with Caroline, if memory serves me. Correct?"

"No, sir. We broke it off last week."

"Oh dear, I'm sorry to hear that. All amicable, I hope. Splits can be messy."

"It's fine, sir."

"Good. I knew her father, you know."

I nodded again, having heard the story about Alistair and Caroline's father being contemporaries at Oxford. It's a small world when your boss is chums with the father of your ex.

"Thank you for your time, sir. I'm going to get back at it," I replied, downing the last of my drink and excusing myself.

Now back in my office, I spent the rest of the day reviewing the markets and laying the groundwork for my next excursion, probably in two weeks. I was destined for Bulgaria and Romania to look at another natural gas pipeline coming out of the Black Sea, with maybe a hop into Turkey at the end. I was looking forward to the trip. It was an exotic part of the world, and the folks I planned to meet with always put on a good spread. Wild game, fresh fish, good wine—certain to be a pleasant experience.

I finally shut my computer down and turned off the lights at nine. I texted Caroline to ask if she was still up and if I could stop by to get my stuff. The message back was a simple, *Yes*, as was her habit. Short and sweet.

Truth was, it was good we'd split. She was a wonderful woman, smart, kind, and beautiful; we simply came from very different walks of life. We lasted two years and some change, but I think she started to get bored with me—maybe exasperated—six months in; my indelicate ass could only enjoy cocktails with friends and posh galas for so long before I needed a strong ale or a few fingers of the hard stuff to keep my sanity.

And if I were honest, my own crap didn't help matters. She wanted to know about my life before moving to England, my time in the Corps, too, but I played it off. I wanted to forget my past and start anew—thus my move to London a decade before. I'd rather be where no one would raise an eyebrow if they heard I was a vet. I'd prefer people not to know and not to care.

But I couldn't erase everything. The few nights I spiraled into a rash of darkness fueled by bourbon grappling with my demons, it unsettled her. It was too complicated, downright nasty, and I don't blame her. No one needs to be saddled with that mess.

When the time came last week, the break was unambiguous and final, nothing to drag out. It's always easier when it's mutual. Now I just wanted my clothes back and to wish her well.

"Have a good night, Mr. Hackett," called the security guard at the front desk as I walked by.

"And you, Tom," I replied. "How's Gwen?"

"Just fine, Mr. Hackett. Thanks for asking. At university now."

"Glad to hear it, Tom. See you Monday," I said, breaching the exit doors.

The cool London air, bordering on cold, greeted me on the street with a refreshing gust. I was inclined to walk home, thinking the exertion would do me good. It would help settle things. The work had been effective in clearing my mind. Now I needed some exercise to put this Gomez-Delgado business to rest.

I looked left toward the car queue and saw Ike standing by the rear passenger door of the Bentley waiting for me. He had a hard presence to him, someone who'd weathered the elements and been in the thick of it more than once. Not surprising given he'd spent twenty-five years in the Paras, doing time with a rifle and boots in the Falklands, Iraq, Bosnia, and Lebanon—nice places to vacation—before joining the firm.

"Good evening, Ike. How are you?"

"Fine, sir. Missed you at the airport."

"My fault. I failed to let you know."

"Nonsense, sir."

"I think I'm gonna walk home, if you don't mind. I could use the fresh air. Why don't you take the rest of the night off."

"It's no trouble, sir. Would you like me to take anything for you? Your valise, perhaps?"

"I left it upstairs."

"It's no trouble, sir."

"You really need to stop calling me sir, Ike. It's kind of insulting."

"Of course, sir. My apologies. Won't happen again."

"See you Monday, usual time?"

"Yes, sir. But," Ike said, catching me before I turned to go. "Is everything all right?"

"Of course. Why?"

"No reason, sir," the old soldier replied, not making much of an effort to conceal his suspicion something unusual had gone on. He knew my patterns well. He was a good man and, in a way, the closest thing I had to a real friend over here.

"I'm fine, Ike."

"Very well, sir."

"Goodnight," I said, turning to go at a not so casual pace. Walking, running, speed, physical activity—I knew it cleansed the mind. Had I not been in oxfords and a suit, I probably would have started jogging, inevitably increasing to a hard run. It would just happen whether I meant to or not, my body yearning to detox itself, letting Gomez go one last time.

Caroline's place was a few miles away, so I took the Tube for part of it. I got off near Kensington Gardens so I could walk the last mile. I reached an intersection north of embassy row and would have blundered across were it not for the cars rushing by. A handful of other late-night pedestrians waited alongside me—fat ones, tall ones, skinny ones, short ones—mostly in their own world, indifferent to the strangers close enough to smell their cologne, perfume, and one bloke's curry-laced breath. I'd drifted into my secluded world too.

Consequently, it took me a moment to notice one individual eyeballing me a little too intently. He wore a suit without a tie and appeared clean-cut, so the thought of getting mugged didn't cross my mind, but I didn't recognize him. I had the urge to ask, *Do I know you*, but refrained, once again looking straight ahead at the far side of the intersection like everyone else. I'd encountered weirder things on London's streets.

The signal to walk flashed and I strode off, continuing my jaunt to Caroline's house, wondering if we'd have sex one last time tonight. I wouldn't complain if we did. Sex was one thing we'd connected quite well on.

Most of the other pedestrians disappeared into the night, and I found myself on a deserted street I rarely paid attention to, rounding the next corner out of habit. But as I did so, I noticed an individual trailing me, perhaps fifteen yards back, who seemed to have suddenly appeared. It was a woman from the intersection, I think.

I increased my pace, more out of irritation than anything else, having enjoyed the solitude of the walk. I reached the next block, crossed over, and took another glance behind. I expected to see the woman farther back strolling along, but didn't. She was nowhere in sight.

I kept walking, but my mind paused, curious where she'd gone since there were no other side streets or alleys she could have turned down. The woman had simply vanished. A sudden appearance and disappearance, but I quickly stopped this line of thinking, dismissing the observation as nothing more than my inclination for paranoia.

I decided to slow down. I'd started to sweat, feeling the moisture on my back and a bead of sweat on my upper lip. I had at least another twenty minutes to go and didn't want to arrive at Caroline's a swampy mess. No one would appreciate that.

Then a dark figure stepped out from an alley in front of me. It was a man, and he planted himself right in the middle of the sidewalk, like a pillar in a river forcing the water to flow around it. I recognized him as the man from the crosswalk who'd stared too intently. He was no more than ten feet away and his eyes were locked on me, the provocation blatant.

Although the last twelve years had made me inclined to de-escalate confrontations—a brawling banker wasn't good for business—something from long ago welled up inside me. All the frustration and confusion from the past thirty-six hours, the arrogance of Doug, the veiled threats by Garrett—it was too much. I snapped.

"Can I help you?" I challenged, advancing with long strides to close the distance. I felt my muscles go tense and I flexed my hands, balling them into fists.

The lone individual stayed firm, waiting for me.

"Hey, you," I called. "I'm talking to you." I pointed my finger like a drill instructor bearing down on a bewildered recruit, halting just out of arm's reach.

"Good evening, Mr. Hackett," the man said calmly. "I require a moment of your time." He spoke with the hint of an unidentifiable accent. Not precisely British English, nor Northeast American. More like a boy who grew up in a household whose parents were first-generation immigrants, conditioned to straddle dialects.

"Who are you?" I demanded.

"I'm a friend, Mr. Hackett. I need to speak with you about our mutual acquaintance, the *journalist Henry Delgado*." The man pronounced the title and name with sardonic emphasis.

"Right. Henry f'ing Delgado," I hissed. "Who sent you? Was it Doug? Garrett? Another reminder?"

The man cocked his head. "We care about Mr. Delgado, like you. It's dangerous work, what he does, no?"

"Is it? Is it really? You sent him over there, and now you hang him out to dry."

"It's business, you know."

"No, actually I don't know. I don't work for the damned CIA like you, like Doug, or like that other shit, Garrett. So, Mr. . . ."

"John."

"Right, John. Look, I got the hint the first time, so whatever you came here for, out with it."

"Please, Mr. Hackett." The man extended his hands, his palms outstretched, pleading, as if I were the one who had made things difficult, which only served to piss me off more.

"You know what, screw it. You know you're abandoning a real hero out there, right?" And I was about to blurt out the name *Kevin Gomez*, but something stopped me, remembering the line from somewhere, *The dead should stay dead*. And Gomez was in fact dead; he was Delgado now, even to these fucks. "Delgado, Henry, Hank," I continued. "I doubt you know it, but at one time he was a warrior with honor and courage, and most of all—loyalty. Something you shits are lacking."

John listened, nodding his head, digesting my words. "Delgado. You know Mr. Delgado good, yes? You work together?"

Work together? The man's question made me pause. And his grammar was slightly off, and ending the question with *yes*. He'd done that moments ago with *no* as if validating a statement with an unnecessary prompt for a response. A worrisome suspicion fractured my assumptions about who this man was.

"Who are you?"

John's mouth pressed into a tight smile, akin to a guilty child caught in a white lie. "I'm John."

"No, wait. We're not doing this anymore until you tell me why you're here."

"Doug sent me to talk about Mr. Delgado. A reminder, as you say."

I scrutinized the man more closely. He wore black pants, black shoes, a white shirt, and a black leather jacket. His cheekbones were high, his hair nearly black, and his eyes were like dark holes. Eastern European or Balkan, I surmised.

Uncertainty mutated into alarm and I lunged forward, grabbing the man by the lapel. "Who the fuck are you?"

He took a small step back to maintain his balance, but he met my snarl without a flinch. Then his features narrowed. An instant later, he delivered a rib-cracking blow to my left side.

I immediately realized my mistake and tried to back away to create some space between me and the man calling himself *John*. But it was too late.

John delivered a crushing downward blow with his other arm and broke free from my grip. His right leg swung out and struck the side of my shin, sweeping both my legs out from under me and knocking me to the ground. Humiliation at being taken down so easily, coupled with the jolts of pain from the fall, sent me reeling.

"You stupid American," spat John, twisting my left arm into a painful lock. "Why did Delgado contact you?" The man's accent degenerated even more, the Slavic tones unmistakable.

"Fuck you," I growled. "Who the hell are you?"

"You not get to ask questions. Why did Delgado send you email? Are you CIA too?"

"I'm not telling you shit."

I tried to shake the man off my back, bucking my hips and struggling to bring my knees underneath me, but another sharp strike hit my side. My reflexes jumped uncontrollably and I lost whatever opening I might have gained.

"You tell me or this get worse," John snarled.

"Fuck you."

John used some type of blunt weapon to hit my outer thigh. Paralyzing pain coursed up and down my leg, and all my strength in that limb went flat.

"You no want to talk. How about we do this with your pretty girlfriend. Yes? She have nice house, nice ass, good life in Notting Hill. We will talk about many things."

Fear flooded inside me. "You son of a bitch! You threaten her, I'll kill you—"

John wrenched the arm lock and I cried out, rage overtaking me. I flailed and thrashed, no longer caring about what hurt or if my arm snapped. You could threaten me, you could beat me, you could try to kill me—so be it. But I will never stand for anyone doing harm to someone close to me, including those from my past. I wanted to destroy this man, slam his face into the pavement over and over again until it was a bloody mess.

"Hey! Hey! What are you doing?" A voice shouted, but from where I couldn't tell.

John's grip loosened, which was all I needed. I bucked again and broke John's hold. Ignoring the pain, I ripped my arm free and pulled up my knee. I managed a look up and saw John retracting, his attention switching between me and whoever was yelling.

"You there, stop!" came the unknown voice again.

I pushed myself free and kicked my heel into John's knee. He cried out in a language I didn't understand, stumbling as he stood up. He flashed me one more look before turning on his heels and fleeing down the street, disappearing over a wall into a garden.

"Wait! Stop!" the approaching voice hailed.

I heard footsteps pounding the sidewalk, getting closer, but I didn't care. I tried to get to my feet, but the pain in my side and leg hobbled me. Still, I had to go. There was no time.

Whoever *John* was, he knew where Caroline lived—another innocent in danger because of me.

I pulled out my phone as I stumbled forward, striving to break into a run. I speed-dialed a number and through winded breaths said, "Ike! Meet me at . . ."

CHAPTER NINE

I rounded the corner onto Caroline's street, running at full tilt. The muscles in my thighs ached and my lungs screamed for more oxygen, but I kept pumping my arms and driving my legs forward. The more it hurt, the harder I pushed. I thought my chest was going to explode, but another twenty yards and I'd be there.

Fifteen . . . ten . . . five.

I grabbed the railing to stop my forward momentum and cut left. I bounded up the steps two at a time and charged through the front door, dread pouring through me as I anticipated what I might find.

In the six minutes and fourteen seconds it took me to run the mile and a half to Caroline's place, my mind had reeled in all directions. At worst, I expected to see Caroline gagged and bound, her face bleeding with big, hulking men standing over her wearing black gloves and holding small batons meant for beating soft flesh. Perhaps there would be another with a gun, aiming it at me as I burst through the door.

"Caroline! Caroline!" I yelled, tearing through the foyer, scanning frantically down the hall and up the stairs and into the kitchen. It was a three-level townhouse, narrow like most flats in Notting Hill, but well appointed due to the money Caroline came from.

As I stormed through the ground floor searching behind furniture and inside closets, I found nothing, the house quiet, peaceful. The light under the kitchen cabinet was on, and down the hall a warm glow spilled out from the salon. Then I heard laughter, like from an audience. The television?

"Caroline?" I called out again.

She poked her head into the hall, then stepped out, dressed in a pair of beige capris pants and a coral-colored blouse, her blond hair falling elegantly around her shoulders. "Mason?" she asked, a hint of annoyance in her voice but not a sliver of concern. "What's with all the yelling? You sound like a madman."

"Are you okay? Is anyone here?" I asked between breaths.

Caroline glanced into the rooms to her left and right, confirming what she already knew. "No one's here, Mason. Why?"

"You're sure? Are you okay?" I stepped into the kitchen, my eyes searching the counter and floor for anything out of place. Next I entered the study, turning on the lights and checking the window locks.

"Mason, what are you doing? You've given me a fright." She stood clutching her arms as if touched by a chill.

I looked into the room where Caroline had been watching the TV, then up the stairs again, peering through the banister to the third floor. Everything appeared as it should. I imagined I'd find the same if I were to check each room upstairs. Yet . . .

"Grab your bags. Now. Come on," I said, heading for the stairs, assuming she'd already packed a bag for the weekend at her parents' place. We'd broken up, but she was still planning to go last we talked.

"Mason. Stop. What's going on?"

I paused partway up the stairs and met her eyes, seeing the confusion and preamble of fear. I'd never seen her scared before; there'd never been any reason for her to be scared. Concerned, maybe, but not scared and certainly not from anything I'd ever done.

My heart went out to her. I hadn't meant to frighten her, but I had to get her out of here. Whoever *John* was, he'd threatened both of us. I found it hard to believe such a thing could happen, but it had. This wasn't a mugging by a hooligan kid with a blade—someone had hunted me down, assaulted me, and then threatened me and an innocent person close to me. It was a bad dream I couldn't wake up from.

Yet this, all of it, was as real as the first shots in a gunfight. Everything had fallen apart in the past hour. Nothing was safe. This wasn't a faraway war zone—this was my home turf, my backyard, on my front step. And I'd put someone I cared about at risk. Caroline. Blameless, innocent Caroline.

"I'll explain once we're on the road. Now come on," I said, continuing up the stairs.

"On the road? What are you talking about? I'm not going anywhere tonight," replied Caroline, chasing after me.

I poked my head into the two guest rooms, the second-floor study and the hall bathroom, then went into the master. I found no one and nothing out of place.

I grabbed one of Caroline's high-priced overnight bags and tossed it on the bed. Fortunately, in preparation for the weekend, she'd already laid out a spread of clothes and personal items. "Come on. We need to hurry. Grab enough for tomorrow—you can send Alice for the rest later," I said, referring to her mother's personal assistant.

"Mason, stop. Please."

"I'm taking you to your parents' tonight," I repeated.

Caroline grabbed my arm as I picked up a pair of her pants. "Mason, stop!" she shouted, the fear in her voice cracking. "You're scaring me, and I'm not going anywhere until you tell me what's going on."

"Dammit, Caroline! Just do as I say," but as soon as the words left my mouth I regretted it.

I took a deep breath and closed my eyes. I could feel Caroline staring at me in bewilderment. This wasn't Iraq, nor was it some backwater trip Ruttfield had sent me on. This was London. Given how much time had passed since my encounter on the street, common sense told me no one was coming through the door with guns and hoods to kidnap us.

I started to make sense of things. John meant to get information out of me and intimidate me, but for what purpose I didn't know. If he had intended to kidnap me or Caroline, it would have been more than just him on the street. Something else was going on.

When I opened my eyes to meet hers, I iced over any and all angst inside me.

"Something's happened," I began, my tone devoid of emotion, "and you might be in danger. I'll explain in the car. You're going to your parents'. You'll be safe there."

"Danger . . . I don't understand . . . what's happened?"

"Caroline—pack." I said the words with an unyielding finality, which caused Caroline to blink once, shock overtaking her, and start mechanically stuffing clothes into her bag.

*   *   *

On the doorstep, I spoke with Ike in hushed tones, making sure Caroline couldn't overhear or see our faces. Ike had arrived a few minutes ago, having come right away when he received my call. If one looked closely, the bulge of a pistol was evident under the old soldier's jacket.

When we were done chatting, Ike handed me the keys to the Bentley and stepped inside the house. He nodded hello to

Caroline in crisp military fashion and disappeared upstairs per my instructions.

Five minutes later, Caroline and I were in the car driving north to Yorkshire. Caroline sat silently in the passenger seat, her hands folded in her lap, staring out the window. She hadn't said a word since leaving the house, and I couldn't tell if she was still scared, confused, resigned, perhaps angry? It could be all of the above.

I needed to tell her something about what was going on. She and I were finished as a couple, but I owed her something. She didn't deserve to be mixed up in any of this—my shit. I'd tried so hard to keep all the horrors of my life away from her and everyone else I knew, but I'd failed again. And what right did I have to drag her out of her home in the middle of the night with no explanation? None.

But I was hesitant to disclose all that had happened in the past forty-eight hours. Whatever I said would surely result in additional questions, some of which I didn't want to answer—not just responses I didn't want to provide, but answers to questions I didn't know. Plus, if *John*—whoever he was—were to find her, the less she knew, the better.

God, what was I thinking? Did I actually contemplate what might happen if someone were to nab and question Caroline? What had I gotten myself into?

I pursed my lips and told myself to stop it. The unknowns were endless and I could go round and round and round thinking about all the possibilities and how they could spin out of control. No good could come from that.

"Mason, are you . . . are you in trouble?" Caroline's voice was barely audible. Her gaze shifted fretfully between me and the world's shadows passing by outside her window.

I kept my eyes trained on the road, the headlights cutting through the blackness. Beyond the lights I couldn't see anything except the distant glow from a town and the red dots of a car's taillights a mile ahead. The darkness was pure, like an edge with nothing beyond.

I was done trying to convince myself of one thing or another. My instincts had been right from the beginning and I needed to listen to them. Screw Doug, screw Garrett, and screw anyone else involved in this mess. I was done being a passive listener and playing by their shady-ass rules.

"Something's happened, but not to me," I finally said.

"What? What do you mean something's happened?"

"You remember that before we met, I was a marine?"

"Yes, of course."

"A friend of mine from back then, he needs help," I said quietly.

"Who? Do I know him?"

"No, I've never spoken of him."

"What has he done? Is he in trouble?"

"It doesn't matter," I replied flatly.

"Of course it matters. I can see you're dreadfully worried, and you're angry. I can feel it. And you just dragged me out of my house in the middle of the night. Please, talk to me."

All I could offer was a troubled shake of my head, wanting to say something—anything—but not having the words. For an instant I was thankful I was driving, not even wanting to look at her. I don't think I could handle being face-to-face, with all my cracks exposed.

"Mason, are *you* involved in something? Is it something you did?" Caroline asked.

"No," I breathed, shaking my head again.

"Then what, Mason? You can't keep doing this."

"Can't keep doing what?" I asked. "Look, things are sensitive—"

"No, stop it," interrupted Caroline. "I don't want another one of your brush-offs. If you're not going to tell me what's going on, what's rattled you so deeply, then you need to listen to me instead."

I glanced at Caroline, now wondering if I was the one who'd missed something.

"Mason, we broke up, but you need to hear this. And please listen." Caroline composed herself and continued. "You have to stop ignoring anything that is emotionally difficult in your life, and you're going to have to let people in at some point. Maybe it's now. Lord knows I wanted to be there for you, but you didn't want that. I don't know if you were afraid or what. But if you keep locking the world out and keep everything inside, you're going to destroy yourself."

"Caroline—"

"I'm not finished. These past two years, I've seen you at some of your lowest points, and I've seen you at your best. Yet this cloud is always, always there, and it's here now. I don't know what it is— anger, guilt, regret—but I am not your enemy. I was never your enemy. You don't need to protect yourself from me. I loved you. I still care for you, Mason. But you've got to stop walling yourself off. You can't live like that, not healthily, anyway."

I pursed my lips, blown away that she would bring all this crap up now. Now was not the time. "Caroline, you don't understand. This is different. There really is a—"

"I don't care, Mason. You're going to have to deal with your crap eventually. And despite your assertions that it was time for us to split, I disagree. I simply knew there was no point in arguing once you'd made up your mind, you stubborn ass.

"But I'll say it again. I still care for you and I want you to be okay. Whatever this is with your friend, I hope you know what you're doing, and I hope you can help your friend, whatever his name is and whatever he's mixed up in."

Caroline's words sent a jolt down my spine, but not for the obvious reason. She may have just ripped me up one side and down the other about how I'm a dysfunctional nutcase, and maybe if we were in a joint counseling session clutching stress balls and using active listening techniques while a psych-moderator guided us toward a more fulfilling relationship, I might have been more open to internalizing what she said—but I couldn't right now. My focus was elsewhere. Emotional health and getting in touch with my messed-up feelings had to wait.

Rather, her words, *whatever his name is and whatever he's mixed up in*, made me realize the mistake I made, and it pounded in my skull like a steel pipe. How could I have been so stupid!

Doug didn't send John. John didn't know Doug and he didn't know Garrett.

John came from somewhere else. He was searching for information, about Delgado *and* me. He'd known about the email and asked if I worked with Delgado, and I'd said Delgado was with the CIA . . .

Son of a bitch! My only consolation was that I didn't reveal his true identity, but still—I might as well have wrapped the garrote around Gomez's neck myself. I'd outed him.

Who was John and how did he find me, and how did he know about the email? John's accent, it sounded like someone from Eastern Europe. Ukrainian? Russian? This John and the people he worked for, were they the ones holding Gomez? If they were, the mistake I'd made just sealed Gomez's fate—killed him.

"Mason. Mason, are you there?"

I turned to see Caroline looking at me, pleading with me from every contour of her face and position of her body. But I couldn't tell her what was going on. Not now. My crap, whatever it was, would have to wait. I wasn't going to make the same mistake twice. I wouldn't make it again.

Given what I was about to do—what in that instant I'd decided to do—Gomez's life depended on it. I wasn't going to let my friend suffer at the hands of Ukrainian militants because of my careless-ness. And they apparently knew of me but didn't know who I was, which made me a threat—which meant I couldn't just let it all go and hope they'd leave me alone.

"Mason, talk to me," she implored.

I grasped her hand. "Caroline, listen to me. I need to go away for a few days. I can't tell you where or why, only that a friend needs help. I'm taking you to your parents' place and you need to stay there until I get back. There is a real danger. I need you to trust me and put all that other stuff aside. Can you do that? Please."

With a huff of resignation, she said, "I don't understand, but I suppose I have no choice."

"Thank you, and I'm sorry I can't say anything more. I truly am."

And I was. Events had occurred in the last forty-eight hours I never could have fathomed. But there was no time to dwell on it. The clock was ticking, and I had too much to do before I left.

I returned my attention to the road, and out of the corner of my eye saw Caroline cross her arms and fix her gaze straight ahead, set-tling into a distant silence.

For a moment I hated myself. After leaving the Corps, I told my-self I'd never be a part of ruining other people's lives again; yet, I'd just tossed Caroline's into the fire and I genuinely feared someone might come after her.

I had to make this right, and I had to do everything in my power to help Gomez. I couldn't be responsible for his death a second time.

CHAPTER TEN

Showing up in the middle of the night and leaving my ex-girlfriend at her parents' estate went about as well as could be expected—a turd in a punch bowl.

Edwin Prescott, a formally titled English gentleman, answered the door and assumed an air of genuine concern colored with a splash of confused wariness. I'd met him three times before and we'd hit it off, including my participation in the family's annual fox hunt replete with tweed and flasks topped off with whisky.

But when I told him he should have a chat with the estate's security manager, the man's countenance tightened and he pressed me for more information. I explained what I could—about as much as I'd told Caroline in the car—but wouldn't go any further, much to Edwin's displeasure. Nevertheless, the man took on an air akin to a commander of the brigade as he set about inspecting the house and grounds.

When I said goodbye to Caroline, she hugged me, but it was cool, like an estranged relative. I suspect saying all she did in the car had been a long time coming. She needed to get it off her chest, and now it was on me. She wasn't wrong—I knew what I ran from in this life—but what could I do about it?

Nothing. I couldn't sort through years of emotional sludge in a few hours, or even a few days. And certainly not now. Other, more urgent matters were at hand.

I was glad she was with her parents. She should be safe here.

I left and got back in the car, shifting my mind to what lay ahead. Mapping out as many details as I could on the drive back, I reached London just after four in the morning after driving much faster than I should have. Instead of going home, I went straight to the office in the city. I caught a couple of hours of restless sleep on my couch, then showered and changed into one of the spare sets of clothes I keep in the closet. I opted for gray slacks, a white button-down shirt, and a black sport coat.

When Alistair Ruttfield emerged from the elevator bank at a quarter to seven—typically one of the first to arrive—he found me sitting outside his office.

"Good morning, Mason. For what do I owe the pleasure? I thought you were taking the weekend off," Alistair asked with a raised eyebrow.

"Sorry to ambush you like this, Mr. Ruttfield, but I need a few minutes of your time."

"Of course. Coffee, tea?"

"No, thank you. I won't be long."

A curious expression came over the elder gentleman's face as he unlocked his private office. I followed him in, and while Alistair went behind his desk and set his briefcase down, I assumed a position a few feet away with my arms by my side. It was then that Alistair took note of the scrapes on my hands and cheek. "My god, Mason. What happened? Are you all right?"

"It's nothing, sir. Fell during my walk home last night."

"Right," he replied, evidently skeptical of the explanation but letting it go. "Would you like to sit down?"

"I'm fine, sir. I really am in a hurry."

"Yes, obviously so. Well then, out with it."

"I need to take a leave of absence."

Alistair didn't flinch. "I see. When?"

"Today."

"And for how long?"

I hesitated. "I don't know. At least a week. Perhaps longer."

"I see. May I ask what is the matter? Though I've encountered the odd request from my people before, I find it unusual to find someone such as yourself waiting outside my office to ask for time off so suddenly."

"Yes, sir. I understand—"

"Mason, I've told you before. Please call me Alistair."

"Yes, of course. Regrettably, I'm unable to fully explain why I need the time off."

"Hmm. Yes, most unusual."

"It's a personal matter."

"I hope not a consequence of your latest trip to Frankfurt?"

"No. Not in that way. It's . . ." I wanted to tell him. I respected him, and Alistair had been immensely generous to me over the years. Not telling him—lying, in a sense—felt like a betrayal. But I couldn't reveal what was going on, what I suspected, nor what had already happened. It would sound crazy, especially what I planned to do next. "It's a matter from my past I can't ignore. I hope you can understand."

A spot of reluctant acceptance overtook my boss. "Perhaps from your time in the service? Old demons."

I allowed a resigned smile. "Something like that."

Alistair thought for a moment, then extended his hand. "Well, I wish you luck in whatever you're doing and that the matter sorts itself out accordingly. Take as much time as you need. Your position will be waiting for you upon your return."

"Thank you, Alistair. I left instructions for my team."

Alistair waved his hand dismissively. "I've no doubt. We'll manage. Is there anything I can do?"

"No, thank you. I'll be fine."

Alistair nodded. "Very well. Off with you, then. Best of luck."

"Thank you."

I departed the offices of Ruttfield & Leason without another word. With the sun up and another day starting for the rest of London, I stopped at a convenience store for a few essentials. Next, I went to Barclays and withdrew forty thousand euros in cash.

Back on the street, I pulled out my phone and dialed an overseas number reaching a cell phone in Kyiv. A familiar voice answered and the conversation lasted fifteen minutes.

With the phone still in my hand, I watched the midmorning traffic motor by and packs of pedestrians hurry about. They probably had *normal* jobs and *normal* lives, perhaps living in the same neighborhood they grew up in, still able to attend Sunday dinner at their parents' house twice a month, maybe every week.

They had *normal* problems too—a salary that paid too little with the bills piling up, a newborn baby who wouldn't let anyone sleep for more than two consecutive hours, an alcoholic brother who hadn't yet been arrested or lost his job but was on the verge, or the ones who maybe had a recent talk with their doctor about a lump found in the breast.

They had *normal* lives and *normal* problems I'd never experienced. I wasn't sure if that was a good or a bad thing. It just was.

I unlocked my phone again and pressed the speed dial.

Ike's voice came over the line. "I'm here."

"Can you pick me up at Piccadilly Circus?"

"On my way."

CHAPTER ELEVEN

LONDON

I emerged from the Piccadilly Circus Tube station and got my bearings. Taxis, buses, and private autos were bumper-to-bumper, rolling, stopping, and inching through the five-street road junction. People of all shapes, sizes, and colors hustled down the sidewalks, across the streets, and into buildings, or stood vacantly deciding where to wander next. This was London, a city on the move.

I glanced back down into the subterranean station to see if I recognized anyone coming up the stairs who'd been with me on the train, or if anyone was paying me more attention than I deserved. The previous night's events had changed everything, and everything and everyone was suspect. Men by themselves walking or standing, women pushing prams, old ladies carrying grocery bags.

If someone was following me, they'd try to appear normal, blend into the mix. They wouldn't have a sign draped around their neck or come up and introduce themselves.

But there would be indicators, clues, anomalies to pick up on, like the kids in Iraq playing in the street. If the kids suddenly vanished, like they'd all been called home for dinner at the exact same time, sure as shit the ambush was about to start. Then would come the gunfire.

I didn't expect anything like that to happen here. This was London. But men swarming out of a van, wrapping a hood over my head, and stuffing me in the back did cross my mind. At this point, let them come.

I didn't have any weapons—no guns or knives—but I was prepared to knock the crap out of anyone I thought might be connected to *John* or somehow involved with Doug's bloody Program. If they slipped up and I saw them closing in, I'd bounce their head off the steel railing and stomp their guts out, doing it with a grin ear-to-ear.

But I saw nothing down in the Tube hole or on the concrete above ground, so I turned and proceeded north up Shaftesbury Avenue, walking past the entrance to the godawful *Ripley's Believe It or Not* and spotting the Picturehouse Central farther up the way. I hadn't gone more than twenty yards when my phone vibrated.

I brought it to my ear and said, "Where are you?"

"Parked just off Great Windmill," Ike said. "Do you see me?"

I looked across the street and spotted Ike leaning against the façade of St. James Tavern. Instead of wearing his usual suit and tie, he wore jeans and a rough, tan-colored jacket. He also had a book tucked under his right arm. It was probably Dickens or Conrad, knowing Ike. The man was never without a book, and often the same tome would show up a few months or a year later, the volume in need of another review, as he would say.

When I approached, neither of us said anything. Ike motioned at an older model Land Rover parked off a side street and climbed behind the wheel. I got in the passenger side.

"Where to?" asked Ike.

"Someplace quiet so we can talk," I replied, trusting he knew better given he'd grown up in this town.

"Right, sure. When was the last time you had something to eat?"

"I can't remember."

"Right. I know just the place."

*   *   *

Twenty minutes later we occupied a booth in a corner pub on the edge of Harringay. It reminded me of a local joint my grandfather used to take me to in Marblehead, Massachusetts, called Maddie's. A casual establishment with booths made out of dark, time-weathered wood and a bartender that lived in the two-room apartment upstairs.

Before Mom died, Grandpa would take me there on Tuesdays when he wanted to play hooky from the Fed. We'd order *lobstah* rolls and thick fries with vinegar and ketchup, and the waitress, Peggy, knew to bring him a draught beer in an oversized, freezer-chilled glass and me a Coke. He'd then tell me stories about the South Pacific when he was a Seabee in World War II, or tales from when he was a Boy Scout hiking the Sierras back in the thirties. FDR, the New Deal, radio shows on Saturdays, church on Sundays, depression and war, all for God and country.

My formative years in a nutshell. I wondered what he'd think about where I am now.

Ike ordered us two meat pies and two ales from the waitress whom he seemed to know, an attractive gal probably in her late forties with blond hair cut short and a charming amount of freckles across her nose and cheeks. The food and beer arrived quickly, the waitress flashing Ike a smile when she reached across the table. Maybe she and Ike had a thing. I hoped so. He deserved someone nice.

The pit in my stomach gnawed at me as I breathed in the meal steaming before me, the aroma enticing. But I stayed myself from taking a bite or sip. I was exhausted and short on sleep. I wasn't ready to fight the inevitable food coma sure to follow a full stomach.

Ike also let his plate sit, lacing his fingers in front of his mouth with his elbows resting on the table. "So, what you got? I've worked for you for seven years, and up until last night you never once asked me to do anything out of the routine. Got my blood flowing a bit, you know?"

"Thank you for your help last night. I never meant to put you out, but you're the only one I could call."

"'Course, but how about you take some of that load off. Let me hear it."

I allowed myself an amused smile. "How much you want to know?"

"All of it. Best to know all the menaces before jumping into the shit. Am I right?"

"Right," I replied, meeting my friend's intrigued stare. I started at the beginning—Gomez's face on the television, the email, the encounter with Doug, the altercation on the street, and all the crap in between. I left nothing out—including my own blunder—presenting the information chronologically in an objective, emotionless manner, not unlike how I would have delivered a briefing if I were back in uniform. Except now I had a cold maturity to things that I hadn't in my cavalier twenties.

It took about half an hour to lay everything out, and I realized this was the first time I'd articulated the situation in its entirety. When I finished, I remained silent for a time, finally digesting the full magnitude and deceptiveness of it all. A faked death, a covert CIA program dating back to the start of the Cold War, the Russians, Ukrainian separatists, crooked industries, mercs and arms dealers, and a mission so secret not a word could be breathed about it. Jesus Christ.

Ike apprehended the hairiness of the matter too, though he never flinched.

"Quite the situation," he offered. "This Gomez. You said you knew him in the Corps. Was he a good mate?"

Ike posed the question in such a way as to suggest the word *friend* and the word *mate* had distinctly different definitions. A friend could mean just about anyone, but a *mate*, a *brother* in arms . . . that was someone whom you've suffered through severe hardship with and, in many cases, experienced what most would consider unspeakable. Death, survival, terror, killing, destruction, mutilation—and a willingness to sacrifice so the other might live.

Yes, Gomez was a mate in the purest sense. We'd been through it all during the five years we'd been together in the Corps.

Yet even though Gomez and I had experienced some of the worst mankind could do to one another—the meat grinder of Ramadi taking the cake—what came to mind most clearly was that morning in Kuwait before any of the real shit happened.

Gomez and I went through training together at Quantico and we'd sweated a lot and bled a little learning how to fight like marines, but our first taste of the real thing—combat—didn't come until March 2003. We were both rifle platoon commanders, each with roughly fifty men in our charge. Nineteen-year-old riflemen, twenty-two-year-old machine gunners, mortar men who looked like they were fifteen, senior NCOs who carried themselves like they were closing in on forty but who were only twenty-six—all of us gearing up to invade Iraq.

Upon our arrival in Kuwait in January, our battalion took up a position eight miles from the Iraqi border, and for the next few months we lived out of fighting holes eating MREs and getting abused by the hot sun followed by ferocious sand storms. We were completely isolated, too. No mail, no phones, no television, not even the *Stars and Stripes*. At one point a rumor rippled through the lines that the pop singer J. Lo had died; a soul-crushing bit of news for a bunch of testosterone-filled jarheads getting ready to kick off a war.

It was an awesome time, a fucking blast, brought down to the basic elements of survival, just a gnat's ass above animals. Living in grit with no way to wash, eating food that tasted the same no matter if it was beef stew or cheese and crackers, skin so dry I had to wrap duct tape around my fingers to prevent them from cracking and bleeding—but I could handle it.

The hardest part—even though I'm an introvert living in my head most hours of the day, a champion of solitude—was the psychological isolation for twenty-three hours out of the day. I was always with my men, so I wasn't truly *alone*, but I was the one they relied on, not the other way around. As the platoon commander, I always had to be on my game, set the example, and make the ultimate decisions. I had a strong platoon sergeant who handled most of the grind—digging deeper holes, maintaining vigilance on the line at two in the morning, honing the men to a ragged edge as they practiced on the firing line and ran patrols five miles out through the desert—but in the end it fell to me and I could only let my true self come out in bits and pieces. I won't lie, it was a burden for a twenty-four-year-old schmuck like myself.

I usually found a break during the daily company meetings when all the platoon commanders and platoon sergeants met at the command post—a spot in the sand midway along the quarter-mile line—to get the daily update. A cup of coffee, a few laughs with the other lieutenants, but soon enough it was back to the holes.

It was draining, the day in and day out, not knowing when or if we were going across the border, what was happening beyond our bit of the desert, and simply rotting in the *cradle of civilization* that God had mortgaged. Often I prayed for the fight to start so at least something would happen, crazy as it sounds. Who dares pray for war?

But one morning while walking the line around four or five, I bumped into Gomez who was also out walking the line making sure his men were awake and alert watching the vastness of the Kuwaiti desert. The first slivers of the sun had just crested the horizon, and Gomez pulled out a pack of smokes, offering me one. I said fuck it and sat down on the berm, lit up, and we shot the shit for the next hour.

We talked about home, some of the dumb stuff in training that hadn't worked so well in the field, our problem marines who even in the desert with nothing but nothing around still managed to get into trouble, and our ideas about what we thought we were about to do once the word came down to saddle up and cross the border with guns blazing. It was the best fifty-six-minute conversation I'd had in two months. We smiled, we laughed, we chain-smoked, and I sat beside my best friend and let all the stress and weight fall off my shoulders.

We ended our little respite with a pact, as clichéd as it sounds. If either one of us found ourselves in a bad spot, the other would do anything and everything within his power to come to the other's aid. I commanded first platoon and he commanded third, so we'd never be too far from one another on the battlefield. We'd do our duty and follow orders, of course—we were marines. But we would also risk our lives to help the other if the shit got thick. That's what Gomez had referred to in the email, which was sounding in my head now and why I couldn't let any of this go.

Yes, Gomez was a mate, and I nodded to Ike telling him as much.

"Right. Brilliant. You carry a lot of nasty baggage from him, don't ya?"

I shrugged.

"Right. Doesn't matter. We all got to deal with our shit in our own way. I got mine, you got yours. What matters is if we can do something about it when it suits us and if the opportunity presents itself."

"Yeah, I guess."

"Yeah. Right," Ike said, nodding. "Then let's do that. What's the plan?" he asked, picking up his fork and stabbing through the crust of his pie, a waft of steam rising up with the scent of gamey meat and brown gravy.

"Still working that out, but earlier this morning I called a contact of mine in Kyiv, a man by the name of Kristyen. I used him as a broker the one time I went to Ukraine for Ruttfield. He says he's aware of the situation with a detained journalist, and he can make contact with the right folks."

"What kind of folks?"

"People connected to Gomez's detention, so I can negotiate his release. Pay them off."

"Really?"

"Yeah. From what I've gathered and from the little time I've spent there, some of these separatists are in it as much for personal gain as they are for national ambitions. Corruption and bribes still rule that part of the world."

"Not surprising, I guess. Bloody mafia, militants, and politicians all in bed, no doubt. Fucking mess. Full of mercs, too."

"Yeah. But that's the gist of it. Get in country and then pay one or two million to get him out. The trick will be to make my offer more attractive than whatever arrangement the big bosses—whoever they are—have over the ones actually holding Gomez. One million might turn into five."

Ike whistled. "Your own money?"

I nodded. My entire savings. I didn't make anything near what the associates and partners pulled in with their commissions and bonuses, but I earned more than my share and knew how to squirrel it away. But I never thought I'd need it for something like this. "Better than anything else I'll spend it on."

"Right, sure. I got an account you can invest in if you're looking to offload a little more."

"If I get schwacked, I'll put you in my will."

"How about you put me in before you get schwacked?"

"Done."

"It's kind of thin though, don't you think? You know a guy, who knows another guy, who will put you in contact with the blooming Russian-backed paramilitaries running a low-level insurgency up and down the border. Cease-fires and demilitarized zones mean nothing over there."

"It's the best I got at the moment."

"Bloody nuts."

"Maybe."

"Right, sure. And this Kristyen, you trust him?"

"As much as I trust anyone right now, present company excluded."

"Sure, right. Not a fucking lick. What'd he say when you mentioned this bit to him? Not exactly typical work for a banker, even one with your expertise."

"It's the money. He's got his fee."

"How much?"

"Ten percent."

"That's it?"

"I didn't argue."

"What if he wants more?"

"I'll figure it out."

"Right, sure. I bet you will. So, when do we leave?"

I smiled but shook my head. "I can't ask you to come with me, Ike."

"Don't have to. I'm volunteering. My supervisor won't mind neither. You're the client. Besides, could be a rash of fun."

"Yeah, I could use you to watch my back. No doubt about it."

"Right on. There you go. I might be getting on in years, but I can still swing a pipe with the best of them. Probably a bit meaner in my old age as it is, which is good stuff in a brawl."

"Yes, for sure. But I can't have you come. I need you to do something else."

Ike waited for me to continue.

"I need you to watch Caroline and the family for me. You're the only one who knows the full story, and they threatened her. Her father's security at the estate is good for trespassers and unwanted party guests, but not this mess. And if anything happened to them because of me . . ." My voice trailed off.

She and her family were in this mess because of me. Again, my fault that others were at risk. I reached across the table and gripped Ike's forearm, meeting his eyes for a time before saying, "You know what I mean."

"Yeah, I get it. I'd rather be taking a trip with you, but I hear ya. I won't let anything happen to them. How likely is it they'll go after her?"

I released my hold and shrugged. "No idea. I think they'd come after me first if I had to bet. But if something goes wrong over there, I don't want them following up with Caroline or the family to use as leverage. Right?"

Ike nodded. "Yeah, yeah. Makes sense, good sense."

"Thank you."

"It's nothing. You're the boss, but I don't let that get in the way of one trooper backing up another. I know what you did back in Iraq."

I let out a short laugh. "Of course. But there's one more thing."

"What's that?"

"I need your help getting across the Channel and onto the continent without anyone knowing."

Ike tilted his head. "I think I can help with that."

CHAPTER TWELVE

The mobile phone sitting on the corner of Petrov's desk began to vibrate. It should have rung over two hours ago, but it hadn't. His people were never late. It didn't matter if they were drunk in Bogota, smitten by a prostitute in Seychelles, or visiting their grandma at the family dacha grilling sausage and chomping on green onion stalks. His people knew that punctuality, among other things, was critical to their longevity with Petrov's business.

Thus, Petrov was very interested in learning why the delay, his mind having sorted through numerous scenarios over what might have happened. He once heard an American say that bad news never gets better with time, which is true, but Petrov believed no news could be worse. Not knowing can be the death of everything.

Petrov picked up and answered the phone. "Da?"

"It's me. I have my report," said a man's voice in Russian.

"Why are you late?"

"I will explain."

"First, where are you?"

"I am secure, finally. But still in our neighbor's yard."

"You had to secure yourself?"

"Yes."

"Go on," said Petrov, pursing his lips to no one but himself. "Who is this man?"

"He is not a professional, and I suspect he's not been involved in the operation before now."

"How do you know?"

"I confronted him on the street earlier this evening as planned. But *he* immediately made assumptions about my connections to Doug Mitchell and his organization. I made no such allusions. He was quite agitated about the entire affair, more so than I expected, as if something had happened when we were not on him."

"The airport?" asked Petrov.

"Possibly. He mentioned someone named Garrett, who I do not know."

"What about him?"

"Nothing, just the name in association with Mr. Mitchell and Mr. Delgado."

"Continue."

"When I engaged him, he did not reveal much more than we already know. Names, affiliations . . ."

"Yes, yes. But what of *him*? Who is he?"

"I have nothing more than what we had acquired from our available resources. US Marine, connected to Delgado many years ago, banker. But still nothing affiliated with our activities, even distantly. He has no connection from what I have learned."

"Except the email."

"Correct."

"Where is he now?"

The line stayed silent for a moment too long.

"Where is he now?" repeated Petrov.

"We lost him."

"What?"

"The encounter on the street ended in an altercation and witnesses arrived. I had to remove myself from the scene."

"Shit," breathed Petrov, his eyes drifting up to the metal rafters. "You're not working for the thugs in Moscow anymore. Stupid, brutish tactics are their methods, not ours. We care about how things look. My bosses—your bosses—care about how things get done."

"Yes, sir. I know. I apologize."

"Fuck your apology. Switch out your team and reset on his known locations. Pick him up. We must know what his role is."

"Da."

Petrov jammed his thumb on the phone's screen to hang up, and he started to replay the conversation over in his head. He needed to think of a way to frame the incident in a better light. They had nothing to show for an incident that may or may not be contained. The person he was about to call tolerated complications even less than he did.

He dialed a new number, and the line rang six times before someone finally picked up.

"Alo," came a polished male voice.

"I need to speak with the boss," Petrov said.

"He has an event," the voice replied firmly.

"He'll want to hear this. Put him on."

The phone went silent and Petrov remained motionless, staring at a water stain just above the door. At times, he made weighty calls from his office suite in Sochi while he beheld the Black Sea. And then there were times like this, where he found himself lurking in the dark corners of the world. For the briefest of moments, he wondered if the man he was waiting to speak with had forgotten what the grime of this side of the business looked and smelled like.

"Mikhail," came a voice that at once conveyed refinement and seniority, and if one listened closely enough—brutality. "Is this a call for good news or bad?"

"I wouldn't disturb you like this if it were good."

"Of course, you never would. You're not that kind of man, are you, Mikhail. Does this have to do with our little problem?"

"Yes. We still don't know who this man is or why Delgado contacted him."

"Why not? This should be a very simple matter. You've known of the CIA's intrusion into my business for well over a year, yet you cannot determine the connection to this man? And from what you've previously conveyed to me, there is nothing *secret* about this man or his past activities. Simple, Mikhail, simple. I expect more from you."

"The connection is unorthodox."

"Our work is unorthodox. That is why I use your little private army of miscreants rather than those shits the big boss in Moscow offers. Find out why the CIA has involved this man Hackett and deal with it. We have consignments moving all over the world, millions of euros' worth. Very sensitive. The deal is shaping up."

"I know, sir."

"Then fix this. If you don't and this shit expands into a problem, my partners, as well as I, will be very disappointed. Things will need to change." The line went dead.

*   *   *

Venice, Italy

The old man, who most of the world knew as Viktor Leos, dropped the phone on the seat, then squeezed the bridge of his nose between his thumb and index finger.

"Here," said the woman sitting next to him in the back seat of the fully armored Mercedes sedan. Her voice was elegant with an undefined Mediterranean accent that amplified the beauty of her thirty-something oval face and natural blond hair. She extended a small glass of ice water. "You need to refresh yourself."

"Thank you, Genevieve," said Leos, graciously accepting the glass and taking a small sip.

Genevieve blinked with an almost smile, then picked up the tablet resting on her lap. "I wish you wouldn't let these matters vex you so. It's not good for your health."

"Ahh, but my interests do vex me. I've done so much good in this world, it always bothers me when something so insignificant causes me problems. Disruption. Disruption isn't good for my health."

"Of course. Should I look into the issue personally? I would be discreet and separate from Mr. Petrov's activities, of course."

"No, not yet. Let that rat Mr. Petrov do his work. I pay him good money. He needs to earn it."

"And if not?"

"We shall reconsider the matter then."

"As you wish. Would you like to review your talking points once more?" asked Genevieve, switching to the next item on the agenda.

"For the event? No. I say what I say. No one knows my businesses better than me. And these people have come to talk to me; I have not come to talk to them. These galas are always good for business other than what they are intended for."

"Of course. I have confirmed the pipeline execs will be in attendance. They will want to use your construction firms, I have no doubt."

"Is Senor Mario already in there?"

"Yes, he's making a count of who's present to ensure the connections are made."

"Mario is a good man too," Leos said as he set the glass of water on the seat tray and took Genevieve's hand in his. He kissed the tender patch of skin between the thumb and finger while briefly meeting Genevieve's turquoise eyes.

"We go," announced Leos as he tapped his passenger window and the door popped open, his driver moving to the side. The warmth of the Venetian sun greeted Leos as he stepped out onto the piazza, and a young man in a black suit and white shirt with perfectly styled dark hair swiftly approached.

"Signor Leos, right this way, please. The gala is in the courtyard and the guests from the International Refugee Commission are eagerly waiting for you to join them."

Viktor Leos nodded as he buttoned his suit coat and flashed his iconic smile—a smile well known from magazine covers and television screens. He then followed the young man toward The Gritti Palace hotel.

CHAPTER THIRTEEN

The sun had already set when the Cirrus Vision jet started its descent over the Czech landscape. In the distance I could see landing lights radiating from a single airstrip. They were getting closer and closer with each passing second, the surrounding forest nearly pitch black.

The darkness prevailed and, for some reason, thoughts of the OSS and an insertion behind enemy lines—the Nazis and WWII—came to mind. Images of partisans holding torches to guide the incoming aircraft, Harrison Ford and *Force 10 from Navarone*. High-speed and low-drag, the plan doomed to fail.

I'd visited the Czech Republic on a few occasions—Prague was a nice place to meet businessmen and other contacts who didn't care for their own country—but I'd never come in like this: a small private plane landing at an isolated airfield and my name nowhere on any flight manifest.

As far as the English and European Union authorities were aware, I had not taken off from a private airfield outside Chelmsford and I was not about to land at this quiet airstrip tucked in an evergreen forest north of Prague. According to the Big Brother databases and files that tracked the world's population, I was back in London down at the pub knocking back a pint of ale.

"We'll be on the ground in five minutes," came the voice over the headset.

"Roger," I replied, taking my gaze from the expansive view and looking at the pilot next to me. His name was Neil Walker, a man in his mid-fifties whose face was more haggard than most due to the amount of fine and not so fine whisky he consumed. The white whiskers on his chin indicated he hadn't shaved in a few days, and his clothes were eager for a wash.

But despite the man's appearance—and the trace of Cutty Sark on his breath—Ike had described Neil as a solid chap who was perfect for the job. Ike knew him from the Paras and their foray into the Falklands back in '82. They'd served alongside one another, walking away from a few nasty scrapes. Ike wouldn't describe Neil as a close friend—they didn't exchange holiday cards—but he trusted the man implicitly. Except when he drank tequila; Neil had a mean streak.

According to Ike, after the Paras, Neil bounced around a bit, eventually setting up a small courier outfit to ferry people and special cargo between England and the continent with his fleet of private jets. He did well, for the most part, and the majority of his work and clients were aboveboard, though often eccentric.

Neil also dabbled on the edge of legality, and when offered the right price, he knew how to move people and cargo quietly and without all the bureaucratic forms and inconveniences. He'd never admit to being a smuggler, but he had a wicked grin that suggested he liked being the man who knew how to move shit.

Given Ike and Neil were war buddies—and in light of the five thousand pounds in cash accompanied by a case of Ardbeg—Neil was happy to help me with my little issue without asking questions. Not a one. All he needed to know was where and when and he was ready to jump into the breach. Not the OSS, but right in line with the SOE.

And so it was. At just past eleven, the jet touched down on Czech soil. In less than a minute Neil taxied to the apron next to a small building, powering down the plane's engine and rapidly sorting through his post-flight checks.

"Like we planned, let me do the talking," Neil said.

"No problem," I replied, removing my headset and reaching for my duffel.

"And don't pull out the cash like a bloody dope. Keep it wrapped in that magazine. These lads may turn the other way, but they don't embrace the idea of taking a bribe."

I didn't bother to respond. The act of bribing a government official or local authority, or any gatekeeper for that matter, was not something I was unfamiliar with. Bribes, fees, taxes, and payments under the table made the world go round, and I'd made my share of contributions over the years.

I suspected internal accounts at Ruttfield would probably raise a few eyebrows if they knew how much I'd paid out on my trips for the firm, but that wasn't a concern. Alistair knew and approved it all, and that's what mattered. *The cost of doing business*, he liked to say.

Neil yanked the door handle and popped the jet's exit hatch. He kicked the step down as he slipped out of the plane and marched swiftly toward two uniformed men sauntering across the pavement, both of them carrying excessive potbellies.

The entire exchange took less than five minutes. Once Neil motioned for me to join them, my clandestine entry into the Czech Republic went smoothly and without incident. Barely making eye contact with me, the two immigration officials stamped my passport—conveniently not scanning or registering it—and without a word they took the rolled-up magazine concealing the cash.

Fifteen minutes later I was opening the door to a taxi when Neil grabbed my shoulder. "Best of luck to you. I don't know all you've got in mind, but I'd say watch your back." He handed me a card. "When you need to come home, give us a ring."

"Thank you."

Neil didn't say anything more. He turned on his heels and walked back toward his plane, pulling out a flask and taking a long pull as he went.

* * *

The taxi headed down the drive to the main road toward the village of Loděnice and then continued on to Prague. The driver didn't have any trouble finding the address in the city center, and he duly deposited me at the hotel's entrance. I paid the driver in cash before stepping out onto the curb and taking in my surroundings.

To the north I could see the edge of Vítkov Park—a green area with trees and walking trails, with a monument to Czech independence at the top of the hill—but all around I heard, felt, and smelled the city's bustling nightlife. Bars, restaurants, clubs, casinos, and the people filling them, surrounding me in a cacophony of activity.

Over the past ten years I'd spent a significant portion of my life in Europe's capitals, and I truly enjoyed the culture, the food, the atmosphere—all of it. In fact, for a multitude of reasons, I preferred Europe to most any city in the US—except Boston, of course—and I embraced the identity of being a solitary ex-pat.

After the marines it seemed like a better fit; a new life with a new profession and a new image. And, no one gave a rat's ass about my time in Iraq. That's what I appreciated most.

Yet despite my affinity for the Czechs and the City of a Hundred Spires, at this moment I felt forsaken. Standing before the Prague Inn—a two-star hotel hidden behind the historic façades that defined the inner city—I realized there was no one, no lifeline. Ike could handle just about anything, but I wouldn't put him out any more than I already had.

I'd fallen out of touch with most of my marine buddies too, though I still sent the annual letters to the next of kin for those I lost. They wrote me back sometimes, a few parents never missing a year to send a note, but I could barely read their words even if it was just a simple, friendly, maybe even heartfelt *Hello, nice to hear from you, and hope you're doing well. God bless.* Seeing the ink on the paper made it hard to breathe . . . but that's another matter. Caroline probably had an opinion on that stuff too.

There was no one else. By my own choosing, I had no one. I was totally on my own and had a sense at any moment armed men would emerge from an alley and seize me.

I wasn't a carefree guest of the EU this time around. I'd broken laws and would probably break a few more before everything was done. I could never let my guard down, I could trust no one, and both the local authorities and the militants who'd captured Gomez—who apparently had a reach as far as Notting Hill—posed a threat.

I, however, knew the wariness I currently felt was a good thing. These were uncharted waters, and the unknowns about who was out there—perhaps watching me right now—were endless. The appreciation for the edge would make me observe my surroundings, spot irregularities, and notice if the shadows were closing in.

I hadn't felt this way for a long time, despite Alistair frequently sending me off to unsavory places to earn the mighty coin. As an agent of Ruttfield, although I'd needed to maintain awareness and be mindful of risky predicaments, fundamentally I'd always been operating within the laws of the land and could count on the host nation's authorities for assistance. It was in their best interest because even the despots and dictators wanted the West's money.

I entered the hotel and approached the desk, attended by a girl in her early twenties with purple hair and enough piercings to make me suspect she steered clear of magnets.

She offered me an apathetic smile, and in simple English I asked for a room. She accepted my cash without undue attention, and when she made a photocopy of my passport for registration, she simply filed it away in a drawer rather than running it through a database. I had to give Neil credit for recommending the place.

As I walked up the stairs to my room, the emotional exhaustion of the past few days took hold. I was ready for the unknown and unpredictable, but I wanted rest. I wanted to drop my bag, lock the door and barricade it with a chair under the doorknob, then lay down and close my eyes. At this moment that's all I wanted.

CHAPTER FOURTEEN

My body sank into the mounds and troughs of the tired mattress, but I didn't fall into a deep slumber. The rest felt good and damn welcome, but achieving nocturnal bliss wasn't wise.

My mind was firing on all cylinders about how the next few days would play out, and my eyes cracked open every hour, demanding I look at the red numerals of the digital clock on the nightstand. If I did doze, I ventured into that half-dream state where reality mixed with the imaginary. It was a familiar condition for me when a show was about to kick off.

When my alarm finally announced 5:00 a.m. had arrived, I got out of bed rested enough to squeeze into the tiny bathroom. I'd paid extra for a room with a shower, unsure when I might enjoy a bit of privacy again. The warm water sputtering against my skin felt good, and when I emerged from the steam-filled space I appreciated the cool air in the room, rousing my body and mind.

Cleaned and dressed, I repacked my bag, headed downstairs, dropped my key at the desk, and went outside. Winter was fast approaching, so there would still be at least an hour of darkness before the sun made its appearance, but the hum of the city had already begun. Where the night before the streets had been filled with revelers and after-hours misadventures, Prague's residents were now shuffling to work trussed up in coats and scarves.

I popped the collar of my jacket. It was time to get on with it. I'd made my plans. I'd thought about it enough. It was time to jump. The crack of the starting gun.

*　　*　　*

I turned west on Husitská Street, joining the advance of scurrying pedestrians. Soon enough I spotted a café up the street. I weaved out of the mix and went in.

I went straight for the counter to order a coffee and buchteln, a sweet bun made of yeasty doughy goodness. I took two bites and settled into my coffee.

I made a casual sweep of the café's interior—the patrons, the servers, the layout—taking note of the people coming and going. There was a mix of businessmen and -women, one or two folks whom Americans would call blue collar, a few harried students, and at least one survivor from the previous night's nonsense.

Could I spot someone following me? I'd never been formally trained in this spy shit, but I had good street sense and had picked up a few things hopping around the world for Ruttfield. But depending on how sophisticated the surveillance might be, I knew they didn't need to put shoes on the street with someone glowering at me from a dark corner. They could track my movements from a distance with high-tech gizmos and cameras, and I'd have no way of knowing.

My only advantage was not drawing attention to myself, hoping I'd landed in the Czech Republic without anyone noticing. Europe was a big place with millions of people. I was in the haystack.

The other question to ask—perhaps the more important one— was *who* might be watching me. Doug and his CIA buddies? The

Czech authorities? Perhaps Interpol, aware I'd broken a few laws to get on the continent? Maybe.

I was more concerned about *John* and whomever he worked for. They didn't get all they wanted out of me, the bastards; I knew that. Kind of like the end of a date, expecting to land in the sack, but getting a door slammed in your face instead. I speculated *John* and his pals would be more direct about their expectations if they showed up again.

They knew about the email and they knew something about my history with Gomez. Yet they used the name Delgado, indicating they might have some insight into Doug's pet Program. All very concerning, and suggesting secrets had been compromised while other lies continued to circulate, further telling me I was on my own and could trust no one.

I watched and listened to the café's activity for another few minutes, sipping my coffee. Nothing struck me as odd. Time to move.

I left a few euros on the counter and departed, stepping back out onto the street. The air felt brisk on my face, with a hint of light appearing in the sky.

I love the dawn, always have, even when I'd been in the trenches or holed up in a hard-point in some shot-up building. The dawn always gave a suggestion of how the day might go. Today seemed good.

From my spot on the sidewalk, I checked the windows across the street, the doorways, the entrances to little alleys. I hunted for the same types of indicators I'd looked for in the café—someone I'd seen somewhere else, someone loitering where they shouldn't be loitering, or someone quickly glancing away. Again, I didn't spot anyone unusually interested in me or anyone trying to appear uninterested. But if there were cameras on me, I couldn't help that.

Letting a pair of determined ladies pass by, I turned left and headed east on Husitská Street—back the direction I'd just come—and then

took a quick right onto Orebitská and another quick left on Rehor-
ova, finding a much quieter, narrower one-way street. I'd plotted
this route the night before, believing it gave me a better chance to
identify a tail.

But there was no one on the street to take note of. Empty.

I checked my watch and saw it was almost six. It would take me
another seven minutes to reach the train station, Praha hlavni
nádrazi. I'd then launch my odyssey east, through Slovakia, make a
train swap, and barrel on into Ukraine.

Kristyen would be waiting for me at the platform in Kyiv tomorrow morning. *Get your ass to Kyiv*, that's what the man had said in
his half-English mash-up. From there we'd travel to Ukraine's separatist region, every hour ticking like the Doomsday Clock.

That was the plan. It was a good plan. Simple, straightforward,
like any other trip I'd taken in the past ten years.

Yet it wasn't. It wasn't a simple itinerary to follow and be on time
for. There were all kinds of intricate steps to tangle with. And the
only way to ensure I didn't botch everything because of a stupid
mistake was to constantly review and re-review the plan.

Before anything kicked off—review the plan. Once everything
started—review the plan. And once a phase was done and it was
time to transition to the next—review the plan. Think about it, digest it, over and over again.

That's what Gomez and I always said when we were slogging
through the brush at Quantico with the rain pouring down, the
insides of our boots like sponges, getting ready to flip the switch. *The
plan—know the plan—study the plan—breathe the plan—consume
the plan—scrutinize the plan—poke holes in the plan—rethink the
plan—know the plan inside and out, backwards and forwards—and
above all, don't be afraid to change the plan.*

Everyone knows no plan survives first contact with the enemy or the first ten minutes of a road trip involving planes, trains, and East European automobiles. The enemy, Mother Nature, and bad luck have a say in the matter. Murphy is a son of a bitch.

But what do you do when that happens? *Change it—adapt it—evolve it—and do it fast.* I could almost hear Gomez's voice rambling in my ear.

Fast. Fast. Fast. The word—the very sentiment of it in its truest form, *characterized by quick motion, operation, or effect*—boomed inside my head. There was no time to waste.

The longer it took me to make contact with the men holding Gomez, the narrower the opportunity to help him. At some point Gomez's captors would move him, put him in a deeper cell, or kill him. The same was true in every kidnap situation. Once captured, the opportunities for escape diminished with each passing second, the perpetrators asserting more and more control over the situation.

Time was ticking. I had to do it this way. It was a good plan. There was no turning back.

I entered Prague's principal railway station and made for the ticket counters. I weaved around groups of travelers, single riders, families going on vacation, workers heading down to the metro, backpackers staring at maps, and a host of other human actions and reactions. The morning rush.

I was another fly in the mix, I told myself.

CHAPTER FIFTEEN

I approached the ticket counter, a row of ten windows with tellers behind thick glass. Expectant passengers were queued up in good European orderly fashion. But rather than getting in line, I loitered off to the side, leaning against a pillar.

I pulled out my phone and a scrap of paper with a number on it. I dialed, let it ring, all the while watching the ticket windows and the mass of passengers moving here and there. My eyes bounced from person to person: a group of scruffy backpackers, a middle-aged man in work overalls mumbling to himself, a father wearing a pink shirt holding the hand of one child while the mother chased down the second.

On the fourth ring a woman picked up. "Ahoj?"

"Hello, this is Erik," I said, my voice quiet but not a whisper. "I was told to call this number about a ticket."

"Where are you headed?" asked the woman, switching to accented English.

"Madrid," I answered, supplying the destination Kristyen had provided me.

"Are you in the terminal?"

"Yes, where I was told."

"Wait a moment."

Silence filled the line.

A minute came and went. Then a minute and fifteen seconds.

I looked at my watch, at the ticket window, and at the police officer posted by a coffee kiosk. He stood ramrod straight with his fingers curled around the shoulder straps of his tactical vest, an MP-5 submachine gun dangling at his side. He seemed bored and ready for his shift to end.

Finally, the woman's voice came back. "Scratch your right shoulder with your left hand."

I did as instructed. A signal to another person, someone watching me. "Done."

"Wait."

The woman hung up and I let my arm drop.

I continued observing my surroundings but also zeroed in on the door to the left of the ticket windows. I assumed my contact would come out from there. We'd go someplace less public to make the transaction, a quick swap of cash for a ticket with an unregistered passport. Under the radar in plain sight.

Then a finger tapped me on the shoulder, and the unexpected touch sent a cool shot down my spine. I turned to find a pimply-faced teenager wearing a station uniform. He motioned with a head jerk for me to follow, and the boy walked off without a word.

I'll never underestimate the youth who work in the underworld. Too often dismissed as inexperienced and immature—teeming with bluster and trash talk—some can be just as ruthless and cunning as their elder criminal bosses. Sometimes they can be more so given their lack of fear from not yet having been tormented by life's brutal trials. Maybe a little less squeamish about punching a blade into someone's gut.

I fell in behind the kid. He led me down a side hall until we stopped by a single, unmarked door. Again, without a word and his manner impersonal, he motioned for me to wait.

But instead of opening the door and going in, the boy disappeared around the corner.

A second passed, and another, just like when I was back at the ticket counters. A sense of naked exposure crept within me. Why would they send a boy to lead me to a door to abandon me?

The door suddenly opened with a metallic clang echoing down the hall. But instead of finding another station attendant, I beheld a police officer with a grizzled beard glaring at me.

Shit was the first thing to come to mind.

Someone with an accosting cologne came up from behind me. As I looked over my shoulder, two hands shoved me through the door. The uniformed officer pulled me the rest of the way through.

A voice said, "Mr. Hackett, you're under arrest."

CHAPTER SIXTEEN

TRAIN STATION, PRAGUE

I sat in a metal chair the manufacturer had designed to be as stiff and uncomfortable as possible. A rectangular table wobbled before me, large enough for two people to sit next to each other but no more. Someone had bolted a grommet in the center of the table, which I assumed could be used to attach restraints to for a good lashing.

The officers hadn't handcuffed me, but the threat remained.

There were no windows, only the one door, and the room was barren of anything else: white walls, gray linoleum flooring, a fluorescent light. I suspected the space was soundproof too. A sterile emptiness defined it, though isolation was a more apt descriptor, giving me the sense that it was a cozy place to sweat or piss yourself.

I'd been in here going on ten minutes. The officers were either giving me time to think, to let my mind wander through different stages of fear and guilt, or the wait wasn't intentional, merely a bureaucratic pause as the gears of Czech law enforcement ground through policies and procedures. It was probably the former, though I wondered what they'd arrested me for.

I knew what I'd done—entered the country illegally, bribed a border official—but did they? I speculated what the punishment for something like this could be. A hefty fine, a few nights—or months—in lockup? Or would it be rope torture à la Hanoi Hilton?

Or might they have nabbed me for something else? Perhaps they'd set up a sting on the people I'd intended to buy a ticket from to break up their operation, and I'd simply been caught in the net as a nice piece of collateral.

No. A chance dragnet wasn't likely. They'd called me by name. They knew who I was.

I'd need to call Brian, my solicitor. Or was he a barrister? I don't know, I always get those two titles confused, even if I shouldn't by now.

Wow. Won't this be a pickle, I thought as I tilted my head up at the ceiling and expelled a slow breath.

*   *   *

The door to my holding cell opened, shattering my cogitations, a large uniformed officer poised outside in the hall.

"Thank you," came an American voice from somewhere down the corridor. "This shouldn't take long."

A man carrying a briefcase, with blue eyes and a sculpted goatee and a flowing wave to his highlighted brown hair, appeared in the doorway. He wore a closely tailored navy suit with a white check shirt and thin blue tie. He smiled, showing a bit of teeth, but it didn't extend to the eyes, conveying his entire presence was disingenuous.

The American slipped inside the room, shut the door, and pulled back the chair opposite me to sit. Without speaking, but keeping his manufactured grin fixed toward me, he set his briefcase on the table, exposing his cufflinks: silver skull and crossbones.

"Mason Hackett," the man said with a smug *I got ya* in his voice. He removed a folder from his briefcase and placed it between us. "My name is Zach Cardon, and I'm from the US Embassy here in Prague." He opened the folder to lay out three eight-by-ten black-and-white photos side by side. "Would you mind explaining what you're doing in these photos?"

I had remained rigid in my chair with my fingers interlaced in my lap during Zach's presentation, but now I dropped my eyes to examine the images before me. Although each photo had been taken at an odd angle, they were clearly of me. One captured me and the immigration officers at the airfield, another was of me emerging from the café where I'd had the coffee and pastry earlier this morning, and the last showed me following the teenage ticketing attendant. Undeniable, every one of them. Cameras all over me from the beginning.

"I don't know what you're talking about. That's not me," I replied. I'd been held in secondary quite a few times, so the lie rolled out sincerely. But I knew things were different this time and no envelope filled with euros or a slick story would make it all better. But I needed to see where this would go.

"Oh, come now, Mr. Hackett. It's clearly you. Look here. In this photo I can see your hair, your eyes, your smile. And that magazine you're handing to the immigration officer, five thousand euros in cash inside, right?"

"I've no idea," I answered, digging my hole ever deeper.

"And here. Look. You're wearing the same clothes. And this one is from a few minutes ago. You called . . ." Zach made a spectacle of touching his suit pocket before removing a tiny notepad. He flipped through a few pages, and if he'd had a pen in his hand he probably would have licked the tip. "Ah yes, you called a number ending in four-six-eight-one and asked about a ticket to Madrid."

I nearly laughed out loud. This man from the embassy—Zach— knew way too much. No one could have put all this together if they'd only started surveilling me at the airfield. Something was up, and I needed to be even more cautious not to talk myself into a trap, whatever the setup might be for.

"Mr. Hackett, or can I call you Mason? That all right?"

"Sure."

"Right. Great. Let's not play games. I'm here to help you."

"Help me?"

"Why, yes. You're under arrest, and the Czech authorities have compelling evidence against you."

"For what?" It was a dumb question, but I needed Zach to keep talking. The more the man talked, the more I might learn about my predicament. And if Zach was talking, I wasn't, which at the moment was a good thing.

Zach smiled. "Right, you'd like to know the charges. Of course. My mistake. Illegal entry into the European Union, bribing an immigration official, and—although the evidence is speculative—intent to fraudulently purchase train passage to . . ." His voice dropped off again before coming back alive with a theatric sense of eureka. "Ahh, I remember. Kyiv. You're trying to go to Kyiv."

I refused to react, but in my mind, *What the hell?* echoed between my ears. Had Neil turned me in?

No. He wouldn't have, not unless they'd nabbed him.

But they hadn't; he'd gone back to England. Before driving away in the taxi, I watched Neil's plane take off and disappear into the night sky. And that drunk didn't know about Kyiv.

The only other people who had half a sense of my whereabouts were Ike and Kristyen, and I would swear on the Bible that Ike would go down in true British defiance before revealing anything. Ike had bollocks the size of coconuts and considered loyalty a law of nature. He'd never give me up.

But Kristyen? Had he sung to the Czech authorities? But why and to what end? I doubted it. He was too greedy and too slick to turn me in before getting paid. He'd wait until after he had the cash in hand before selling me out. Or, had the people holding Gomez, the people who'd found me and Caroline in Notting Hill, had they identified Kristyen?

"Why are you silent, Mason? Trying to think of how to talk your way out of this?"

I leaned forward as if to study the photos more closely, then sat back again. I met Zach's smug face. "I'm wondering where this—" I flicked my eyes at the pictures—"where this story is coming from."

"You mean how we know what you've been up to since you left England?"

"And you say you're from the embassy. What does that mean? Are you State Department, Defense, Treasury, can't tell me?"

Zach shifted in his seat and adjusted his cufflinks, twisting the skull and crossbones so they were straight up and down, perpendicular to his wrist. "To put it plainly, my organization is well connected, and the Czechs prefer to call us when they catch wind of an American entering their country illegally."

"Are you FBI?" I asked.

"No. A colleague called me, from the same organization you spoke with back in Paris. That's why I'm here."

I remained impassive, but I had inferred as much. As soon as Zach appeared in the doorway, I wondered if Doug was lurking about. Doug probably had the CIA watching me the entire time—physically and technically—but let me get this far to make the evidence incontrovertible.

But why?

I didn't have to work in intelligence to know surveilling me so extensively for this long wasn't a simple endeavor. It took people, resources, time—all of which had to be pulled from other requirements. Priorities refocused on me. Why?

Did Doug and his posse consider me so much of a threat to the Program that, rather than intercepting me back in London, they'd let me cross into mainland Europe . . . to do what?

And why didn't Zach come out and say *Doug*? What was with the *colleague* bullshit? If you're going to call me out, why not do it?

"Who sent you?" I asked.

Zach matched my stare. "A mutual acquaintance."

"Who?" I asked more firmly.

Zach snickered. "Doug. Your friend."

"My friend. Right. He sent you?"

"He did."

"Am I so important to warrant a full-fledged CIA surveillance op?"

"He thinks so, and I would agree. You're messing with sensitive stuff, Mason. Things could go sideways pretty quick if you were to continue blundering about."

"Why?"

Zach shook his head. "That's not your concern. But now that I see you're done being cute, I'll be direct with you. As I said a moment ago, the Czech authorities have enough evidence to charge you with illegal entry into their country, bribery, and conspiracy to fraudulently obtain passage across international borders. Without me, you're fucked. Tracking?"

I frowned but didn't utter a word.

"If you were anyone else in Czech custody—and I wasn't here— you'd have the right to consult with the embassy's consular section. But given you're simply a private citizen, there's not much they could do. You broke numerous Czech and European laws and the United States respects the laws of other countries, usually, but particularly when we have good relations like we do here. However, given your connections and that we know what you're trying to do—as ludicrous as it may be—my organization has a little pull. So, I have an offer for you."

"I'm listening."

"Surrender yourself into my custody for escort back to the UK. For the next month you'll wear this." Zach removed a tiny black bracelet from his briefcase. "It's like a police tracker for dopes on parole, monitoring your location with all kinds of anti-tampering measures and stuff I don't understand." He placed the bracelet in front of me. "Also, you agree to drop this crazy business about helping a certain person of interest."

"And?"

"And all this goes away."

I thought for a long moment before asking, "Why in the world would you offer such a thing?"

Zach abruptly stood, collected the photos and bracelet, and returned everything to his briefcase. "That doesn't concern you."

Zach stepped toward the door, then turned to give me a final look. "Think of this as your one and only lifeline. Your decision should be simple. Go home or get locked up in a Czech prison."

He pounded on the door with the meat of his closed fist. The lock popped and the door opened. "I'll be back in an hour. Be ready to go. Or not."

CHAPTER SEVENTEEN

Three hours passed before Zach returned, and in that time I came to grips with the situation. I didn't like it, but I didn't have a choice. It wasn't like I was going to break out of this cell and make a mad dash for the prison block wall. That'd be stupid and likely result in a tight grouping of hollow-point 9mm rounds lodged between my shoulder blades.

Zach came across as a shady turd and seemed to be withholding a hell of a lot more than Doug had, but I didn't have much to go on or any other options. Agreeing to go with Zach was the only way. I'd be escorted back to England and slapped with a CIA-made kiddie tracker. Embarrassing, frustrating, uncomfortable—yes, all of the above.

But that wasn't the worst of it. Gomez was still being detained by militants in the midst of a Russian-backed war. The US government had abandoned him and now, because of my incompetence, I'd failed miserably at a rescue attempt.

I may have been naïve to think paying off Gomez's captors would succeed, but getting wrapped up by my own side in less than twenty-four hours was pathetic. I should have known Doug would be watching and I should have taken greater precautions.

The question was what to do now.

"All right, Mr. Hackett," said Zach. "Time to go."

I peered up and met Zach's superior look, but kept my expression impassive. If there was one thing I was good at, it was not letting anyone else see what did or did not get to me.

I raised myself out of the chair, zipped up my jacket, and asked, "My bag?"

"He's got it," replied Zach, motioning at a new face standing outside the holding cell. He had the smell of American too, though he was evidently the muscle, his arms stretching the fabric of his suit jacket and his chin too square. "That's Rick. Rick—Mason. Mason—Rick. All good? Great."

"You couldn't handle me on your own?"

"Last-minute addition. Even I don't have all the answers. Isn't that right, Rick?"

Rick didn't say anything, his demeanor a lot less slimy than Zach's. But I noticed his eyes were focused on Zach as much as they were on me, watching us both, which made me wary.

"When's the flight?" I asked, wanting to insert questions and actions into the mix to see how Zach and Rick reacted. They came across like they knew each other, but something was off.

"Slight change of plans," said Zach. "Come on."

"What's the change? You sending me to the Riviera instead?" I quipped, coming around the table and exiting the cell, dimly waiting for Rick or Zach to tell me which way to go.

"Couldn't get a suitable flight out today. So, we'll stay the night in a hotel and fly out first thing. That work for you?"

"Do I have a choice?"

"No, but there's no reason to be impolite."

"I should thank you."

"You should."

"Rick, you make the res?" asked Zach.

Rick grunted, which I assumed meant yes. It was like they were taunting each other.

"Everything still in my bag?" I asked.

"Thoroughly searched, of course," replied Zach over his shoulder as the three of us proceeded down the hall. "And the money is there too, in case that's what you were asking about. You can count it at the hotel if you want. Won't bother me."

We reached the end of the hall where a uniformed gendarme stood by a solid metal door. Zach nodded, said thanks, and walked through with Rick and me in tow.

We emerged into the public area of the train station and headed toward the exit, the bright Central European sun piercing the grand windows making me squint. Having been stuck in a holding pen for the past four hours with no notion of what was happening beyond the blank walls, it felt like I was emerging from a cave, once again mixing with life on the surface.

Outside, Rick led us to a parked sedan.

"Sure you don't want to take my car?" asked Zach. "I got the office's SUV down the street."

Rick shook his head and waved his arm to the far side of the vehicle for Zach to get in. "It's good we switch it up. I'll call for Hans to get the SUV."

"Right," muttered Zach, getting in the back seat and me beside him. Rick got behind the wheel and pulled into traffic.

"That was very efficient," I said, looking out the window at the city passing by.

"Did you expect to get discharged like Jake Blues?"

"You just dated yourself. But no, merely an observation."

"Like I said, we have a good relationship here. And, as long as you stick to the rules, all the records of your activities in the Czech Republic will disappear. You'll be able to travel back any time you want without a blip. Though next time I suggest you do it like a normal, law-abiding person. Isn't that right, Rick."

Rick's eyes flashed to the rearview mirror, but again the man stayed silent.

"And my record with your organization?" I asked.

"Your record? Can't erase those files," Zach replied with a laugh. "But they'll never surface. We're good at keeping secrets. We've buried a body or two. Unless, of course, you attempt another boondoggle."

"Right, boondoggle. How well do you know Doug?"

Zach shifted in his seat, seeming to remove something from his right hip under his suit jacket, as he said, "Well enough. He made a call and—"

Before Zach could finish his sentence, Rick reached back over the seat with a small-caliber automatic in his hand. The shot was swift and the pop inside the vehicle made my ears ring. The bullet struck Zach just above his left eye making a small red hole, but the deadly projectile didn't exit, pinging around inside his skull tearing up the brain. Zach's lifeless body slumped against the seat, and Rick turned back around to take the wheel and continue driving through downtown Prague.

"What the fuck!" I yelled.

"Quiet. Listen. He was gonna kill you and me. He was going for his gun. Look."

I drew my eyes from the back of Rick's head and saw that Zach did indeed have his right hand wrapped around a pistol.

"Son of a bitch," I said. "Who are you? What's going on?"

"Not right now," Rick said, a smoothness to his response, like this wasn't the first time he'd killed someone and then turned to another task with detached focus.

The sedan picked up speed as we swerved around a lorry and then turned down a side street. I sat back and tightened my seat belt, scanning the outside as well as watching the back of Rick's head as he maneuvered onto another thoroughfare.

"Listen carefully," said Rick. "Doug didn't contact Zach. Zach works for *them*."

"Who's them?"

"The people holding Delgado. Now listen. We have to move. Look out the back window, tell me what you see. Cars following, anything like that. Zach wasn't alone."

"Christ," I murmured, starting to take stock of what just happened and doing so in an instant. Zach dead, killed by a man who up until now hadn't said more than ten words. Doug. The people holding Gomez. People on us.

But I didn't fear Rick, not yet. If he'd wanted to kill me, he wasn't going about it very well. And he must have believed I wasn't a threat to him either. But thoughts of another *John* situation like back on London's streets, presenting one thing but being another, concerned me.

Unfortunately, there was no telling at this point. I just had to go with it.

"Where are we going?" I asked, checking out the back window but not seeing anything indicating someone was in hot pursuit.

"Away from here. Safe house."

"Tell me what's going on."

"They're onto you. They've been tracking you ever since you got that damned email. They sent Zach in to take you out."

"Who? Who the hell is after me?"

"The same people who have Delgado, the man you know as Gomez. These are people you don't want to mess with." Rick took a breath and picked up more speed. "Do you see anyone following us?"

"No," I said, turning back around. Contrary to my initial impression of him—a cagey thug whose biceps had more intellect than his brain—Risk was speaking and acting with razor precision. "Dammit. Who are the people after me? The Russians? Separatists?"

"I'll explain when we get there. Just sit tight for now. But stay sharp. Like I said, Zach's got friends but I don't know how many."

"Was Zach really CIA?"

"Fucking traitor. Yeah, the bastard was CIA. We'd suspected him for about a month. But him snaring you proved it. He wasn't even supposed to be in Prague. He came out of Berlin and got on the ground just a few hours ago."

"Was he part of the . . ." My voice trailed off, wanting to levy the question but not sure if—

"Was Zach part of the Program?" Rick asked, reading my mind. "No. But he'd been sniffing around in the wrong places at the wrong times, which is why he was on our radar and we were watching him."

"And you?"

"I really do work with Doug. I was on my way to intercept you when—"

A massive impact blasted our sedan off the road and caused it to flip. I felt myself hurtling through the air and heard and saw metal crush and glass shatter. Then nothing.

CHAPTER EIGHTEEN

Rick had less than a second to react when the Sprinter van lost control and veered into oncoming traffic. The van slammed into the front of our car going upwards of one-hundred-twenty kilometers an hour with a force that rocked every one of my organs.

The van originated in Germany, the driver a man of Turkish descent with a wife and six children and a mother-in-law who never ceased criticizing him. He worked for a Stuttgart-based logistics company, and on this particular day he was transporting half-inch sheets of hardened steel to a vehicle armoring company in Prague. He hadn't slept well the night before, and after being on the road for six hours, he'd fallen asleep behind the wheel. He woke with a start and jerked the wheel into oncoming traffic.

Our vehicles struck head-on akin to two cannonballs colliding in midair. The additional weight from the sheets of hardened steel stacked in the back of the van magnified the impact to an exponential degree, with a sound that cracked the ears of anyone on the street. Our lighter sedan skidded sideways across two lanes of traffic, with smoke whooshing from the tires. We hit a short wall and flipped over, settling upside down with that damn silence that always follows a sudden accident.

When I came to, my head was ringing with a high whine, and I felt a crushing pressure on my shoulders and chest. I struggled to breathe. It took a minute for my vision to clear. I tried to move my arms, but my entire body seemed out of balance.

I realized I was upside down, suspended in my seat by the safety belt. Though in a fog, I determined that the source of my pain was due to my unnatural state upside down against gravity. I didn't see any apparent injuries to my chest or stomach, just the belt cutting into my skin through my clothes.

A mass of broken glass covered the car's roof like a sea of crystals. I noticed fluid dripping in the back, but my head was too messed up to realize the danger. My hearing was still muffled from the violence of the accident, but I heard people yelling, sirens, and the grinding of the sedan's fractured engine struggling to turn over.

Just outside I glimpsed the mashed front end of a van and what appeared to be the upper half of a human body sticking out of the windshield. It'd been sheared in two at the waist by a flying guillotine.

Responsiveness finally came back to me. I looked to my right to see Zach's lifeless body also dangling by the seat belt. The front passenger seat had collapsed onto his legs, pinning his corpse into the seat.

And up front I saw a large, flat piece of metal had blasted through the windshield, and there were four or five square metal pipes that had punctured the front of the sedan like crossbow bolts. I was lucky one hadn't hit me, but couldn't tell if Rick was still in one piece. The shredded airbag obscured my view.

Then I smelled it: the viscous odor of diesel and the accompanying acrid smoke when it burns. It'd been nearly fifteen years since I'd smelled a suffocating diesel fire, but it was unmistakable. Visions of Humvees destroyed by IEDs, burning hulks with ammo cooking off, bloodied bodies trapped inside or sprawled in the dirt flashed through my mind.

Instincts kicked in.

I struggled with the release of my safety belt and yelled, "Rick! Rick! Are you okay?"

Rick's dangling arms flinched.

"Rick! Wake the fuck up!"

My belt release clicked and I dropped a few inches onto the vehicle's roof. I squirmed onto my stomach and shook Rick's shoulder.

"Rick! Come on!" I yelled, but the CIA man didn't respond.

I heard a pop and looked to the rear of the car. Flames and thick black smoke were penetrating the rear hatch with a hazy, wrathful glow.

I rolled over and kicked my heel into the passenger door. On the fourth try it surrendered. I squeezed through the twisted metal and broken glass, not caring about the cuts and scratches raking my skin.

Out of the sedan and onto the sidewalk I struggled to my feet. The bystanders who had initially gathered to help were now backing away. The undercarriage of the sedan was fully engulfed in flames, screaming with heat.

I bent down and moved back toward the car. Shielding my face from the fire and choking smoke, I dropped lower and reached in through the window. I shook Rick again, yelling his name. "Rick! Rick! Wake up!"

Rick's eyes finally fluttered open, going wide. Despite the man's injuries, he knew something was terribly wrong and that he was in grave danger.

"Your belt! Release your belt!" I shouted, yanking on the door handle. I pulled and pulled, with drops of burning diesel dripping down the side of the chassis onto my hands. I slapped away the burning fuel, numb to the second-degree burns on my bare flesh, and continued heaving on the door.

It finally sprung open and I fell on my backside.

Anyone who had ventured near the crash site when the accident first happened by now had fully dispersed, most getting far away to seek cover from the possibility of an explosion. Those who still hung close by screamed at me to get away. I ignored them.

I scrambled back on all fours and tried to reach through the mess of crushed seats and torn metal to free Rick, but I quickly realized there was no way. The steering wheel and the dash had collapsed into him, trapping his legs.

I looked into the man's eyes and saw genuine fear, something I suspect he'd rarely felt before.

"Mason, help me. Get me out of here."

"I'm trying," I strained.

The flames on the car's undercarriage were roaring, now working their way down the side panels and into the cab. Rick started to scream. It was the deep scream of intense pain that assaults your ears. It comes from the depths of an agonized soul feeling unimaginable pain.

The only time I'd heard someone scream that way was when they were on fire burning alive. I'd seen it happen twice before, long ago in a dark, horrible place, and now it was happening again.

Another splash of burning diesel dropped onto my arm and caught my shirt on fire. I swatted it out, reaching in one more time to help Rick. I managed to pull a small duffel out of the way and tossed it behind me. I went to reach in again but a surge of smoke and fire jetted into my face, blowing me back.

I couldn't see, I couldn't breathe, I was overwhelmed. It was no use.

I turned and crawled away from the hulk that was now fully ablaze. I heard Rick's screams die out. Although he would live for a few more seconds, perhaps a minute, the fire and smoke had filled his lungs, scorching his throat and voice box, rendering him mute.

I got to my feet and stumbled backward, picking up the bag I'd tossed, and turning back around when I was maybe thirty feet away. Not a safe distance, but I didn't care.

The sedan burned like an inferno with thick black smoke rising into the sky. I could see Rick's body hanging inside, but it was no longer moving. Zach's body had suffered the same fate.

Beyond the burning car rested the smashed front end of the Sprinter van. The upper half of the driver's body hung out the windshield, and there were multiple steel plates on the pavement or falling out of the front of the van. Given its proximity to the fire, no one was going near it either.

It had started to rain and emergency vehicles were arriving. Police officers, fire crews, and medical personnel were getting out and trying to assert control over the chaos. They would come to care for me as soon as they cordoned off the scene, and then I'd be rushed to a hospital, probably questioned by the authorities. It'd be a mess to explain.

I looked around, and an SUV jammed in the snarled traffic caught my attention. A man with dark hair had the door open and was standing on the running board, straining to get a better view of the accident scene. Our eyes met, and I knew he wasn't some random driver late for his lunch date.

I made my decision in less than a second.

I tucked the bag under my arm, turned, and ran. With all the panic and confusion, no one stopped me. I dashed down a road I didn't catch the name of, then down an alley.

Despite the shock of everything that had just happened, my thinking was clear. I needed to get the hell out of the city.

CHAPTER NINETEEN

A hand shook Delgado's shoulder to rouse him, but he hadn't been in a deep sleep. He wasn't asleep at all, actually. He knew exactly where he was and what was going on. But he still needed to play the part and live the lie: a Spanish journalist—Henry Delgado—scared out of his mind and about to crap his pants.

Yet he knew the lie was futile at this point. They *knew* who he was.

His interrogators had switched tactics soon after the first twelve hours. In the beginning it'd been the typical fare—punches, kicks, pressure just shy of bones snapping or complete asphyxiation. Easy stuff. Good stuff. If all they were doing was beating him, it meant they didn't have anything solid. It hurt—no getting around that—but it was tolerable. They hadn't gone completely medieval on him. He'd stayed strong and sent the mind somewhere else.

But no more. The thugs with the fists and boots and pipes went on a coffee break, replaced by the talkers. At first, Delgado had called them P1, P2, and P3, the *P* standing for *Prick*. He'd given them more personal names after he'd gotten to know them.

P1 became *Smoky* for the endless supply of cigarettes he sucked down and the accompanying shit-breath that could kill a horse. P2 became *Tapper* because the man never stopped tapping his heel, and if he did, he'd tap his pen or his finger or some other appendage. P3 was *Asshole* because he simply came across as one.

Although the few guards he'd seen and his previous abusers had worn a variety of mismatched military clothing, these three didn't. Straight up black jeans and black jackets for them. They were professionals working as a team. Whoever was in charge had sent in the big guns because he or she knew they had something valuable on their hands.

He estimated his first session with these guys had lasted about six hours—three hundred sixty minutes of awesomeness. They'd rotated every hour or so, sometimes working together and at other times going at him solo. He tracked the time by their rotations and the number of cigarettes Smoky went through.

He approximated the second session lasted twelve hours.

This was the third.

They were good, he had to admit. They asked direct questions requiring specific responses. Then they'd chitchat to get him to say more. Casual conversation topics about how he was feeling, where home was, how they were sorry about the previous mistreatment, what news articles he was working on before Ukraine—questions and comments designed for him to repeat himself. Wear him down through frustration, confusion, and circles.

And he had to talk. He couldn't clam up with name, rank, and serial number like a POW. That's what soldiers, sailors, and marines do. Laws of war and the Geneva Conventions.

He couldn't be any of those. If you were untrained and innocent, you had to talk because the average person always believed there was a chance they could convince their captors of their innocence. It was human nature—reaching, yearning for that sliver of hope.

But in an interrogation like this, there was no convincing. They had you. All they were trying to do was trap you in a lie or contradiction to trip you up. And as things spun further and further out of control, the more you revealed.

They were asking him the same questions over and over again, but doing so in different ways and over time. Adding his exhaustion and the lingering pain from round one with the warm-up crew, it was hard to keep things straight. But the real kicker was how they were mixing his life as Henry Delgado with who he really was, the man he'd said goodbye to long ago—Kevin Gomez.

Somehow, they knew who he was and they'd told him they knew it all—name, hometown, college girlfriend, Marine Corps... There were a hundred ways they could have figured it out. He'd been operating for over fifteen years as Delgado, and even the tightest covers had holes.

But he'd never know how they did it. The people he was going up against—the people outside the doors he hadn't seen but who were calling the shots—he knew they weren't in the habit of revealing their methods. They wouldn't be as elusive as they were if they made a show of their methods and operation. Still, that didn't prevent him from going around and around about the possibilities. DNA links, big data image comparison, deep surveillance, a mistake from long ago.

Or, his worst fear: a leak—the entire reason he'd been in Ukraine— someone on the inside betraying it all—a tentacle inside one of CIA's most sensitive activities—a traitor feeding the enemy.

"Kevin? Kevin? Are you awake?" asked Smoky, tapping the smoldering cherry of his cigarette against Delgado's eyelid.

"Ahh. Ahh. Yes. Please," Delgado pleaded.

"Kevin, it's okay. We must talk more. It's okay. I must ask you about a friend of yours. A good friend, but someone you haven't talked to for many years, until recently—Mason Hackett."

Delgado inhaled deeply. Years ago, well before this operation, he'd left instructions with a firm to send an email automatically in the event he was ever kidnapped, killed, or mysteriously disappeared. It was a long shot to someone who thought he'd died in the sands of Iraq—Brother Hackett. His old friend might be able to do something—and *they* knew about him.

The safety protocol Delgado thought he'd established may have just blown up in his face. He braced himself for what was to come.

CHAPTER TWENTY

I sat behind the wheel of a Škoda Octavia, the car I'd stolen from a parking garage four blocks from the crash site, and which I'd switched out the license plates on twice during my drive. I reached the edge of Brno an hour ago, a medium-sized city southeast of Prague off the E50, and parked just off the road with a view of the trees and the farmhouses built a century ago. The first rays of dawn were creeping toward me over the toiled fields and crumbling stone walls, the day shaping up to be a pisser.

I stared at nothing, reliving the crash and thinking everything had changed.

The trauma of the accident had been severe—the collision, the fire, a man shot, a man burned alive, another sheared in half—but I'd seen enough in life where that stuff didn't get to me, even if it should have. Rather, the events surrounding the accident that were in connection to the broader predicament I was now in were what unsettled me.

I was being hunted.

There'd been no sign of the SUV I'd spotted at the crash site, nor anyone else seeming to be on my tail, but as my detention at the train station proved, my adversaries—whomever they were—had other ways to track me. At this moment, my only hope was that the disarray caused by the accident and me no longer in possession of anything electronic—I'd found my phone in Rick's duffel and chucked it out the window while going 140 kph—had thwarted any means to ascertain my whereabouts. Only time would tell.

And what of my adversaries?

Zach had presented himself with credentials and real knowledge of Doug, Gomez, and me. He wasn't like the goon I'd encountered on London's streets. Zach had been convincing and knew details, and the way he and Rick interacted, I'm confident he was a bona fide CIA officer.

And then Rick shot and killed him. A fast, clean shot through the forehead as if he was aiming for Zach's groomed eyebrow. I'm pretty sure Zach was going for his gun too, but Rick acted sooner.

Rick claimed Zach was working for the same people holding Gomez, and that he was the one actually connected to Doug and on my side. But Rick's dead too, a charred corpse on one of Prague's pristine boulevards. I couldn't ask him the multitude of questions radiating in me.

Yet for a reason I cannot explain, I believe Rick had been telling the truth. Whether Rick and I would have enjoyed a cocktail together while marveling at the local talent is another matter, but I do think he was trying to protect me from Zach and whomever he was in league with. Russians, Ukrainians, something else . . . the haziness was concerning and grave.

So, what to do now?

The question of whether to turn tail and head home or keep going to help my friend and get answers had been overcome by events. Gomez was still being held by some bad dudes, and they were on me pretty darn thick, too. Hiding in my basement wasn't an option. My only choice was to keep going to find answers and to help Gomez. I couldn't live with myself without either, even if I found a place somewhere on the West African coast to spend my dying days. I had to keep going.

The real question was how.

I glanced at the duffel bag on the seat next to me. During my escape from Prague while racing away in this lovely stolen car, I'd already rifled through the duffel to find my bag and phone, but I hadn't had an opportunity to see what other surprises might await me.

I unzipped the duffel to find my clothes and money—hallelujah—but what snagged my attention more profoundly was the beautiful nugget sitting at the bottom: a Glock 19 pistol secured in a small, inside-the-pants leather holster.

I pulled it out and admired the weapon. The blued metal and black plastic were clean, not a scratch anywhere. It had tritium dots on the front and rear sites, which would glow in the dark for low-light shooting. I pressed the magazine release and saw it was topped off with fifteen 9mm rounds. Racking the slide with a swift pull and locking it to the rear, the sixteenth round popped out of the chamber. I inspected the cavity and saw it was clean and smooth, like the exterior—a well-maintained pistol carried by a professional.

Whether that professional had been Zach or Rick, I didn't know, but at this point it didn't matter.

I needed a new plan, my initial idea to cross into Ukraine via Slovakia using Kristyen no longer viable. Zach had known all about it and I had to assume other individuals with less than honorable intentions did too; people would be watching. Given the EU also had me on their radar, I couldn't cross at another spot farther down the border. If I used my real passport, I'd light up Interpol with a big fat warning message blaring like a fire alarm.

A false passport wasn't an option either, principally because I had no idea how to get one. I was no spy, trained to use aliases and covers and legends. I had common sense and could tell a nice tale when cornered, but I knew better than to fake the funk.

No. What I needed was distance between me and the Czech Republic, as well as an expert in the *traditional* travel routes that didn't bother with the EU's red tape. I also needed to get a message to someone.

I slid the full mag back in the magazine well and pressed the slide release, sending it home with a metallic clap. I removed the magazine once more, contemplated topping it off to fifteen as I'd found it, but didn't. The 19 tended to double-feed when packed to the top, so I let the magazine stay at fourteen and put the extra bullet in my pocket. I reinserted the mag and slipped the pistol under my right leg.

I had to get to Bucharest to make a phone call and then pay someone a visit.

CHAPTER TWENTY-ONE

THE ISLAND OF CRETE

Viktor Leos gazed out over his patio and the two-acre lawn and garden that made up his backyard. The space would have been larger were it not for the treacherous slopes and blinding white cliffs that surrounded his hillside residence on the north side of Crete. His grandmother had been from St. Petersburg—Leningrad at the time—but Crete was Leos' ancestral home and where his family had lived for centuries.

Leos smiled. From where he sat with the Mediterranean sun warming his face, he took in a full view of his youngest daughter's twelfth birthday celebration. Children playing games, lamb kabobs grilling over open coals, colorful streamers fluttering, manicured animals wandering, a live band, dancing, and waiters and staff floating about—he'd spared no expense. His little *kopítsi* deserved every ounce of doting for the joy she brought him.

He reached next to him and took his wife's hand, kissing the side of her index finger. She smiled back at him, the fine lines around her eyes and mouth always a little more pronounced when outside under Greece's sun. But she wore her forty-seven years well and she could still catch an eye when she graced the small town down the hill or hopped over to the mainland to indulge in the boutiques. She was especially fetching when she wore a flowing dress as she did today, her figure a little thicker than it was when Leos plucked her at twenty-seven, but still ravishing.

Lilijana was a good wife and knew her part. She cared for the children, stayed on Leos' arm in the public's eye, and most importantly, never asked questions about his business. She was more than sharp enough to know what he did, and he couldn't prevent her from seeing the news when one of his commercial interests splashed the headlines, but it wasn't *her business.*

Leos supposed that's why they'd been content these past two decades. We each know our place, he thought.

"*Archigós*, my sincerest apologies for the interruption," said a Spanish voice from behind, always using the Greek word for "boss" whenever he referred to his employer, no matter what language he might be speaking in.

"Senor Mario," Leos said, drawing out the last of his name. "My dear man, what is it? Didn't we see each other enough at the gala in Italy? It's my daughter's birthday. My little kopítσι."

"I know, Archigós. But something has happened I think you should know."

"And it can't wait an hour. Your toast, my adored," pleaded Lilijana.

Leos patted his wife's hand. "Senor Mario wouldn't interrupt our day if it wasn't important, would you, Mario?"

"Of course not."

"That's right. Mario's worked with me for twenty years, from before I found you. I trust no man more."

Lilijana offered her husband a joyless smile, which vanished when she gave Mario a final look.

Leos again patted his wife's hand as he stood. He kissed her gently on the forehead, buttoned his linen jacket, and motioned for Mario to precede him. He never once turned back to see his daughter petting the white and black Arabian horses in procession. A tiny gift for her passion.

Leos joined Mario, Genevieve, and Ismael in the shade on the portico. He kissed Genevieve on the cheek more tenderly than politely, and then said, "Ismael, my dejected Israeli, so good to see you. Now what the fuck is going on? Am I to understand you are the one spoiling my daughter's day?"

Ismael gave a curt nod and said, "Mr. Leos. I do my job."

"Right. Yes, you do. Good money too. Now out with it. That was the downfall of your predecessor. He was never quick enough with the bad news. Always wanted to protect me, he said. But that never made sense. My interests are my interests and I need to know all problems. Isn't that correct, Senor Mario?"

"Yes, Archigós."

"Exactly. It's all about survival. Me and my family, of course." Leos belted out a hearty laugh, but his audience maintained respectful smiles.

"Of course," said Ismael.

"Well come on. Out with it, man."

"Right. I got a message from our man in Prague. The one with the internal connections."

"That's my man Jan, right?"

"Yes," answered Mario.

"Right. Always know my people's names. Good business works that way."

"Yes, Mr. Leos. He said there was an incident. His contact said two American officials died in a car accident, and one was shot in the head."

Leos narrowed his eyes and looked at Genevieve, who nodded and said, "Our friend out of Berlin we sent in."

"Yes, he was a damn cocky shit. Dead?"

"Yes."

"But who was the other? Our little problem? The mysterious Mr. Hackett?"

Genevieve shook her head.

"Then who was the other American? You said both were Americans. Who was he?"

"The other individual who died was also American intelligence, I think," replied Ismael. "And there was a third man who fled the scene."

"Him, yes? Mr. Hackett?"

Ismael nodded.

"Where is he? That was the whole point of taking him. No more games. Put him in a dark room and bleed it out of him. Now where is he?"

No one spoke, the coastal wind rustling the clothes of the three messengers. Leos' face darkened and he took a moment to look about at nothing. A waiter carrying a tray of champagne flutes glided by, a guitarist hurried inside the residence, and a quartet of boys dashed around the stone wall with sparklers alight.

"What is the conclusion, then?" asked Leos. "You are paid well. I expect you to have answers."

"Our friend, he was the one shot," said Ismael. "A single bullet to the forehead. We don't know why the other official was in the car, but he was driving and the police found a gun in his possession. And as I said, the third man—Hackett—has disappeared."

"What else?"

"There's nothing else."

Leos nodded and crossed his arms, contemplating the polished stone under his shoes. "Thank you. Now listen. Get whatever else comes out of Jan and alert the rest of our contacts east of Prague. The official ones. You know the names. That's your job and you're good at your job. You understand?"

"The ones with the retainers," added Mario.

"Right, the retainers. Ismael understands. He's Israeli, and Israeli intelligence never works with stupid."

"Right, Archigós."

"Good, good. Go." Leos dismissed Ismael with a wave, then turned to Mario. "He's with us what, three years?"

"That's correct, Archigós."

"He's in Erik's old place in the village, right?"

"That's right."

"It's a good place. I hope he doesn't spend too much time there. Erik did. Didn't pay enough attention."

"Right. I'll keep an eye on him."

"Good. Now, Genevieve, where do you think our man is heading?"

"He will keep going," answered Genevieve.

"You're sure?"

"His past suggests it."

"His past, his past . . . but why is he involved?" Leos looked up to the clouds. "Why did our man Delgado send him that email? What is the connection?"

"They were soldiers together," said Mario.

"Yes, yes, we know these things. But that was a long time ago when Delgado was still Gomez. And Gomez died. You say we know his past, but we know nothing."

"I'll keep looking," said Genevieve.

"Yes, yes, I know you will. You never let me down. But don't use Petrov and his apes anymore. That man needs to handle our man Delgado." Leos paused, thinking for a moment. "Put some whispers out in my old circles. The unsavory friends we used to have. Mario knows the ones, don't you, Mario?"

"Of course, Archigós. Good friends, good people."

"Fucking criminals, all of them. Killers. Have them drop some nets and catch this fucking man. Add a finder's fee. Enough to make it worth their attention but not make them think our man's too important. Never trust those shits."

"I'll take care of it," said Genevieve.

"I know you will." Leos took her hand and kissed it gently. "You take care of me."

Genevieve walked off, and Leos' eyes never left the contours of her hips under her ivory-colored skirt.

"Archigós, one more thing."

"Mario, my only friend. Make sure my wife and I have a nice dinner tonight. Private. We need some personal time."

"Of course, Archigós."

"And tomorrow I need to confer with Genevieve again. Same arrangement as last time."

Mario nodded.

Switching back to business, Leos asked, "What was the thing?"

"Tolesky."

Leos rolled his eyes. "Yes."

"Delgado was trying to arrange a meeting with Tolesky. That's why he was near the border."

"Yes, I know this. Tolesky does well, but he's careless sometimes. Use that. Maybe make him a little looser, let things slip a bit. Sometimes it's good to expose a little leg to keep the folks distracted. We'll keep them looking over there while we go over here."

"Right. Hess has him now."

"Sochi?"

Mario nodded.

Leos frowned and said, "Fine," turning his attention to the water and the whitecaps until he noticed his wife waving at him, beckoning him to come.

"My family is beautiful and I must attend to them."

"Yes, Archigós."

"You are family too, Mario. You understand."

Mario nodded and Leos walked off, a bright smile coming to his face and his arms spread to embrace his lovely daughter and loyal wife.

CHAPTER TWENTY-TWO

ROMANIA

Twelve hours passed on my drive from Brno, Czech Republic, to Romania. I pushed hard the entire day, only stopping for gas and to relieve myself. It rained all through Hungary, never once letting up, and by the time I reached the southern hook of the Carpathians, darkness had blanketed the landscape.

I stopped in Piteşti, a town with numerous thoroughfares heading in every cardinal direction. If I suddenly popped on the grid, even the CIA and NSA would have trouble guessing which direction I went, and I could only hope that my other pals interested in my whereabouts were less capable. But with a bit of luck I wouldn't pop, at least not right away.

I found a local pub where the town's serious drinkers go and where I hoped no one would pay any mind to my disheveled appearance, singed clothes, and trailing smell. I paid the owner forty euros to use his phone in the back office. He happily obliged me for what I said would be no more than a five-minute call, probably less.

I shut the door, sat behind the desk, picked up the receiver, and dialed a number by heart. It came alive on the third ring.

"Yeah?" answered Ike.

"It's me. You understand?" I asked.

Ike didn't hesitate. "Yes. Good to hear your voice."

"Got a piece of paper? I need you to get a message to someone."

"Go for it."

Over the next minute and seventeen seconds, I gave Ike a telephone number, a name, and told him to call it using a clean phone. I asked him to pass along a two-sentence message and ask a one-sentence question. I told him I'd make contact again in two hours, but from another number, and said I'd call the burner I'd given him before departing England.

"I got it. Easy," replied Ike.

"Thanks."

I was about to hang up when Ike asked, "Hey, you doing all right?"

I paused, not expecting the question. It should have been a simple answer, *Yep, just peachy.* But small talk hadn't been a part of my existence for days. Plus, you typically give someone you know a more genuine, perhaps revealing response. But all I said was, "Yeah, I'm fine."

"Really?"

"Yeah."

"Good."

"How are they?"

"No issues. Quiet."

"Good. Thanks."

"Keep your head down."

"Yeah. You too."

We both hung up, clean and efficient, but with loads of information passing between us in those few words. It was a relief, actually. With a man like Ike I could do that, trusting we were on the same wavelength where every detail didn't need to be expanded upon. We each just knew, the tone in our voices sometimes saying more than the words. I passed him instructions, he'd asked if I was all right, and I asked about Caroline and her family.

All was well, even if it wasn't.

*   *   *

An hour later I found a similar establishment in a town farther west called Târgovişte. At the bar, I had a plate of Mici—grilled minced meat rolls—and a beer. It was the first thing I'd eaten since the accident, and I'd forgotten how hungry I was.

It's astonishing how hot food on a ceramic plate and a drink from a real glass can snap you back to normalcy after you've been running on the edge for so long, even if it's just for a moment. It was a reminder of our humanity, and my need to sometimes just sit, go through the mindless activity of raising the fork to my mouth, and let my thoughts drift without structure. At the very least, it seemed to order the disorder inside me and make me feel like I had at least a teensy bit of control over things, even if I didn't.

With the two-hour mark nearing, I made the same request of the pub owner as I had at the other place. He pointed at the back and let me be.

Sitting behind the office desk, I could hear my heart beating. I didn't expect to receive any earth-shattering news from Ike, but it would be my first intentional contact—albeit indirect—with someone else whom I didn't know whether he was my friend or an enemy, although I was banking on the former. He had to be.

I picked up the phone and dialed, and Ike answered on the first ring.

"Did you reach him?" I asked.

"Yes. Message passed and I asked the question."

"What did he say?"

"Nothing about the car accident. It was hard to tell over the phone, but I don't think he even blinked. Not sure what that means, but that's what my gut says."

"Fine," I replied. I didn't need the man to respond, only to receive the message. But my inquiry was different. "And the question?"

"Vague."

"What did he say exactly?"

"His exact words were, 'I don't know for sure—my source is gone—but I believe the same as your friend.'"

"Okay," I said. The response may have been vague for Ike, but I had a pretty good idea what it meant. I would think on it later.

"Okay. Did you do it clean?" I asked.

"All calls were clean and distanced, including now. This phone's going in the drink. Here's a new number." Ike rattled off a ten-digit number for a new, nonattributable cell phone, which I wrote down and tucked in my pocket.

"Thanks."

"Right. You still good?"

"Yeah. Still working through it."

"Should I expect you to come out the other end anytime soon?"

"Not yet."

"Right. Good show. Keep your head down."

"I will. You too."

"Easy day."

I hung up and stared at the far wall with a pinup calendar hanging next to the door with a busty brunette holding an assault rifle, and a corkboard on the right filled with business cards, receipts, and yellowed flyers. A pile of cigarette butts filled the glass ashtray on the corner of the desk. If I had a pack of smokes, I probably would have lit up.

Ike had called Doug, and Doug hadn't reacted one way or the other in response to my message about the car accident. *Rick shot*

Zach and the car accident killed Rick. I had nothing to do with it.
Wise or unwise, I didn't care. I wanted Doug to hear the message
just in case he launched the assassin squad to hunt me down and
blow my brains out. It was all I could do from here.

His answer to my question, however, was what I really needed
clarity on. I'd deduced that Rick was Doug's *source*, and if Rick had
survived the crash, he would have told Doug what he'd learned after
going up against Zach. Rick may have even shared the info with me;
my gut says he would have.

Rick had said the people holding Gomez were the same people
after me, and via Ike, Doug had corroborated that. But who was it
really? The news said Ukrainian separatists, but back in Paris,
Doug had said it was the Russians and then made all these nebu-
lous references to mercenaries and international businessmen and
corporations.

The jumble made me think the connection to Russia's security
services was genuine, but there were other, nongovernmental players
involved.

But what the fuck did that mean?

My head began to hurt. I wanted to move, to pace around, to get
the gears flowing, but this tiny office hadn't been designed for open
space. Sauntering down the sidewalk also didn't seem wise. Maybe
the drive would help. I could think on the road.

And I needed to get to Bucharest before it got too late. The man
I needed to see, I didn't want to wake him. I'd rather not startle him
in the middle of the night; he had to be fully lucid when I dropped
my request on him.

CHAPTER TWENTY-THREE

I reached the outskirts of Bucharest a little after eight, no clearer on the twisted layers surrounding Gomez's situation or my role in it. The first thing I did was find a sleaze-ball hotel, just in case I needed a place to lie low. I wanted that set up and out of the way before my next move.

Now I stood before a row house in one of the newer neighborhoods on the city's edge. The line of houses had been constructed with what I'd come to describe as the modern, simplistic style of European buildings. Flat façades colored concrete-gray, geometric lines and windows, with a cool industrial appeal. Functional, like Ikea for residential construction. Dwellings for the struggling middle class who'd escaped the monolithic high-rises left over from the era before 1989.

Inside I could hear the occupants—kids, parents, grandparents—a happy family laughing in the comfort of their home. They'd probably just finished dinner, having scooped generous helpings of meat and vegetables from the bowls and platters crowding the table. Hugs and kisses before bed were coming soon.

I wondered if the man of the house would help me. He would hear me out, for sure. He was a businessman, always digging for angles and opportunities. But once he knew the deal, would the man flash me a conspiratorial smile and say, *Count me in*, or kick me out and call the police.

There was only one way to find out.

I raised my fist and knocked three times, causing the metal door to rattle on its hinges. I took a step back and waited, hearing a father's voice trying to quell the commotion inside. A dead bolt scraped against rusty metal and I took a breath.

The door opened to reveal a haze of smoke and soft orange light, with a man in his late thirties just inside. His clothes proclaimed he wanted to be ten years younger and he held a cigarette between his fingers. His hair had too much product in it, the stubble on his chin looked more like coarse sandpaper than whiskers, and his red tracksuit and gold chain rounded everything out.

"Hello, Stanislav. How are you?" I said.

"Mr. Hackett, is that you?" The Romanian crinkled his brow as if he didn't trust his eyes, then a broad grin appeared on his face. "Ohhh, my friend! Come in, Mr. Hackett, come in."

I smiled and entered the home as Stanislav grasped my hand for a vigorous shake.

"I did not know you were in Bucharest. What brings you to my home? Did I forget—"

"I apologize for my unexpected appearance," I interrupted. "I wish I could have called."

"No, Mr. Hackett. There is no need to apologize. It is my pleasure. I'm just . . ."

Stanislav regarded me more closely, someone who knew me as an agent for a powerful financial firm. Three days' growth on my face, disheveled hair, evidence of a few scrapes and cuts, fire-singed clothes, and an accompanying odor preceding me—I must have been a sight.

"I do apologize for my appearance. If there's somewhere we could talk, I'd like to explain."

A young boy, no more than seven or eight, came running down the hall. His younger sister peered out from the kitchen, a mix of curiosity and shyness on her face. They'd both grown so much in the years since I'd seen them last, each with round faces and curious eyes.

"Costin! Costin! Back to the table," ordered Stanislav in a paternal voice.

A woman stepped out from the kitchen, a dishrag in her hand, whom I recalled was Stanislav's wife. Her expression suggested she recognized me too, though wary. I offered a smile, instantly feeling like an intruder who'd disrupted their innocent lives. I'd thrust apprehension on this family.

Stanislav, noticing my sentimental regard for his home and the people in it, smiled with embarrassment. "Mr. Hackett, please forgive my family. It's not often we get visitors like yourself."

"Please, call me Mason," I replied. "It is I who must apologize for interrupting your evening."

Stanislav shook his head. "No. No. You are an honored guest. Come, we shall talk."

He pointed toward the rear of the house and blurted something in Romanian to his wife, leading me through his slim, two-story home to the postage stamp plot of dirt that mimicked a backyard. Cinderblock walls at least seven feet high surrounded the area, with a sun-bleached pink wagon in the corner tipped on its side and a dirt-scarred soccer ball next to it.

Stanislav motioned for me to sit in a plastic chair when his wife appeared and set two glasses of beer and a bowl of olives on a small, wooden table. I did as my host requested.

Nearly two years ago, I'd contracted Stanislav's expertise for a vast, private tour of Romania, Bulgaria, and the Black Sea coast. Stanislav owned a small tour company with a specialty in excursions off the beaten path. I'd required Stanislav's intimate knowledge because I'd been researching the development of energy infrastructure coming out of Russia, and I'd only gotten so far using traditional sources.

Stanislav had more than hit the mark, showcasing the construction sites, plans by local governments, and networks under development—critical details for the success of major land and sea ventures in the less governed areas of the world yet absent from the earnings reports and the news cycle. He'd done so well back then, I believed he could help me now.

Stanislav lit another cigarette with the butt of the first, then lifted his glass in a small toast, taking a drink. "So, Mr. Hackett, what can I do for you? Perhaps another tour?"

"Something like that. I need your help and I'll pay, but I must have your discretion."

Stanislav took a drag and motioned he was listening.

"I'll just come out with it. I need to get into Ukraine, and I need to do so without anyone knowing. You see, I need to help someone, but it's complicated."

"Without anyone knowing? A lover?" the Romanian said with a laugh.

"No," I replied, leaning forward and interlacing my fingers. "The authorities can't know."

Stanislav's smile dissolved and his eyes narrowed. "Because you need to *help* someone?"

I nodded. "A friend."

"And what makes you think I can do this? This is illegal, no? Illegal border crossing?"

"Yes, that's exactly it," I said flatly. "You have connections."

Stanislav raised his hands defensively. "I have a legitimate business, Mr. Hackett. I do tours. I am no smuggler."

"I didn't say you were. I wouldn't suggest anything of the sort."

"Good. Good. I have a family. You see, yes?"

"Yes, I do. But you know people and you know the areas. You showed me, remember?" Which he had, on more than one occasion suggesting he knew about the people who ran the secret underworld. A little bluster, for sure, but some of it had been genuine.

Yet the Romanian shook his head. "I don't like your accusation, sir. I'm a legitimate businessman who—"

"I know that, but you *do* know people."

"This offends me, Mr. Ha—"

"Don't bullshit me," I snapped, icier than I intended, causing my host's face to hitch back. I softened my tone. "Please, I'm desperate. I have money, and I need your help."

Stanislav stood up and expelled a troubled breath, staring at the cracks in the brick wall. He shook his head while scrunching his chin, then turned and pointed his finger at me.

"You're asking me to smuggle you into Ukraine, avoid the European authorities."

I nodded.

"To where?"

"I need to get to Mauripol'."

"Mauripol'? It's a war zone. Are you crazy?"

"I know what it is. I don't need you to go with me. Just get me across the border."

Stanislav scoffed. "I don't understand. Why in the world are you doing this?"

"This wasn't my first choice. I had other plans, but things didn't work out. It's complicated."

"Complicated? You ask too much, and you disrespect me think-ing I would do this."

"I'm not here to disrespect you. I trust you."

"Ha. We do a tour together, I show you around, and you think that makes this okay?"

I narrowed my eyes, becoming increasingly annoyed by the man's protestations.

"I cannot. My business, my family. I cannot do this. This is not like America. If the authorities don't shoot people, they make you disappear. It's not so different from when the Soviets were here."

"Again, I'm not asking you to go with me. But you know the peo-ple who do this for a living."

"You insult me."

"Dammit, Stanislav. I said I would pay. Enough to make it worth your time." I stood up, removing an envelope of cash from my pocket and plopping it on the table.

Stanislav gaped at the envelope. "What is that? Put that away—"

"Stop it," I hissed.

The color drained from Stanislav's face, the bluster ceasing.

I approached Stanislav to within a few inches. I couldn't force the man to help, but he was pissing me off. Despite my earlier hesita-tions, I thought at the very least the man would put me in contact with someone. That's all I wanted. Simple. Easy. Just a name and a number and I'd take it from there. No connection back to him or his business.

But no. Now I sensed it was a matter of pride for Stanislav to hold his ground.

The idea of grabbing him by the collar and pushing him back against the wall crossed my mind, but I stopped myself. The image of roughing Stanislav up in front of his children was too distasteful, and it repulsed me that the thought even crossed my mind.

I'd seen how *enhanced interrogations* and *physical stress* had worked in Iraq, and it revolted me. That bastard Captain Hart liked to do that. A prior enlisted man who'd gotten a commission just after 9/11, and who had a following of wayward sergeants and corporals awed by his salty demeanor and callous approach. I'm pretty sure Hart murdered a detainee or two who tried to *run* or *resist*, not that anyone would ever question those things. Shit happens in war.

No, I could never do any of that shit, no matter how desperate I was.

"Please, Stanislav," I said, trying again. "I came halfway across Europe. You must—"

"No, you must leave. I cannot do this. I cannot help."

I grimaced. "Stanislav, if you can't help, you must know someone who can. Just a name."

"No. You must go." Stanislav downcast his eyes, pointing at the tarnished sheet metal door leading to the back alley.

I exhaled and picked up the envelope of cash. But before leaving I faced the Romanian once more. "My friend is going to die if I don't get to Ukraine, and I'm all out of options." I held up a piece of paper with a phone number and the name of a hotel on it. "If you change your mind, I'll owe you everything."

Stanislav raised his eyes to meet mine but did not take the slip of paper. "Out," he said.

I turned to leave, but not before stuffing the slip of paper in Stanislav's breast pocket.

CHAPTER TWENTY-FOUR

As I stood motionless in the alley behind Stanislav's house, I heard the Romanian slam the back door. The sound possessed a deep finality that was coupled with the otherwise quiet evening and a vacant road marked by an abundance of weeds sprouting from the cracks in the asphalt. The stench of days'-old trash and animal waste hung in the air.

Replaying the conversation in my head, I pondered whether I had come at Stanislav too directly, dropping everything on him so suddenly that he had no choice but to resist. And then, as I pressed, he dug in. I'd let my exhaustion, stress, and fear—yes, fear—get the best of me.

I needed time to think, to figure out my next step, but I had to get off the street. I walked down the alley, around the corner, and emerged back on the main road. I could get back in the Škoda, but my gut told me it was time to abandon it. I opted for a taxi.

Thirty minutes later I was in my room in a hotel I doubt even a broke student backpacker would stay at. Drugs, prostitution, and other less than wholesome activities defined the establishment. Room rates by the hour, bottles and needles on the lobby and hall floors. All of it contrasted violently with the building's exterior, which had an architectural design left over from the influences of

France's Second Empire style: mansard roofs, columns, decorative ledges. Everything was a contradiction, with exteriors nothing like what they hid within and nothing as it seemed.

But screw it. The only thing that mattered was the hotel accepted cash and didn't bother asking for identification.

The room itself wasn't too bad. A sink and a pot but no shower, a bed with a sheet that might have been washed, a rickety chair that should have collapsed a long time ago, and a dead bolt on the door. The sounds of Bucharest's nightlife vibrated through the single window, the street below full of cars and people. It was nearly ten and things were just getting started.

My stomach growled, the Mici from the pub a few hours ago only doing so much.

Well, I had time and I had money, and some food would help me think. Maybe a drink. Perhaps a few. Not to get rip-roaring drunk, but enough for the fresh ideas to break through the biases and subconscious barriers. So far my rational mind hadn't gotten me anywhere. I needed a new approach.

I was about to head out to grab a bite when my phone vibrated. I checked the screen but didn't recognize the number. With my index finger I pressed the answer button and brought it to my ear. "Yes?"

"It's me. You recognize?"

"Yes," I answered, hearing Stanislav's smoke-scarred voice.

"Good. I have a friend. They will meet you tonight. To help you with . . . your situation."

"Thank you," I replied, at once heartened and curious about Stanislav's reversal to help me. "How do I contact them?"

"They will find you. Are you at the hotel?"

"No. I'm at the one across the street," I said.

"Fine. No problem. They find you."

"Are you sure? Do you need the—"

"No. They are good at finding people."

"Right."

"You remember the name of the owner of the restaurant in Constanța?" Stanislav asked.

It'd been well over two years, but I recalled the evening. We'd eaten dinner at a restaurant on an elevated patio overlooking the Black Sea, and the owner had given Stanislav and me the royal treatment. I pictured the owner's face: tanned, weathered, white hair, eyes as black as onyx, yellow teeth, and a bit overweight wearing a white, open-neck shirt. *My name* Alex, *and my restaurant is now your home.*

"Yes, I remember."

"Good. They will find you."

"Is that—"

"That is all," said Stanislav, cutting me off again. "I want no more of this. This is all I do."

"Okay. I understand. But my *gift* to you."

"I don't want your gift. You understand? I am not doing this for a gift, and I don't want to see you unless you come as you do before with contract and normal request for service. You understand?"

"Yes, I hear you."

Stanislav abruptly hung up, leaving me with the phone still pressed against my ear.

Almost immediately a knock came at the door. I took a step back against the wall, feeling for the pistol tucked in the small of my back.

Another knock came, harder this time. "Hey!" shouted a woman's voice. "You, open up."

I gawked at the door. A woman?

Creeping forward, I peered through the peephole, finding the hazy image of a woman standing in the hall glancing restlessly to her left and right. She looked dressed for the night, like a pro from downstairs, probably determined to sell me the honeymoon package.

I was about to tell her to go away when she pounded on the door again. "Fuck, Mason! Open the goddamned door," she yelled.

Disbelief hit me like a brick.

With my hand on my pistol, I unlocked the bolt and cracked the door. "Who are you?"

The woman pushed past me, barging in. I nearly raised my gun and fired, but something made me pause, telling me she wasn't a real threat. I watched her quickly survey the room before turning her attention back to me.

"Shut the fucking door. I'm Alex."

*   *   *

"We don't have time," said the woman who called herself Alex. "We must hurry. But first, money. You pay ten thousand euro now, five thousand when job is done, yes?"

I swung the door shut with a heavy thud, still gripping the pistol by my side.

Alex sauntered a few steps into the center of the room, placed her hands on her hips, and looked around as if she were an appraiser, contemplating whether the small, shifty space was suitable or not. I, in turn, examined her.

She wore close-fitting black jeans and heavy leather boots. Her black T-shirt was exceptionally tight, stretching the fabric over the contours of her breasts, but failing to cover a thin line of skin just above her waistline. Her small leather jacket was also black, and it displayed the scars of being worn daily, regardless of winter or summer.

Her face, however, captivated me the most. She had brunette hair but must have dyed it with a deep maroon to give the suggestion of color in the right light. She wore it neck-length and a little tousled, which framed her round face and high cheekbones. Her deep blue eyes were like intense orbs, and she'd used plenty of makeup to create a dark, smoky shade to contrast with her burgundy lips.

She stood with confidence, even a bit surly. The combination would have put anyone off balance, even other women.

"Are you deaf?" the woman asked, tapping her ear. "You hear me? Ten thousand now, then we go."

"Who are you?" I asked.

She flashed me a mocking smile. "Stanislav. He call you, yes?"

I nodded.

"You need help, yes? Need to get to Mauripol', yes?"

I nodded again, incurring a flashy smile and a twinkle in the woman's eye.

"Well, I here to help. But money first."

"How did you find me?" I asked. She'd already established her bona fides—she'd obviously talked to Stanislav—but her sudden appearance, having just hung up with Stanislav, gave me pause.

Alex rolled her eyes. "You give Stanislav name of hotel, but you not stay there. You tell him you stay across the street. Smart. But you still smell like American. You not fit—" the woman tossed her eyes around the room again—"you not *fit* in this place."

I exhaled, assuming Stanislav must have sent her to the hotel written on the piece of paper I'd given him before he called me. She then found the misplaced foreigner—me—and had probably been standing outside the door listening to our conversation.

"What's your name?" I asked.

"I tell you. Is Alex."

"Yeah, I heard you. Alex what?"

The woman shook her head, puckering her lips. "No. We stick with Alex, just like you stick with Mason. Good for me and good for you. Now—"

"Not so fast. I get it, Stanislav sent you. I know him but I don't know you, and I've already been screwed on this little adventure. I need you to tell me who you are and why he called you after he told me he wanted nothing to do with this."

Her mocking smirk returned, but her eyes were argumentative, no doubt perturbed at having to explain something she considered a done deal.

"Okay. I don't know why he called me after he told you *no*. I just know he called me. You come to Stanislav for help, to get into Ukraine, but don't want complications. You offer money, good money. You have some *friend* who needs help. Well, I help people. I transport people and things the government authorities don't like to know about. Is good business. Now, you pay, and we go. No more chitchat. You keep asking questions, I leave, because you starting to smell like security."

I held my ground, continuing to scrutinize the woman, calculating the risks more with my gut than anything else. I hadn't known what I'd wanted or expected when I contacted Stanislav—a contact to help me cross the border into Ukraine, I guess—but I hadn't envisaged this, a woman akin to a Bond villain tromping into my room and bowing up to me with fire and piss. My options were limited. In fact, outside of her I had nothing. And I did trust Stanislav would not intentionally screw me. He wanted my future business.

The big question was, could I trust her? Or, perhaps a better way to think about it, should I trust her?

I reached into my pocket and tossed Alex the same envelope I'd offered Stanislav.

Alex caught it, opened it, and dragged her fingers across the stack of bills. "No," she said flatly. "This only five. I say ten."

"No. I give you five now and fifteen once across the border. Like I said, I've been screwed once already, and I need you committed to get the rest."

Alex crossed her arms. "Show me the fifteen."

"No."

"Then no deal."

She went to toss the envelope back, but I raised my hand. "I have the money. Didn't Stanislav tell you who I am?"

She shrugged.

"Then you should know I'm good for it. I won't stiff you. You'll get your money and an additional five, for a total of twenty thousand, but only if we quit this back-and-forth and get going."

Alex cocked her head and said, "Okay, we go. But I hope is not too late."

"Too late?"

"Yes. Security services find your stolen car. It seems they receive tip."

"What? How?"

Alex shrugged. "We hypothesize later. Come."

She went to the door, peered out, and slipped into the hall, moving briskly toward the stairs. I stuffed my pistol back in the holster, snatched my bag off the bed, and followed. *Here we fucking go.*

CHAPTER TWENTY-FIVE

ROMANIA

Alex led me out the back of the hotel, looking to her left and right and over her shoulder. I did the same until we reached a dented-up four-door Dacia in the next alley.

"Get in," Alex said.

A wave of stale cigarette smoke and other curious odors greeted me as I slid into the passenger seat, but the interior looked clean enough. When she started up the engine, it sounded in good working order. Alex kept the headlights off and rolled slowly down the alley.

"Do you think the police followed me here?" I asked, checking the side mirror and looking ahead, searching forward and back.

"Not police. SRI. They have your name."

The acronym sounded familiar, but I couldn't recall what it referred to. "Federal security?"

"Serviciul Român de Informații. Domestic intelligence, like your FBI. Gestapo."

"Crap. They know who I am? But I've done nothing here."

"Like I say, I think they have tip."

"How do you know?"

"In this business one must have sources. I make call and they tell me anonymous tip come in about you. Description, crimes, murder. All very interesting."

"Holy shit."

Alex laughed. "You interesting man to be wanted by SRI. Perhaps I charge you higher fee. Perhaps I charge you good fuck, too."

"Excuse me?"

Alex laughed again while my face flushed.

We reached the end of the alley, and she flipped on the head-lights, turning into traffic. Alex then crushed the accelerator and the Dacia sped into the mass of cars with alarming speed.

I gripped the door handle, stealing a glance in her direction. She'd assumed a slouched position leaning against the driver-side door, one hand on the wheel. All she needed was a cigarette dangling from her lips. Thoughts of, *Who the hell is this woman?* and *What did I just get myself into?* ran through my mind.

"Where are we going?" I asked.

"You want to go to Ukraine, yes?"

"Yeah."

"Good. We go to the border crossing, drive over. Is a good spot. You have a passport, yes?"

"Wait, what? What are you talking about?"

Alex winked. "I make joke. I think you get shot if we go to border checkpoint."

"Very funny. Where are we going?"

"Murgeni."

"And where is that?"

"Near Moldova. A nice river nearby. Prut."

"Moldova? Why there?"

"Is a good route. Is much easier to reach Ukraine from Moldova than Romania."

"Why?"

Alex shrugged. "They like my money better."

I nodded, assuming the Moldovan border guards were easier to bribe.

"And you know this route well? You've taken people like me across without any trouble?"

"No trouble. You pay, and it's my service. But I may add a fuck, too," Alex said, flashing me another look. "I'm serious."

I frowned incredulously, which evoked another laugh from my newfound guide. I'd come across some brassy people over the years—my time in the Corps and then with Ruttfield thrusting me up against some swarthy personalities—but Alex strutted about in her own unique way.

"You look nervous. I like it," she said, hitting the accelerator and speeding around two slow-moving cars, hanging out in oncoming traffic a little too long.

"How long till we get there?" I asked.

Alex tapped the clock on the dash. "After midnight. You can sleep if you want. We talk later; we have time."

"Sure," I replied, but not daring to close my eyes.

Alex pulled a business card from her pocket and handed it to me.

"What's this? Tour guide?" I asked, flipping the card over and reading the text in English.

"Yes, is good. A real business. My brother owned it."

"You're a tour guide?"

"It makes my job easier," she said defensively. "Gives me a reason to transport people like you."

"And the authorities believe it?"

Alex shrugged. "Don't know, never had to use it. But is a good idea, yes?"

"Sure," I said.

Silence followed, and Alex reached for the radio, settling on a station playing Eastern European rock. I was grateful she didn't blare it but suspected she was that kind of girl: loud, provocative, tough, and in your face. Sometimes it was an act; sometimes it wasn't.

But what did it matter? Not a lick.

All that mattered was her ability to get me into Ukraine. I was grateful.

CHAPTER TWENTY-SIX

A little before midnight, Alex turned off the highway following a side road through a deeply forested area. This part of the countryside didn't have any streetlights, and the moon's absence made the night nearly pitch black.

Knowing Romania's history and having read a bit of Bram Stoker back in the day, I wasn't surprised stories of vampires, witches, and werewolves emerged out of this wilderness. A roughness gripped the land and the air felt different in my lungs. I breathed deeply, tasting it, wanting to revere its earthiness for a reason I can't explain, only knowing it intrigued me. This land deserved respect, like the formidable power of a rival who had an army perched across the border during a tenuous peace.

"Are we close?" I finally asked, breaking the silence after three hours of nothing.

"Did you see that sign we passed? We are outside Murgeni."

"Near the border?"

"Yes. Close to the border. We stop for the night and cross in the morning. Border patrols are nicer then."

"Nicer?"

Alex smiled. "They like me and my money."

"Right," I said.

Alex turned onto another road, this one plagued by an abundance of potholes. Farther down, cutting through the darkness, the soft light from a cluster of buildings came into view. There were perhaps four or five structures, most of them single-story, and a larger one with a second floor.

"What's that?"

"Village. Is good village."

"And we'll spend the night there?"

"Yes. You will see, you will like it. I take care of you," Alex said, placing her hand on my thigh and squeezing it. I kept my composure neutral this time but gave her a look, eliciting another laugh from Alex before she returned her hand to the wheel.

After another fifty yards, she turned left onto a drive leading to a small gravel lot next to the two-story building. There were three cars parked—all of them in bad shape—and I could see activity going on inside through the small, four-paned windows, the shadows dancing within.

"Come on," said Alex, getting out of the car and heading toward the entrance, not bothering to see if I followed. Reaching the door she pushed on through, allowing a flood of orange light to escape. She went in, leaving me alone by the car.

"How bad could it be," I mumbled to myself.

I marched across the gravel lot and pushed through the bar door, a dose of cigarette smoke, dim lighting, the smell of stale beer, and Romanian rock music greeting me. I squinted through the haze and noted maybe ten or fifteen men and women of all ages, shapes, and sizes sitting at tables or the bar. But Alex was nowhere in sight.

Everyone stared, which made me uncomfortable. I'd been the outsider on countless occasions before; my work at Ruttfield making it a common occurrence more often than not. Usually I was fine with it. But here my foreignness was much more pronounced, and without Alex, I felt naked.

Someone smacked me on the shoulder. It wasn't hard enough to be a punch, but it was strong enough not to be friendly. It resembled the kind of smack a bully would use on the playground to shove a smaller child out of the way.

I turned to face the offender, only to find an old man half my size with a face like leather, motioning for me to get out of the way. I did as requested, incurring a grunt from the man as he took his jacket from a hook by the door.

Someone else then grabbed my triceps. I spun around more forcefully to break the individual's grip, this time coming face-to-face with Alex glowering at me.

"Hey, don't fight him. Come on," she said, a glass of beer in one hand, the other motioning toward the bar. I pursed my lips and trailed her around the tables and chairs. Now that the other patrons saw me with Alex, most went back to their drinks, with just a few curious faces continuing to shoot me hard looks.

"Alexandra!" shouted a young man from one of the tables. The guy then bellowed a phrase I didn't understand.

"Fuck off," rejoined Alex as she kept moving. The man guffawed and returned to his drink, while one of his buddies smacked him on the shoulder.

When we reached the bar, another elderly individual who looked like he'd lived his entire life weathering the elements with only a few teeth left, leaned toward Alex and whispered something. She smiled, and I watched her slip a few bills into the man's hand. His face warmed like a drunk who'd downed his final ration for the evening, and he slid off his stool to make room for the two of us.

Alex yelled, "Pyvo," at the bartender, a woman with a face as callous as any man. She turned, dropped a mug of beer in front of me, and returned to the far end of the counter.

"Seems like you're a regular," I said, taking a seat and eyeing warily the pint before me.

Alex offered a half-smile. "Nice place. Good people. Is safe."

"Who was that guy?" I asked, watching the man who'd given up his seat putting on a hat before going outside.

"No one," she replied, her tone flat. "Food? You want food?"

"Yeah. Something heavy, please."

"Is different every time, but filling."

"Good?" I asked.

"Ehh. You eat, you decide. Maybe you get sick, maybe you don't."

I chuckled and sipped my beer. Then, over the rim of my glass, I saw a hand grab Alex's shoulder and spin her around. My first thought was someone was about to jab a finger in her face or grab a clump of hair. I tensed to intervene, but instead watched a bearded face with lips puckered move in for a kiss.

The union lasted no more than a half-second before the perpetrator, who turned out to be the young lad from the table who'd called out earlier, buckled over when Alex's knee smashed into his crotch. She wiped her mouth with her sleeve and smacked him on the back of the head.

The spectacle drew a barrel of laughter from the other customers, including the bartender. The suitor also laughed heartily as he hobbled back to his table clutching his groin. Alex raised her arms like a gladiator reveling in the roar of the crowd, then turned back to the bar to down another beer.

CHAPTER TWENTY-SEVEN

The Romanian–Moldovan Border

I woke to sunlight coming through the soot-smudged window. We'd stayed in a guest room on the second floor of the bar. I'd slept in a chair, grateful the cushions were so deeply worn I'd sunk into them, but now cursing the resulting pain in my spine.

Alex had occupied the bed. The night before, she'd downed at least six or seven beers in a two-hour spat. When she'd led me up to the room—courtesy of the owner, she'd said—she'd stripped down in front of me without a drop of hesitation. I couldn't help but gape at her tight body and lacy underwear, falling victim to a sultry laugh from her as she snuck under the sheets.

I rubbed my eyes again and looked at the bed, expecting to find her passed out and snoring. But instead, I saw the light on in the bathroom and her clothing gone.

The bathroom door opened and Alex emerged, fully dressed and drying her face with a towel.

"Come on. We need to go," she said, not a trace of last night's drinking evident, and fresh as a coed after morning swim practice.

"Right," I replied, standing up and stretching, my back popping like steel cables breaking loose from their anchors.

She tossed me a toothbrush and said, "Like Waldorf. Let's go."

Five minutes later we headed downstairs through the bar area toward the exit, the space looking entirely different now cleaned up, empty, and with the dawn's light seeping through the few windows. But before going out, Alex approached a small display that I'd failed to notice the night before. A picture of a young man—no more than twenty-five and with a familiar pair of eyes—hung on the wall, and below it was a small ledge with a candle and crucifix.

As Alex walked by, she kissed her fingers and touched the picture and, without saying a word, opened the door and walked outside. I followed.

Once we were in the car with the motor running, I asked, "Who was that on the wall?"

"No one. Is none of your business."

The tires kicked up gravel as she revved the engine and backed up. She sprayed even more gravel getting back on the dirt road.

"Okay. Listen. Is important," Alex began, checking her mirrors, her voice firm and crisp. "This is how things work now. You don't talk, ever. No one wants to know who you are and you don't want to know them. This never happened. You are not in Romania, you don't cross border, you don't exist. Understand?"

I nodded. "Yes."

"Good. Okay. We will meet a man at the end of the road by the river. He has boat. You don't talk. When I say you get in the boat, you don't talk. You don't say, *yes* or *okay*. Nothing. You understand?"

"Yeah. I got it."

"Good. We cross river. On other side we meet Moldovan border police. Again, don't talk. I talk, I pay. You don't talk, you don't smile. You don't exist. Is very simple, yes?"

"Yes, you handle everything. I got it. Then what?"

"After river, we drive. Everything over. Simple."

"Can I talk then?"

Alex tilted her head. "Depends. You have something interesting to say, is okay. If not, then no. You don't exist, remember?"

I chuckled. "Sure. Got it."

"Good."

*   *   *

Everything went as Alex said it would. We crossed the river aboard a less than seaworthy dinghy, and she paid off two uniformed Moldovan police who seemed just as charmed by Alex's flirting, like she was a Greek siren. If truth be told, I was starting to wonder if she was.

The car waiting for us happened to be another Dacia. It was green, but otherwise smelled and looked the same. Except the radio didn't work, inducing Alex to say a few choice words as we drove off.

After ten minutes of bumping and jostling over the ruts and washouts, we reached a paved road. But in contrast to the previous night, Alex did not test the max speed of the car. Though evidently at ease on this side of the border, she drove carefully. This wasn't her country.

"So what's next?" I asked.

Keeping her eyes on the road, Alex said, "We do the same thing. We reach the cross point, spend the night, next morning you go into Ukraine. But one difference. You pay, and I go home."

"Okay, easy enough. And I don't talk, right?"

My comment made Alex lend a wry smile. "You smart man."

CHAPTER TWENTY-EIGHT

Moldova

For a time we drove in silence, and normally I would have been content staring out the window lost in my thoughts. Alex seemed content behind the wheel too.

But I had the urge to talk.

Once I crossed the border into Ukraine, I'd be back in the breach, on my own again, unable to trust anyone with anything. In the realm of civilized normality, it's easy to say, *I don't trust anyone* and act like you don't care. I've heard countless impudent teenagers, saucy socialites, and phony ruffians say that exact phrase. It's predictable when someone says it, the proclaimer's cocksure manners the prelude to the delivery.

But when you don't even have faith in the safety of your bed, it's more complicated. Trust, when it comes to actual life and death, is on a level most people can't comprehend. Either that or they're just fucking stupid and deserve a thinning of the gene pool. There are no rules, no laws, no justice, no equality, no pity when it comes to base survival—you either make it or you don't, and no excuses or whining matters.

I'm not suggesting I possess any mythical insight into any of this, but after days of skirting the underworld, always wondering if the people I encountered were going to help me, ignore me, turn me in, or kill me, the strain of isolation had begun to bear down. Everything had become suspect.

Over the past twelve hours, however, I'd come to feel a sense of familiarity with Alex. Talking with her, even with her feisty borderline combative manner, was refreshing, almost uplifting. Like after emerging from a dank and foul-smelling cellar, the cool breeze against your face is something you want to close your eyes and savor.

The truth is—and in total contrast to how over the years I'd convinced myself I was—I wanted to talk to Alex, if for no other reason than to avoid thinking about what lay ahead. I'd come to realize she possessed an arresting complexity to her character. Long hours in the car, as well as seeing her dress, undress, and pass out drunk on a bed, had given me ample opportunities for observation.

At times she emanated a bold persona, taking on the world with her chin thrust forward and her hands on her hips, daring anyone to challenge her. But she also had moments like this, where she seemed far off, reflecting on a matter she might never discuss with anyone but herself.

Watching her now, she remained focused on the road, her keen stare indicating she often had time to contemplate her thoughts. I imagined most of her trips occurred in silence, not with a passenger hoping to chitchat.

Yet I wanted to engage her and hear her thoughts in this state. I believed this is when I might get the truest response. And I needed some truth. There were just too many lies, too many betrayals, too much deception.

I don't know how Gomez did it, living in this world that I imagined he did—spies and cheats and liars, plotting to double-cross you at every turn. It could eat you alive or drive you mad.

"Those were your people last night, weren't they?" I finally asked. Alex didn't respond, acting as if she hadn't heard my question.

I waited another minute before trying again. "Are you from that village?"

She gave me a sideways look. "Why do you ask questions? Is simple business arrangement, no?"

"Maybe for you," I replied. "You do this kind of thing often, I assume, transporting people you don't care to know."

Alex shrugged. "Is not dating service."

I chuckled. "No, it isn't. But it's personal, at least for me."

"Everything is personal," she said as much to herself as to the air between us.

"You transport a lot of people like me?"

"I don't know you. But no. Most people are—" she appeared to search for an appropriate phrase in English—"less nice, less honest."

"I guess that makes sense. Ironically, I think you're the most honest person I've met on this little fiasco of mine."

"Ha! *Honest*. I don't think so. You trust no one. You not trust me. I see it in your eyes."

"Perhaps."

"Perhaps yes," she declared.

"Then I'll ask again, was that your village?"

"Yes, it is my village. I know all the people. They are like family."

"That man you gave the money to and kissed on the cheek, is he your father?"

"Uncle. He is a good man. He taught me many things growing up."

"Like what?"

"You ask many questions."

"It's called conversation."

She flashed me a half-irritable smirk. "He taught me to shoot, how to be tough, to survive."

"Really? Is that normal in your village?"

"For a little girl, no. Some boys don't like, but it is okay. Good life lessons, I think you say."

"Yeah, that's one way to put it. Did he want you to know how to hunt?"

"Hunt?"

"Yeah, for food."

She shook her head. "Is different. He was a soldier under the Soviets, but he was not a communist. He is afraid one day Russia come back. That's why he taught me to shoot and be strong. Is a hard life here if Russia comes back."

"He thinks the Russians could return?"

"Yes. We Romanians are very independent people."

"I've heard."

"Yes. We are free and we are independent. We simply want to live."

"Is Moscow trying to stop that?"

Sincere astonishment appeared on her face. "Do you not see the news? The dictators are taking power. The nationalists are coming back. Russia is meddling. There is no room for life unless you want *that* life."

"What do you mean?" I asked, though already having a suspicion what she was referring to. Only a hermit would not have seen Moscow getting back in the ring with a chip on its shoulder.

"People are forgetting what war is like, what oppression and power is like. The Soviets, Bosnia, corruption. Romania has many scars and our prosperity is fragile. Is like a roller coaster. We prosper, we decline, we struggle, we shift, we survive. Up, down, up, down. But we must always be free. Russia cannot come back."

I studied her as she spoke. Her initial comment about Russia was not surprising, but I sensed more here. She couldn't have been more than thirty years old. She would have never known the Soviets, but she would have experienced the turmoil after the fall of communism. She would have grown up in the violence, corruption, and instability she just referenced. Yet Romania had been on the upswing for nearly two decades, making me wonder what else beset her.

"Who is that shrine to?" I asked.

Alex stayed silent, her hands on the wheel, her breathing rhythmic, her lips parted. I knew she heard me, but as the seconds passed I doubted she would answer. Whoever the shrine was for, it was deeply personal, perhaps still raw.

After a minute, she then asked me, "Who is this man you go to help?"

"I thought you didn't want to know these things?"

"You started the conversation. Now I want to know. Who is he?"

If I was ever going to learn about the man in the shrine, which for some reason genuinely intrigued me, I'd have to open up myself.

Ha! If Caroline heard me say that, she would have either remained impassively composed without evincing a shred of emotion, good English stock, or she would have fainted. Hell, I never thought I'd say something like that.

But to be honest, I think I needed to talk to someone about Gomez, especially someone who knew nothing of my past. Sometimes they have the freshest insights. Not canned like a psychiatrist session or all kumbaya-like sitting in a circle with other miscreants, but totally clean. Safe, too, because I could take it to heart or tell the person to piss off, or say nothing at all. No additional baggage either, like a friend or lover might have.

"We were in the Marine Corps together. We were . . . we were close," I said, stumbling over the words.

"In war?"

"Yes."

"Why was he in Ukraine? Is not a nice place right now. Fucking Russians."

"He was working there. Now he's being detained by militants out near the border. I'm sure the Russians are involved too."

"What did he do to get detained? He is not businessman selling shoes."

"I'm not sure," I replied, only half lying.

Alex crinkled her chin and asserted, "He spy."

I shrugged.

"He spy," she repeated. "Is the only thing that makes sense. Or mercenary. You say he works for your government."

"I didn't say that."

"Your silence did. And there is no reason for an American to be in the separatist region if they are not a spy."

I didn't respond one way or the other, but Alex had nailed the obvious. How simple it was.

"So," continued Alex. "He is a spy. What are you going to do? Are you spy too?"

"No," I said, shaking my head. "I'm not a spy. I'm exactly what Stanislav told you."

"Banker."

"Something like that."

"Is crazy, you know? Your friend was in the separatist area, yes?"

"Yeah."

"Hm," uttered Alex with a disapproving shake of her head. "Even if you make it to separatist region, you are in trouble. They will see you as soon as you arrive, banker man, then they will capture you. If you are lucky, they shoot you. If not," she said, cocking her head, "you wish you were dead. And they take all your money."

"Perhaps you're right. But I do fine taking care of myself."

Alex rolled her eyes.

"I made it this far, didn't I?" I challenged, flashing her an amused smile.

"Yes. You are here, you journey a long way. Good job. So maybe they only cut off one finger."

"Thanks for the confidence."

"Is reality. But I am still confused why you do this for your friend."

"It's not complicated. My government refuses to help, so I will."

"Your government will not help? Ha! I am not surprised."

"Neither am I," I muttered.

"But you think you can help, yes?"

"I owe it to him."

"Because you are good friends?"

"Yes."

"Is stupid reason."

"What?"

"Is stupid. You fight in war together, yes? Iraq, Afghanistan?"

"Iraq."

"You two were comrades, yes? You see many horrible things. You are brothers."

"Yes."

"But is war. People die, people save lives. Is over. Iraq big mistake. Everyone knows this. You owe nobody nothing."

"I see things a little differently, I guess."

"Yes, because I don't think you tell me the real reason."

"Oh really."

"Yes. I think you may not know the real reason yourself."

"You think I don't know why I'm doing this, that there's something else?"

"Yes. Is true."

"And why do you think that?"

"My uncle was a soldier. My brother was a soldier."

"Your brother, the one who owns your fake travel agency?"

Then it donned on me, recalling the photograph with the shrine and the familiarity of the face.

"That memorial is to your brother, isn't it?" I said.

Ignoring my comment, Alex said, "In battle, soldiers risk their lives for each other. Is comradeship, is brotherhood. But after so many years, no. Help him find a job, loan money, yes. Risk life like this," she said flipping her hand in the air, "it does not make sense."

"Says you."

"Yes, says me."

"Okay, if you've got it all figured out, then what is it?"

"Guilt."

"What?"

"You have guilt, and something else. You are angry. It comes out when you sleep, when you stand, when you look at people around you. Is everywhere. I see it."

Her comments slammed into me with the force of a battering ram. Caroline had said the same thing just a few days ago, and so had Melissa, and Jenn, and Tara . . . every woman I'd dated for more than a heartbeat since Iraq. They said I put on a good show for the general public sitting in the bleachers, but below the surface I carried an anger that gnawed at me like an animal chewing through its leg. It'd taken months for the others to see that darkness in me—I hid it well—but Alex saw it in a matter of hours.

Alex was right and Caroline had been right. I hated admitting such a thing to myself—who wants to be described as *angry*—but deep down I knew. I regret things every minute of every day, feeling a weight ceaselessly compacting my lungs, preventing me from breathing. The men I killed, I can rationalize what I did, even if I still see their faces. But some things haunt me like a ghost in the walls, always there and appearing at the worst times. Except this one—the ghost of guilt—it had bored into my soul.

Gomez was just one thing among many comprising the mess. Like those three kids . . .

I told Tara, a woman I dated years before Caroline, about them, a long time ago. I was stone-cold sober when I told her the story, thinking I could open up like that, but she never looked at me the same afterward. I felt like a freak, a murderous freak. I vowed never to reveal that stuff to anyone ever again.

But those kids . . .

They just happened to be in the house when we breached the door. We'd already slugged it out through four city blocks on that damned op, the first one Doug had been a part of. We'd killed some hard-core fighters already and taken our share of casualties along the way. Batter down the door, toss in a grenade, wait for the explosion with a concussion that hits your lungs, then storm in guns up with foggy vision and ears ringing.

I didn't know they were in there, those kids. But they were.

It was their fucking home for God's sake . . . They should have been there. *We* shouldn't have.

But when the charge went off and I ran through the door, I shot. Seven rounds total. Double-taps in the first two kids, three in the last. None of them could have been older than eight or nine. But they were there, and I shot them.

Kids. Children. Hiding behind a door and a couch, tears running down their faces, terrified.

Then their sister, probably five years old cowering in the corner, stared at me, eyes frozen like I was the devil. I guess I was that day. I'll never forget her eyes or the look on her face. She screamed hysterically for an hour, her parents nowhere to be found. We'd probably killed them somewhere outside in one of the alleys or behind a wall, likely mixed up with the real insurgents. Or maybe they were fighters too. Who the hell knows . . . I can still hear the little girl's screams.

We eventually had to move on, working our way deeper into the city, toward that damn objective that was crap. Doug and his damned classified op.

I ordered my men to leave them there. We had to keep advancing, clearing out the *enemy*, the fucking muj. I have no idea what happened to the girl or the bodies of those boys. That op was bad all around.

Gomez heard about it later that night, including the kids. I'm not sure how he heard the news, and I never asked, but he came to see me and we sat outside the hooch in the darkness watching the shitter fires. He didn't say anything, but he was there. He showed up, and sometimes that's what you need.

But I wasn't going to talk about any of that here to Alex, and definitely not my anger. I don't even know if that's the right word to call it. Bitterness, resentment, cynicism maybe?

What I feel about Gomez, what I grapple with when it comes to my men, those who died and those who survived, it's hard to articulate in my own head, much less to someone else. And what we did, and why they told us to do it—I didn't want to talk anymore.

"Mason," Alex said in a gentle tone I never would have expected. "It's not important. I am sorry I say something. I understand, and I help you."

"Yeah," I uttered, slowly coming back. She hadn't pressed me, demanding I share what was going on in my knotted-up head. She'd just let me be, and I could tell it was genuine. She was comfortable letting me be. And at this moment, her silence is what I needed.

"You're already helping me," I finally said.

"No. I provide a service, yes, and you pay. But now I take this personal. Is not just business."

"What do you mean?"

"I make sure you are taken care of. You will see."

"Thank you," was all I could get out.

CHAPTER TWENTY-NINE

"He's becoming confused." The interrogator held a cigarette close to his lips, pinching it between his thumb and index finger.

"But that is a good thing, yes?" asked Petrov, staring at the interrogator, his wiry arms crossed.

"Yes. Yes, of course. He knows we know who he is. Delgado, Gomez, international journalist, CIA, marine, Mexican shit . . ." spat the smoking interrogator. "He is all these things, yet none of them. He has lived as no one and as everyone for so long, when he speaks I can see his mind shift with the moment. But he is getting tired."

"Fine. Yes, very interesting. We know who he is. You need to do your job."

"I am doing my job."

"I need to know why he came here and why he contacted the man Hackett."

The interrogator pulled back his chin and took a final drag on his cigarette before dropping it on the chipped linoleum floor and crushing it with the toe of his shoe. He regarded the door leading to the cell and twitched his nose. "Yes, I know. We are getting there."

"You must work faster," Petrov said, his voice nearly breaking.

The interrogator, the chief of the *troika*, extracted a pack of cigarettes from his breast pocket and snapped a match to light it. "Yes, you said so when we started. What is the rush? I explained when we arrived that these things take time. And he is good. He is trained."

"That's why I summoned you, because others failed."

"Why so urgent? We have stopped him and we are here." The interrogator motioned at the facility. "The hole where undesirables disappear."

Petrov tore his eyes from the interrogator and looked at the steel door, picturing Delgado on the other side bound to the chair, his head wobbling from the lack of sleep, constant questioning, and leftover pain from the past few days. He was certain Delgado knew more than anyone else about the Program, and he had come to the border to do more than arrange a meeting. Petrov needed this information—to know why—not only to satisfy that bastard Viktor Leos, but also the vipers in Moscow who wanted their cut.

And there *was* an urgency—a deal was shaping up, and once it went, there would be no turning it off. If Petrov didn't determine what Delgado was up to, he feared what Leos and the others might do. He knew they didn't hesitate to eliminate their own to clean up messes or bring matters to a close—they'd contracted him to do it for them more than once—and he feared that he might meet the same fate one day.

"It is a matter of state and money, and none of your fucking business. You do as you're directed," Petrov said. "You must question me less and question him more."

"Yes, Colonel," replied the interrogator, his words laced with narky contempt.

"Perhaps it is time to use more direct means. You brought your supplies, yes?"

"Of course."

"Then prepare him. We will use such methods in the next two days. I give you that time."

The interrogator took another long pull on his cigarette followed by a heavy cloud of smoke flushing out from his nostrils. "Is that all, Colonel?"

"Yes, continue your work," ordered Petrov.

The interrogator flicked his cigarette against the wall and opened the door. As he went in, Petrov caught a glimpse of Delgado strapped to a chair in the center of the room, a black hood over his head. Behind him stood that imp Mykola, the *major*, his arms crossed and a revolver dangling from his hand. The interrogator swung the door closed with a thud that reverberated up and down the hall.

Petrov turned on his heels and walked back to his provisional office at the other end of the factory. He went inside and locked the door behind him, pulling a mobile phone from his tunic pocket that had only one number in it, which dialed a direct line to an office in the Kremlin.

An old man on the other end picked up after two rings. "Da?"

Without introduction, Petrov said, "It will take a few more days. He is complicated."

"Are you surprised?" asked the old man, his hoarse voice murmuring across thousands of miles, himself a withering shell of what he once was.

"No," replied Petrov.

"Very well. Then call me when you have your final report."

"You shall have it in a few days' time."

"Good."

"And Mr. Leos. He still does not know you apprise me separately?"

"No. I keep this relationship clear."

"Good, continue to do so. Leos has many friends here, his business interests are beneficial to the president, but Leos doesn't need to know we also have interests in him."

"Of course."

The line went dead.

Petrov set the phone on the file shelf against the wall and removed a different phone from his trouser pocket. He dialed, and this number rang in the Russian city of Sochi situated on the Black Sea.

"Allo?" a man shouted, loud music blaring in the background along with girlish laughter and squeals.

"Where are you?" asked Petrov.

"I'm at the fucking club. Where do you think?"

"Have you found Tolesky yet?"

"Yes. I'm entertaining him now."

"Good. Keep him there."

"Yes, yes, but he's anxious. He whines he's losing business, blah, blah, blah."

"What business? The only deal he should be worried about is ours."

"I don't fucking know."

"Remind him of his priorities."

"I know the priorities."

"I know you know. Tell him," said Petrov, grinding his teeth.

"Okay, okay, okay, boss. I will tell him and keep him and entertain him well."

"Good."

Petrov hung up and tossed the phone on the desk. He lay down on his cot, closing his eyes and pinching the bridge of his nose, whispering to himself, "Mr. Delgado, you come to Ukraine to meet a Russian arms dealer who is connected to my business. Why? What do you want and who is Hackett?"

CHAPTER THIRTY

Alex and I filled the remainder of the drive with lighter conversation. I think both of us had exhausted our supply of sensitivity DNA, needing to escape back to a place that didn't require emotional intelligence and verbal sympathies.

We stopped for a bite around noon and then continued on until we reached a rural village east of Tiraspol, a few miles from the Moldovan-Ukrainian border.

Snow flurries had been coming down for most of the day, which had slowed our travel, and it was almost evening. The snow covering the ground, coupled with the sparse forest and looming shadows, gave me a sense of venturing onto a frontier. We were, in a way. In addition to being the name of a country, Ukraine also meant *boundary* or *borderlands*.

And now it also symbolized the edge for me. I'd crossed countless lines to get here—physical and figurative, legal and ethical—but this border embodied the line of departure. All systems go. Tomorrow I'd be amid the true enemy.

"Is this a place like last night?" I asked, motioning at the nondescript boardinghouse through the trees.

"Is okay. Food okay. Dry room. Is easy," Alex answered.

"Should I expect another reunion when we walk in?"

"I may know people, but no family here."

I took that to mean even though she'd been here before, it wasn't *her* place. Less ball busting.

"Anything I should watch out for?" I asked.

"Yes. You no talk, you no exist. Is important."

"It might look weird if I don't say anything, even to you."

"You can talk to me, is okay. But you are American. You no speak Romanian or Ukrainian."

"I speak a little Russian," I said only half-seriously.

"Your Russian sucks."

I laughed. "True. Anything else?"

"No."

"Lead the way."

The sun had just about disappeared below the horizon when we got out of the car and walked across the snow-covered ground. The boardinghouse was a two-story wood building. The façade had blackened over time, giving it a charred look with few windows. The only sign of life came from the two chimneys, from where smoke drifted up through the tree branches.

Upon entering I quickly shut the door behind me to keep out the cold, then turned around to survey the room. Three round tables filled the floor, two of them occupied by men ranging in age from their mid-thirties to their fifties. A barmaid stood by a short counter that held trays and plates. A fire burned at the far end of the room, the wood smoke mixing with the cigarette haze stifling the air.

Alex hesitated for a moment before moving to the empty table. She sat down, as did I, and she nodded to one of the men nearby. The man, dressed in heavy-duty overalls with messed salt and pepper hair, nodded back. This exchange seemed to signal to the other patrons to stop staring and go back to their food and drink.

I met Alex's eyes, and she allowed a nearly imperceptible smile.

"Food?" asked Alex, speaking softly so only I could hear her.

I nodded, remembering her words of caution. Although the other customers were no longer staring at us, I could still feel their awareness of my presence swirling around me. And I wondered who else was in the house.

Alex motioned for the barmaid, who walked over to our table. She stood over us with her arms crossed and spoke in a clipped tone I didn't understand. Alex answered with a simple, "Tak." The woman nodded and disappeared through a door, presumably the kitchen.

"She'll bring food and drink," Alex said.

"Only one choice?" I asked.

Alex nodded. "Is not Intercontinental."

"I'll lodge a complaint," I replied. "Do they have a room for us?"

"I not ask yet."

The kitchen door opened and the hostess reappeared with two bowls balanced on one arm and two mugs gripped in her other hand. She put them down on the table with a slosh, uttering something as she did so.

Alex handed her a few coins and spoke, and a curt exchange ensued between them. There were a few gestures toward the upstairs, and everything concluded with a sharp nod by the woman as she walked away, disappearing through another door.

I looked expectantly at Alex.

"Yes, we have room."

A small sense of relief came over me. I hadn't realized how on edge I'd been, it having crept up on me from the moment we entered the boardinghouse. But now, with warm food on the table and the prospect of a dry room to spend the night, I eased off a bit.

We both turned to our bowls and ate in silence.

*   *   *

I was finishing up the last few spoonfuls of stew—a salty dish of mystery meat drowning in wilted cabbage—when the two men at the table behind us got up and left. Alex had eaten half her bowl with a few sips of beer, but didn't seem interested in licking her plate clean or knocking back the pints like the night before.

Assuming we'd go to the room soon, I asked the all-important question. "Does our room have a bathroom?"

Alex shook her head. "Out back."

"Right," I replied, envisioning a trudge through the snow in darkness.

"Here," she said, offering me a mini-LED suitable for a key chain.

I took it, said thanks, and went out the back door into the frigid night air. The temperature must have dropped twenty degrees while we'd been inside, and the wind had picked up. I thanked God I could stand to do my business.

Squinting into the darkness, I saw the outline of a shed fifty feet into the trees. Those who had gone before had made a path through the snow, but the continuous flurries had applied a fresh coating of light powder.

The stillness of the forest was at once peaceful and barren. Although I'd just left the warmth of the house and had seen numerous homes and cars on the drive here, an extreme sense of outlands defined this place. Thoughts of the Russian tale *Peter and the Wolf* came to mind, and I again felt for the pistol in my pocket.

As I was about to reach the outhouse, I heard the crunch of tires on frozen ground and glanced over my shoulder to see headlights veering into the boardinghouse lot. I didn't find it unusual more locals had come for an evening meal or drink, but I wished Alex and

I had retired to our room first. The fewer people who saw us, the better.

Nevertheless, I reminded myself this was Alex's territory. She may not be as sparky as she had been the previous night, but she knew her business. I had to give her that. Everything had transpired as she said it would, and when she wasn't slamming back drinks, beguiling men with her feminine wiles, or crushing the nuts of those in her path, she operated with cool efficiency.

The sound of two car doors slamming cut through the darkness, but the lot was on the opposite side of the house and obscured from my view. Not thinking any more of it, I went into the rustic facilities.

A few minutes later, I trudged back to the warmth of the house. Even if I was destined to spend the rest of the night upright in a chair with Alex sprawled on the bed, I was looking forward to the much-needed rest. The previous night's travel and this day's many hours on the road had worn me down, and I yearned to close my eyes.

Tomorrow, after the border crossing, I'd then say goodbye to Alex when she handed me off to the next link in the chain and then off I'd go, alone and unafraid.

But amusingly, I was more interested to know if I'd ever see Alex again. Part of me hoped to, but it was a ridiculous thought, I told myself. Even if it were possible, it wasn't a good idea. It'd be all kinds of complicated. Yet . . .

I opened the back door and returned to the smoke-filled room. I squinted through the haze, waiting for my eyes to adjust, but I instantly sensed something was off. The hostess had vanished and the three older men who'd occupied the other table had left.

However, two men who hadn't been there before sat at the table with Alex.

They were younger, probably in their late twenties, but coarse and unkempt. Even sitting down, one appeared noticeably short, probably no more than five-foot-five, but the other one seemed like a solid fellow with a broad chest. They had lustful leers on their faces as they leaned in close to Alex, perched on each side of her.

Alarm shot through me, and the concern on Alex's face confirmed my fear.

The two men at first seemed surprised at my sudden appearance at the back door. They quickly flashed me the universal look of *piss off*, uttering a few words I didn't understand. They then went back to cozying up next to Alex.

Shorty must have groped her thigh under the table because Alex swatted him as she scooted back in her chair. But she didn't get far. The other one grabbed her arm.

Alex's face turned to venom and she smacked the bigger one hard across the face. The blow shocked him, and his face flashed a look of disbelief. But while the big one regained his composure, Shorty went to grab her other arm.

Alex almost made it to her feet, but Shorty took hold of a clump of her hair and yanked her down. She yelped, flailing against his grip.

I launched across the room, covering the few feet in less than a second. I snatched a heavy beer mug off a table as I passed by. Both men were focused on subduing Alex—trying to muscle her—and they didn't see me coming.

I swung the mug at the back of the larger man's head. I aimed to connect the hard stoneware with flesh and bone. Unfortunately, the ongoing struggle, along with the tables and chairs in my path, caused me to come up short. I rendered a glancing blow, hitting more shoulder than head.

Alex, struggling, threw another punch, but she was off balance. Shorty drove his fist into her neck, causing her to cough and choke.

I recovered quickly from my clumsy attack. I hurled my mug at the taller one. It hit the man in the cheek. He reeled back, losing his grip on Alex.

I lunged to get between Alex and Shorty, but caught movement out of the corner of my eye and ducked. The leg of a chair glanced off my back.

I spun around to see the larger one coming at me. The man had a rage in his eyes and swung the chair wildly.

I dodged again.

The man overextended and lost his balance.

I launched forward and drove my palms quick as pistons into the man's jaw, nose, and neck. I kept striking him as I closed the distance until I could reach out and grab the man's head. I pulled the man's face down as I drove my knee up. I felt the bone and cartilage in the man's nose crumble from the impact.

I did it again, driving my knee a second time into the man's face, trying to rupture eyes and break teeth. I shoved the man to the ground. I raised my leg and drove the heel of my boot down through the side of the man's knee. I heard the joint snap.

I whipped around, ready to launch myself at the other one, but instead, found Shorty on the ground curled up in the fetal position. Alex, with a bloody lip and fury in her eyes, kicked the man repeatedly in the head and neck. She cursed him with each blow, knocking him senseless. The man could only flinch lethargically.

I took hold of Alex's arms, and her right hand would have knocked me silly if I hadn't blocked it. "Come on!" I barked.

It took a moment for her to realize I was the one restraining her. Her eyes flitted around the bar, taking in the busted-up tables and chairs and the crumpled bodies of her two attackers. The chaos of the moment left her and she regained control.

"The car. Come on!"

We bolted from the boardinghouse, our feet kicking through fresh snow and over frozen gravel. We jumped in the vehicle. Alex stomped on the gas, spitting dirt and rock with a clatter against the side of the building. The car sped off down the road into the darkness.

CHAPTER THIRTY-ONE

The Moldovan–Ukrainian Border

The Dacia hurtled over the bumpy road heading south. Alex gripped the steering wheel with both hands, her eyes riveted on the road. The darkness was pure, the only visibility provided by the vehicle's headlights. And the snow kept falling in thick, clumpy flakes.

Alex's lip had stopped bleeding, but a smear of blood remained at the edge of her mouth. Her cheek throbbed red. She swiped a tear from her eye, then returned her hand to the wheel.

"Are you all right?" I asked.

She didn't answer.

"Alex, are you hurt?"

"I'm fine," she blurted.

I stared at her. She appeared physically okay, but she was anything but fine. She seemed a pressure cooker ready to blow. But whether she was furious, upset, distraught, or all of the above, I couldn't tell.

Alex spun the wheel, turning down another road, this one even darker than the one before. Again, her lead foot hit the pedal, the car bouncing and skidding over the rough ground.

"Where are we going?" I asked, bracing my arm against the dash.

Alex didn't answer, still clutching the wheel, locked on the emptiness that lay beyond.

"Alex."

She shook her head dismissively.

"Alex! Stop!" I shouted.

She slammed on the brakes, but rather than tires squealing, we slid over the snow with a rough chop. The trees lining the road and those ahead of us disappeared, replaced by nothing. The car's headlights shimmered off something in the distance.

When the Dacia finally stopped, I released my grip from the dash and sank back in the seat. I peered out of the windshield, thinking we were on the edge of a field or a wide-open space but unsure. All I cared about was we were stopped and not wrapped around a tree or upside down in a ditch.

I faced Alex, part of me wanting to lash out at her for driving like a madwoman, but another part desperately wanting to know what happened back at the boardinghouse. I knew it was more than a fight. Whatever it was had unsettled her cool-as-ice world.

I heard her taking deep breaths and exhaling through pressed lips. She stared at nothing but the blackness in front of us.

"Alex, what was all that about? Who were those guys?"

She shook her head like she was about to say something, but caught herself. She wiped another tear from under her eye. I waited, letting her regain her composure

Finally, her voice just above a whisper, she said, "You ask about shrine. The picture."

I recalled the photo of the young man smiling. He exuded an air of vibrancy, the world at his feet with life just starting. So much to do and become, so many places to go. Yet he was gone from this world.

"The shrine is for my brother, Emil. A good, good man. A soldier, once, like you. He fight in Afghanistan. He medic, he help people."

Alex paused and I waited, watching her fortify herself to continue. Closing her eyes, she went on, "He came home, left army. He wanted to be a doctor. He was smart." She lifted her chin and looked up, as if she could see the night sky through the roof of the car.

"One night two years ago he was celebrating acceptance to medical school. It was late, and on his way home he sees commotion in a car. He goes to help. There are two . . . men . . . raping a girl. A young girl. My brother surprised them and they run, but he recognized the two men. He knew them. He took the girl to the hospital and in the morning he tell the police. The two men, they are from border region. But is hard. They are Moldovan, he is Romanian."

She shook her head again, another tear dropping down her cheek. "Emil, my brother, found murdered two days later. Beaten and robbed."

"My God," I whispered, wanting to reach for her hand but staying myself.

"God not involved. Is those two men who raped girl. They killed my brother."

"They knew who he was?"

"Yes."

"And those two men tonight?" I asked, already knowing the answer.

"Same."

"Jesus. What the hell did they want with you?"

"They know I am sister. They are evil men."

I sat up, myself feeling a simmering rage at what I'd just heard. "I should have let you kill them."

Alex laughed humorlessly. "You did not know. And besides, you are not murderer. You are strong, you are brave, but you are not murderer." She turned to look at me. "You are a good man, like my brother. You help people. This man in Ukraine, your friend, he is lucky to have you as friend."

"We'll see," I replied. "I'm so sorry about your brother. About all of it."

"Is nothing," she replied, her expression hardening, the tears drying up.

"What do you do in Mauripol'?" she asked, the story of her brother and the anger from the fight now tamped down into her inner depths. I could tell she was done wading into those dark memories. She would speak no more of it.

"What do you mean?" I asked.

"Who do you meet? What do you do? How do you find your friend?"

I exhaled. "I'm still working that out."

Alex turned to face me. Her eyes, her intense green eyes, staring into mine.

"I have some ideas," I said. "But the details . . ." My voice trailed off, and I watched Alex inch closer to me across the bench seat.

"I help," she said, her tone softer than before. "I know people who can guide you."

"Oh," I said, as she slid another few inches, her gaze never breaking.

Despite having been on the road for days and now having survived a brawl, I could still detect the trace of her perfume. I could feel the warmth of her body too, her leg now almost touching mine and her leather jacket brushing up against my shoulder.

I couldn't pull my eyes from hers. I didn't want to. The intensity of everything—the fight, our escape, and this moment—consumed me.

And her body, I could picture the contours of her hips, her small waist, and her breasts. She was mysteriously sensual, sultry, and she exhibited no inhibition.

I felt a heat rising in me, something I hadn't experienced in a very long time. Caroline and I had had great sex, but this was different. The attraction to Alex seemed deeply internal and immensely powerful, like an actual physical draw to her. It was as if my muscles were going to bring my body closer to hers, whether I was in control or not.

She took my face in both hands and kissed me firmly, pressing her chest against me and lacing her fingers through my hair. Although gentle, she drew me in, demanding our bodies touch.

I kissed her back, cupping the back of her neck with my palm. She eagerly pressed closer, shifting her hands to my shoulders while attempting to shake off her jacket. She then pulled away to get her arms free of the sleeves.

I shook my jacket off as well. I beheld Alex and smiled, as did she. The rest of our clothes came off just as quickly. Then we reached for each other . . .

CHAPTER THIRTY-TWO

I woke to the morning light breaching the car windows, the rays warming my face. I found myself wedged against the passenger door, my legs extended across the seat and under the steering wheel. Alex lay tucked against me, her face more peaceful than I'd ever seen it.

I took in our surroundings, finally able to see where we'd spent the night. Snow and ice covered a lake spreading out before us, the shoreline no more than thirty yards from the bumper. Not a scrap of civilization was visible. Only the evergreens populated this place; deep green trees that contrasted perfectly with the fresh, pristine snow. A flock of birds took off from the far side of the lake, and for a moment I wished we could stay here and live in a dream.

"Is Kuchurhan—how you say—fake lake," Alex said, stirring on my chest.

"You mean reservoir?"

"Yes. Is Ukraine on other side."

"It's beautiful," I said. "It reminds me of a lake in New York. My parents had a house there, and we used to go there for the summer. Sailboats, walks in the town, fireworks. My mother would make the best French toast, with cinnamon and a trace of nutmeg."

With her chin resting on my chest gazing at me, Alex said, "I not know those things. Is different here."

"Right. I can only imagine."

"In few hours you not imagine," she said, sitting up, rubbing her eyes and yawning. "You will be there and see for yourself."

I watched her stretch in the cramped car. A small red mark remained on her cheek from the fight, but the evidence of the cut on her lip had disappeared. The solemn disposition she'd had the previous night had also vanished. It was as if the night's sleep and our intimacy had healed her, erasing the fury of the brawl and aftermath.

Once more, I wondered if I'd see her again after this morning. Sex aside, I was drawn to Alex. The stress, the uncertainty, the proximity—all of it had undoubtedly heightened whatever feelings I may have had. Yet I couldn't dismiss my yearnings so easily. I could see she felt something deeply too, in her own way.

I chuckled to myself. Perhaps if I made it out alive, I'd come back and take Alex to dinner, all normal-like. Cocktails, crab dip, wine, filet mignon, and crème brûlée—ha!

"What is funny?"

I turned to see Alex smiling at me. "Nothing," I said.

"I like you, Mr. Mason."

"And I you, Alexandra."

I detected the tinge of a blush on her cheeks but feared to say anything more. I had to change the subject. "So, will this play out like yesterday? I don't talk?"

Alex momentarily downcast her eyes. And when she looked up, her gentleness—perhaps vulnerability—was gone. We were back to business. "Is similar, but no boat, and I not go with you. These men take you to Odessa, and then a business associate will take you to Mauripol'."

"Business associate?"

"Yes. I say I help you. We work together sometimes. He is an honest man."

"His name?" I asked, our efficient, no-nonsense method for discussing procedures returned.

"Orest. His name is Orest."

"How will I recognize him?"

"Men at border will take you to him. But he is in his fifties, with short beard and brown hair, and with belly. He likes to graze like a cow, always looking for food."

"Right," I said, tilting my head in amusement. "These men at the border, how well do you know them?"

"We do business before, but they not border police. Is different. They keep police away, and they run side business."

"Mafia?"

Alex shrugged.

"Do you trust them?"

She shrugged again. "I not trust anyone, and you should not either."

"They're not *honest* like Orest?"

"Is all business for them. You understand?"

Yes, I understood. This entire event boiled down to one thing—money. I hadn't gotten this far because people were nice, nor because they took pity on me and wanted to help. Not in the slightest. No one risked their neck for a hug and a handshake.

Which reminded me. I reached into my pocket and removed a stack of euros, extending it to Alex. "Here's the remainder, based on our agreement."

Alex eyed the money aversely like it had no place between us. Then she grabbed the cash and stuffed it in her pocket. "We go."

Alex turned the key in the ignition, put the car in reverse, and backed away from the picturesque lake. She did a three-point turn, crushing a bush and scraping a tree in the process, and sped back along the trail. After three more turns, never once passing any suggestion of human existence, we drove down a narrow, unimproved road.

In the distance, no more than a hundred yards away, I saw a drop arm across the trail. On the other side, three men stood wearing black jackets, black pants, and black watch caps—a style I was tired of seeing. Behind the trio, an SUV idled in the middle of the path. I glanced at Alex as she steered toward the waiting gaggle, and like the other morning, she had a guise of pure business about her.

Alex slowed our vehicle and rolled to a stop a car's length from the drop arm. She should have turned the engine off and we both should have gotten out, but when I stole another glance in her direction, I saw her grasping the wheel with a confused look.

"Is something wrong?" I asked.

"I not see Peter."

"Who's Peter?"

"My contact, and the one to take you to Orest. We make the plans, and he should be here."

"Perhaps he's in the car," I said, referring to the idling SUV.

Alex shook her head. "No. He always stand outside so I recognize him."

The hair on the back of my neck stood up as I detected the unease in Alex's voice.

"What about the others? Do you recognize any of them?"

"The one on the right. He work for Peter."

"Does that mean we're good, or . . ." I turned to look out the rear window, searching to see if a vehicle or another group of men had come up from behind, but saw nothing. I checked the tree line to our left and right, not seeing anyone on our flanks, either.

"Is okay," Alex finally said. "Nothing ever easy. But remember." She took her hand off the wheel and grasped mine, interlacing our fingers. "Do not trust anyone."

I looked at her, but she still stared straight ahead. Then it struck me; this was her goodbye. I squeezed her hand, wanting to say something indelible, but I pulled away instead. What was the point.

I popped the door handle but waited until Alex moved to open hers. She gave me an inexpressive wink, then got out.

Alex and I met at the front of the car and advanced to within a few steps of the drop arm. With my hand in my pocket and my fingers wrapped around the pistol, I studied each of the men on the opposite side of the border.

Their faces were callous, like they could each knife a man and not show a scrap of remorse. The one on the right whom Alex recognized was the shortest of the three. He had a broad, thick frame, like a tree trunk, and his face had the contours of strength mixed with fleshy fat. The man in the middle was tall with an average build, with a day's rough growth on his face. The last of the three couldn't have been more than a teenager, but his beady, bloodshot eyes were creepy, like he abused kids or fucked animals or something.

"Sasha," Alex called out in English, "where is Peter?"

The shorter one, Sasha, shrugged and said, "He's occupied. He had other business to attend to, so he sent me."

"He tell you what is deal?"

Sasha nodded, pinching his double chin.

"Tell me what it is. Is not good business for you to fuck up."

Sasha smiled. "We take package to Odessa and give to Orest. Orest is waiting for us. Very simple, no papers. Easy day, yes?" Then he shifted his attention to me. "You. What is your name?"

"Mason."

"American?" Sasha asked, a trace of surprise in his voice.

"Yes," I replied, not seeing any reason to lie. I'd have to open my mouth at some point.

"Okay, good. Come." Sasha waved for me to walk around the drop arm and cross into Ukraine. I shot a glance in Alex's direction, who nodded.

This was it. No room for extended farewells. Off we go.

I made my way around the steel barrier. Sasha extended his hand, but as I went to shake it, I saw the taller one step forward and motion for Alex to approach. The tall one said something in Ukrainian, and I assumed this is when the money would change hands. I wondered how much she had to pay them for this little service, and if once on our way, they'd demand a second, additional payment from me. I wouldn't be surprised; everyone needed to get paid.

But when the tall one removed his right hand from his jacket pocket, my heart stopped.

The man drew a pistol. He raised it and fired once at Alex. The bullet struck her in the forehead. Blood, skull fragments, and brain matter exploded out the back of her head. Her lifeless body surrendered and dropped to the ground.

I tried to cry out, but someone yanked my arm and a blow to the side of my head rendered me senseless.

CHAPTER THIRTY-THREE

I reeled and my head spun as heavy knuckled fists hammered my face and body. Sasha and the other two Ukrainians threw me in the back of the idling SUV. I barely caught a glimpse of what was happening.

Yet I was absolutely certain about one thing. They'd shot and killed Alex. A pistol barrel inches from her forehead. Bang! The bullet shattered her skull, bored through her frontal lobe, and exploded out the back of her head. She'd crumpled to the ground in a lifeless mess, left lying in the middle of the trail. Murdered in an instant—because of me. She'd been here because of me.

I tried to cry out again. The shock of Alex's murder, the realization I was being taken, physical pain—it poured through me like liquid fire.

A fist struck me in the face and my nose throbbed. Other hands tied a gag around my mouth, synching it down and tearing out strands of hair. More hands bound my wrists and legs with zip ties. Thoughts of where they were taking me and why hadn't they killed me like they did Alex flooded what little consciousness I held onto.

I heard car doors slam and felt the vibration of the vehicle as the engine came to life. The driver backed up fast, causing me to roll and slam into the rear seat. I struggled to right myself onto my back, anything to see what was happening.

They hadn't blindfolded or hooded me. Why? Did they not care if I saw where we were going? Did it matter? What did it mean if it didn't?

The driver hit the brakes and turned, again sending me into the rear seat like a sack of shit. The vehicle jerked forward and back, then sped off. I tossed and rolled, my head smacking around like a bobble toy.

I strained to see out the windows but saw nothing except the tops of trees whipping past. I struggled against my restraints, feeling the blood build up in my hands from the plastic biting into my wrists, but it was no use. There was no way I was going to bust out of the zip ties.

Wait. The gun. Had they taken my pistol?

I rolled over but didn't feel the lump of a weapon in my pocket. It should have been pressing into my gut, but I felt nothing. It was gone.

The vehicle picked up more speed, no longer on a dirt road with potholes and washouts. We were driving on blacktop, rocketing at a hundred miles an hour.

How long had we been driving? Maybe five minutes? If I could track time and determine a general direction, I'd have a better sense of where we might be going. I knew on the map where the border crossing had been and I knew the vicinity of major towns. It wouldn't be much, but it was better than nothing.

The words *Get out! Get out! Get out!* screamed in my head.

The next few minutes were critical. The best chance to escape was immediately after being captured. I heard my instructor from SERE school, Gunny Beach, drumming the principle into me while he stood on the podium. My captors were trying to establish control, which meant they didn't have control. Opportunities to escape existed. *See them. Take them.*

Now. Now was the time. I had to be ready. I had to be willing to risk everything. These fuckers were killers. They wouldn't hesitate to kill me; I wouldn't hesitate to kill them. I *wanted* to kill.

The engine's whine slowed, the vehicle's speed decreasing. Were we stopping or simply making a turn? How long had it been? Ten minutes max. We couldn't have gone far.

The vehicle turned, but once through it, we only sped up slightly. We made another turn.

We were arriving somewhere. I was certain. But were we still in Ukraine or had we crossed back into Moldova?

It didn't matter. Knowing where I was on a map was less important than what I needed to do in the next few moments. I needed to absorb everything—sights, sounds, smells—I needed to take it all in.

The SUV stopped. A car door popped open and cold air burst into the cab.

Men spoke. Was it Ukrainian? Russian?

The rear door opened and the tall one and the teenager reached in for me. There was no point in struggling while bound like this. *Pay attention and look for an opening*, Gunny Beach had said.

The two men wrenched me from the back of the SUV and brought me to my feet. We were still in the forest, but now in a small clearing. I saw a run-down shack a few yards away. And there were three other vehicles here, both SUVs like the one I'd just ridden in, but nicer.

Then my hope sank. Six additional men were clustered together, all armed. They came across like they'd spent their entire lives fighting, thieving, and killing.

* * *

Sasha stepped in front of me, a baleful look on his fleshy face. The stench of stale cigarettes wafted off him, with beads of sweat dripping down his cheeks.

"You are an interesting man. Powerful people want to meet you. You are worth something. Alexandra, however," Sasha said as he shook his head, "she should not have fought those men at the bar the other night. It was a mistake. They are friends of mine. They call me, tell me about a man they fight who speak English traveling with whore Alexandra."

The confusion of the last twenty minutes suddenly made sense. These fuckers killed Alex because of the damned brawl. Those fucking rapists must have known Alex's work, known her associates and contacts, and then called this piece of shit to have her killed and me taken. The incestuous network of criminal filth made me want to vomit.

And this man Sasha said I was wanted by powerful people. I was back in their crosshairs.

"Fuck you!" I growled through my gag, lurching forward. "I'll fucking kill you!" But the tall one and the kid held me fast.

"Shh," Sasha said, wagging his finger. "It's not wise for you to fight right now. You will die quick. But, if you be good, I will take off the gag, you understand? You be good?"

My eyes bored into this short, fat troll of a man. I wanted to pound his face over and over again. Put two bullets in his chest and one in the head. Kill him, and then leave him for the wild dogs and crows to pick apart. He deserved nothing more for what he did to Alex.

But I nodded anyway, taking a deep breath as I did.

Sasha smiled, showing brown and crooked teeth, and he removed the gag from my mouth. With the cloth gone, I opened and closed my jaw to loosen it, then stretched my neck.

"What are you going to do with me? Who are they?" I asked, nodding at the six other men in the clearing. Were these the same men who'd been on my tail since London?

"They transport you for a fee. Like I said, you are valuable. They decide what next."

"Who are they?" I asked again, my voice steady.

Sasha huffed. "They will tell you if they want. We do our part."

He looked at the tall one who was holding my right arm and gestured for him to cut the restraints around my ankles. The plastic ties snapped loose, and I was shocked at the sudden sense of freedom. But the cold steel Sasha pressed into the base of my skull erased the tease of liberation.

Sasha positioned himself behind me and stood on his toes to whisper in my ear, "If you run, I shoot. This is easy for me. I am not so worried about what these men pay. I have what you gave Alex. Understand?"

"Yeah," I replied.

The next two minutes were fast and efficient like I was nothing more than a commodity passing through a supply chain. Sasha ushered me over to the waiting armed men. One with a scar on his nose searched me. Another with a shaved head tossed an envelope to Sasha. They exchanged a few words I didn't catch. My new captors put me in an SUV, but this time they let me sit in the back seat without a gag, only my arms bound. The abundance of firearms this group carried must have given them confidence I wouldn't stand a chance if I tried anything. A minute later the three SUVs, with me in the middle one, headed off, leaving Sasha and his two partners in the clearing.

Wham-bam and off we go in less than five minutes. Professionals.

I looked around at my new friends. Three men were in the car with me. The bald one sat in the front passenger seat. I suspected he was the leader of the group, or at least someone with authority. The driver had some years on him, probably in his mid-fifties, and had a mop of gray hair. The one who sat in the back next to me wreaked of body odor. He appeared well-kept enough, but he stank like a high school locker room.

All three of them were armed, the one next to me, Stinky, with a submachine gun of sorts. I didn't know what it was, except it appeared to be a cross between an MP5 with AK-like parts. Not that it mattered. I had no doubt it'd kill me with ease.

Once the three-vehicle convoy reached the paved road and headed in the direction I thought was east, the bald one turned around.

"Name?" Baldy asked.

"Mason," I replied flatly.

"Full name?"

"Mason Hackett."

"You are a businessman, yes. What business?"

"Ruttfield and Leason," I answered, assuming they already knew this information or could uncover it on their own easily enough. I chose not to make things more complicated for myself over a trivial question. They already knew who I was—I needed to find out who they were.

"Fine. Here is the deal. You do as you are told. A man want to see you. You talk. Then maybe you go home. Is very simple. You understand?"

I glared at Baldy, who spoke impeccable English, who'd just laid out in the simplest terms that all I had to do was shut up, play along, and I might go home. Give me hope so I didn't cause problems.

Simple and straightforward, almost like the general contractor who says he's going to knock down this wall and refinish that cabinet and boom, your brand-new gourmet kitchen with a Tuscan tile backsplash. All I had to do was say, *Okay, boss, you're in charge. Where do I sign?*

Yet it wasn't simple, nor clean, nor tolerable.

That fuck Sasha and his men had murdered Alex in front of me, blowing the back of her head out like a water balloon. My blundering efforts to help Gomez had been crushed, my balls in and out of a vice since I started this crazy adventure. And at this point I had nothing to go back to. I had nothing more with Caroline or anyone else, and I'm sure the pink slip would come once Doug took Alistair out for a scotch and regaled him about the trail of bodies in my wake. Then I'd probably find myself in a CIA prison snuggled up to Bubba or Pablo or Ahmed. Goddammit!

For the second time in my life, I didn't care if I lived or died.

But despite it all, I felt quite liberated. I had nothing to lose. I wanted to cause problems.

"You got scammed," I said, putting acid in each syllable.

Baldy crinkled his brow, evidently not expecting such a response. "What do you mean, *scammed*?"

"Those assholes you paid. What they didn't give you was the two hundred thousand euro I had on me, which they decided to keep for themselves. You missed it."

"What are you talking about?"

I leaned forward, causing Stinky to press the barrel of his gun into my side. But I didn't care. I was *valuable*, and they wouldn't kill me until they got to the bottom of what I'd just tossed out. A taunt the size of a manhole cover, hitting the concrete with a massive iron clang.

"You got taken by those three dopes. How much did you pay for me? Five, ten, maybe twenty thousand? To deliver me to someone else? How much will they pay you? I doubt two hundred euro." I looked Baldy up and down. "You're the dope."

Stinky jammed the barrel harder. I grimaced but didn't give an inch.

"You gave up two hundred thousand euros in cash, right under your nose. Yeah," I said, thrusting my chin out, "you go ahead and pass me off. It sounds like you're just the middle shit missing out on the big payoff. Hell, why do you think people want to talk to me?"

Baldy stayed focused on me but gestured for Stinky to settle down.

"Thanks, asshole," I said, casting Stinky a nice *fuck you* look. Turning back to Baldy, the boss man, I said, "I'm valuable and you know it. Sasha knew. He said powerful people want to see me. Truth is, I don't know why, and I doubt you do. But that's my problem. You, however, miss out on the easy cash. Cheers, fucker."

Baldy studied me, the jackass American lecturing him on how he'd screwed up. He may not have understood everything I said, but he definitely got the gist, and he was evidently rethinking what to do next. Maybe he'd drill me between the running lights with the hand cannon dangling from his stupid-looking shoulder holster.

Screw it. I'd gone this far.

"Yeah, that's right, my friend. Great idea those three pricks sold you on. Hand me off, tell you I'm a sure thing, keep the cash they took off me, and go back to drinking vodka while you're left with this mess. And do you know what else?"

Baldy shook his head from side to side.

"They didn't like that a girl beat up two of their bed buddies. That's right, a girl. A girl they just murdered. You might not care she's dead, but I doubt you knew it happened. Pretty twisted, if you ask me. But the bottom line is you got swindled. A nice fuck up the ass with nothing to show for it. How's it feel?"

Baldy didn't say anything for a good while, which caused me to wonder if I'd gone too far. Maybe they did know and didn't care. They had their orders.

But something in the air made me think otherwise.

Baldy barked at the driver, who slammed on the breaks, skidded through a one-hundred-eighty-degree U-turn, and tore off back the way we'd just come.

CHAPTER THIRTY-FOUR

Baldy shouted orders into his phone, grasping it like a handheld radio in front of his mouth.

The third SUV in the column accelerated past our vehicle and the one in the lead, screaming ahead. It took a hard right off the main road, smoke coming off the tires.

We were going to intercept Sasha and his crew. That's the only thing that made sense. But as for what would happen once we caught up to them, I hadn't a clue.

I needed to think of something fast. Even if Sasha handed over the cash with a smile and a peck on the cheek, the question of my future was wildly unknown. Hoping for the best wasn't a good plan.

I scanned the inside of the vehicle. I needed something sharp, something to cut through plastic. Getting out of these cuffs was my first priority; I wouldn't last more than a few seconds with my arms tied behind my back.

I remembered seeing Stinky with a cutter but hadn't seen where he stashed it. I was too busy getting smacked around like a one-legged fool at a king's court. But it was a good bet he'd put the cutter in his pocket.

Perfect, I thought. The man who likes to poke people with submachine guns has the cutter. One burst from that thing would zipper me full of bloody little holes. And with my arms tied behind my back, it wasn't like I could kung fu his ass. I needed to find another way.

Out of the corner of my eye I sized up Stinky. He had an average build and he possessed the bearing of someone who could be cruel, but he wasn't an ox. He'd shifted the submachine gun down between his legs and he didn't have a seat belt on. Once we caught up with Sasha, he'd probably stay in the vehicle to guard me.

I started to think of a course of action that might work. I didn't have another option. Risks be damned.

The longer I stayed with these men, the more likely they were to kill me, either because it made business sense or because they didn't want the hassle. Moreover, once they realized the two hundred thousand I'd been talking about was actually only twenty thousand, there'd be no more chitchat.

Our SUV turned off the main road onto a dirt one. We trailed the other two vehicles. It might have been the same road from before, but things were moving too fast and the landscape looked the same everywhere. Snow, ice patches, freezing temperatures—if I managed to get away, I'd have to contend with that pickle too, but that was the next problem.

Right now, all that mattered was escaping Baldy's crew and avoiding Sasha and his two slobs. Easy day.

The SUV curved around another bend, entering a denser area of the forest. This was good, maybe. If I ran, more places to duck and hide, or get lost.

Hitting a washout, the SUV bounced. The shocks slammed with a hard clank. I banged into the door, stabs of pain shooting down my shoulder and arm.

The road straightened out and the vehicle picked up speed again, rattling over the frozen mud. Tree branches snapped as we whipped past.

My pulse quickened as the adrenaline hit my muscles. My body went taut and I took deep breaths through my nose while simultaneously willing myself to settle. If I was too amped, my fine motor skills would be crap. I might do well in a brawl, but I'd need dexterity to cut myself free and handle a gun—if I could get one.

Baldy's phone rang and he picked up. He listened, uttered something that sounded like *Da*, and clicked off. He snapped an order at the driver, who increased the vehicle's speed even more.

Thirty seconds later we slid through a tight turn, coming up fast on three vehicles herringboned in the trail. Men were out pointing fingers and yelling at each other. Our SUV made a hard stop behind the last vehicle. Without a word, Baldy and the driver jumped out. Stinky didn't budge.

I stayed still in my seat, not glancing at Stinky. I didn't want to give the man a reason to do anything but sit there, submachine gun dangling between his legs.

Through the windshield I watched Baldy and his gang confront Sasha, the tall one, and the skeevy kid. I couldn't hear anything, but with guns out and the hand and arm gestures and the way the men were standing indicated the exchange was heated and only getting hotter, a Mexican standoff Ukrainian style.

Stinky shifted his attention between the dispute outside and me. He adjusted himself in the seat, bringing the submachine gun out so it pointed aimlessly at my gut. I silently swore, wondering if I'd waited too long.

I was running out of time, the seconds ticking off like a gong in my head.

Screw it. I couldn't wait any longer. I had to go now.

I leaned forward, bearing down, and retched. I forced the blood to rush to my face. Gasping for breath, I then leaned back and stared up at the roof. A second later I retched again. Then again. Every time I buckled over, I inched closer to the middle seat.

Stinky recoiled against the window with a disgusted twist to his mouth. "*Layno*," he grumbled.

My face flushed and I gagged, turning toward Stinky's feet.

Stinky scooted and yelled, "Nyet! Nyet! Nyet!"

I dug my toes into the floorboard and lowered my center of gravity.

Stinky pressed himself against the door, doing everything he could to avoid the expected hurl of vomit about to spew from my mouth.

He never saw it coming.

My body, cocked like a spring-loaded jack and aimed at Stinky, exploded into him. I drove my forehead into the man's nose and eyes. Bone and cartilage cracked. The back of the man's skull collided with the door window.

I fought through the haze and slammed my forehead into Stinky again, aiming for the nose and eyes again. The third time I connected with Stinky's temple, knocking him unconscious. Squinting through the pain, I found blood dripping from Stinky's nose and thanked God the submachine gun hadn't gone off.

I flopped into a sitting position and reached with my bound hands behind me to rummage through Stinky's pockets. In the third pocket my fingertips found the cutter. I pulled it free. I fumbled with the blade as I manipulated it behind my back.

Through the windshield I watched Baldy jam his finger into Sasha's chest. Everyone had guns drawn, but they still had them pointed at the ground. But as soon as someone raised a weapon, the shooting would start. You could bet it all on black for that to happen.

I felt the cutter slip off the plastic tie, the blade scratching my wrist. I tried again. I struggled to get the angle right with enough force to cut through the bind.

A car door slammed, but it hadn't come from the vehicles up ahead. I could see all of them, and no one had gotten out.

I glanced over my shoulder, and the sight made my nerves shock cold. A fourth SUV had arrived. The driver was out and walking toward the fray. He was ten yards back, and he'd pass by my vehicle in a second.

I willed myself to maintain control and slow my fumbling hands. I deliberately gripped the cutter and worked it back and forth in a consistent motion. I felt sharp scrapes against my skin and thought I felt something warm dripping down my palms, but I kept working.

In the rearview mirror I could see the new arrival's attention staying focused on the standoff up ahead. He barely glanced at me as he came even with the rear bumper.

Finally, the plastic restraint snapped in two and my wrists popped loose. The sense of freedom was immediate.

A gunshot rang out, causing me to look up. In the middle of the pack, Baldy gripped a pistol that had been pointed at Sasha's face, who was now sprawled on the ground on his back, arms splayed out like a cross.

Oh shit was all I could think.

I looked out the passenger window. The new arrival was right next to me, eyeing the situation down the trail. He drew a gun, then caught movement inside my SUV and peered through the window. His eyes went wide.

I threw open the door, slamming the edge into the man's chest and knocking him back. I then launched from the back seat, diving for the man's pistol.

Up ahead, another shot rang out.

Then another, followed by a burst.

Gunfire went off everywhere in every direction.

I grabbed hold of the new arrival's hand. As we struggled, the pistol went off inches from my head. The sound cut through the air, making my ears ring.

Hugging the man's shooting arm to my chest, I kicked, kneed, and head-butted the man to the ground. When we fell, I dropped all my body weight onto him. His hold on the pistol loosened. I ripped the gun from his hand and, bringing it over my head like a club, crashed the butt of the pistol grip into the man's temple. He went limp.

More yelling and gunfire. The gunfight between Baldy's and Sasha's men raged. Three more men went down, but I couldn't tell from which side.

Instinctively, I turned my pistol on the man I'd just wrestled it from—the new arrival—and shot him in the head. I looked back inside the SUV at Stinky, who still lay slumped against the far door. I shot him in the head too.

I grabbed a clip of ammunition from the dead man's belt and readied myself to bolt off the trail into the trees. A burst of automatic fire, however, sprayed the frozen ground in front of me. I dove for cover.

CHAPTER THIRTY-FIVE

I crouched behind the SUV. Another burst of automatic fire peppered the front and side panels of the vehicle. High-pitched pops rang out as bullets cut through the aluminum and ricocheted off steel.

At least five of Baldy's men were still alive, but I couldn't see if any of Sasha's men were still in the mix. Men yelled, guns fired, and everyone scrambled.

I couldn't stay hunkered behind the SUV. It was only a matter of time before Baldy sent one, two, or three of his goons to finish me off. I had to make a break for it.

From my position—tucked behind the SUV and keeping as much of the engine and wheel wells between me and the melee up ahead as possible—I couldn't see much. I knew we were a mile or so off the main road in a dense forest, but that was all.

As thoughts about which direction to run raced through my mind, two more shots cut through the air. In contrast to the others zipping by since the shit hit the fan, these seemed more deliberate and closer. Someone was closing in.

I was out of time. I had to go.

I made one more turkey peek around the edge of the SUV, but didn't see anyone. I took a breath, then bolted from the cover of the vehicle's body across the openness of the road and dove into the trees.

The comfort of the forest—trees, rocks, dirt—received me like a blanket, but not before another burst of automatic fire let loose. The bullets cut through the branches and evergreen needles, embedding in the tree trunks around me with muted clips and pops.

I ducked down and ran harder, weaving around the brush and downed logs like a running back busting through a defensive line. I used my hands to block the branches trying to scratch and cut my face.

Shouts from at least two different voices came from the road. I had no idea if it was Baldy or one of the others. I didn't bother to look back. I needed to put as much distance between me and them as I could.

Pushing harder and harder and ignoring the burning in my lungs and fire in my legs, I came upon what I guessed was an overgrown firebreak. It ran perpendicular to the direction I'd been heading. I went right to break up my trail, then after about fifty yards, I cut back into the dense forest and continued on.

The shouts and gunshots faded with each step, but I kept going. I ran and ran until my body was a wobbly mess, nearly falling down as I gasped for air. I fell back against a tree and looked around.

At first all I could see was forest, but as my heart rate stabilized and I focused, I remembered to look up to find the sun. It was still early morning, and if I could pick out the sun through the overcast sky, I could ascertain some general cardinal directions.

Unfortunately, it was snowing again and all I could discern was a wide expanse of sky slightly brighter than the rest. Good enough.

Examining the terrain around me, I noticed a gentle rise in elevation to the left of the direction I'd been traveling. That made it northeasterly, I thought, and deeper into Ukraine. Going back to Moldova made no sense.

I started up the hill toward higher ground. It'd be easier to spot someone following me, and hopefully I'd get a better view of the surrounding area. Perhaps I'd be able to identify a village, anything that might offer shelter.

I ran but not at an all-out sprint like before. There was no way I could sustain such a pace—no one could, not in these conditions—and I had no idea how far I had to go.

That was the other problem. Where was I going and what would I do once I got there? Should I try to reach Odessa and link up with Alex's contact, Orest? I didn't have a means to contact him. Not to mention, I had no money, no phone, and I barely spoke the language. All I had were the clothes on my back and some mafia-man's pistol.

I'd need to figure these things out, and I knew I would eventually, but right now I had to focus on a more pressing matter: survival. I was alone without adequate clothing or gear, isolated in a Ukrainian forest in early winter. I may have escaped Baldy, but the current situation was equally dire. The weather—the cold, specifically—was a killer.

After another ten minutes of slogging through snow a foot deep, I reached a small clearing. It was no mountain, but I was up high enough to see the landscape beyond the trees right in front of me.

I squinted, hunting for any sign of human activity. A town, a village, a road, anything. But I saw nothing. My heart sank, and I ran my fingers through my sweaty hair, recognizing the perfect conditions for hypothermia and frostbite. Shit . . . Shit! Shit! Shit!

Then I heard what sounded like a howl.

A howl! Are you fucking kidding me? A howl! A wolf?

Christ almighty. First Baldy, then the cold, now wolves?

I kept searching the distant terrain for anything, anything that might suggest shelter or warmth. Then I saw it, what looked like a line weaving through the forest. I could barely make it out through the snow getting whipped up by the arctic gusts, but maybe it was a path or a road. And if so, it would lead somewhere. Perhaps somewhere beautiful, with lovely sweet warmth—a house, a shed, a fire, a sauna with beer and a little white towel that would barely cover my ass.

"Damn, it was cold!"

I looked at my hands, which were dry, cracked, and flirting with a light shade of blue. I felt the cold on my face, my soaked feet, and my sweaty chest and back. If I kept moving, I could survive for a few more hours, but once the sun went down, my blood would turn to ice, my skin would harden, and I'd stumble into oblivion, a tasty frozen treat for the critters.

I heard another howl but had no idea where it was coming from. The wind blasting my ears was distorting everything.

I had no choice. Finding that trail was my only option.

I started off down the hill, again at a jog, but considerably slower than before. It was more of a shuffle, my feet dragging over the snow.

But when I eventually reached what I'd hoped would be a perfect road leading me to toasty ecstasy, I discovered it was nothing. Nothing! No trail, no road, not even a damned path. Nothing.

I plopped down against a tree, exhausted and shivering uncontrollably, like I'd just completed an ironman race across the Siberian tundra. The hair on my head was frozen, and the skin around my snot-smeared nose and tearing eyes fought against an icy burn.

I hugged myself and rubbed my arms, but it didn't do a bit of good. My body could no longer warm itself. The furnace had gone out and the icy gales were blasting through me.

I had to do something, I had to keep going, somewhere. If I didn't, if I stayed here, I'd go into shock, hypothermia, freeze to death. One, two, three. Game over.

My vision was no longer clear, the blurriness a permanent shackle preventing me from seeing anything clearly. And all I could hear was the roar of the deadly wind teasing me as it rushed through the trees, hunting me down.

I wanted to close my eyes, just for a bit, just until I caught my breath. And I did close them for a second before opening them again, knowing that doing that would be the inviting, sleepy path to a frozen end. I'd never wake up.

But my eyes wanted to close. I couldn't keep them open. I tried to raise my hands to rub my face, but my arms were so heavy. I felt myself leaning forward, falling, everything blurry, going dark . . . and something running toward me. Something gray, howling.

CHAPTER THIRTY-SIX

When my eyes finally cracked open, I found myself propped up in a chair sitting in front of a stone fireplace. The heat from the glowing embers had restored some of the sensation to my legs and feet, but the cold had been replaced by a dull ache. The process of thawing my blood, muscles, and bones wasn't exactly pleasant.

Nevertheless, I was alive—I knew that much. I wasn't frozen, covered over in snow, my corpse waiting to be torn apart by wolves or bears.

Yet I had no idea where I was. I slowly looked around and ascertained I was inside a small farmhouse. A kitchen area, a rough-cut table, a frayed jacket hanging by the door, cloudy windows—and a man sitting just a few feet away with a shotgun across his lap and a gray dog by his feet, both of them staring at me.

The man had disheveled white hair, a weathered face, and excessively smudged clothing that suggested he'd worked in the woods all his life. He sat there staring with an impassive expression common to those individuals who'd spent their lives hacking out an existence in the harshest conditions.

I tried to smile, but I'm not sure I succeeded, the muscles in my face as thick as sludge.

"Where am I?" I asked.

The man didn't move or make any indication he'd heard me. He stared like a lifeless portrait hanging on a museum wall, the dog too. I couldn't even see the animal breathing.

"Do you speak English?"

Again, nothing.

I shifted in my chair to face my host more directly, and it was then the dog finally proved it wasn't a statue. It let out a soft growl, and I wondered if he was the one I'd heard howling in the forest.

I stopped moving and tried in broken Russian to ask where I was. But again, no response.

No matter. I smiled again, both to express my gratitude and that I meant no harm. I was alive, and somehow this man had found me and brought me here. I'd escaped from what would have been certain death if Baldy and his men had gotten to me, and I would have died if left out in the cold.

Certain death . . . I chuckled to myself. I never thought I'd use such a term. Even in downtown Ramadi I'd never felt that way. Plus, back then I'd had a troop of rough and tumble jarheads to watch my back. But now, someone was either trying to kill me—or they weren't. A middle ground didn't exist. Here, I had nothing. No backup, nowhere to go. Even the weather was trying to snuff me out.

And Alex, the only person I could have called an ally . . . she was gone. The cold had numbed me to her for a short while, but now the memories were back. Sasha killed her, but I teed her up. If I hadn't hired her to take me into Ukraine, the chance encounter with those two rapist fucks never would have happened. More innocents, dead because of me.

I tried to focus on the man of the house again, wondering what would happen next. I needed to get to Odessa, but I also should let the man know that less than an hour ago I'd killed three members of a mafia gang—a gang that someone *powerful* had ordered to track me down and capture me. A small detail I'd be remiss keeping to myself.

Who knows? Baldy or another team of killers on the hunt might be following my tracks right now and—

The front door blew open and I almost tipped out of my chair as I whipped around to see who it was. I feared the worst. The old man and his dog, however, unconcernedly looked over their shoulders at the visitor, a young man no more than thirty.

The new guest said something to the old man, eliciting a simple grunt in response, and shut the door behind him. The gray dog got up and padded over, displaying a body the size of a wolfhound. The young man scratched behind the dog's ears, then removed his dark blue overcoat, revealing a trim, almost scrawny frame. He wore a simple pair of pants and a button-down shirt, and I pictured him at ease working at a desk or studying in a university library. He wasn't a farmhand, and I doubt he ran with Baldy's crew.

"American?" the young man asked in clear English, hanging his jacket on a wall hook.

"Yes," I answered.

The young man nodded, walking over to the corner of the house that served as the kitchen. He selected three stoneware mugs and a kettle, which he pumped water into. Pulling up a chair opposite me, he hung the kettle over the fire and nodded at the old man, whose eyes suggested he found something amusing.

"My name is Georgiy," said the young man. "And this is my father, Vanko. He says he found you in the forest. And who are you?"

"Mason Hackett."

"Hello, Mr. Hackett. It's not often my father finds a stranger half-frozen in the woods, particularly someone who obviously shouldn't be anywhere near here."

"My car broke down," I said. "I started walking and got lost." I had no idea why I was lying, but I wasn't ready to divulge all that had happened.

Georgiy nodded, then faced his father to translate. The old man had returned to his impassive self, grumbling something. The dog came back over and lay down next to him, but the beast was no longer interested in me, opting to rest his snout on his paws and stare at the fire.

Georgiy bobbed his head and scrunched his chin, an apparent contemplative expression for him. He removed the pot from the fire and poured steaming water into the three mugs. He took three tea bags from a hand-carved box above the fireplace, dropping one in each mug. He handed a cup to his father and one to me.

"Thank you," I said, bringing the steaming mug to my lips and breathing in the aroma of the black tea. I could finally feel my hands and was surprised how the mug burned my fingertips.

"My father says you are lying," Georgiy said with little interest.

"Oh," I said, not questioning why he thought that, simply acknowledging it.

"You look like you've fought off an army, not someone who had car trouble."

"Oh," I said again.

"Nor do normal people carry guns."

I suddenly realized the pistol I had in my pocket was gone, now presumably someplace out of reach.

"Who are you? CIA? American Special Forces? Smuggler?"

"No. God, no."

"Mr. Hackett, it would be best if you start telling the truth. We Ukrainians can be quite hospitable, but that is coupled with a severe suspicion of strangers, and we can be effectively rough when necessary. My father would like to shoot you and be done with it."

The old man adjusted the shotgun from its casual position on his lap to an angle pointed at my stomach. I grimaced. I was tired of people pointing guns at me, and I almost told the man to point it somewhere else. But they were right; enough with the bullshit.

"I'm a banker out of London," I offered. "I've no doubt you're more than capable with a computer. You can look it up, Ruttfield and Leason. But that's not why I'm in Ukraine, nor does it have any relevance on how I ended up lost in the forest. You're right. I shouldn't have lied, but once I tell you the rest you may understand why."

I paused to allow time for Georgiy to translate. The old man's face didn't crack.

"I'm here in Ukraine to help a friend. Seven days ago, separatist militants captured him in the disputed area, and he's still being held. I'm here to get him out." For something that had been so complicated, saying it as I did made it sound so simple.

Georgiy pondered my statement for a moment, then asked, "Why was your friend in such a dangerous area?"

"I'm not sure. But in full disclosure, I do know my government sent him there."

"Why?"

I shrugged. "I don't know."

"CIA?"

I shrugged again.

"Who detained him?"

The young man's question made me pause, and I wondered what side Georgiy and his father were on. Were they pro-Ukrainian, pro-Russian, indifferent? Given how far they were from the disputed region, odds were they weren't separatists. But that's what made this conflict so vicious—neighbors had become enemies, families had split, and sometimes people never revealed their true loyalties, exacerbating the distrust and making everyone suspicious of another's true intentions.

Yet, given my situation and the fact I'd just tacitly acknowledged Gomez worked for the CIA, I thought what the hell, why stop now. "Russian-backed paramilitaries, I think, or some other mercenary outfit. It's unclear, but I know they're after me now too."

Georgiy nodded, but not with concern. He was gathering information like an interviewer. "Your friend, he was working against the Russians?"

"Yes. That I'm sure of," I replied, even if it was more complicated than that. At this moment, keeping the lines clean and direct was best. "You know how we Americans view the Russians."

"Yes. Yes, we do. But you still haven't explained how you ended up here."

"Yeah, about that."

I started with Alex and Romania, quickly getting to the border crossing that went bad. Alex murdered, me taken—if I'd been anywhere else I might have paused to reflect, but in this setting I kept my composure. I could dwell on the shit later. Georgiy needed to know about Sasha and Baldy. Alex was gone but Georgiy and his father were alive and helping me. They needed to know if a wrecking crew might show up at their doorstep.

But neither of them seemed phased by my harrowing tale of escape and evasion. I even closed by saying, "I hope this doesn't come back on you or your father."

Georgiy waved his hand dismissively and said, "They won't bother us, even if they followed you here."

The old man cleared his throat. "You go to help friend escape, yes?"

I eyed the father, realizing he'd understood everything I'd said since I arrived. I had to smile.

"Yes, I'm going to rescue him," I said.

"How?" asked the old man.

"Up until this morning I had a plan, but it's fallen apart. Now, I just need to get to Odessa. From there I'll work things out."

"Why Odessa?"

"It's a major city. I can get money there, refresh. Prior to things going bad this morning, I was supposed to meet someone named Orest. But I don't have much to go on."

"Do you have a phone number? An address?"

"No, only a physical description."

"You know Orest is a very common name, right?"

"Yeah, I know."

"What is friend's name?" asked the old man.

"Henry Delgado," I answered.

"Delgado," said the old man, pondering the name. "And why you risk this. Is very dangerous."

"We were close once, in another war a long time ago," I said, my voice distant.

The old man narrowed his eyes and sat back, setting the shotgun down butt first on the ground. He looked at Georgiy and spoke in rapid Ukrainian.

Georgiy then said, "Your plan sucks. If you're going up against the Russian dogs, I have a better idea."

CHAPTER THIRTY-SEVEN

Goooooaaaaal! shouted the commentator on the TV, his long-winded announcement of FC Barcelona's goal against Valencia.

Leos jumped up from his desk with his hands raised in the air and cheered along with the others, Mario on his left, Tony on his right with some girl, and Martina—always in her black business suit and pouring over the corporation's numbers—in a chair off to the side. Andres sat up close by the flat-screen, and nearly spilled the tray of tapas on the glass coffee table—cold meats and cheeses and other delicate creations.

Leos tossed back the remainder of his wine and reached for the bottle. "Barça plays with such passion, but Spain cannot compete with my country's vineyards. Andres, more wine."

Andres grinned and rushed out of the office to retrieve another bottle from the kitchen. Leos owned the entire floor of offices in this high-rise set in downtown Barcelona, and he'd designed a custom kitchen with a wine cooler that could house over one hundred bottles of the world's finest vintages.

As Leos sat back down and selected a tiny clam that had been simmered in white wine, garlic, olive oil, and parsley, Mario touched his shoulder. He motioned at the phone on the desk with its light flashing.

"Quiet, quiet," said Leos, reaching for the receiver.

Everyone stayed their banter and muted the TV.

"Halo," Leos said into the receiver.

On the other end, Genevieve spoke fast and direct. As he listened, Leos' ear-to-ear grin remained, but his blue eyes cooled. Without warning Leos swept his free arm across his desk, clearing it and sending dishes, glasses, papers, pens, paperweights, and futbol magazines crashing to the floor. Everyone except Mario and Martina recoiled, and the girl shrieked.

"Gamoto!" shouted Leos, slamming the phone down on the desk and jumping up, turning his back to the group to face the floor-to-ceiling window.

Mario reached for the receiver and said, "It's Mario. What happened?"

Genevieve relayed to him the same thing she'd told Leos. One of the gangs on the Moldovan–Ukrainian border had secured Mason Hackett, but in less than an hour, a shootout between rival groups erupted and Hackett had escaped.

Mario told Genevieve to hold on and turned to Leos. "What do you want to do, Archigós?"

Leos didn't acknowledge Mario's question. He stayed motionless, tranced at Barcelona's cityscape outside the window.

"Leos?" Mario repeated.

"Your source inside says our man Hackett is going to rescue Delgado. And we know Delgado was complicating our business. This is not right, very bad, lots of money. We can't have this. None of this is good, and I am very disappointed with the incompetency of our partners. I don't want any more complications. We need to make them all go away."

"What do you want to do, Archigós?"

"Tell that Russian shit Petrov to finish up. He has twenty-four hours. I don't want to hear any fucking thing about time and patience and his process of getting information. I don't give a fuck about his fucking *Program*. Fuck those CIA shits and fuck Petrov. I want Delgado done with, like before, same thing."

"Karl, that one?" asked Mario, referring to a forgettable man Leos ordered killed a few years ago.

"Yes, that fucking one. They know too much and the trail is too ugly now. Like a fucking goat's ass. Wipe the shits clean. My business needs to be clean."

Mario spoke into the receiver. "Genevieve, did you hear the Archigós?"

"Yes," answered Genevieve. "I'll have it cleaned up."

Mario hung up the phone and Leos turned back around.

"Everyone out," ordered Leos. "Now."

Tony, Andres, Martina, and the girl dropped whatever they were holding and scurried out of the office. Mario, knowing his boss, remained.

When the door clicked shut, Leos said, "Mario, why is this so hard? It's one man. What's the problem?"

"It's unusual, Archigós."

"Fucking inconvenient. I'm getting concerned. Our deal is coming together, but we may need to change it up. Tolesky, Petrov, Delgado, our man Hackett, our man in Prague, the goddamned Ukrainians—too many problems. Too many ears and mouths. I don't like it. My clients rely on predictability—tech, energy, entertainment. My businesses deliver and when they don't we spin them off. I've made my business because I make the connections and I deliver. It's the same with *this* business. I don't like it. We need to change the deal. The customer, the Africans, they get it. They know things change."

"Yes, Archigós. All they want is the shipment of parts."

"Right. That's right. We need to change the deal."

"How do you want to do that, Archigós?"

Leos waved his hand, pointing at the game. "Later. I need to think about it. We've done this before, but never because of some shit like this. It will be easy. Perhaps we deliver next door or something. I need to think on it."

"Of course."

"Once Genevieve closes things up, we bring her in. She's smart. She understands."

"She's ruthless," quipped Mario.

"Like us years ago, Mario. Maybe we watch her too. Never trust a woman you're fucking, right?"

Mario smirked, then turned his attention to the match.

FC Barcelona was on another breakaway, but Valencia's left defenseman tipped the ball off its line and the players quickly spread across the field. There would be no more goals in this game.

CHAPTER THIRTY-EIGHT

By the time Georgiy and I saw the outskirts of Odessa, the moon shined brightly in the cloudless night sky. Driving in a jeep-like vehicle that flaunted more rust than paint, we pulled into the parking lot of a run-down, abandoned factory, probably built during one of Stalin's five-year plans.

During the hour drive from the farmhouse, Georgiy had convinced me that Orest may very well be a swell guy, but the chances of finding him were slim to none. Georgiy had a better idea, which involved this place.

The young Ukrainian assured me the men I needed to talk to were inside this building and they'd hear me out. I needed to tell them everything, just like I did at the farmhouse. No lies and nothing held back.

But that's as far as Georgiy would commit. These people had their own priorities, he'd said, and hopefully my needs would align with theirs.

I wasn't thrilled about the uncertainty—I'd been abandoned, knocked around, and tripped up enough this trip—but if I could persuade this group to help me, I couldn't ask for more. According to Georgiy, these men were members of a pro-Ukrainian paramilitary cell. If anyone could get me into the separatist zone and on the trail of Gomez, they could. His confidence gave me hope, but I'd save any real optimism for later. Rather, now I was irredeemably determined.

"Come on," said Georgiy, putting the car in park and getting out.

I followed, heading toward the building's entrance.

"They're going to search you. It's no problem you have a gun—most people do—but don't object when they take it."

"Sure. Anything else?"

Georgiy shook his head. "No."

"I can't thank you or your father enough."

"My father hated the Soviets and he hates the Russians. So do I. If you end up killing a few Russians to help your friend, we hope they die slowly," Georgiy said, flashing me a smile.

"Right," I replied, meeting Georgiy's eyes and noting how casually people in this region spoke of death and killing, actually meaning it.

Inside the factory, I sensed an unseen activity. We stood in a damp, musty space measuring roughly thirty-by-thirty. There was no sign of life, only the moonlight coming through broken windows and what appeared to be an emergency light casting a dim yellow glow over the entrance to a hallway. Still, I sensed someone was watching us, perhaps through a lens.

Taking a closer look, I spotted a crude camera mounted in the upper left corner of the room. Next to it, I identified the signature of a directional charge and command wire, not unlike a claymore mine.

The presence of these items generated an equal degree of alarm and comfort inside me. They indicated these people were professionals who took security seriously. Yet, they faced a real threat requiring weapons that could obliterate a man's body.

"This way," Georgiy said, heading toward the hall with the light.

I followed. Once we entered the corridor—a confined space meant to channel intruders into the fatal funnel of a machine gun—a light at the far end flickered on. A solid-looking man wearing dark green camouflage clothing stepped out from around the corner. A Kalashnikov-style rifle lay slung across his chest, and I instantly noticed how different it looked compared to the brown wood and black metal AK-47s I'd seen in Iraq. This one, in contrast, was all black with a collapsible stock and short barrel, replete with a rail mounting system holding a mini-light and optic. The way the man held the weapon indicated he possessed the skills of a trained operator, too.

Combined with the camera and anti-personnel mine I'd spotted, the image made me wonder how often this group came under attack here in Odessa.

Georgiy greeted the guard and stepped aside, presenting me like an unsuspecting hog to the slaughter. The guard motioned for me to raise my hands and then he frisked me. He quickly found my pistol, pocketed it, and continued the search.

The guard then met my eyes, as if his silent glare was the final scrutiny into my intentions. He jerked his head toward the hall door.

"This is where I leave you, Mr. Hackett," Georgiy said, extending his hand. "Good luck."

I went to say something, but Georgiy turned to leave before I could get the words out. The young man's departure seemed surreal. I'd known him for less than six hours, but in that time he'd sheltered me, saved my life, connected me with a Ukrainian militia, and asked me to kill some Russians as a favor. And once again, I was on my own.

"Go," said the guard.

I took a breath and pushed through the door, finding a windowless space with all the markings of a waiting room: a small table with a coffeepot, a television, a refrigerator, a couch, a few chairs, and three men in similar military attire as the guard. Two of the men gave me a disinterested look, then went back to watching a soccer match on the TV. The third stood, muttered something to the guard, and waved for me to follow as he stuffed the last bite of a sandwich into his mouth.

We entered another windowless room, but this one had more of an office flare to it: a round table, chairs, and a desk. Behind the desk sat a steely individual with dark hair freshly buzzed, near-black eyes, a scar that curved under his left ear, and a sinewy yet powerful look-ing frame under a tight black T-shirt. The man raised his head from the map he was studying, sized me up, and returned his attention to the materials before him.

"I am Borysko," he said. "Commander of the twenty-third Ukrainian militia of Odessa. Sit." He directed me to a metal chair across from him. "My cousin says you need help. You want to go to the separatist region, yes?"

"Yes," I replied, not having known before this moment that Geor-giy was related to this guy. Everything suddenly made sense, includ-ing why Georgiy hadn't cared about Baldy and his mafia crew. I was pretty certain Baldy wasn't inclined to tangle with this group, the difference between a backyard militia from Arkansas and British commandos.

"Why do you want to go to separatist region?" Borysko asked. "You want to see the sights? There's war there."

"I need to help a friend who's been kidnapped."

Borysko leaned back in his chair, staring at me as he did so, and lit a cigarette. "Yes, Georgiy told me. Your friend, he worked for your government, yes? CIA? Special ops?"

"Something like that."

"Name?"

"Henry Delgado," I replied, incurring a slight head tilt from Borysko.

"And you're a banker, from London?" he asked.

"Yes."

Borysko's brow rippled with skepticism. "Why do you help this man? What is he to you?"

"Didn't your cousin tell you?"

"He told me things, but I'm asking you. Why?"

"I owe it to him, from a long time ago."

"But why?"

"Do my reasons really matter?"

"They do when it may risk the lives of my men."

"I'm not asking you to help me rescue him. All I want is to get to Mauripol'. I'll figure it out from there."

Borysko let out a curt laugh and stood, walking over to a table against the wall that held three glasses and a bottle half-full of a clear liquid. He poured himself a few fingers and pointed to me.

I assumed it was vodka, remembering what a business associate from Finland once told me. *We do business over vodka. If everyone is drinking, everything is good. If not . . .*

I nodded.

Borysko poured again and returned with the glasses, but he didn't offer it yet. "You figure it out . . ." He twirled the liquid in his glass, staring at it contemplatively, like the distilled spirit held a dash of insight. "Figure it out . . ." he repeated. "I doubt that. You are not a man to just figure it out. What is your plan?"

I narrowed my eyes. "What do you care?"

"Is dangerous. You could get killed."

"Isn't that my business? You don't strike me as the humanitarian type."

A genuine grin opened up across Borysko's face, and he handed me the other glass. "True, and you are right. Is your business. But is my war. Is not in my interest to deliver an American to a combat zone without a plan. It would be *inconsiderate*, I think is the word."

I nodded. I didn't know Borysko beyond the past five minutes, but his manner struck me. He possessed a directness I hadn't been around since I was in the Corps. No nonsense. Get right to it without the small talk, especially for grave matters. I knew right where he stood, and he should know the same about me.

"My plan is very simple," I said. "I'll make my presence known in the local area and that I'm there to secure my friend's release. Then I will pay lots of money."

"Ha! They shoot you on sight."

"Possibly. But they'll also be curious, particularly when they know two million in cash is on the table."

Borysko's mocking expression vanished.

"I'll take precautions, of course," I continued. "Some money now, more later, inviable smart contracts, and the like. You know, banker shit. But you're right, I could end up with a bullet in my head. I'm simply counting on a most basic human instinct—greed."

Borysko studied me, then stared at nothing as he took a long drink from his glass.

I took a sip from mine. "Will you help me?"

CHAPTER THIRTY-NINE

Borysko's men put me up for the night in a room on the second floor of the factory. A metal cot, flimsy foldout chair, and rickety aluminum table filled the space. Coupled with the window and bathroom down the hall, it was the cleanest, most comfortable, and safest place I'd spent the night in days.

Still, I didn't drift off into nocturnal bliss and dream about perfectly prepared rib-eyes and unicorns. Rather, I conjured up Alex's smile, her cheekiness, and the sparkle in her brown eyes each time she'd taunted me. I could hear the notes of her voice too, along with her throaty laugh.

My memories of her were fresh; it'd been less than twenty-four hours since her murder. Yet with everything that had happened since then, it seemed like another time long ago. I missed her, and then I chided myself for having such a feeling. I'd known her for a mere three days.

What the hell was I thinking? Crazy, right?

Yeah, it was crazy. But it hurt. I liked her, desired her, and had toyed with a ridiculous dream that we'd see each other again after this nonsense was over.

But no. That would never happen.

Whether you count my time in the Corps or not—people close to me get hurt, die, or disappear. It's only a matter of time and it's goddamned tragic, like I'm cursed.

When the sun's rays gradually peeked through the dingy window, my eyes were open, staring at the ceiling with my hands resting on my chest. I hadn't slept at all.

* * *

Borysko came to get me shortly after dawn. He'd traded out his tactical getup for street clothes, and handed me something akin to an energy bar and a bottle of water. We exchanged a few words, then headed outside to a waiting van. I knew where we were going because we'd discussed it the night before.

Borysko had agreed to deliver me to Mauripol' for the discounted price of two hundred thousand euro. It was quite a steep taxi fare, but I appreciated the perks: knowledgeable guides through a combat zone, relative trust, and an armed escort. Whether they would protect me if things got sporty, I didn't know, but they'd defend themselves at least.

But before we kicked off our little odyssey, Borysko wanted the money, understandably so.

"Do you have a preferred bank?" Borysko asked in his best English accent.

"For this kind of withdrawal, I'll need to speak to the manager. Is there a UkrSibbank branch nearby?"

"Of course."

"Good. And I'll need some new clothes."

Borysko displayed an annoyed frown.

"I can't waltz into a bank like this and withdraw that kind of cash," I said, gesturing at my mud-stained pants, jacket, and torn-up shoes. "Is there a men's clothing store nearby?"

Borysko wrinkled his brow and said something to the driver. Ten minutes later, he and I walked into a boutique in the city center. I emerged sporting the standard slim-cut dark suit and white shirt that served as the uniform for European financiers, while carrying a bag with a version of *roughs* inside: dark jeans, long-sleeve pullover, jacket, and low-cut boots.

Feeling like a new man minus the shower, we drove a few blocks over and pulled up to the entrance to a UkrSibbank.

"You're coming in, I assume?"

Borysko nodded and opened the sliding door. We both got out.

"Good," I said, "but please hang out in the waiting area and let me conduct the transaction."

"But how will I know you won't double-cross me?"

I gave Borysko a dumb look. "And how would I do that? I came to you and I'm paying you. You either take the money or you don't. I'm the one who should worry about being double-crossed."

Borysko smiled. "You make good point. I like that. Okay, *banker man*, I will sit and read paper while you make a deal." He opened the door and swept his arm across like a butler beckoning me to enter.

I headed straight for an open teller and smartly asked to see the manager, indicating I needed to make a significant withdrawal. A minute later, a flimsily built fellow with gray stubble on his chin and a teardrop belly emerged from the back.

He approached, extended his hand, and said in halting English, "Hello. My name is Symon. Can I help you?"

"My name is Mason Hackett with Ruttfield and Leason out of London, and I need to make a sizeable withdrawal. May we speak in private, please?"

The Ukrainian banker nodded and directed me toward a small cubicle enclosed by windows located at the end of the counter. Once

Symon shut the door and sat down, he asked, "You say you are with Ruttfield and Leason?" his recognition of the firm evident.

"Yes, a partner. I'm on business here in Odessa and need to withdraw a large sum of cash. It will need to be wired, of course. Here." I handed him a piece of paper. "This is the account number, routing number, institution, and amount required."

The man's face betrayed his shock when he saw the figure. "Yes, sir. Right away."

"Do you have an account with us?"

"Not yet."

"You must have an account with us to make a transaction."

"Then open an account for me, please."

"Yes. Splendid. But I need to make checks first. Passport? Do you have a passport?"

"Of course." I smiled and handed over the smudged and creased document.

The banker left the tiny cubicle with its fishbowl windows and disappeared into the back offices to go through the protocol of identity verification and account opening. When I first walked in I noticed an ATM and a decent number of bank staff using computer terminals. I didn't expect everything to happen at the speed of the London Stock Exchange, but I was hopeful. I wondered what language the actual withdrawal forms would be in.

I was adjusting my suit jacket when Symon suddenly returned.

"That was fast," I remarked.

The banker smiled disingenuously, sat down, and handed me back my passport and the slip of paper. "My apologies, Mr. Hackett. I cannot open an account or make the transaction. The accounts are frozen."

"Frozen?" I blurted incredulously, but my reaction was for show. I'd suspected this might happen. This smelled of Doug . . . And I'd just used my passport, albeit knowing the risks.

Symon the banker had undoubtedly run it through an international finance network, effectively bringing me back up on the grid. Ukraine didn't belong to the European Union or NATO, so they weren't linked with the border and immigration trap-lines like the other countries I'd passed through, but they did have Interpol, which made me wonder if the police were on their way.

I looked over my shoulder at Borysko, whom I found leaning forward and resting his forearms on his thighs, staring at me intently like he knew something had gone awry.

"You work with Mr. Borysko, yes?" asked Symon.

I twisted back around to face the banker. At the mention of Borysko's name my spirits lifted, and I knew the police weren't on their way to arrest me and toss me in a hole.

"Mr. Borysko and I are acquainted."

"You arrived with him."

I shrugged.

"I not call police. Your passport, it has notice to contact police. I not do this if you work with him."

I thought for a moment, now willing to show the rest of my hand. "We have business together, if that's what you're asking."

Symon nodded, then leaned to the side and waved for Borysko to join us. Borysko entered the tiny office, and he and Symon exchanged a few words.

Borysko turned to me. "So. You are wanted by Interpol."

"I'm sure I told you that," I replied.

"Yes, you did. But you didn't tell me you don't have money."

"My accounts are frozen."

"Yes, this man told me. This seems to be a problem for you."

I exhaled a heavy breath. "I told you I could get the money, and I will."

"How?"

"I'm going to make a phone call."

"Phone call? To who? Mommy?"

I grinned. "You're not the only one with connections. I thought this might happen," I said. "So I have a backup option. But before I do this, I need you to do something for me."

"Another favor? I'm not sure you have many left."

"You'll want to do this one." I turned to Symon the skittish Ukrainian banker and told him what needed to happen.

CHAPTER FORTY

My call to Ike was brief and direct, just like last time. The old soldier was already awake, the time difference only two hours, and I suspect he'd made his rounds on Caroline's property an hour or two before. I imagine when the phone rang he had a cup of coffee in his hand, turning the pages of a Sherlock Holmes story. All secure, as he liked to put it.

Inside of two minutes, I told Ike what I wanted, which was a bit different than my previous calls. I asked him to contact someone in London who was not expecting the call, pass very specific instructions, and convince this individual not to deviate from them no matter how unusual it seemed. I trusted Ike could do it, and I also trusted the man I needed to speak to would play along.

Thirty minutes later, I used the bank's phone to dial the number to a small conference room in Ruttfield's headquarters in London. Alistair, my boss, picked up on the second ring. I expected to hear a note of surprise in his voice, but there was none. He sounded cool and clear, just as he did every time I called him when on a trip. I'd told Ike to tell Alistair it was me who'd be calling; I guess he just took it in stride, which is probably why he'd risen to the level he had in life.

I didn't regale Alistair with all the nasty details about what I'd been through since leaving London or how I'd landed in Odessa—and I'd told Ike not to either—but I knew the old gentleman wasn't a fool. When I requested he wire two hundred thousand euros to an account in Odessa under another man's name, however, the silence on the phone thundered. But I think that was just me assuming—it was just silence. Still, I felt my heartbeat crank up, and I imagined Alistair gazing out the window across London City's skyline.

When Alistair did finally speak, he did so simply and precisely, as if nothing was amiss—pure businesslike. Yes, he would wire the money, acknowledging he understood I needed assistance to come home, and that I was suffering from an *unexplained passport discrepancy*. The money would come out of the firm's account, with the understanding I would pay it back in full upon my return to London in the coming days.

However, he said my status with the firm would come under review once all the facts were available. Although much was still unknown, the very nature of the situation suggested it was not in keeping with Ruttfield & Leason's professional and ethical standards. He said these things as if reading from a script, making me wonder if that mouse from personnel was standing beside him, listening in, and wagging his finger.

But Alistair's final words caught me off guard. Once he'd finished telling me I was under review, he said, "Mason, this is off the record, not as your boss but as your friend. Be careful. I know generally where you are and that there are some nasty individuals running around. Nothing like you haven't tangled with before, but I think these circumstances are different this time."

"Thank you, sir," was all I could say.

When I hung up, I stared at a spot on the desk for a long moment. Alistair was a good man, and I felt guilty putting him in this situation. But I had no choice.

I looked to Borysko and Symon and said, "Check the account."

Both men got behind the computer terminal, and I heard Symon tap the keys to pull up the transfer record. I knew the money had arrived when Borysko grinned. He was about to open his mouth to say something, but the desk phone rang, cutting him off. All three of us watched it, rattling in the cradle with a ring that jarred the ears.

"Who would call this number?" Borysko asked, shooting me a look.

"I have an idea," I said before Symon could answer. I reached for the receiver. "Hello?"

"Mason, I'd recognize your voice anywhere," said a voice I also recognized.

"Hello, Doug. Not worried about names this go-around?"

"Not this time. And don't bother asking how I got this number or how I'd know you'd be standing next to the phone when I called."

"You're fast," I replied, guessing they'd been monitoring Rutfield's lines for something like this.

"It's what we do, man. Don't act surprised."

"I hope you're not going after my friends?"

"Nah. No reason to. Besides, they haven't done anything I didn't anticipate."

"How fortunate," I remarked. "You believe me about Prague, right?"

"I do. Don't care about that right now."

"What about Rick?"

"Good man. He was an ally on your side, but I'm not calling about that either. If you make it out of this alive, I'll explain then."

"All right. Fine. You obviously know where I am. What do you want?"

"I'm calling to give *you* a message."

"What?"

"Good luck going after Delgado. He's in play, doing what he set out to do. From here on out, we'll do what we can. It isn't much, no backup on strip alert, but the few people tracking this shit show are beating the turf with eyes and ears wide open. I hope you get him."

"What? That makes no sense to me."

"It will if you succeed in getting Delgado out. Can't send the cavalry, but if we can support from afar, I got some good people on it."

"Your caginess kills me."

"Not like the people you're about to go toe-to-toe with. Do you have access to the internet?"

"Yes," I said warily.

"Good. Look up *The Hess Group*. You won't find much, but that's what you're going up against. Good luck."

The line went dead.

*   *   *

I replaced the handset in the cradle and locked eyes with Symon. "I need to use the internet."

The Ukrainian banker swallowed and scooted back in his chair to make room for me in front of the computer, but I shook my head.

"Not here. Somewhere private. Where's your office?"

Symon looked at Borysko, who shrugged indifferently. Symon then stood and led us toward the back. We walked down a narrow hall and entered a room with a metal-framed desk and single chair. There was a small rectangular window, no bigger than a TV tray, up near the ceiling that no one of average height could see out, but it cast the only light in the sterile room.

Symon sat behind his desk and typed in his password to unlock the computer. He then duly got out of the way, motioning for me to have at it.

I sat down only to realize the language on the screen was in Russian. Google was still Google, but everything else was in Cyrillic. Fortunately, I saw the keyboard had a dual English-Cyrillic setup.

"Can you switch this to English?" I asked, motioning at the screen.

Symon shook his head. "I don't know how."

Rolling his eyes, Borysko pulled out his phone and spoke harshly to someone on the other end. After he hung up he said, "I fix."

Less than a minute later, one of Borysko's henchmen from the van—Olek, I think—burst into the office out of breath, as if he'd sprinted from the street through the bank, racing to put out a fire. Borysko snapped instructions at him, causing Olek to display an eager, childish grin.

"Mr. Hackett," Olek said, "I fix. No problem." He squeezed into the room, forcing us all to crowd together with shoulders rubbing. He hunched over the desk, and his fingers danced over the keyboard until he tapped the mouse three times. "Bingo!" he announced, jabbing the enter key with a fencer's thrust and raising back up to his full height, smiling proudly.

"Go, go," ordered Borysko with an impatient wave of his hand before lighting a cigarette.

"Thank you," I said.

Olek slid past me, unfazed by his boss' abrupt dismissal and still smiling like a boy who finally got asked to play with the older kids.

I sat behind the desk again, brought Google back up, and typed *The Hess Group* in the search bar. Doug was right, not much came up, but there was enough, and I'd come across footnotes about the company in my travels the past few years.

Working my way through the links, I refreshed my memory. The Hess Group described itself as an international security firm providing various protective and investigative services to clients, but everything else—the media, forums, and the like—depicted Hess as a Russian private military company. It wasn't as big or widespread as Russia's larger firms, like Wagner, but Hess was on the field playing a similar game.

My own encounters in Iraq with members of DynCorp and the former Blackwater came to mind; former US military personnel turned private contractors who provided security and protective services to the US government. Some deemed these companies to be the latest form of organized mercenary work, and a few were straight-up soulless in how they did business, catering to the highest bidder and racking and stacking with lethal efficiency.

The Hess Group was registered in Argentina but had corporate offices in Caracas, Saint Petersburg, and Sochi. News outlets reported Hess had performed paramilitary work in Chechnya, Venezuela, and Lebanon, and most recently in Ukraine. The evidence was spotty, but a few media platforms accused Hess of being an extension of Russian military intelligence, their orders coming straight out of the Kremlin alongside millions of dollars in contracts.

I wondered if that crew I saw in Syria, my trip right before Frankfurt, was a Hess unit. The coincidence would be uncanny, including Alistair's comments.

As I scrolled through more articles, I noticed Borysko leaning over my shoulder with his eyes scanning the screen. A cigarette dangled from his lips as the smoke wafted across my face.

"Would you like to take over?" I asked.

Borysko gave me an embarrassed look, snatched the cigarette from his mouth, and stood up. "Sorry," he muttered. "Why do you look up Hess?"

"Do you know them?"

"Yes, of course. They are all over the Donbas. Very ruthless, crazy."

"How so?" I asked, recalling a YouTube video showing a group of Russian mercs mutilating a bunch of bodies in Syria—sledgehammers, iron rods heated red hot, and hatchets.

"They like to torture and murder. I think many were too crazy even for Spetsnaz. They are, how you say, *rejects*. Or perhaps they are paid to do such things. Does not matter. Hess is very ugly."

Yes, they are, I thought. "Are they where we're going?"

Borysko shrugged. "Yes, maybe. Hard to tell. They not have name tags."

"Could they be the ones holding my friend?"

He shrugged again. "Is possible. I ask if I see someone. I make inquiries. No problem."

It was my turn to roll my eyes. "Right, sure."

I returned my attention to the computer screen, but my thoughts shifted elsewhere. On the banks of the river Seine in Paris, Doug said Gomez was going up against the Russians and bad-actor corporations, and moments ago he'd pointed me in the direction of a private military firm doing Moscow's bidding. He'd also hinted at tension between governments and international conglomerates, mentioning a change in the balance of power. And then there was Rick and Zach, suggesting someone connected to Doug's special Program had been compromised . . .

What the hell had Gomez gotten himself into?

CHAPTER FORTY-ONE

An hour later walking out the front door of the bank, I was still just as confused about Doug's phone call and the connection to Hess, but I trusted what he told me. He actually wanted me to rescue Gomez, long shot that it was.

Borysko, six other men, and I got into two SUVs and drove northeast along the Black Sea heading toward Mauripol'. I rode in the front seat of the first vehicle with Borysko behind the wheel. I recognized the two men in the back from the night before, Serge and Denys.

Unlike yesterday, today everyone wore their best civilian threads: dark jeans, dark shirts, dark jackets, black boots, and sunglasses. Like the mafia, black was the unofficial national color for this kind of work. It matched the black assault rifles everyone carried, an accessory giving the outfit a nice pop, I thought.

Both vehicles were rolling arsenals. Every man had a tricked-out long-gun and pistol, with multiple magazines topped off with 7.62 and 9mm rounds. The backs of the SUVs, however, contained the real interesting stuff. PKM light machine guns, hand grenades, boxes of ammunition, and most notably, RPGs.

These little toys weren't like the ones on the nightly news: worn-out tubes shouldered by men wearing headscarves and shouting *Allahu Akbar*. Those were RPG-7s first produced in the late 1950s and now commonplace among the world's low-tech armies. No, the ones we had were later models, somewhere between an RPG-22 or 26, and dressed up to party with better optics, longer range, a higher explosive yield, and deeper penetration.

I supposed we might encounter almost anything. The international war correspondents who'd braved the conflict zone had captured it all on camera: infantry, tanks, helicopters, artillery. In the disputed zone, there'd been all-out battles with maneuver elements engaging in a full-scale conventional war.

We could find ourselves in a similar predicament. Best to be ready.

And the notion of what we were doing—driving into a war zone with the car radio jamming Okean Elzy—did nothing short of amuse me. Unlike some Hollywood war movie, where on patrol or right before a fight everyone is stone-faced and silent with ramrod military discipline cover-and-aligning nuts to butts, we were trucking along in style with toons playing.

"I think I'm going to need my pistol back," I said. "Unless you have another one you could spare."

Borysko gave me a sideways glance.

"Once you drop me in Mauripol' and I'm on my own again, I'm going to need it. And it seems to me like you guys are prepared to shoot your way through any bit of trouble we might run into between now and then, so why don't you—"

Borysko shouted an order to Serge in the back who, in turn, handed me a semiautomatic pistol along with three magazines loaded with 9mm ammunition.

"Is Fort-17. A good Ukrainian pistol," Borysko said.

I took it and tested the balance in my hand. It felt good. I'd never used this kind of pistol before, but it shared similar qualities to a Sig Sauer.

Borysko pointed at one of the magazines. "To load . . ."

But I tuned him out and proceeded to manipulate the slide, hammer, and magazine release. "No de-cocking mechanism?" I asked absently.

"No," Borysko replied slowly, switching his attention back and forth between the road and my handling of the weapon.

"But still double action, yes?" I asked, turning it over.

"Yes."

"Right."

I checked the number of bullets in each magazine to ensure they were topped off, smacking them in my palm to firmly seat the rounds. I inserted one of the magazines into the magazine well and racked the slide, putting a round in the chamber, and manually de-cocked the hammer.

I turned to face the two men behind me. "Got an extra holster?"

Borysko, his eyes still flitting between me and the road, let loose a gravelly smoker's laugh. He reached his right arm back over his shoulder and Denys passed up a black holster, which Borysko tossed in my lap, again with a laugh.

"Where did you learn weapons like that?" asked Borysko, more serious now.

"Didn't Georgiy tell you?" I asked, undoing my belt and attaching the holster to my right hip. "I was in the military."

"Special Forces?"

I grunted. "Marines."

Borysko smiled. "John Wayne. Iwo Jima."

I chuckled, securing the pistol in the holster and pocketing the additional magazines. "Yeah, fucking John Wayne."

"This man you are going to help, he was in the marines too?"

I nodded, turning to look out the window at the green and white countryside rolling by. "Yeah, we served together."

"When?"

"Why's it matter? Thought this was a simple business transaction for you."

"You are not a simple banker. You are paying me to deliver you to a war. And you say you are going to help a *journalist* who you served in war with. This all very interesting to me."

I detected a slight mocking tone in Borysko's voice, as if he knew more than he was letting on, but I went with it. "We were in Iraq together, a long time ago. Same unit. We lost a lot of good people," I replied, the names of the fallen ticking off in my head. "We always said if the shit got really thick, the other would do anything they could to come to the other's aid. So, here I am."

"Noble."

"Right, sure."

"And this man would do same for you?"

I hesitated in my response. It was a good question, and one I hadn't thought about until now. I'd come all this way and wrestled through some hairy situations—nearly dying a few too many times—but would Gomez do the same for me? I would like to think he would, that he had taken our pact as seriously as I had, but the notion gave me pause, even if there was only one response I could give Borysko.

"Yes, he would."

"But the war is over, no? You are no longer in military."

"That doesn't matter. He needs my help."

Borysko thought for a moment, contemplating my matter-of-factness, and causing me to wonder how different this man and his crew were compared to the men I'd fought alongside in the Corps. Although I'd paid a healthy fee for his services, Borysko didn't strike me as a simple knuckle dragger working for the highest bidder. The family connection to Georgiy and the old man, coupled with an apparent professionalism alongside intuitive questions, made me believe Borysko had ethos.

"You know why we fight, Mr. Hackett?"

"Russia invaded your country. You're protecting your homes and your families," I said.

"Yes. Our freedom. The Russians are dogs. They are the same as the Soviets, they are the same as imperialists, and they are defenders of no one," Borysko said, hitting the gas to pass a lumbering truck. "You lose many men?"

Again, the names of the fallen ticked off in my head, as well as the new additions to the list—Rick, Alex . . . "Yes."

"And what about family?"

The question made me pause, wondering if Borysko was asking if I'd lost any family members to war, or perhaps in the 9/11 attacks.

No, I hadn't. Not recently, that is. I lost an uncle in the eighties during a military training accident that always seemed to make my elder relatives pause, but everyone else had died of natural causes including my grandfather and father. WWII and Vietnam vets respectively.

Our wars were always fought far away on foreign soil.

I knew America was unique like that. Wars were fought elsewhere on someone else's turf. Not since Pearl Harbor and the Aleutian Islands campaign had there been a battle on US territory. And 9/11, although terrible and unspeakably horrific, had been a terrorist attack, not a battle. We didn't have to worry about the Canadians or the Mexicans rolling across the border in tanks and slugging it out in the northwest suburbs of Chicago.

But for the rest of the world, wars occurred in people's backyards. When the opposing armies rolled in, civilians either fled or got caught in the mix. And there's no glory when grandma is killed in a mortar barrage because she's too slow to get down into the cellar. It's just ugly.

"No," I finally said. "I guess I'm lucky."

"We are not so lucky," Borysko went on. "The Russians and their slaves don't just come for land. They want to exterminate Ukrainians, all people disloyal or a threat to Russia."

"You know this personally, don't you?" I looked over my shoulder at Serge and Denys, and then back to Borysko, all of them impassive.

"Yes. I had a wife, I had a brother, uncle, cousins."

"What happened?" I asked, realizing the conflict—a little border dispute—had been right on this man's doorstep. I may have lost many friends, people dear to me, but these men had arguably suffered things much closer. We all carried burdens.

"We all were from a village near Berdyans'k on the Black Sea. It was a mix of Ukrainians, Russians, good people. For years we get along, everything is okay. Then, after Crimea . . . neighbors kill neighbors, families, kids, friends . . ."

"The Russians?"

"Militias. I lose my wife, I lose my brother. Killed in my house."

"I'm sorry."

"Don't say sorry. Is not your fault."

"Still, I can't imagine."

"Ehh." Borysko shrugged.

"Is that why you fight? Revenge?"

"No. Revenge is hopeless. I fight because I am loyal, and even in their deaths, I will protect who they were," Borysko said, lighting another cigarette and settling back to drive in silence.

At that moment, I decided I really liked Borysko.

CHAPTER FORTY-TWO

The strap tightened around Delgado's neck with the snap of a noose, cutting off the flow of oxygen. His larynx felt like it would collapse and his face ballooned with arterial blood.

Another guard bear-hugged his right arm and shoulder, the hold vice-like. And two others clamped down his left arm, one on each end, prying it open to full extension. Delgado couldn't kick his legs or twist his body because of how they'd bound him with coils of rope.

But despite it all, Delgado glared at Tapper standing before him. The interrogator held a syringe in his hand. He smiled with a crooked curl at the edge of his mouth, then honed in on Delgado's exposed arm and a prominent vein at the fold of the elbow. He gripped Delgado's bicep to make the vein throb. The needle punctured the skin and slid into the vein, Tapper pushing it steadily. The clear fluid—a medical cocktail you would never find in a hospital—flowed into Delgado's bloodstream. Within seconds Delgado felt his brain start to swim.

The men holding Delgado eased their grips, including the strap around his neck. Air rushed into Delgado's lungs but the relief was muted. His body floated and his hearing distorted into a bad audio recording.

Delgado allowed himself to relax; he knew this sensation. No one could fully control the feeling the cocktail brought on, no matter one's willpower, prior exposure, or training. Drugs were drugs. But Delgado forced himself to concentrate on the convolution of lies, disinformation, and truth he needed to keep spilling.

Whether he delivered this information according to the original plan through a clandestine meeting with a Russian arms dealer, or now under interrogation hopped up on some psychoactive juice, it didn't matter. The transmission of the information is what mattered.

"Mr. Delgado," Tapper said, sitting down and tapping his pen on the desk. "We know you are Kevin Gomez. We have established this many times."

"Yes, yes. That's my name! Kevin Gomez. Gomez. Gomez, Kevin."

"Yes. Yes, you are Kevin Gomez. We have questions for you."

"I like questions. And I have many answers. I like pizza too. Can we order pizza?"

"Perhaps later. First we must talk. About why you want to meet with a man named Tolesky, and why you involve a man named Hackett."

"Yes. Talk, answers . . ."

CHAPTER FORTY-THREE

We'd been in the car heading east for almost four hours when I noticed Borysko touch his hip and adjust his shirt, ensuring he had a clear path to the pistol holstered on his belt.

I was familiar with the motion. It's what I used to do in the marines if I thought we were about to get hit; an instinctive fidget that could shave off the split-second separating life from death.

Without a word I did the same with my shirt and pistol, while simultaneously making a slow scan of the road ahead and the surrounding countryside. A gray sky that smelled of rain, brown and green rolling hills dotted with snow, and a handful of farmhouses well in the distance completed a romantic landscape if it were any other time.

What did Borysko see? Did he see anything? Or did his shift in demeanor mean nothing except that he'd become tired with how the edge of the pistol cut into his hip.

I was about to dismiss my paranoia when Serge said something in Ukrainian I didn't understand. His tone, however, caused the hair on my forearms to stand up.

I realized no other traffic was on the road.

For the entire trip, we'd driven behind, in front of, and passed other cars. This section of the road was no more desolate than any other part. Yet I hadn't seen another car for quite a while.

Borysko hadn't noticed *the presence* of something—he'd noticed the absence. Memories from over a decade ago cut into my consciousness. Visions of empty Iraqi streets seconds before the RPG blew a truck to bits. People emptying the bazaars so the machine guns could fire down the alleys at the marines on foot. A stretch of road no one drives until the Americans strike the IED, with soldiers losing limbs and eyesight.

"What's wrong?" I asked.

Borysko didn't answer, nor did either of the men in the back. All of them kept staring out the windows to the front and flanks, observing their sectors.

I returned my focus to the road ahead. If something was about to happen, it would be there.

My pulse quickened when I saw it. Two hundred yards away I spotted a bend in the road curving to the right. The road cut through a hill, leaving two steep slopes on both sides of the pavement. Any vehicle driving through the curve would be channeled and exposed to elevated positions on each side.

This type of terrain was typical for any highway set amid hills and mountains; but here, right now, in this situation, my thoughts tumbled toward an ideal ambush site.

As our SUV neared the bend, the rest of the road came into view. I spotted two trucks parked perpendicular across the road, blocking it. Five or six men armed with rifles scurried about, one of them with his arm raised, palm out, ordering us to stop.

Borysko muttered a curse under his breath but kept his foot on the gas. We had one hundred fifty yards to go, closing fast.

My eyes darted to the crests of the low hills flanking the road. I spotted brush, saplings, rocks, and a machine gun position dug into the hillside. In the side mirror I looked beyond our trailing SUV and watched two pickup trucks drive out from a field up onto the highway, perhaps three hundred yards back. The trucks trailed us slowly, occupying both sides of the highway.

We were boxed in. Roadblock to the front, two trucks for containment to the rear. We couldn't stop, couldn't turn around, and there weren't any side roads. Judging by the snarl on Borysko's face, these people weren't friendly.

"Who are they?" I asked.

"Separatists. Is trap. We fight."

We were a hundred yards away from the roadblock, still driving at speed. Borysko barked sharply in Ukrainian, and Denys behind him spoke into the radio.

I gripped the door handle and synched down my seat belt.

Besides the front and back, I didn't see anything on our flanks, but that didn't mean there weren't other teams positioned on a hill or in a clump of trees, aimed in on us. Ditches ran parallel to the road on each side, and I wondered if there were anti-personnel mines primed to clack off if we didn't cooperate.

We were fifty yards away and closing.

The men at the roadblock scrambled into defensive positions, realizing we weren't slowing down.

"I hit brakes, we fight," Borysko said through clenched teeth.

"Got it." I drew my pistol and checked the chamber, then glanced over my shoulder to find Serge and Denys adjusting themselves so they were perched to jump out with rifles up.

Borysko waited for another half-second, gritted his teeth, and slammed on the brakes. The SUV's tires squealed and smoke erupted from the burnt rubber. Borysko turned the wheel left, putting the vehicle into a skid until it stopped perpendicular to the road.

I looked out my window, now in full view of the roadblock and close enough to see the waiting militants' eyes go wide in astonishment.

They started shooting.

The machine gun on the hill opened up, bullets cutting into the SUV's thin aluminum skin.

"Fuck!" I hissed, diving across the center console to bail out through the driver's door.

Borysko was already on the road and firing over the SUV's hood at the ambush site.

Serge and Denys were on the road too. One of them fired at the trucks coming up on our rear, while the other opened the SUV's rear hatch.

I crawled out the driver's-side door and saw our second SUV skid to a halt behind us. It made a barrier offering a small degree of cover.

Now on the ground, I realized at this range I couldn't do squat with a pistol.

"Serge!" I shouted over the gunfire, trying to get the Ukrainian's attention. He was firing his rifle over the hood of the SUV at the roadblock. "Serge!" I shouted again, this time catching his attention and causing the man to duck down and take a knee. He reloaded and met my eyes.

"Rifle?" I shouted.

Serge pointed at the back of the other SUV, then stood back up to continue firing.

I stayed low and scooted across the pavement. When I reached the other SUV, a boom followed by an equally loud whoosh cut through the sound of the small arms fire. The air sucked from around me as if someone had opened an airlock. One of Borysko's men held a stubby tube, having moments before fired an anti-tank rocket. Less than a second later an explosion came from the direction of the roadblock.

The sights, the sounds, the smells—I remembered them all. This wasn't a simple shootout between gangsters with pistols and popguns—rather, an all-out battle with military-grade weaponry raged. It didn't matter where one was or who was involved, they were the same. Battles were battles.

I pulled a rifle from the back of the SUV.

The automatic fire coming from the roadblock started up again.

I ducked down, jamming a thirty-round clip into the magazine well.

When I looked back, searching for a position to move to and fire from, I saw two of Borysko's men had gone down. They were bleeding from holes in their chests, stomachs, and legs.

Borysko, crouched by the back of the SUV, glanced at his two men dying. But all he could do was grit his teeth and keep firing. His AK hammered on full auto.

I thought to join him but stopped. Another burst of automatic fire peppered the two vehicles and surrounding pavement. I again looked at the two Ukrainians, both of whom had fallen and lay exposed in the road. Both men still moved—a hand twitch, a leg kick, a chest heave. They were alive but bullet-ridden, with their life dripping out of them.

I didn't think. I darted the few steps over to the closest one.

Fully exposed in the road, I caught a glimpse of the roadblock and saw one vehicle on fire—likely from the anti-tank shot—and multiple men hunkered around the other vehicle and in the ditches. They were firing at me and the others.

Bullets zipped past with a distinctive crack and zing.

I grabbed the wounded Ukrainian's collar and dragged him back behind the SUV. Then I went out again and grabbed the other one.

I should have been shot. At least one of the hundreds of bullets flying through the air should have hit me. But none did.

The two Ukrainians, however, were both ripped to pieces. Thoughts of trying to patch their wounds flashed through my head, but I didn't have a medical kit. However, I did see both men had tourniquets on their chest racks, which I grabbed and synched down on the worst-looking limbs. If anyone was still standing in the next few minutes, they might have a chance, but that was all I could do for now.

I looked around. I needed to get into the fight, but staying here on the road was futile. We were sitting ducks smack in the kill zone. We wouldn't last much longer. We'd all be dead as dogs if someone didn't try something to break out. There was no other way.

I swore and picked up my rifle. I snatched a chest rack from the SUV's back seat and rushed to Borysko.

"Have your men cover me," I shouted over the hail of gunfire.

"What?" asked Borysko, a squint of incredulity on his face.

"Just do it," I barked.

I turned, crouched like a sprinter, took three rapid breaths, and launched forward. I burst from behind the vehicle and ran across the open pavement to the side of the road. Bullets whizzed past and kicked up tar and stone around me. I dove into the ditch that ran parallel to the highway.

I found myself facedown in icy mud. Although I could hear the firefight fine, I couldn't see any of the roadblock positions. If I couldn't see them, they couldn't see me. I glanced behind me, heartened to find no one to my rear.

I checked the action of my rifle to be sure a round was seated in the chamber. I raised myself to a knee. In a low tuck, I dashed down the ditch toward the roadblock. Despite my heavy breathing and the air rushing past, I heard the gunfire up on the road increase. I hoped it was Borysko and his men pouring it on.

I kept going.

Thirty yards away. Twenty yards. Ten yards from the roadblock.

Not slowing down, I raised up just enough out of the ditch to bring my rifle to bear and fire multiple shots at the area around the burning car. A man who'd been lying in the prone position spotted me coming and rolled over to get into a better position. I sent three rounds into him as soon as he exposed himself.

I was five yards away, but instead of keeping on toward the road, I veered right to go around the small hill. I charged up the slope, rifle at the ready. When I crested the hilltop, I spotted the machine gun position with two men manning the automatic weapon. I fired six or seven times, hitting the two militants with multiple bullets. Their bodies spasmed in shock and pain.

I didn't stop.

I bounded over the dying men and ran down the hill, unloading my rifle at everything I saw. For an instant I wondered if Borysko and his men had spotted me and shifted their fire, or would they keep peppering the ground I was about to charge into . . . but it was too late for such thoughts.

Once down the hill I reached the edge of the ditch by the road and paused, combing the ground for anyone still moving. Four bodies were sprawled on the road, bleeding from multiple wounds, and more charred bodies were visible in the flames from the burning vehicle.

A sudden movement caught my eye through the smoke on the opposite side of the road, and I let loose another burst of automatic fire until the bolt locked. I pulled out the empty magazine and inserted a fresh one, all the while searching the ground and the car windows for anyone who might still be alive.

The shooting had stopped. It was quiet. No one was firing.

I knelt, inhaling deeply. Then it hit me. I was still alive.

CHAPTER FORTY-FOUR

I stood over the bodies of three Ukrainian fighters. Roman and Vasyli died from gunshot wounds, and the third—Olek, my computer friend—succumbed to injuries incurred from a grenade. They no longer looked like themselves, the blood drained from their faces and their features locked in a death mask the moment their lives were snuffed out.

All around smoldered the remains of battle. Piles of spent shell casings, burnt metal, mangled bodies, acrid smoke, ringing in the ears, total exhaustion, grime ground into the skin, and the sound of the wind rushing over the earth. I hadn't seen a sight like this in over fifteen years, but you never forget it. It's seared into you—there's nothing else like it.

Borysko, who stood next to me, smoked a cigarette, indignantly inhaling and exhaling the tobacco smoke. "Now this war take another cousin," he said.

I looked up but didn't say a word.

"Him," uttered Borysko, motioning at Olek and shaking his head. "I'm sorry."

"No, don't be sorry," replied Borysko, taking hold of my arm and locking eyes with me. "No," he repeated, hammering the word into the air. "Why did you risk your life to help them?"

"What do you mean?"

"You ran out. Fucking bullets everywhere. Pulled them behind the car. Why?"

"We were in a fight," I replied as if the reason was obvious. "We were under attack and they were lying out there, in the open, dying."

"Right, under attack. Then you charge those men." Borysko waved his arm at what was left of the roadblock. "Crazy."

"There was nothing else to do," I said.

"Ha! Nothing else to do?" Borysko released my arm, took a step back, and appraised me up and down. Then he moved a step closer and raised his hand with the cigarette, poking his finger toward the Russian border. Rage seemed to burn inside him, on the verge of erupting.

"The Russian and her dogs are *our* enemy. They kill our families, they destroy our homes. Yet you fight them like they're *your* enemy. You understand this, yes?"

I fixed on Borysko and nodded. *Yes, the Russians and the mercenaries they command are your enemy, Borysko, but they are also mine.* I had to fight them any way I could, and not only because they held Gomez or because Alex and Georgiy feared their return, but because of all of it.

The Russians were bullies, they were cruel, and they only cared about power and weakness. And although at Ruttfield I'd had to view things through a profitability lens, deep down I hated them. I knew the wider the sphere of influence Moscow wielded, the worse it would be for everyone else, Europe especially. I despised those individuals and groups who made other people live in fear. No one should have to live in fear.

A part of me started to think that even if I couldn't help Gomez, hitting the goddamned Russians and all the mercs and criminals fucking up this region was a good alternative. Perhaps I'd get a little redemption for the trouble I'd brought upon Caroline, the death of Rick, Alex's murder . . . maybe even my own guilt from so long ago. This time I wasn't an invader accidentally killing kids in their homes; rather, I was helping people fight back.

"This was not in the bargain," Borysko went on, motioning at the surrounding carnage. "You did not have to fight like you did, but you did."

I remained impassive, watching Borysko.

"You are a warrior, with us." Borysko extended his hand. "We are not taking you to Mauripol'."

"What?" I blurted.

Borysko leaned in to just a few inches from my face, his frown indomitable. "We take you all the way to the border region and help you find your friend. I *know* your friend, and I know where they are holding him. This fight is now our fight."

CHAPTER FORTY-FIVE

Later that afternoon, we arrived in an area barely a village that was just east of Mauripol' and ten miles from the Russian border. Borysko led me into a farmhouse built like every other dwelling sprinkled among the trees and feral fields: rectangular, two windows on each of the four walls, an apex roof made out of thatch, a dirt drive, and perhaps a shed or dirt pile. Standard stuff for the poor who called the disputed region their home.

Borysko hadn't said anything more about his knowledge of Delgado. I'd asked, considered pleading, but Borysko ignored my questions. And although our *partnership* had evolved since the ambush, I didn't feel I could press the man too hard. Rather, something told me he would share everything he knew soon enough—like now.

We sat at a table in the center of the concrete room, with two men lounging on the opposite side of the table, each with a cigarette either clinging to his lips or burning between his fingers. They were somewhere between forty and sixty, with dark features and weathered faces one normally acquires from a lifetime on the water fishing or in the fields farming. Perhaps they'd had those professions in the past before the war.

No longer.

These two men—Taras and Nikita—commanded the two resistance cells in Mauripol'. They spent their days plotting ways to kill Russians and their Ukrainian puppets.

In Mauripol' and the other villages scattered throughout the separatist region—which ran north from the Black Sea up to Luhansk, east to the Russian border, and west to Donetsk—a brutal civil war had raged since 2014. It involved militant groups, separatists, loyalists, Ukrainian armed forces, the Russian military, paramilitaries, neighbors, families . . . everyone. Russia effectively controlled the separatist region by covertly backing the pro-Russian population, but the guerrilla war simmered.

The uniformed Russian military sat perched right on top of the internationally recognized border between Ukraine and Russia. If one listened to the Kremlin, these forces were present to defend Russian territory from the criminal Ukrainian militias and terrorists who attacked and murdered ethnic Russians.

The Russian military hadn't *violated* the border either, except on rare occasions to keep the peace and protect the innocent. The Russians are quite noble and believe that sometimes they must exert a heavy hand to make sure the children don't get out of line.

In reality, Russian Spetsnaz and contract mercs were crossing the border like it was their backyard. Dressed in civilian clothes but armed to the teeth with guns, cash, and materiel, they directed the actions of the pro-Russian Ukrainians, in addition to running their own paramilitary ops. Arms flowed too; there was never a shortage.

The situation was brutal, violent, and a poorly kept secret. Ukrainian loyalists would bomb a pro-Russian business, and pro-Russian militias with their Russian handlers would round up and execute the suspects. At times, tanks and helicopters would cross over the border to neutralize a *terrorist* threat. Other times, neighbors would kill the man down the street and take his plot of land or store in town, claiming this or that as justification. And when the Russian president got bored, he enjoyed stacking up his mechanized battalions for a no-kidding invasion, only to call the dogs off a few days or a week later.

Sometimes the situation across the region was hotter than others, but there was always a low boil. Peace negotiations at the UN were for show; day-to-day existence in the region was hostile.

Taras and Nikita lived in this cauldron and knew better than anyone what was happening in and around the coastal town. They might not have the capacity to do much about Russian interference or separatist activity, but they acted when the opportunities presented themselves.

"Well?" I asked.

"Yes," said Borysko, turning his attention from our hosts to face me. "We have much to talk about concerning your friend Delgado."

"How do they know him?"

Without turning back to Taras or Nikita to ask the question, Borysko said, "We used to work with him."

"'We?'" I asked, meeting Borysko's reticent stare.

"Yes. We."

"And what was your work with him?"

"It was very small. I help him get information two or three times."

"And them?" I asked, referring to the two cell leaders.

"Same. All together. Very inclusive, but small. Mr. Delgado was a cautious man, yet he paid well. That was the deal. He support us, we support him. Win-win, as you say."

"Right. Of course," I remarked, noting how transactional life and death were here.

"What information was he looking for?" I asked.

"He would not say. He a very cautious man, yes. Secretive. He a good CIA officer," Borysko said with a conspiratorial smile.

Outwardly, I didn't react to the comment about Delgado being CIA, but inside I accepted it for what it was. Delgado aka Gomez had been running clandestine ops with these men, using them, paying them, and they knew it. I didn't think that meant these men viewed their relationship with Delgado poorly. On the contrary, the impression Borysko was giving me was that they were satisfied with the arrangement, with everybody benefiting. But I wondered how far this type of loyalty would go.

"Our work with Delgado was very simple," continued Borysko. "We would broker introductions for him, and he would talk with them, sometimes for many hours. Sometimes not long. Only once did things not go so well."

I cocked my head, waiting for him to explain.

Borysko shrugged. "One man, a Turk, I think. He was arms broker. He didn't like what Delgado say, or something. I not sure. But he get angry."

"What happened?"

"Delgado shoot him. Was very fast. Pop pop. Two to the chest. The Turk not have time to blink," Borysko said, chuckling.

"Right. Was he always meeting with arms dealers?"

"Mostly. Businessmen, arms dealers, mercenaries . . . Hess."

I narrowed my eyes, not in an accusatory way, but in a manner that indicated I was accepting the revelations of truths that had been withheld from me. "You knew all along."

Borysko shrugged. "Not completely, but I make connections. And I not know you before. Is good to be cautious when a man shows up, asking about someone like Delgado, yet mysterious himself, yes?"

"Yes," I agreed, then turned to consider Taras and Nikita, both of whom hadn't budged while Borysko and I spoke except to smoke their cigarettes and light new ones.

"Delgado didn't tell you what he was doing here, but what do you *think* he was looking for?"

"I think he was very interested in arms and mercenary networks. He not care about Russian GRU or SVR. He think they are, how you say, clumsy. It was the others, like Hess, he wanted to know about."

"And?"

"He say one day that he think those kinds of people were connected to problems outside Ukraine, but he not say what. Was very strange."

"Do they know?" I asked, again referring to Taras and Nikita.

"No."

I nodded. "Do you know how he was captured?"

"I don't, but they do."

"Ask them," I said.

Borysko nodded and posed the question. Nikita spoke and Borysko translated. "He says your friend wanted to meet with a Russian broker to get information about a man named Tolesky."

"Who's Tolesky?" I asked.

Borysko raised his finger to stay quiet. "Tolesky is arms dealer from Sochi. Your friend had a guide, but not one of us, we not know him, but the guide betrayed him. When he organized the meeting and your friend was waiting at a house north of here, Russian paramilitaries captured him. Guide betray him."

"Who took him? Hess?"

Borysko shrugged.

"Why? Why did the guide betray him?"

Taras shrugged, and Borysko said, "Paramilitaries took him to the border but didn't cross over."

I leaned forward in earnest. "Borysko, why did they take him? Why was he betrayed?"

Nikita lit another cigarette while Borysko asked the questions.

"Your friend had deep connections inside Russian activities. Intelligence, military, the security firms. Inside a war zone is the best place to meet. But this mission was different."

Borysko motioned for Taras to wait. Turning to me, Borysko said, "Tolesky is major arms dealer. He supplies weapons all over the world. Here, Syria, Libya, Somalia, Venezuela. I hear he likes South America and wants more business there. He well-connected man, and he makes lots of money for people. Even some American politicians and businessmen."

"What?"

"Just my opinion. Everyone is dirty and likes war. Is good business if you not the one fighting."

"I don't understand."

Borysko scrunched his mouth. "You think about it, then we discuss over vodka if we live that long. Is not important now."

"Then what is important?"

"These men tell me this. During Delgado's last trip before his capture, he was different. He said he could no longer trust the people he worked for. He could only trust one."

"Who? Why?" A deep uneasiness formed in my stomach.

"They don't know who. But one night your friend was very distraught, like he felt betrayed, the deepest betrayal. All he said was his government—his country—was no longer what he thought, and he needed to find someone to learn the truth."

CHAPTER FORTY-SIX

I leaned against the kitchen wall on the ground floor of the farmhouse and stared out the window at the fading sunlight. The landscape appeared empty, as though only the minimal amount of trees, bushes, grasses, houses, sheds, and roads were allowed here. The sky was gray and overcast, and not another soul was visible anywhere—no one was outside. This was the frontier, the border, the edge—nothingness. It was abandoned, isolated and alone.

Taras and Nikita's account of their final conversation with Delgado magnified the sensation I felt. The Gomez I remembered wasn't a bare-your-soul kind of guy. He didn't talk out his innermost thoughts and fears for others to overhear. For him to have appeared distraught and to have voiced his concerns about trust and betrayal in front of these two men, the situation must have been severe, heavily weighing on him.

Why was he trying to meet with Tolesky, and what truth was he looking for? Did he fear his own government? Did he fear Doug? And what of these arms dealers and mercenaries, what of Hess?

The threads were many, but I couldn't see the connections except in the vaguest terms, and I honestly wondered if anyone knew the entire story. The men here—Borysko and his compatriots—knew their part. Rick had known his piece. And Doug seemed to know the most. But I suspected even he didn't have it all.

Only Gomez could put the missing pieces in their proper place. He was the key and was the one who went on this mission. He was the one who sent me the email, pulling me into this in a way that I couldn't refuse. And he had reasons for his actions.

I wanted to save my friend, but after all I'd been through, there had to be more to it.

I shifted my gaze from the window and eyed the trapdoor to the cellar. I heard Borysko's voice and the voices of the two cell leaders coming from down below. I wanted to know what they were saying, but Borysko told me they needed to speak among themselves.

They were debating whether they would help me. I knew Borysko would, but I was uncertain about the other two. I didn't know what the benefit to them might be. They surely wouldn't do anything purely on my behalf. They had to see the connection to Delgado aka Gomez.

They'd said they knew where Delgado was being held and that he was being guarded by a mercenary outfit. Did they think an armed rescue was even possible? Given the same group had been trying to knock me off since London, my initial idea for a ransom payout no longer seemed like a good idea. So it would have to be a rescue. I saw no other way.

I walked over to the kitchen to pour myself another cup of coffee, but when I grabbed the pot, I heard a vehicle's engine and the sound of tires on gravel. I pulled back an edge of the curtain to see outside and saw a truck pulling up with its lights off.

Taras and Nikita hadn't mentioned anything about more people joining our evening salon, and neither had Borysko. I looked across the room at the AK and kit I'd acquired during the ambush, but it was too far away.

Rushed footsteps trampled the hard dirt outside.

Someone in the cellar yelled, followed by feet pounding the stairs.

I drew my pistol, steadied my shooting stance, and aimed in on the front door.

A fist pounded on the wooden frame outside.

"No!" shouted Borysko as he emerged from the cellar's trap-door.

I broke my focus on the front door and let my pistol fall.

"Don't shoot. Is friend," said Borysko. "We have problem."

"What?" I asked, watching Taras and Nikita surface from the cellar.

Nikita moved to open the front door, letting a freckled teenager into the farmhouse. He barely looked old enough to shave, but both Nikita and Taras engaged him as if he were a mature fighter.

"What's going on?" I asked.

"They're moving your friend," answered Borysko.

"Where?"

"Across the border into Russia, we think." Borysko nodded at the kid. "He has team watching the building where your friend is. He says trucks just showed up and everyone is leaving."

That, I thought to myself, or they were about to execute Gomez and they were eager to dump the body on their way to the after-party. "How does he know they're taking Delgado and if he's even still alive?"

"He knows. He good," stated Borysko.

"If they move Delgado into Russia, he's gone," I said.

"Yes." Borysko ran his fingers through his hair. "We must intercept, yes? Vehicle interdiction, you say."

"Yeah," I replied, nodding with a hard determination. "Will they help?"

"Yes. If Delgado is gone, is as bad for them as it is for you, just different. Money, support, those things. Is not much, but is enough. Come on."

Taras, Nikita, and the kid looked at us expectantly and then hurried outside. I followed Borysko, grabbing my rifle and kit as I passed by the table.

CHAPTER FORTY-SEVEN

Delgado tried to open his eyes but the bruises, swelling, and traces of the drugs fought hard to prevent him from doing so. He resorted to prying his lids open with his fingers.

His vision was still blurry, but his cell looked the same. His captors had left him unbound after the chemical party, probably assuming he was so doped up he couldn't find his fly to pee much less a way to break out of here.

He had no idea how long it'd been, and without any windows, there was no way to determine if it was night or day or time to hit the showers and call it a day. Which then made him wonder how long he'd been here. Between the beatings, the hours of interrogations, and now the drugs, the days had run together.

They couldn't keep him forever, he thought. He was fairly confident he was still in Ukraine, having kept his wits about him enough that first night when they took him to know that he hadn't crossed the border into Russia. He supposed keeping him on this side of the border in Ukraine's unregulated disputed region made things convenient. Territory with questionable levels of authority had always been a place to hold individuals that no one knew what to do with.

No recognized law enforcement to speak of, no mayor to vote for, no tax collector to take your last dime, and no one to care if you buggered this person or that.

The question he should be asking himself was, what's next? After they'd had their fun playing or determined he was no longer worth babysitting, they'd have to make a decision. It took people, effort, and time to hold and or move him, but killing him would be a fast and simple way to end the comedy.

The sound of a sudden bang came from outside his cell, causing Delgado's head to painfully twist toward the door. Then there were two bangs in rapid succession, followed by two more. They sounded like gunshots, double taps, but Delgado wondered if he thought they sounded that way merely because moments before he'd been contemplating a heroic death, blindfolded and on his knees with a pistol at the base of his skull.

But if they were gunshots, who was shooting whom? He hadn't caught any signs of other detainees enjoying the all-inclusive resort, and the sounds had been clean and sequential, like someone walking down the line and popping away rather than an attack of sorts with all the chaos that goes with it.

It was something else.

Fuck 'em, he thought. If they were coming for him next, he wouldn't go down like a heifer in the stocks, waiting for the bullet to the head while chewing on cud. Make it hard on the bastards so they had to work for their notch on the buttstock.

Delgado rubbed his face to force his senses to wake up, then struggled to his feet to shake out his joints. Moving hurt like hell, but it got easier with each step. He thanked God they hadn't broken any real bones, just a few fingers. He could work around that. And what was pain right now anyway; if they were coming to do the deed, who the hell cared if he had a headache or if his knees were stiff. It was time to shake it off.

Delgado staggered to the door and leaned against the wall, pressing his ear to the cold metal, listening for anything.

Voices, footsteps . . .

CHAPTER FORTY-EIGHT

Five of us—Taras, Nikita, Borysko, the kid, and me—streamed out of the farmhouse. Borysko waved me to the far side of our SUV, and I slung my tac vest on over my shoulders and buckled the clips as I got in.

Taras, Nikita, and the kid jumped in the other SUV and tore out of the driveway, headlights off. The vehicle's shadow bounced as it hit the dirt road and they sped into the darkness.

Borysko put our SUV in gear and followed them, also blacked out.

I checked the action of my rifle to ensure I was loaded and topped off.

"How far to where they're holding him?" I asked.

"Kid say twelve kilometers," answered Borysko, squinting through the windshield and picking up speed. Nikita's vehicle stayed fifty yards in front of us.

"Will he still be there?" I asked, adjusting the pouches holding my magazines so I could draw them quickly.

"We find out in ten minutes."

I sank my ass into the seat and held onto the door handle. "Right. Fucking go, man."

"Ahhhh!" growled Borysko.

CHAPTER FORTY-NINE

Mikhail Petrov gathered up the stacks of loose, handwritten notes and stuffed them inside his briefcase. The information these papers contained was gold, absolutely priceless. No one in over seventy years had gained so much about the Program. No one. Even the consultant they captured back in '84 broke and revealed everything he knew, but his knowledge of the Program was infinitesimal compared to Delgado's.

Delgado was a senior operator and in the Program's leadership ranks, and he'd come here poking around a transaction he should have known nothing about.

But he'd told the *troika* everything, the medical cocktail forcing the real breakthrough. The three interrogators were impressive, experts in their craft. It was an art for them, and worth every euro.

Petrov heard a commotion outside and drew his pistol. He'd told his men to dispose of the four Ukrainian separatists—including that shit major—who'd been guarding the exterior of the facility. They were no longer needed, but they couldn't simply go home to the family farm or shop after what they'd been exposed to.

Petrov went to the door and opened it. He poked his head out and saw two of his men ushering a person down the hall, one on each side. The one on the right, Aybek, a Kazak, nodded, signaling that all the loose ends had been snipped clean. Petrov's mood eased; his plan to get across the border was rolling out nicely and he smiled as he appraised the prisoner.

A hood was over the man's head, and his arms were bound behind his back—bloody Delgado. Although Petrov's crew had turned the screws tight, the man's posture appeared taut, like he still had some strength in him. Once across the border, they'd have to rectify that.

As the two guards passed by, Petrov fell in behind them. All four men exited the building to be greeted by darkness and a cold gust of pre-dawn air. Building lights illuminated a concrete lot where a sedan and two gun trucks sat idling.

The guards stuffed Delgado in the rear cab of the middle truck, and Petrov got in the back seat of the sedan.

"Once they're ready, head toward the border crossing," Petrov instructed the driver. "But not too hard. I must make a call as we go."

"Yes, boss," said the driver.

The three vehicles, with Petrov in the lead and Delgado in the middle, drove like a motorcade to the main road that led east toward Russia.

CHAPTER FIFTY

The SUV surged forward as Borysko hit the gas coming out of a turn. He steered with one hand while using his other to hold a phone to his ear. I steadied myself with the door handle. The dirt road we were speeding down had a ridiculous number of washouts and rocks on it that were rattling the hell out of the SUV.

"Any updates on if they're moving yet?" I asked, referring to the group holding Gomez.

Borysko clicked off his phone and stuffed it in his pocket. He'd been talking with Taras, who was still ahead of us.

Borysko nodded. "Just left. On road to border."

"Fuck. How long till they reach it?"

"On main road, fifteen minutes."

"Can we catch them?"

"Yes, we try."

"What about Denys and Serge? Are they closing in?" I asked.

While Borysko and I made the rendezvous at the farmhouse, Denys and Serge had been at another safe house getting food and waiting for the call. Now, they were also on an intercept course.

Borysko nodded. "They will hit front; we come up the ass."

"Then we go," I said, playing out how the vehicle interdiction, or VI, would happen.

"Then we go," repeated Borysko, taking another turn as hard as physics would allow.

CHAPTER FIFTY-ONE

APPROACHING THE RUSSIAN BORDER

Petrov looked out the passenger window of the sedan, barely making out the contours of the fields and patches of trees passing by in the darkness. The phone against his ear reached two and a half rings before the man on the other end picked up.

"Tell me you're not still in Ukraine," said Leos.

"We are headed to the border now. We will cross over in the next twenty minutes."

"Fine. Marvelous. Easy work, my little friend. Now, once you meet with our partners, hand the man over as soon as possible. He's Moscow's problem now. I want nothing more of him."

"Yes, of course," answered Petrov.

"And what of your report? I need some light reading and to know why this shit is fucking with my business."

"I have all my notes with me. I'll transcribe them and send them off once I get to Sochi."

"Right," Leos curtly replied. "Genevieve is waiting for you at the airfield and will accompany you to Sochi. Treat her well. She speaks for me. She has some things to discuss with you."

Petrov rolled his eyes but did not dare let his annoyance appear in his voice. "Excellent. And when will you and I meet? We need to discuss what to do next."

"Soon. Just get our man out of Ukraine and you rendezvous with Genevieve. That is my concern right now."

"Of course."

The line went dead, and Petrov went to close his eyes to gather his thoughts in anticipation of his meeting with that *woman*, but a spot of movement up ahead caught his attention. Squinting into the darkness, he spotted a rectangular object moving at a high rate of speed. It took him another second to realize it was a vehicle on a parallel road.

Petrov then watched as the unidentified vehicle sped forward and cut left onto the road in front of his motorcade.

"Nyet!" yelled Petrov.

CHAPTER FIFTY-TWO

We were still blacked out, now just one hundred yards behind the motorcade.

I caught a metallic flash in the distance as Denys' vehicle cannonballed up onto the road in front of the three-vehicle motorcade. The lead vehicle, a sedan, swerved and pumped the breaks to avoid colliding with Denys' SUV.

"Hold on," growled Borysko next to me. He slammed the gas and our SUV shot forward.

Taras, Nikita, and the kid were behind us. I glanced in the side mirror and saw their SUV speed up too. I returned my attention to the scene ahead of us, adjusted my grip on my rifle between my legs, and shifted my torso, braced to launch myself out the door.

The next few minutes were a violent blur.

Denys' SUV first zoomed farther ahead of the motorcade to create some distance. Then Denys hit the brakes and entered into a skid, sliding his vehicle ninety degrees to the road to block it.

All three motorcade vehicles careened left and right, trying not to hit Denys or each other. Their tires screeched as they stopped in a rough herringbone.

Borysko, still on the gas, pulled up fast and stopped twenty yards behind the jam-up. Taras and Nikita's vehicle held back another fifty yards to provide overwatch.

As I opened my door to get on the street, I saw a handful of men pouring out of the motorcade vehicles, like angry wasps defending the nest. They dropped into firing positions around their vehicles or flat on the pavement.

Then the shooting started. Deafening cracks, pops, zings, and bangs, a gunfight up close right on top of each other, shattered the forsaken landscape.

The men in the motorcade, though returning fire and trying to organize themselves, seemed completely unprepared for our attack, as if the very idea of a hit so close to the border had been unfathomable.

The crossfire intensified, and we all ran the risk of being struck down by our own people, but the situation demanded it. If Gomez crossed the border into Russia, his demise would be certain. And given the time we had to react, there was no other way. Either we hit the bastards hard and fast on this stretch of road, or nothing.

Both Borysko and I fired our rifles from the shoulder as we walked, steadily closing in on the motorcade's rear truck. I saw at least two men go down. And I held my breath for the return fire that would drop me or Borysko. But I kept aiming and firing, aiming and firing, shooting the motorcade's vehicles and the shadows around them, closing in.

Then I heard an engine rev and tires screech. The sedan at the front of the motorcade lurched toward Denys' vehicle that still blocked the road. The sedan gained speed and struck one of Denys' men, Serge or maybe Denys himself, and then slammed into the left front panel of Denys' SUV. The sedan pushed through to the open road on the far side. Bullets ricocheted off the sedan's body, but it kept going until it disappeared into the night.

I cursed at the car's escape, but there was nothing to do at this point. I could only hope Taras and Nikita had seen it too and could call in another cell to intercept the sedan. Until then, we had to survive the fight we were in.

Borysko thought the same, yelling at me to focus on the remaining two trucks, now shot to shit. He and I kept moving forward, firing and reloading with smooth, machine-like movements. Our comrades up ahead kept the heat on too.

As Borysko and I got closer, the firing increased. The survivors of the motorcade, Denys, Borysko, and I, we were all nearly on top of each other. I felt the bullets zipping by within inches of my head, but there was no point in ducking or flinching. Out in the open like this, there was no place to hide. If a round was going to hit me, I wouldn't have a say in the matter.

Then, instantly, the intensity of it all ceased. No shooting, no movement—nothing. This forgotten plot of land at the edge of the world held its breath.

Borysko and I were just ten feet away from the rear truck. Three bodies lay sprawled on the ground, shot to pieces. All the truck's doors were open, with no one left inside. I looked up to the second vehicle, where I hoped Gomez would be if he was actually here. I spotted the driver's door open and another lifeless body splayed on the ground, but the rest of the vehicle was closed up.

I looked at Borysko who met my eyes. He nodded and yelled something in Ukrainian. I heard Denys respond, and felt relieved knowing at least he was still alive. Borysko then motioned for him and me to move forward.

We approached the SUV with weapons up, alert to any sign of movement. Borysko took the right side and I took the left.

The driver lay half out of the door, with a pool of blood glistening in the moonlight. The SUV's body and windows were spider-webbed, making me think it was armored. If Gomez was inside, that may have protected him. That is unless a guard still in the SUV had already popped Gomez between the eyes. I'd find out in a moment.

On the other side of the SUV, Borysko snapped his fingers to get my attention. He then reached forward and yanked the passenger door open. I heard a cry of protest, and then Borysko shot twice. He looked at me and gave me a thumbs-up.

My turn.

It was then I noticed that dawn's early light had just crested the horizon. The darkness was fading, shapes, colors, and details coming more clearly into view. I took a breath and lowered my rifle, slinging it behind my back. I drew my pistol, and with my left hand I reached forward to touch the cool door handle. I yanked it once and stepped back, pistol up and ready.

CHAPTER FIFTY-THREE

The cab was dark, and at first, I didn't see any sign of life. I don't know what I expected to find after all this, but the stillness caused a crater to form in my chest.

Gomez wasn't here, I thought. He was either in the sedan that escaped and was cruising toward the border, or there'd been a mix-up. Maybe another vehicle in the motorcade had broken off, split from the convoy, and taken Gomez a different way. A decoy. Or Gomez had never been in the motorcade. Maybe they'd shot him and left his body on the floor of the warehouse. Or maybe something else happened I couldn't fathom, and I'd never know.

But something compelled me to take a step closer to see farther in, to confirm my fears, my heart sinking with each inch I moved.

Then, in the shadows, I spotted a boot. Peering deeper, I found a pair of bright white eyes staring back at me. As the individual's profile took shape, all the despair I'd been feeling just moments ago vanished. "Gomez?"

"I'm going to lodge a complaint with my travel agent," came a raspy voice.

"Gomez? Delgado?" I said again.

"Yeah. Brother Hackett?"

"Yeah," was all I could muster, still struggling to believe it was really him.

"What took you so long?"

At that comment I burst out laughing. I lowered my pistol and reached in to pull my friend free from the vehicle. And once Delgado found his footing and I cut his restraints, we found each other's faces and stared for a long moment. A thousand words passed between us.

The best friend I'd ever had, whom I hadn't seen for fifteen years and believed dead, was now before me. The ghost who'd sent me a cryptic email was now a physical being before me, gripping my shoulders while I took in his bruised and battered face.

We both could very well die in the next few minutes, his captors coming back for round two, but at this moment I was overcome with fearless exhilaration. But despite all the questions and thoughts that had been churning in my head ever since I saw Delgado's mug on TV, all I could say was, "We need to go."

Delgado looked around and spotted Borysko. He nodded with a familiar smile.

"Are you two it?" Delgado asked.

"Sort of. It's complicated."

"Ha! Tell me about it," Delgado said with another cough.

"Come on," I said, pointing back at our SUV down the road. I took Delgado's arm, but he stopped me.

"Wait. You guys have a radio?"

I shook my head and turned to Borysko.

"Radio?" Borysko held up his handheld.

"No. Wait." Delgado hobbled to the driver's door, dragged the body out the rest of the way, reached in, and retrieved a green, boxy tac radio. "Give me one minute."

I glanced at Borysko, who shrugged. He brought his handheld to his mouth and spoke, taking a few steps toward Taras and Nikita's truck.

"What are you doing?" I asked, returning my attention to Delgado.

He was punching the keys on the faceplate and manipulating the dials. "You may not be the cavalry, but I have a 911 number. I just hope someone is listening."

Delgado brought the handset to his ear and keyed the mic. "Black Strike One, Black Strike One, this is Lost Soul, come in, over."

Delgado met my stare and I smiled.

"Black Strike One, Black Strike One, this is Lost Soul, come in. Am in contact with main forces with three PAX total requesting immediate extraction. *Landslide, landslide, landslide.*" Delgado un-keyed the mic and waited, checking the keypad display to make sure he was on the right frequency and transmitting.

No one answered, but Delgado's words echoed in my ears with a force that hammered with fifteen years of pain, regret, and loss—*Landslide, landslide, landslide.*

"Black Strike One, this is Lost Soul, authenticate with . . ." Delgado listed off a sequence of numbers and letters phonetically. He spoke in clipped statements telling whoever was supposed to be listening that he'd escaped and was inside Ukraine near the border. But still no one answered.

Delgado paused to make a quick survey of the surrounding terrain, then asked, "Do you have a line on an HLZ?"

Borysko, half listening to us, half chattering on the handheld, muttered, "A farm east of Mauripol'. I get grid."

"Right," replied Delgado, keying the mic again. "Request emergency extraction east of Mauripol'. Will provide HLZ when known. Again, request emergency extraction. I say again, *landslide.* Lost Soul, out."

Delgado looked up from the radio. "I hope someone's listening."

"Who are you trying to call?" I asked.

"The good guys. If I ever got isolated, this was supposed to be the personal recovery procedure. Report with location and get instructions."

Delgado keyed the mic again, speaking with an earnestness not lost on any of us. I prayed someone on the other end of the line would respond. If they did, our chances of getting out alive would increase exponentially.

"We need to go now," shouted Borysko, trotting back over to us. "Nikita say he hear chatter. Forces coming this direction."

I looked back at Taras and Nikita's SUV, which in the early morning light I could see was slowly rolling our way.

"Who's coming?" I asked.

"We wake the border with our little party," he said with a chuckle. "Russian army and their separatist puppets are coming."

"Fuck—"

The rest of my words were drowned out by the blast and rush of a rocket coming from the far tree line, streaking toward us. The warhead slammed into Taras and Nikita's vehicle, turning it into a fireball with metal debris blown in all directions.

"Run!" shouted Borysko.

Gunfire again filled the air, bullets saturating the ground around us. A second rocket slammed into Borysko's and my vehicle, destroying it. I dropped to a knee to seek cover.

Borysko shouted and dashed toward Denys' SUV.

I grabbed Delgado and we followed.

Denys' SUV was backing up to get us. It stopped and Denys jumped out from behind the wheel to help me load Delgado into the back seat. Denys then dropped. Bullets hit him in the shoulder and neck. Still struggling to hold up Delgado, I saw Denys' body twitch and then go limp.

I pushed Delgado into the back seat and yelled at Borysko to help me. He rushed around the front of the SUV, took one look at his cousin, and shook his head.

"Leave him. We go."

Borysko got in the driver's seat and I crawled through the back into the front passenger seat. I didn't see Serge, who must have fallen during the fight, as I'd guessed.

Borysko hit the gas, hauling down the main road and then jerking onto a dirt access road. I held on as he drove, and in my head the names of the fallen called out—Taras, Nikita, Denys, Serge, Olek... They were all gone, just to save one man.

But just when I thought things couldn't get worse, I spotted a dark, menacing object pop over a grove of trees to our left.

"Gunships!" I yelled.

CHAPTER FIFTY-FOUR

Borysko swore and the SUV picked up speed. Both Delgado and I stretched to see out the windows to locate the gunships. I'd caught a glimpse of two Mi-24 attack helicopters, mean bastards that could wreck anyone's day, and I expected them to commence a gun run on top of us.

But rather than coming in hard and fast with their 12.7mm Yak-B Gatling guns roaring, the two helicopters screeched through the morning dawn heading north. One fired two rockets and the other opened up with its cannon, both directed at targets beyond our line of sight.

"What the hell?"

"They engaging our resistance cells," Borysko said. "Border is erupting." He pulled the handheld from his chest rack and turned the volume up so Delgado and I could hear. A mess of voices and static came across.

"What's happening?" asked Delgado.

"When we come to get you, we alert all cells in area. Now everyone is fighting."

"Holy shit," I said.

Borysko shrugged. "It happens," he muttered, finding another turn off the hardball road and heading down a dirt trail in the opposite direction of the gunships.

"Where are we headed?" asked Delgado.

"Mauripol'. You know? Is village east of city with good fields for landing zone. Is good?"

"Yeah, let me call it in."

As Delgado worked the radio again calling into nothingness for extraction and Borysko Baja'd across the Ukrainian landscape, I kept my head on a swivel scanning for enemy units in the area. For a time—just a minute or two—we drove and didn't see anything.

But as we crested a small hill, I spotted a handful of gun trucks on a parallel road coming from the direction of the Russian border. They saw us, too, because the lead truck opened up with its heavy machine gun. The rounds went high and wide, but that didn't mean the next burst would.

"Fuck! I lose them here," Borysko said, cutting down another road behind a farmhouse.

I held on, and Delgado worked the radio again, sending out a distress call, but with no one answering.

A violent cascade of pops cut through the vehicle's windows and aluminum doors. The sudden change in air pressure inside the vehicle assaulted my ears. I had to shield my eyes from the shards of glass, metal, and plastic flying through the air.

"Contact left!" bellowed Delgado.

A military-style truck with a machine gun mounted on top was bearing down on us from a side road. The soldier behind the gun let loose another burst of automatic fire, the weapon jumping on the mount like an enraged colt trying to buck free from the harness.

CHAPTER FIFTY-FIVE

Petrov's heart rate had just started to return to normal when his car stopped at the edge of the airstrip where the Hawker 850 waited for him. Now that morning had arrived, he felt slightly better as he tried to come to grips with the audacity of the attack he'd just survived. He couldn't believe someone had dared such an ambush so close to the border.

But that wasn't the worst of it . . . he'd lost Delgado.

To save his own life, he'd had to go. Through an onslaught of shouts, he'd ordered his driver to ram the vehicle blocking their path and not slow down until he crossed the border into Russia.

But Leos wouldn't understand. All he cared about was shutting Delgado down and removing that man Hackett. Petrov wondered if it'd been Hackett who mounted the attack. Possible, of course, but it also could have been loyalists. He doubted he'd ever know the full truth.

Nonetheless, whoever had dared such a fight, they were paying for their mistake now. As his vehicle had been screaming east toward the border, Russian military units had launched west into Ukraine to put everything down. The Russian commanders had received flash orders to hunt down the perpetrators of the ambush too. Delgado and Hackett—if indeed it was him—would be dead soon.

Petrov opened his car door to get out on the flight line and board the plane, but stopped abruptly when he saw three people waiting at the bottom of the stairs. He didn't recognize the two men on each side, but the woman in the middle was unmistakable and he wondered why that bitch Genevieve was here.

As he proceeded toward them with his briefcase in hand, he shouted over the aircraft's idling engine. "Genevieve, so nice to see you, though I suspect these conditions are quite rough for your tastes," he quipped, noting her coat and hands tucked up in the sleeves.

"Where is Delgado?" Genevieve asked.

Petrov frowned and halted a few steps away. "We were ambushed by a far superior force. I barely escaped with my life, but the vehicle transporting Delgado was overwhelmed. A loss, yes, but I'm confident the man and the perpetrators of the attack—whomever they were—are no longer alive given the military's response. Fortunately, I have secured everything that matters," said Petrov, giving his briefcase a brisk shake.

"What of Hackett?"

"What *of* Hackett?"

"He perpetrated the attack, yes?"

"I have no knowledge yet of who ambushed us. But if it was Hackett, we will know soon enough when I receive the reports from my teams cleaning up the mess. Now," Petrov said, taking his eyes off Genevieve and making a quick scan of the rest of the airfield, "am I to assume you're accompanying me to Sochi? If so, I suggest we board and continue this conversation—"

*   *   *

Genevieve raised a tiny pistol she'd concealed inside her coat's sleeve and shot Petrov in the forehead. He fell back and hit the ground flat. Crimson blood started to pool on the concrete around his head, and his uniform's lapels flapped loosely in the breeze.

The individual on Genevieve's right stepped forward to retrieve the briefcase and search the body. He found a passport and two phones, which he handed Genevieve.

Then the four of them—including Petrov's driver—boarded the aircraft.

CHAPTER FIFTY-SIX

Delgado looked out the rear window of our SUV. "Fuck, they're still coming."

I turned to see for myself. Three Russian gun trucks were in hot pursuit. "How far into Ukraine will they follow us?"

"Yesterday I think a mile. Today . . ." Borysko shrugged. "Maybe more."

"Can you outrun them?" asked Delgado.

Borysko was about to respond when two flashes followed by rushes of smoke came from our two o'clock.

"Rockets!" I yelled, watching the projectiles screaming toward us with angry black-gray smoke spitting out the ass-end.

But the rockets sailed past, contrails in the air. One slammed into a tree and the other went erratic, spiraling up into the sky.

"Who the fuck?" yelled Delgado.

"There! There!" shouted Borysko, pointing to a mass of trees off to our right.

I spotted three, maybe four men in a defensive position, now shooting rifles at us. They wore civilian clothes, but even at over a hundred yards I could tell they were built like fighters.

"Who are they? Are they our guys?" I asked, hoping futilely they were friendly Ukrainian loyalists.

"No. They separatists, mercenaries, Spetsnaz." Borysko spat. "Too many sides to count." He stomped on the gas again, racing down the dirt trail aiming for an opening in the tree line.

"Better kick it in gear," said Delgado, urgency in every syllable.

I glanced over my shoulder and saw Delgado still looking out the SUV's rear window.

"Those trucks are on our ass," he said.

I cursed, but all I could do was hold on. Russian troops crossing into Ukraine were pursuing us like a hot date, and paramilitary separatists—Ukrainian or Russian, take your pick—were staffing the receiving line with 7.62mm cocktails and high-explosive appetizers.

"What's on the other side of those trees?" I asked, scanning the thick grove to our front.

"Fields. Village," said Borysko. "We okay there. We hide, disappear."

"Right," I breathed, but not at all buoyed by my Ukrainian friend's comment. Our little rescue op had rattled the border and knocked loose anyone in the mood for a brawl. We needed to get out of here, Delgado and I. Borysko could melt into the countryside; he was a local and knew the networks, and they knew him. But we were flashing lights that everyone would instantly know didn't belong.

Even if we dodged all the bullets and rockets, the probability of an informant giving us up was pretty good even if they only caught a fleeting glimpse of something unusual, and especially after this little tussle. The separatists and their Russian backers would be eager to take us out.

"Delgado, what about now? Will they extract us now?" I asked.

Two more bullets, maybe a third, cut through the rear of our SUV, shattering the side window. Cold air rushed inside the cab along with the raw noise from outside.

"Fuck," hissed Delgado. "Yeah, let me try." He took hold of the radio and called out over the airwaves again, asking Black Strike One if they would come for us now that we were in Ukraine.

I faced forward just as we penetrated the tree line. We slid around a bend in the trail and headed deeper into the grove. The trucks trailing us quickly disappeared from view, as did the dismounts that had been to the north.

I heard Delgado transmitting over the radio, but didn't hear any response. He repeated our general location and direction of travel. I again prayed someone was listening.

The trees and bushes flanking the trail whipped past, and Borysko accelerated and braked as he steered us down the wooded trail. We were now at least five miles from the border.

A minute passed, then another, with no sign of the trucks on our tail, dismounted troops aiming in, or those killer gunships overhead. I took a deep breath, thinking about our next steps. We needed more distance if we could get it—the farther we were from the border, the better. And we needed a field suitable for a landing zone.

So simple, but so uncertain. Timing, location, luck—everything could work out easy peasy lemon squeezy, or Murphy and General Slugwort could kick in and derail it all.

I looked down the trail, maybe fifty yards, and saw it opened back out onto a rolling field.

"You know where we are?" I asked.

"Yes," replied Borysko. "Village not far. To the south. We pass by and we okay. We call Nikita and then you call your friends for pickup. Okay?"

"Yeah," I said, turning back to see how Delgado was faring with the radio, but my head only made it partway around.

The inside of our vehicle erupted with broken glass, shredded aluminum, and shattered plastic. My eardrums popped from the explosive boom and overpressure, and a hot, sharp pain jetted through my leg while hundreds of tiny searing prickles hit my face, neck, and hands. A flash of fire and smoke consumed the outside of our truck, and I just barely saw the image of the tree before we crashed into it.

The next few minutes were a blur, and I struggled to ascertain if what was happening was real or a mash of dreamed confusion. Through the haze—both in the air and in my head—I concluded someone had detonated a mine or IED to the left of the trail just as we were about to emerge from the grove of trees. It must not have been too big—our vehicle was still in one piece—but shrapnel had perforated it like a colander, some holes as big as my fist.

Borysko was a bloody mess, the left side of his face and body slashed open. He still moved, but it was slow, as if he wasn't sure whether he was alive or dead. In the back, Delgado was slumped over. I couldn't tell if he was breathing or if he had any more holes in him than when we started.

I coughed, feeling fluid and grit in my mouth and lungs. My left leg hurt like hell, the pain somewhere down by my calf. I wondered what else was wrong, but the smoke, muffled ringing in my ears, and intense shock to every cell in my body numbed my ability to speculate how bad off I really was.

Then my door ripped open and a knot of hands yanked me out and threw me on the ground. I felt them do something to my legs and arms, but couldn't see anything except flashes and shadows through the blinding sun assaulting my eyes.

When they were finally done with me, I turned my head to the side to see uniformed men pull Delgado's body from the back seat and drop him down beside me. I think he coughed but wasn't sure. He was limp all over.

This was the end. We were done.

CHAPTER FIFTY-SEVEN

A squad of Russian soldiers half-carried, half-dragged Delgado and me to a waiting van. My leg screamed but felt bound. When I looked down, I saw that someone had bandaged my wound.

Through the commotion, I saw another group of soldiers taking Borysko to a different truck. Even though his body was sagging and his toes trailed through the dirt, I could tell he wasn't dead yet. Dead bodies always look different than live ones, even if the person is unconscious.

A helicopter swooped overhead and strafed an unseen position somewhere south of us before veering off to come around and do it again. An armored personnel carrier, maybe twenty yards away, fired its machine gun at a row of houses, tearing up wood siding and shattering windows.

Although confused and disoriented, I was with it enough to question why we were still alive. Why hadn't they shot and killed us on the spot? Amid all the chaos, had Delgado's captors wanted us back alive? And where were they taking Borysko? I feared his fate would be worse than ours.

These soldiers were unlike anything I'd seen up to this point. They all wore similar light green and brown camouflage uniforms, their rifles were equipped with advanced optics and suppressors, and all of them covered their faces with masks or scarves.

I suspected these men had been dispatched to locate, capture, and transport us to a dark place in the bowels of some Russian hole. A place where no one ever surfaced.

My heart sank with each forced step that brought us closer and closer to the waiting van, but I couldn't imagine what might be going through Delgado's mind, if he was even conscious. To be rescued and to have fought through so much, only to be recaptured—wounded and bloody—and heading back into hell.

The soldiers crammed us into the van, with bolts of hot pain shuddering deep inside my leg. My head smacked against a rigid seat bench, and my shoulder hit the doorframe so hard that for the next few minutes I had no strength.

When the agony roaring inside my body finally settled, I realized Delgado sat next to me but wasn't able to keep himself upright. He slouched against the side of the van, his eyes closed, his face ashen, with dried blood forming around a gash on his forehead.

I'd seen the look before. The life was escaping out of Delgado's broken and beaten body.

I tried to call out my friend's name but produced only a whisper.

The soldiers who had tied us into the seats didn't seem to notice or care. They were professionals and this is what they did: snatch valuable targets amid violent chaos—alive or dead—and transport them to whoever would dispose of the mess.

The van door slammed closed, imprisoning us inside with nothing but a few rays of light penetrating the windshield. The whup-whup-whup sound of a gunship passed overhead, but no gunfire this time.

It was all over. Borysko was gone, we'd been captured, and I didn't doubt the remaining pockets of Taras and Nikita's men had been decimated. They were either dead lying in ditches, their bodies charred in burned-out vehicles, or they were being lined up against a stone wall ready for a bullet to the back of the head. The end.

Had it been worth it? Hell if I know. Delgado and I were insignificant for that particular question, our lives inconsequential except as the catalyst. But what about the others? Rick, Alex, Roman, Vasyli, Serge, Denys, Olek, and lord knows how many of Taras and Nikitas's men—all dead. Blood on my hands?

Sure, who else could it fall to.

Or were they simply the casualties of a broader war, all of them willingly crossing no-man's-land and knowing the risks. This war of the world that had pitted East against West since the start of the twentieth century, we kept it going like a forever war because war is business and business is good, and we are nothing without violence and tragedy. The lives we chew up, and for what?

The van started moving, jostling me about, with Delgado's limp body suspended upright by the seat belt. The vehicle tilted left then leveled out onto flat ground. It picked up speed, heading toward an unknown destination that would surely culminate in terrifying pain, probably death. I hoped it'd be quick, for both our sakes.

Perhaps when the Russians realized I was nothing but a washed-up vet who'd become a greedy banker, who'd gone on a fool's errand because of some stupid sense of philosophical guilt, they'd just kill me rather than waste any time or energy. That would be best. A simple disappearance in the Russian machine where life meant nothing more than a split of birch tossed in the woodstove.

"Pereyezd na bazu."

I heard the words but couldn't translate what they meant, my ability to understand Russian lost somewhere back in our torn-up vehicle. The passenger spoke to the driver, both Russian soldiers with fresh haircuts and clean uniforms.

Through wrinkled vision, I squinted out the windshield and listened for anything I might discern outside. The helicopter swooped overhead again, seeming to move above and parallel along the same road we were traveling.

Up ahead, perhaps a quarter-mile away, a truck pulled onto the road. Then another truck, and another truck—three in all—but not blocking it. Men got out of the vehicles, armed, but without uniforms. They weren't like the wild paramilitaries we'd encountered, nor the ramrod special ops guys who'd nabbed us—but they were lethally confident with every step and gesture.

Hess . . .

My arms were bound, but I could still move my shoulder. I nudged Delgado, hoping my friend still had some life left in him. "Delgado," I whispered. "Delgado. I think they're passing us off to someone else."

Nothing.

I nudged him again. "Delgado, can you hear me?"

He let out a hoarse breath. It wasn't a word, but it was some kind of acknowledgment.

"I don't think we're gonna get out of this one."

The cluster of vehicles and people was less than fifty yards away. As our van approached, one of the men finally stepped into the middle of the road, causing our driver and his partner to exchange a few words. I settled into my seat, as uncomfortable as it was, resigning myself to thinking my next class of accommodations would be a trunk.

The van slowed and the soldier in the passenger seat pulled a paper from his pocket. He rolled down his window like he was getting ready to show the men up ahead their orders. All according to simple procedure, I thought. The bureaucracy of authoritarianism and imperial agendas made it all the way down to the tactics of covert wars.

I closed my eyes to savor my last few moments of peace. I breathed deeply. My chest hurt, but the air tasted good. Almost fresh.

The vehicle stopped and I opened my eyes. I heard the Russian soldier in the passenger seat say hello . . . then it happened.

Four loud pops erupted in the front cab of the van. They were in such rapid succession they almost sounded like a single shot.

Outside the van a cacophony of sustained automatic fire erupted, mixed with a series of double taps. I expected to feel bullets ripping through my body, but realized nothing was tearing through my flesh or peppering the walls of the van.

A rush of bright light blinded me and I blinked.

When my vision finally came back into focus, I saw hands and arms yanking the two Russian soldiers out of the cab. They were lifeless with heads cracked open from gunshot wounds.

Through the windshield, I saw men in civilian clothes pouring sustained automatic fire in the direction from which we'd just come. And beyond this riot, a smoke trail streaked through the sky and slammed into a hovering helicopter. It turned into a fireball as it fell from the sky.

Before I could put together any sense of what was going on, the van door slid open. A man with hard features, fully kitted out with a chest rack, rifle, drop holster, and an earpiece on his helmetless head, held up a picture with his free hand next to my face. The man looked between me and the picture, then grabbed my shoulder so we were eyeball-to-eyeball.

"Mason Hackett? Are you Mason Hackett?"

I stared at the man blankly. He'd spoken English with a Southern drawl.

The man cupped my chin and shined a light in my right eye, followed by the other. He looked past me at Delgado, now slumped against the far side of the van. Putting the light away, he focused on me again. "Sir, we're Americans here to get you out."

Stepping back, the man with the drawl motioned for two other men to cut my restraints. As they worked, he pressed a toggle switch by his throat. "Black Strike Base, Black Strike Base," he said, staring into the distance. "This is Reaper element. We have possession of the pigskins. I say again, we have possession of both pigskins. Touchdown, touchdown. How copy?"

As the other two men lifted me out of the van onto my feet, the man with the southern drawl paused his transmission, listening to someone far away.

"That's A-firm. Require urgent dust-off for two PAX. Both PAX critical with multiple gunshot and shrapnel wounds. Request surgical team aboard the bird."

The man paused again to listen, while a fourth individual took hold of me. He eased me to the ground, laying me out on a stiff board. "Sir, my name is Doc Sten," said the new arrival in clear English with a very familiar firmness to it. Years ago, I'd known all kinds of men who spoke with a similar tone, including myself at times. It was the kind of voice that could overcome the bullets and the bombs, coming across like it was nothing but an easy day.

"Sir, can you hear me?" repeated Doc Sten.

I nodded.

"Good. We're Americans here to get you out. CASEVAC will be here in seven minutes. While we wait, I'll give you a quick tune-up, blend up some margaritas too. How's that sound?"

The reality of what was going on continued to sink in, and I turned my head to see someone hovering over Delgado, wrapping bandages and administering shots.

The next few minutes were a blur of pokes and prods, with men running and yelling and the occasional burst of gunfire. Whether it had been five minutes or an hour, I couldn't tell, but eventually the sound of another helicopter overwhelmed the scene.

When two men picked me up on the backboard and ran me into the swirl of dust, I finally lost consciousness.

CHAPTER FIFTY-EIGHT

While the aircraft's engines spun up to prepare for takeoff, Genevieve dialed a number and brought her phone to her ear.

"Yes, my dear," answered Leos.

"Delgado escaped and as of yet we have no knowledge of his or Hackett's location. We're waiting on the reports from the units that responded, but I have doubts."

"And Petrov?"

"Taken care of."

"Good. The reports will come in when they do. I'll see you in Sochi. We can talk more then about what to do. This is an uncomfortable problem, and we need to talk about the deal, make some adjustments."

"Of course."

Genevieve hung up and settled into her seat. An attendant handed her a glass of champagne, which she took a sip of as she pulled out the two phones they'd removed from Petrov's corpse. Scrolling through the call log and contacts of the first, she deduced it was Petrov's primary phone, which she had contacted him on once or twice, along with all the other businessmen, government officials, friends, prostitutes, and anyone else who needed to talk to the swine.

She noticed the other phone, however, was special. It had only one number in the contacts and call log, and she recognized the prefix was to a phone in Moscow, Russia—inside the Kremlin. She pressed *call* and waited as the line rang.

The line came alive and an old man's voice said, "Da?"

"Who is this?" asked Genevieve.

A long silence hung on the line, and then the call terminated.

CHAPTER FIFTY-NINE

Leos slipped his phone back into his pocket and returned his attention to Tolesky. "Did you hear my conversation?"

"I'm sitting right here," retorted Tolesky, sweeping his arm along the leather couch that faced the panoramic window looking out across the coastal edge of Sochi and onto the Black Sea. "If you wanted privacy, maybe you should have stepped away."

"I didn't need privacy. What did you hear?"

"That Petrov is dead, Delgado and Hackett have escaped, and your trollop is coming here."

Dimitry, a brute of a man with tattoos up and down his arms and across his chest under his tight T-shirt, smacked Tolesky in the back of the head, causing Tolesky to jump up as if he were ready to brawl.

"Sit down!" commanded Leos, raising his voice but not budging from his perch on the desk. "I have a mind to tell Dimitry to take you down to the water and shoot you for the fish to eat. Make a comment like that again and I will. I'm sure Dimitry as the new boss of the Hess Group would like a good first contract."

Dimitry smiled a toothy grin and rested his palm on the pistol on his hip, and Tolesky whipped his head toward Leos, a dab of color having drained from his face.

Leos then threw his head back and laughed. "I'm just kidding. It's a joke, like your comment about Genevieve, a joke. But sit down."

"Yes," replied Tolesky.

Leos's demeanor went to granite as Tolesky lowered himself back onto the couch. "Good, because we have good business to do. Good for you, good for me, good for many people. But we need to change the deal."

"What?"

"Relax, you'll still make the consignment, but to a different location. And some of the containers will be switched out."

"I don't understand."

"You will, and you will get an additional bonus. Is five million okay?"

"Euro?"

"Yes, you greedy shit."

"Okay."

"Good. Senor Mario has the details."

Mario stepped forward from his post by the door and laid out a series of contracts on the table in front of Tolesky.

As Tolesky read them over and started signing, Leos raised himself up and turned his back on the group. He stepped closer to the window and took in the majestic view of blue sky, seawater, beaches, and the tops of lavish resorts. It was not as beautiful as his ancestral home on Crete, but there was no better place for conducting this side of his business, and it was time to make some changes.

CHAPTER SIXTY

VIENNA, AUSTRIA

The room measured ten-by-ten with a builder's-grade carpet, white walls, a rectangular fluorescent light, and a cheap print of the Golden Gate Bridge hanging on the back wall. I sat in a chair with a thin cushion and backing held up by small metal legs, which some lowly logistics officer had probably purchased twenty years ago. Before me on the circular table was a glass of water, which I hadn't touched, and a steaming cup of black coffee in a paper cup, which I also hadn't touched.

"How's the leg?" asked the man sitting across from me. He'd introduced himself as *Bill,* and his tailored suit seemed in contradiction to the embassy badge hanging from a lanyard around his neck. You could always tell the real embassy staff because their clothes came from department stores, a government salary only going so far. The snappy dressers were *special.*

"Still hurts," I replied, reminded of the bandage wrapped around my calf from where the chunk of shrapnel had gone through. "Same as when you asked me the first time."

"I'm concerned for your well-being. You've been through a lot."

I grimaced and shook my head, not caring about the enmity dripping from every word and gesture I made. "Right, that's been apparent since I landed in Vienna and got whisked away to the embassy. Any news on Borysko?"

"Who?"

"Don't play dumb. The Ukrainian loyalist that helped me rescue Delgado. Any word if he's alive?"

"He's not our concern," replied Bill dismissively.

"Yeah, right. Why am I not surprised. And Delgado, well, he just disappeared."

"That I can answer. We've been over this, Mr. Hackett. Henry Delgado was severely wounded and needed expert care from American doctors. He's already back in the States and doing well. Trust me."

"Trust you? Not in a million years," I replied. "So, what happens now? I get my memory wiped? I go to jail?"

Bill laughed like a sleazy businessman who'd told his wife not to worry about the underage secretary. "Memory wiped, that's a good one. You've seen too many movies."

"And you're not State Department, or FBI, or anything but intelligence. I can smell it on you. Now look, I've been here for six hours and I've answered all your questions, from the time I first saw Delgado's face on the news to when we got picked up by the cavalry. Am I being charged with a crime or is this gonna drag on indefinitely?"

"You're not being charged with anything. That's in no one's interest. Besides, that would be DOJ, which I'm clearly not. But you did stick your nose into something you shouldn't have and you broke a few international laws in the process. Assaulting some authorities, fleeing the scene of a deadly car accident, not to mention the people you killed, though I doubt we'll hear anything about that."

I didn't respond. This was the third multi-hour session at the embassy. I'd already answered and expounded on every single question I'd been asked, no matter how damaging or incriminating my comments might be. I was done lying.

"We're going to let you go, Mr. Hackett, to return to your life. You rescued one of ours, which hasn't gone unnoticed."

"You're welcome."

Bill cocked his head. "But there's still one thing I don't understand. Why'd you do it? Delgado was your friend, but I don't see why you did this simply because you two were war buddies."

"Why can't it be that simple?"

Bill eyed me skeptically. "Because I've been in this business a long time, and people don't risk everything—their life, their livelihood—on something that had next to no chance of succeeding."

"Yet, I did succeed."

"Yes, you did. Still, the odds were stacked impossibly against you."

"You ever serve in the military, Bill?"

"No. But I *do* serve."

"I'm not saying you don't. But you didn't serve in the military, did you?"

"Correct."

"Right. Then without getting into a big debate, let's say my experiences were different and, because of them, it was clear to me what I had to do."

Bill waited for a long moment before saying, "Whatever. Here's the deal. In three hours you're getting on a plane back to London. Back to your life, whatever's left of it. But once you land, you're restricted to English territory. You can't leave. Your passport is flagged and you're on the no-fly list, unless we call you back to the States, that is."

"I don't understand. You said I wasn't being charged."

"You're not, but there's still a mess that needs cleaning up. We need to be able to find you quickly if we have additional questions. It's for your own good, really."

"I won't be able to work. I have to travel for my job."

"Should've considered that before you thought it was a good idea to invade Ukraine all by yourself." Bill gathered up his papers and stood. The Marine guard outside the room opened the door and stepped in. "You remember Tracy? The gal who set you up with the hotel when you first got here."

"Yes."

"She'll be by shortly to take you to the airport," said Bill as he extended his hand. "Goodbye, Mr. Hackett. Good luck."

I hesitated, then stood and shook the embassy man's hand, though it was nothing but a perfunctory formality of the civilized world.

CHAPTER SIXTY-ONE

I stood before my townhouse in the East End of London. The brick needed a power wash, the concrete steps needed some mortar, and apparently my lawn guy had taken another week off. The patch of grass was barely a postage stamp with two struggling bushes, but still, it needed tending.

I'd lived here for seven years, filling the place with the few items I needed—a couple pots, a couch, a bed, some kettlebells—and liked it well enough. I wasn't here that often, but I appreciated the quiet and stripped-down simplicity.

The neighborhood suited me, too. A local pub on the corner, hardworking people, and a line straight to the Thames for heart-pounding runs to purge the demons. I'd lost count of how many times I'd made that run; I'd do it rain or shine, hot or cold, sometimes in the dead of night.

Thus, I found it curious why I fumbled with the keys in my hand and kept looking up and down the street, and for what I don't know. I wondered if I sold the place, could the broker get rid of my stuff in the process. I didn't really need anything, except maybe some of the clothes. And my footlocker, of course. I had a few things from my grandfather tucked inside that I wasn't ready to part with.

I should probably call Caroline at some point. Ike told me that she and the family were secure when he pulled off, but he'd said she'd been worried about me even if she'd not voiced it. It's complicated, I think, as it always is when it comes to relationships. She deserves better—I knew that much.

Yet it hadn't been complicated with Alex, at least not for the brief time we knew each other. Maybe it would have been if we'd been together for more than a heartbeat. But I'd never know . . .

My stomach growled and I thought lamb chops might be nice. A Tube stop away, there was another local pub that made a decent plate. Maybe I'd head there to ruminate. There's something therapeutic about eating alone if you can stomach the pity stares.

I turned to go but stopped when I saw a car driving down the street much too slow, approaching me—a black sedan with fully tinted windows. Not another soul was on the street, and the sun was falling behind the row of houses across the way.

The car stopped next to me, and I watched the driver's-side window roll down. Ike's bold-ass mug appeared. "Sir, you look lost."

"You following me?"

"Maybe."

I chuckled. "You know I live here."

"Yeah, of course. You still seem lost."

"Thanks."

"My pleasure, sir. Just making an observation."

"You ever going to stop calling me *sir*?"

"Nope."

"Thought so. It's good to see you."

"And you. We'll need to knock a few back here soon, but before that, I got someone that wants to talk to you."

The rear window rolled down and Alistair leaned his head out. "Please join me, Mason. We should discuss a few things."

Alistair and I hadn't spoken since the call from Odessa, and since then I'd wondered how our next meeting would go. I had hoped to have a day or two to get my head straight, maybe procrastinate a little, but it didn't surprise me seeing him here. It's why he was who he was—couldn't let something sit if he could do something about it.

I walked around the front of the car and got in the back, settling into the leather seat but nudging myself up against the door. The interior was plenty large, but I felt like I needed space.

Alistair, his suit as crisp as if it still hung on the hanger, reached forward to tap Ike on the shoulder. "Why don't we drive around for a bit."

Ike put the car in gear and drove off.

"It's good to see you back safe and sound," Alistair began.

"Yes, sir. Thank you."

"Ike gave me the synopsis of what you'd gone to do."

"Did he?"

"Yes, but not to worry. Despite the unusual nature of things and our previous call, I've kept it strictly confidential. No need to add to any rumors that might already be floating around."

"I appreciate it, sir. And I do apologize for—"

Alistair leaned across and took my wrist. "There's nothing to apologize for. I don't fault you for making the choice you did and doing what no one else would. I'm glad you did."

"Sir?"

"We do what we must. It's who we are."

"Yes," I replied, returning the man's stare.

He released my arm and pulled up his right pant leg. A jagged, discolored patch of scar tissue marked a spot midway up the man's calf. "A bullet fired from an Omani rifle, July 1972. Its cousins cut down a very dear friend of mine, Ralphie. Nice chap from Birmingham."

I offered my boss a curious look. Despite having known the man for over a decade, I'd never seen the scar or heard anything about this. It dawned on me I'd never seen the man in shorts. Alistair was formal to the core, always dressed conservatively and only exposing personal elements of his life at a distance.

Alistair smiled with a conspiratorial glint. "Before I joined my family's firm, I served in her majesty's Special Air Service, akin to America's special operations."

"I'm familiar," I said, duly impressed by Alistair's former membership with such an elite unit.

"I was a young man then, about the same age you were in Iraq. I felt compelled to test my mettle in the darker corners of the empire."

"I offer my deepest respect, sir."

Alistair winked. "Nonsense. It's what we do, and you are of the same ilk."

"Right," I said, but only able to accept his compliment in part. My regrets still lingered, and I suppose they always will.

"Anyway, after my first tour with the Regiment, I was invited back. A true honor to be asked back to serve with such a unit, and a requirement, I might add."

"But . . ."

"I declined. I had other responsibilities, though one never really leaves, I might add. If you've been there, it's seared into the soul."

"I never knew."

"Few do, and I'd like to keep it that way."

"Absolutely."

"So, now that we have that over with, we need to discuss your status at the firm."

I nodded, noticing the lines on my boss's face and around the eyes like he too had once surveyed the horizon and contemplated if death was near.

"Are you hungry?" asked Alistair.

"Sir?"

"I asked if you were hungry. It's nearly seven."

"Yes, I am. I was on my way to a nearby pub for some lamb, actually."

"Excellent. Ike," Alistair called out, grabbing Ike's attention, though I have no doubt he'd been listening to every word. "Mr. Hackett would like some supper. There's a pub nearby, you know the place."

"Yes, sir."

"Splendid," said Alistair, turning back to me. "We shall discuss your status with the firm then. I believe they have a braised lamb shank on the menu, which is quite good. You won't be disappointed."

"Thank you," I replied cautiously.

*   *   *

Ike found a parking spot near the pub, a rustic-looking place on the corner of Bethnal Green and Ellsworth. We all got out and headed inside.

As soon as I passed through the swinging door entering the place, I stepped to the side to allow my eyes to adjust to the dim lighting and to take a look around. I'd never been here before and preferred not to go blundering about. I expected Alistair and Ike to join me, at the very least to pick an open table. Alistair, however, slipped right past me heading down the aisle along the bar and deeper into the pub.

Ike came up beside me. "We have a table in the back. Come on."

I eyed him curiously, now suspecting they'd planned to take me here all along.

As I trailed Ike, I saw Alistair reach a corner table and slide in next to a fellow already sitting there, waiting for us. A scowl immediately appeared on my face, but I kept walking. I locked eyes with the individual—Doug—and fought back the urge to take Ike by the arm and demand to know what the hell was going on.

When we reached the booth, Ike slid in on the bench across from Alistair and Doug, but I stayed standing, observing the three men.

"Mason, please join us," Alistair said. "I believe you already know Mr. Mitchell."

I hesitated, wanting to blurt out, *What the fuck is this?* or *How do you know this shit?* or any number of inappropriate yet completely justifiable questions, but I restrained myself. It took another moment before I sat down next to Ike and rested my forearms on the table, interlacing my fingers before me.

A server quickly appeared, a shaggy twenty-something who mumbled what could only have been a request for our drink order. Both Alistair and Ike ordered a pint, but Doug raised his glass to indicate he was still working on his whisky.

"What's your best single malt?" I asked, my eyes still boring into Doug.

"Ehh, I think we have a Balvenie something, maybe," said the kid.

"I'll take a double, neat, and make sure it goes on his tab," I replied, pointing at Doug.

"Sure. Cheers. Anything else?"

"That will be all for now," Alistair said, dismissing the server. Turning back to us at the table, he said, "Well, I'm glad we're all here together like this."

"How do you know this man?" I asked, still eyeing Doug, who matched my stare, the whites of his eyes contrasting sharply with his black skin in the dim light.

"Mr. Mitchell? We have similar interests. As do you, Mason," Alistair replied.

"Sir, I don't know what this man has told you, but I guarantee half to three-quarters of it is a lie."

"Perhaps. It's the business. But there are other aspects of our relationship that take priority."

"Relationship? Relationship? Sir, you don't know this man like I do. I'm guessing he's spun some yarn about the gauntlet I just went through, but I doubt he's revealed much about our history."

"He's told me some."

"Has he? Like how in Iraq he was assigned to my platoon as a jackass straphanger sent from on high, and on multiple occasions some crazy order would come down. Then off we'd go, hit some righteous target, and it'd either be a dry hole or we'd end up in a slug match and kill everyone in the house, maybe the neighbors too."

"Are you really bringing that up?" asked Doug. "It was a war, Mason."

"Yeah, no shit. It's what happened after—the fucking inquisition in the basement of the Pentagon."

"That's a separate matter, one we will not discuss here, and there's more to it than what you know about," Doug said coolly.

"Ya think?"

"Gentlemen! I come bearing gifts," announced a new voice off to my side.

I shot the speaker a glare, a tall man with black hair and the beginnings of a goatee speckled with gray. Were it not for his olive-colored skin, the lingering bruises on his face would have been severely more pronounced. He stood at the edge of the table holding three pints of beer and my scotch.

"Delgado?" I blurted out. My friend stood before me, the man I had once known as Kevin Gomez, but my mind had finally made the permanent shift. He was no longer Gomez—he was Delgado. He was still a man I knew and would call a friend, yet in a new life.

"Hola, mi hermano. Take your drink," said Delgado, grinning.

I reached up and took the tumbler from Delgado's outstretched hand, but found myself at a loss for words seeing him standing there, acting like we'd just kicked off happy hour after a long day in the office. Alistair and Ike reached for their pints, and Delgado set his on the table and dragged a chair over, settling in at the end.

"Brilliant," said Alistair. "Now that we're all here, I think we should get down to business. It's apparent more questions need answering before we move forward."

Move forward, I thought. Move forward with what?

My scrutiny shifted from Delgado to Alistair, skipped Doug, and glanced at Ike before settling back on Alistair. I wondered why my boss was the one talking. What did he have to do with any of this, besides perhaps for firing me in response to getting his firm wrapped up in this garbage?

With an amused smile, I said, "Clearly, I'm the one who needs to catch up. I'm listening."

"First," began Alistair, "although we all know each other, I think it's important for Mason to understand how. When you had Ike call me so you could make contact from Odessa, I put a few things together and reached out to our mutual acquaintance, Mr. Mitchell."

"You know each other?"

"In a way. Mr. Mitchell and Mr. Delgado, and others, have been involved in an activity of sorts that caught my interest over two years ago. I'm sure you remember the chat you and I had at the firm's retreat. The one about private military companies and how they were changing how international corporations could do business."

"Yes, I remember. You said you expected them to create more opportunities for companies to move into places that historically would have been inhospitable for business without government troops or security."

"Yes, natural resource extraction, shipping lanes, and the like. With the rise of private military companies, or PMCs for short, CEOs have been able to hire private armies and navies to protect their assets and interests. You yourself, Mason, have seen them in the Middle East, Africa, the pirate-infested waters off Somalia."

"Yeah, I know. But what does that have to do with these guys?" I asked, though my thoughts had already drifted toward Delgado's recent detention and Doug's correlation with the Hess Group.

"Because of my unique interest in PMCs, over the past few years I began noticing anomalies in the illicit arms markets and the associated presence of these people. As my curiosity grew, which was in relation to Ruttfield's investments, I made some inquiries. Very hush-hush of course. But eventually this man showed up," Alistair said, pointing to Doug.

"You're shitting me?"

"Not in the least."

"Why did you reach out to him?" I asked, my question directed at Doug.

"Your boss was asking the right questions of the right people," he replied. "He popped on our radar. A little bit of digging revealed his connections to British intelligence from back in the day."

"What?"

"The Regiment, Mason. Like I explained in the car. One never really leaves," Alistair said, with a bit of a resigned shrug.

"Anyway," continued Doug, "we wanted to get ahead of things and politely requested he stop sniffing around."

Alistair nodded. "Which I agreed to do, under the condition of being kept in the loop on certain matters. I had the firm's interests to consider. So, when Ike told me you had gone to help a friend, Mr. Delgado formerly known as Mr. Kevin Gomez, I made some assumptions."

"Jeez. Wait. When did you two first meet?" I asked, referring to Alistair and Doug.

"Two years ago," answered Alistair.

"Barcelona?" I asked, eyeballing Doug, now wondering if our random encounter two years ago had been connected.

Doug raised his brow non-committedly. "It's a game, Mason. You know."

"And you two?" I asked, now referring to Delgado.

"This morning, over crumpets," replied Delgado.

I lifted my head and looked at the wood beams that adorned the ceiling. *Holy crap* was all I could scrape together. I could barely believe what I was hearing, and I knocked back the last of my scotch.

"This is much bigger than you realize, Mason," said Doug.

"Then explain," I shot back, feeling the blood rise in my face.

"It's not just PMCs," said Doug. "It's America's entire military industrial complex."

"Oh Christ," I blurted. "What is this, a fucking Tom Clancy novel?"

Delgado chuckled but didn't say anything, taking a long pull from his beer and waving for another. I did the same and motioned for Doug to continue.

"I've already told you about the Program, which Alistair and Ike are now fully aware of too. However, this next bit I'm about to explain is about a sub-compartment of the activity. Three years ago, Delgado and I initiated an operation. At first, our goal was to disrupt the international black arms market. We were seeing massive amounts of weaponry end up in the hands of warlords, rebel groups, and problematic countries—think Iran and Venezuela—which we hadn't seen before."

"Hasn't that been going on since the breakup of the Soviet Union," I said. "*Lord of war* and all that crap, supplying the chaos of the '90s?"

"Somewhat," Doug said. "This was different. More advanced systems, weapons that would give the US military a run for its money, and it was both NATO and Warsaw Pact stuff. It first showed up in Iraq and Afghanistan, but now it's expanding. And it wasn't just unaccounted-for Soviet surplus or a misdirected shipping container here and there. The presence was massive, and in some cases straight from the factory to the conflict area. That's when things changed and we began seeing connections to the industry's dominant defense corporations that build the weapons and equipment for the world's biggest modern militaries."

"I'm not following," I said.

"They were connected," Alistair said. "When you think of an arms dealer, some shady Eastern European fellow with a prostitute on one arm and a nickel-plated pistol in the other, that kind of man was no longer in the picture. Instead, men in suits with MBAs began working with the corporations that build military satellites and submarines—as well as the terrorists' AKs and RPGs—under the guise of legitimate business and being financed by Wall Street or the London Stock Exchange. Ruttfield at times."

"To put it simply," Doug said, "the black, gray, and white arms markets coupled with big business and upstanding government types are all in cahoots funding and supplying the world's conflicts, like a self-licking ice cream cone to generate profits and maintain power and influence. Maybe not coordinated with smart contracts, delivery schedules, and foreign policy decrees, but definitely with tacit agreements and head nods and payoffs to go around."

"Okay," I said.

"But then things fell apart," added Delgado.

"What do you mean?"

Doug leaned forward. "We, Delgado and I and a few others, were trying to infiltrate the networks and map them so we could then throw them into chaos and madness. Standard CIA shit. But a year ago our efforts started coming up dry. Networks began dropping without a trace, supply chains dismantled and redirected, and one of our highly placed assets ended up dead."

"We thought we had a leak," Delgado said. "We suspected someone had penetrated our op, tipping off the bad guys, changing behavior, and then killing our man."

"Zach, the guy in Prague?" I asked, my thoughts returning to the accident.

"Not Zach. He was never on the inside. He was sniffing around the Program, but never had the goods. But the world can sleep easy now that he's gone, dirty bastard," said Doug.

"Yeah, not Zach," continued Delgado. "But the fear of someone like Zach in our inner circle was why I went to Ukraine. We knew a Russian arms dealer by the name of Tolesky was all up in this mess. So, I went to Ukraine to make contact, with the goal of putting some false information in play. Basically, put a message into the network and see where it comes out on the other end, which would hopefully point us toward the leak."

"You went over there to tell some arms peddler a bogus message?"

"Yeah. As the info made its way through the network, it might point to our problem."

"Later," injected Doug, halting Delgado's line.

I shook my head. "But you got captured," I said to Delgado, ignoring Doug.

"That variable was in our calculation, and we accepted it as a necessary risk. And if I was captured, I could still put the false info in play. It just might be a little more difficult for me personally."

"They could have killed you," I said.

Delgado shrugged. "It's the job."

"And he refused to go get you," I said, pointing at Doug.

"Not refused," Doug injected. "It's more complicated than that. We had means on the back end, which I didn't share with you."

"And the email?" I asked.

"Part of my personal back end," said Delgado.

I looked from Doug to Delgado. "Nuts. Snap, crackle, pop, nuts."

Delgado shrugged again, this time with a smile.

"Delgado's detention actually worked out in our favor," said Doug.

"Ha! Do tell."

"Turns out one of the targets we've been trying to get a line on—a former GRU officer named Mikhail Petrov—showed up to take responsibility of my interrogation. He was an exec with the Hess Group," said Delgado.

"The private military company I told you to look up," remarked Doug.

"There was no better way for me to put the feed material in play, which I did."

"Congratulations," I quipped. "But you said *was*."

"Petrov's dead," Doug chimed in. "Killed by one of the heavies pulling the strings, we think."

"Who?"

"The same people who gave the orders to go after you in Prague, and again in Romania, Moldova, and Ukraine, until you shook them and linked up with Borysko's crew."

"Who? Hess?"

"Hess is part of it, perhaps the most violent part, but still only a facet of something much broader. We're not certain, but there are indications one of these three men, if not all three, are the real bosses, calling the shots but keeping a safe distance to avoid any stink. They reap the rewards down to the penny and play global politics with their government partners who call in favors and debts."

As Doug spoke, he laid out three photos on the table. I'd expected to see black-and-white surveillance footage capturing shady activities from a perch around a corner or in the distance, but they were anything but. Each photo was of a different man in full public view, at a press conference, on TV, or some other public shot. And I could tell just by looking at them that they were businessmen, not thugs or mafia bosses. Two of the men I didn't recognize, but one photo included company signage for an international defense contractor and the other for a global car manufacturer. The man in the third photo, however, struck me as familiar. He was shaking hands with a woman with a display for a refugee aid organization in the background.

"Who's that?" I asked.

"Viktor Leos," said Doug.

"Why does that name ring a bell?"

"Because he rolls around in US national security circles as a broker for international weapons deals, as well as heading a multinational conglomerate that has a commanding presence in everything from microchips to natural resource extraction to fucking Hollywood. He holds multiple citizenships and owns properties throughout the world too."

"Ruttfield has also done business with this man," injected Alistair.

The ticker tape of recognition began scrolling by in my head.

"You think he's involved?" I asked incredulously. I knew about Leos' holdings, and was taken aback that he could possibly be associated with any of these kinds of intrigues. But then again, I didn't really know the man, only his reputation as one of the wealthiest and most powerful businessmen in the world.

Doug shrugged, and Delgado winced as he took another pull from his draft.

"It all makes good sense when you think about it," began Alistair. "Major defense firms involved in legitimate *and* illicit activities. They supply the major powers of the world, provide genuine contract support in the world's trouble spots, but they also supply the opposition. Not unlike the fox guarding the henhouse while also managing the supply of new chicks. And speaking of your and my countries specifically, defense spending is an enormous portion of the economy. Just imagine for a moment the potential profits if major defense firms could nudge a government into a fight somewhere. Billions."

I shook my head in dismay. I knew what Alistair was getting at. For years he'd been sending me around the world investigating the gritty end of this business as it pertained to the interests of Ruttfield's clients. But this possible connection to Leos, US intelligence, and everything I'd just gone through—I didn't know what to think.

"Okay," I said. "I know you're not telling me this just because you like my sweet personality. I've been an unwitting part of this for quite a while, I take it, so what gives?"

"We need your help, active involvement and fully onboard," said Doug.

"Really."

"Yes," said Alistair. "My interests in this matter go beyond my firm. As I said, one never really leaves this world. But I can't go running around like I used to."

"Right," said Doug. "And our interests are purely twisted, for the fun of it. Good patriotic CIA hoopla."

"Again, I'm not following. Come out with it, already," I said.

"At the ground level, you understand the financial networks and players we're trying to infiltrate. You know them a hell of a lot better than me," said Delgado. "Plus, I need someone else to watch my back and get in the mix on the street. There's no one else I trust more."

"Are you asking me to . . . to get in on the op with you?"

Delgado nodded. "What do you say, my friend, are you in?"

There it was, the point of this entire drama—*the ask*. Delgado's question reverberated in my head . . . and I don't know why but I immediately thought of Alex. I pictured her face the moment I met her in that shady hotel in Bucharest, her smile when she ruled the bar in her home village, the sound of her voice as we talked while driving through Moldova, the smell of her naked skin when we made love by the lake, and the final look in her eyes before a bullet cratered her forehead.

My hand beneath the table tightened into a fist. "Hell, yeah. I'm in."

ACKNOWLEDGMENTS

Writing is a solitary endeavor, but no book comes to print without the support and encouragement from those around you. This book would never have happened were it not for my two agents, Judy Coppage and Sam Dorrance, who have been with me from the beginning. I must also thank Oceanview Publishing for inviting me to join the team; it has been a pleasure working with Pat, Bob, Lee, Kat, Lisa, and Christian throughout the publication process. A special thanks goes to my trusted readers and writing confidants, Mark, Annie, Irv, Jeff, Eric, Phill, Joel, Rachelle, Mike, and Tim. I would be remiss if I didn't also mention the late Richard Marek, who six years ago drilled into me the principles of character development. I am indebted to my parents, as well, for all they have done for me throughout my life. And finally, to my loving wife and children who believed in me and supported me through the ups and downs and everything in between—thank you.